THOSE IN PERIL

BOOK ONE OF THE PHASES OF MARS

Edited by
Chris Kennedy and James Young

Theogony Books
Virginia Beach, VA

Chris Kennedy/Theogony Books
2052 Bierce Dr., Virginia Beach, VA 23454
http://chriskennedypublishing.com/

Those in Peril/Chris Kennedy and James Young -- 1st ed.
ISBN 978-1948485999

For all who have gone down to the sea to protect the ones they loved...
and never returned.

Preface by Chris Kennedy

Welcome to the "Phases of Mars!" This book came about when James Young asked me one day, "So, when are you going to publish an alternate history anthology?" After a moment, I replied, "As soon as you put it together." He accepted the challenge, and "The Phases of Mars" was born. Ultimately, the Phases of Mars will encompass at least three volumes. The first of these, "Those in Peril," deals with naval warfare, the second, "To Slip the Surly Bonds," will deal with air warfare, and the third, "Trouble in the Wind," will deal with ground warfare.

James put together a great selection of naval warfare within this book—there is something for everyone inside! From ships with sail, to steam, to today's modern aircraft carriers, "Those in Peril" traces several centuries of naval warfare…that wasn't. From adding a psychic…to making a different choice of friend or foe…to something insignificant toppling a kingdom, this book has it.

Enjoy!

Chris Kennedy
Virginia Beach, VA

Contents

*****

Naked
by Kacey Ezell

The heat was the worst. Or maybe it was the humidity. Either way, Lydia felt the air surround her like hands over her mouth and nose, smothering her in the scorching wetness that was January in the South Pacific. She'd grown up in Southern California, and though the winters were balmy, they were nothing like this. She sighed at her reflection and started braiding her brown hair back close to her skull. It was already starting to frizz out beyond recognition.

"Lydia," her uncle's voice hit her seconds before the man himself leaned into her open doorway, making her gasp and turn in that direction. His normally handsome, slightly weathered face was ghostly pale under his tan, and a fine sheen of sweat broke out along his hairline. Sure it was warm, but this was excessive.

"Uncle Horatio!" she said, tying off her hair and heading over to him. Careful not to invade his privacy, she extended her senses to pick up the edge of his outer mind. Achy, swirling misery greeted her, making her pull her power quickly back within her own barriers. "You look awful, what happened?"

"I don't know," he said. "I woke up in the middle of the night with aches and fever. I feel like death. I…I don't think I can make today's flight."

"Oh no," Lydia gasped softly, her fingertips coming to her lips. The flight was the whole reason they'd made the trip out this far. Horatio was better known as Lieutenant Commander Horatio Driscoll, Naval Aviation Photographic Unit. But to Lydia, he'd always been her mother's younger brother, Uncle Horatio.

When he'd shipped off to the South Pacific to take pictures for the Navy, Lydia had accompanied him as his darkroom assistant. That was the polite way to put it. It was more accurate to say she'd *run away*, but that didn't sound as romantic and official. Not that it mattered to her, she'd just wanted out of Whittier, and away from the stifling life and attentions of people who'd known her—and her power—since she was a little girl.

Uncle Horatio hadn't exactly been pleased at first, but he was sympathetic to her plight, and he had managed to pull some strings to allow her to stay with him, reasoning that at least that way he could assure the family that she was safe.

Of course, then he took her to the South Pacific, where conditions were anything *but* safe, but they had agreed not to tell the family about that part.

And truth be told, it wasn't that bad. Uncle Horatio got her set up with a darkroom at Henderson Field, and while he was gone on assignment, she processed and developed the negatives that he and the other photographers brought in. Then, after work, she'd meet up with some of the nurses from the hospital and have dinner. It was hard work, but a lot of fun.

But Uncle Horatio didn't look like he was having much fun at the moment.

"Are you going over to the hospital?" she asked.

"I will, but…I need you to take this flight today. Styver said that he really needed some shots of a PBY crew in action."

"Me—?" Lydia squeaked, her voice cracking in surprise.

"Yes, you'll be great. I've already cleared it with the squadron CO. You're a fantastic photographer, Lydia. You have that knack of catching people's emotions right on their faces. That's exactly what Styver wants. Help me out, will ya?"

Lydia drew in a deep breath and nodded, despite her shaking hands.

"Of course," she said. "Of course, Uncle. You brought me here, I owe you. Of course, I'll help you out. But you have to promise me you'll go see the medics."

"I promise. Now here, I brought you my camera and bag. You need to be on the flightline in an hour…"

* * *

Forty-five minutes later, Lydia's hands were still shaking.

"You the photographer?"

She looked up to meet the light blue eyes of the young sailor who'd shouted the words over the roar of aircraft engines. Something leapt inside her mind at the sight of his handsome, open face, but she locked it down hard and forced herself to focus.

"Y-yes. Lydia Driscoll."

"Good to meet you," he said with an easy grin. He shifted his lanky frame and stuck out a hand. Lydia hastily tried to switch the camera to her other hand and dropped it to bang awkwardly against her stomach on the strap. She felt her cheeks heating up as she took his offered grip. "I'm Aviation Ordnanceman Second Class Eric Warner."

"Nice to meet you, too," she mumbled. Or tried to mumble. The engines were still turning not too far away, so she had to shout to make herself heard.

"This way," he shouted back, giving her hand a quick squeeze before dropping it. Then he turned and beckoned for her to follow as he walked down between a line of parked aircraft toward the one that had been making so much noise.

She walked closely behind him, careful to keep well clear of the wings, even though the PBY's turning props were high above her head. She climbed into the aircraft after him, and when he pointed at a headset, she pulled it on over her ears. He did the same.

"Can you hear me okay? Give me a thumbs up if you can," he instructed. She copied his gesture, then looked around for a place to not be in the way. Warner stepped into the PBY's starboard "blister," a dome-shaped window that allowed for maximum visibility on that side of the aircraft. There was a blister on the port side, too, and a serious-faced man stood there fussing with the waist gun on that side.

"You can sit there, on those ammo cans," Warner said, pointing to a spot on the port side, forward of both blisters. Then he nudged the port gunner with his elbow. "Seth here doesn't say much, but he's a good man. If you have any questions, you can speak by holding down this button here. Just press your lips right up to the boom mic on the headset. Perfect. Say hi to the photographer, Seth."

"Hi to the photographer, Seth," Seth said without looking up. Lydia startled herself with a laugh. But because she didn't push the button, the sound was lost in the pulsing drone of the PBY's props.

"All right, that's enough chatter back there," someone said through the headset. "Are we all secured?"

"Aye, sir," Warner replied, giving Lydia one last thumb's up and stepping into his own blister.

"Right, let's go." The noise from the props got louder and slightly higher in pitch, and Lydia could feel an ache beginning just behind her ears. The PBY lurched forward, which was backward from Lydia's perspective, and began to taxi. She suddenly remembered her job and lifted Uncle Horatio's camera to snap off a few shots of the men working with their weapons, and leaning out into their blisters to look around the aircraft.

Before too long, the PBY wheeled about in what felt like a ninety-degree turn, and the prop noise ratcheted up even higher. The aircraft frame felt like it was shuddering as the sound built all around her, until finally it leapt forward with so much force that Lydia nearly tumbled off her ammo can. She had to reach out to steady herself on the nearby bulkhead.

Both men stood with legs splayed, braced in their blisters as that same voice said "rotation" in her headset. Then the PBY pitched up, making Lydia glad she'd found her handhold, and began to climb into the sky.

Even with the protective headset, the noise was punishing. Lydia could barely hear as the men spoke about important, flight-related things. She tried to make out the words, but they just disappeared into the background drone of the engines and props, and the rush of air around them.

The PBY banked to starboard, and Lydia caught a glimpse of the airfield through Warner's blister. She got her camera up just in time to take the shot, and then lowered it as she realized it would probably be censored, anyway.

Warner turned and said something to her, but she couldn't make out his words. He pointed to his position, as if offering to swap places with her so she could get a good view, but she shook her head. It probably wouldn't do to have him off his weapon for that long, plus, she could tell he was busy looking around and speaking often into the boom mic that rested against his lips. She took a few shots of him, and then sat down morosely on her ammo can, wondering how on earth Uncle Horatio managed to do this when he couldn't communicate with his subjects. If only she could *hear* them…

A thought occurred to her so suddenly that she nearly dropped the camera. Her mouth went suddenly very dry, and her hands began to tremble once again, but the sheer audacity of it made her wonder. She *had* to get some good shots, otherwise Uncle Horatio could very well face disciplinary action. After the way he'd played fast and loose with the regs to allow her to accompany him, she knew he couldn't afford a black mark. And now he needed her help.

Lydia took a deep breath and let the tiniest bit of slack in the bonds of will she'd wrapped around her own mind. She pictured a heavy steel door, like the ones meant to contain fires aboard a ship. Then she allowed the door to crack open an infinitesimal amount, just enough to let her power start to trickle forth. She would brush against Warner's outer mind, just enough to get a sense of how he felt, and what he meant.

I hope it's enough, she thought.

The starboard gunner turned to face her with surprise in his eyes, and threw his barriers wide open, welcoming her in to all his delicious maleness. Lydia's power leapt forth with joyful acceptance, and without meaning to do so, she found herself locked in a psychic net with the young ordnanceman.

You're psychic? Eric asked, his mind tone incredulous. *Why didn't you say?*

Why would I? she asked back, too amazed at this turn of events to prevaricate. *People hurt witches, or at least lock us up.*

Don't call yourself that! Eric said, with surprising ferocity. His wide eyes narrowed in a frown, and he turned back to his blister to look outside. *That's a horrible thing to say!*

Everyone else says it, she said. *It's just a word.*

Not to me, he said. *My mother's psychic.*

Ah, so she taught you how to link?

Yeah, he said. *But she never felt as strong as you. She kept her power hidden, though. It always made me sad. She said it wasn't safe to let everyone know, so I guess you're right. I just never thought...she always linked with us kids. It was useful when we'd be out running around in the mountains.*

Oh? Lydia asked, happy to change the subject. *Where are you from?*

Northern California, he said, and his lips curved in a tiny smile as he craned his head to look aft around his weapon. *Little town called Auburn.*

Then he keyed his button and spoke into his mic: "Friendlies, seven o'clock," he said. "Looks like a flight of Corsairs."

"Roger," came the pilot's voice from up front, and unlike before, the words were clear and distinct through Lydia's headphones.

Wow, she said. *This is so much better! I can actually hear what's going on. It must be because I'm hearing through your ears, too.*

Yeah, same for me, Eric said. *This is cool. We could link Seth in, too...*

I'd rather not, she said quickly. *I don't want...I mean, you seem trustworthy, but...*

Oh, he said, and she could feel sadness seeping through their link. *It's not just hypothetical, then? Someone really did hurt you?*

Well, not exactly, she said. For just a moment, she wondered how on Earth she had gotten to this point. She'd only met Eric a few minutes ago, and now here she was ready to share the deepest secrets of her soul with him. Was that the bond? Her grandmother had warned her that it could be a seductive thing, especially when linked with a man not a member of her blood.

Well, what, then, exactly? Unless you don't want to say, he added, as he turned his head away from her to continue doing his job. She had to give it to him, he was super professional, even while holding a conversation with her.

*There's a boy back home. A man, really, I guess, but I've known him since he was a boy. He's always kinda had a thing for me, and I've tried to be kind...*Lydia thought, then trailed off in her mind.

But you're not interested in him, Eric filled in.

Not that way, no. He's got a cruel streak that I don't appreciate, Lydia thought. She shuddered as she pushed away a memory.

Anyway, awhile back, he actually proposed. He'd done it before, but I always put him off, saying I'm too young, etc., Lydia continued. She clasped her hands between her knees, the camera laying on her legs.

Well, this time he came to me and said that it was high time we got married, and if I didn't say yes, he'd turn me in to the law for using my psychic powers to convince people to do bad things, Lydia said after a few moments. She turned to look out the blister past Eric, her stomach flip flopping.

When I asked what evidence he proposed to show, he said he would...well. He'd hurt some people, some people who'd been mean to me when we were young, and that he'd say I had coerced him to do it.

Eric was silent for a long time. Lydia watched the back of his blond head as he turned this way and that, scanning both sky and ocean for enemies.

You were right the first time, he said after a long moment. *He's not a man at all.*

I guess you're right, she said. *Anyway, that's part of why I'm leery of letting people know about my talent. My hometown mostly knows, and it hasn't turned out well.*

Another flight of Corsairs flashed past in a climb.

Is that why you're out here? Eric asked after several long moments scanning to make sure the fighters weren't after a threat.

Pretty much. I followed my Uncle Horatio, and he pulled strings to let me stay when I told him what awaited me back home.

Eric paused and scanned toward something distant. Lydia heard some rapid radio chatter, but was unable to follow what was being said.

Sounds like a good man, Eric said, smiling over at her.

He is. The best, Lydia said.

So, what I'd like to know—

Lydia never found out what Eric wanted to know, because their pilot's voice crackled over the intercom system in their headsets.

"Change of plans, boys. Just got a call. Downed Corsair not more than ten minutes flight from here, in Rabaul Harbor."

"Rabaul Harbor?!" Seth asked, his voice ratcheting up in pitch. "That's sticking our head into the lion's den, isn't it?"

"Yep, Jap harbor guns shot down one of our pilots," the pilot replied. "He got a call off, so he's still alive for the moment. We're not going to leave him to die or be captured."

"Hell, no, we won't, sir," Seth said, racking his weapon. Without realizing that she meant to do so, Lydia lifted the camera to her face and snapped off a shot of his steely-eyed, determined expression.

Okay then, a rescue mission, Eric thought to her as he prepped his own weapon. *You just hang tight, Lydia, this won't take but a minute.*

Lydia felt the tension rise, not needing a psychic link to know that what they were about to do was apparently much more dangerous than a normal mission.

Can I photograph you guys? Lydia asked. *I mean, I won't get in your way, right?*

Of course. Just stay there in your seat and hold on, Eric thought. Lydia could feel the tinge of false bravado in his thoughts. *The pilots may have to do some fancy flying to avoid getting shot down like the guy we're going to get.*

Unbeknownst to the distracted gunner, Lydia could feel Eric's half-hysterical, dark humor. If a Corsair couldn't dodge the harbor guns at Rabaul, how was the slower, bulkier PBY supposed to do it?

Lydia didn't have an answer, so she said nothing as they banked to make a sharp turn to the left and headed toward the mouth of hell itself.

* * *

"Dropping down over the water! Gonna get low to try and keep clear of those damn harbor guns!" the pilot said into his microphone up front. Lydia closed her eyes and held onto the bulkhead with one hand and her uncle's precious camera with the other as both blister gunners fired long, rattling blasts from their guns. The aircraft banked hard to the right, then back down to the left in a maneuver that made her feel like her stomach was about to fly out of her mouth.

"Can you guys see anything back there?" another voice—that of the copilot—asked. His tone carried a shrill edge of anxiety. "It's hard to make anything out up here. There's so much smoke, I can't see where there might be any wreckage or anything!"

"Kinda busy, sir," Seth grunted as he turned his gun and continued firing. "Damn enemy fighters are like flies on roadkill out here!"

Eric didn't say anything, he just focused grimly and continued firing as the Japanese fighters swung down and spat searing lines of fire toward the PBY. A trickle of frustrated despair ran through his mind.

I don't know if we're going to find this guy, he thought in response to the pilot's question. *The smoke is too thick, and I can't take my eyes off these damned fighters for a second!*

Hang on, Lydia said as a thought appeared with crystal clarity in her mind. *Maybe I can help…*

What—?

His thought cut off as Lydia withdrew from their link. What she was about to try would take all of her attention, and even then, her power might not be enough. But she had to try.

She took a deep breath, closed her eyes, and consciously dropped her barriers. She reached out with her mind, stretching her awareness as far as she could. Eric's psyche pulled at her, but she flinched away from the siren call of his mental landscape and kept searching.

Beside her, she tasted the hint of Seth's fear and fatalism as they tangled in his outer mind. He kept scanning and firing.

Forward, the two pilots, men she hadn't even met, mere voices in her headset, hung on with grim determination as they fought to keep the PBY flying low and fast through the smoke that clung close to the water's surface.

Then out, further forward, sweeping for any sign of anything…

There!

Terror clawed at her throat as choking water the temperature of blood swamped her mouth and nose. Her eyes fought to see, but all was black agony and flashes of light that had nothing to do with the external world. Pain wreathed every tortured breath as panic gripped her…

"I found him!" Lydia shouted out loud as she ripped her mind back to her body. She didn't key the mic, but Eric was looking at her and saw her lips move. He turned his upper body in her direction, and she quickly reached out to reestablish the link between the two of them.

Where? Eric asked, urgency throbbing through their connection.

Up ahead, and off to the right—starboard, a little. He's in a lot of pain and blinded.

"Sir, possible sighting ahead to starboard," Eric said over the intercom. "Looks like that's the source of some of this smoke. Could be the wreckage. Can we get closer?"

"Roger," the pilot's voice came back emotionless and focused. The PBY banked to the right, and Lydia could see the dark, greasy wisps of smoke starting to stream past Eric's blister.

Here, Lydia invited, opening her mental channel to the gunner wider. *I bet I can find him again. I'm going to warn you…he's in pretty bad shape.*

I'll handle it. Eric said.

All right, Lydia said. She took a firmer grip on his mental landscape and reached out again. Not so far this time…

There! The beacon of agony and fear called to her, and once again, she felt the searing impact of the wounded, dying man's mind.

Somehow, Eric held it together, even though his knees buckled as the pain and terror flowed down the conduit from her mind to his.

"Got 'im, sir!" the gunner transmitted into the mic. "11 o'clock low, four hundred meters!"

"Contact," the pilot said. "Slight left turn, on the approach. I'll get us as close as I can, let's hope he can swim through the wreckage to us."

Swim? Lydia's mental gasp rocketed out from her mind to Eric's. *Eric, there's no way! He can't even see!*

"Sir, he looks like he's in pretty bad shape from here," Eric said, "I think I'm going to have to go in after him."

"You think you can get to him in time? And not let him pull you under? Or he could be dead already!"

"I've been a lifeguard since I was fifteen, sir," Eric said. "I'll knock him out if I have to, but I can see he's alive. It don't sit right to leave a man behind, sir. Not without giving it a try."

"Damn straight, Warner. All right, go for it."

With that, Lydia felt a *bump*, which struck her as strange. They were landing the aircraft on the water, shouldn't it be more of a splashing sensation? The noise from the props changed again as the pilots maneuvered the now-watercraft through the debris from the wreck.

You may want to avert your eyes, Eric thought to her as he stepped away from his weapon and hung his headset on its hook. He began unbuckling his pants and toed out of his boots. His shirt came off over his head, leaving the long, lean muscles of his back bare, and then he shucked off his pants and kicked them over against the bulkhead.

Before Lydia could do more than blush, he took a few running steps and dove out the rear door. She surged to her feet and followed, bracing herself in the door as her eyes and mind followed him, watching to be sure he surfaced again.

"Starboard's out!" Seth yelled into his mic, even as he continued firing at the circling Japanese fighters.

"I have him in sight!" Lydia said, keying her mic for the first time. "Uh…it's the photographer. I can see the starboard gunner, he's approaching the downed pilot…He's calling out to him. The pilot looks really badly hurt…burns on his face and his eyes…Starboard has him—

"Shit! That harbor gun just fired! Brace!" The copilot's voice cut through Lydia's commentary just in time for her to hang on tight while the PBY bucked skyward as a shell exploded in the water on the other side of the plane.

Get down, under the water! Lydia had the presence of mind to scream at Eric. *The harbor guns are firing at us!*

She felt Eric wrap his arms around the wounded man and duck under the water. Once submerged, the gunner used his powerful legs to drive them through the water toward the shadow that indicated the PBY's position.

The barely alive pilot struggled in Eric's arms, but the gunner used all of his considerable upper body strength to haul the slighter man in toward his chest and keep moving. They surfaced, and Lydia felt Eric drag in a breath of air. His legs burned with fatigue, and the PBY still seemed so far away…

No! You're so close! Lydia shouted, leaning precariously out the door. *I can see you! You're less than a hundred yards away. Don't give up, Eric! Just keep swimming towards me.*

He's heavy, Eric sent back, and Lydia gasped as the exhaustion seared through her.

I know, but you can do it! You're going to save him! Just keep coming towards me! You can do that.

Happy…to…for…you…

The words didn't register at first.

Eric Warner! Are you…flirting with me?

A…little…

Lydia squared her shoulders and leaned further out, conscious that the turbulent air from the props and the spray had already plastered her blouse to her skin. She wasn't indecent yet, but she wasn't far from it. Her mother would snap at her to cover up, but if acting like a hussy saved two lives…

I think you should take me out on a date, she thought to the gunner fighting to drag the now-limp pilot toward the PBY. *Somewhere nice and fancy. I have a red dress I'll wear for the occasion. You like red, don't you?*

*I…do…now…*Eric thought in a mixture of amazement and, Lydia realized, a touch of lust followed by a massive rush of embarrassment.

Fifty yards! Come on, Eric, you gotta earn that date!

"Photographer!" the pilot's voice pierced her attention as the PBY heaved up and then down again in the turbulent, explosive-ridden water. "Sorry, I didn't get your name! How's our gunner doing?"

"H-He's close, sir," Lydia stuttered into the mic. She'd been so focused on Eric and his struggle that she'd totally forgotten about the other men on the aircraft. "He's about twenty-five yards away and gaining every second."

"Port, get back there and help her. Those harbor guns aren't letting up, but the fighters are breaking off for the moment. They're going to circle back around to try and strafe us, I'll bet. We really need to get out of here!"

"Excuse me, miss," Seth said then, tapping her on the shoulder. "Better move back, now, I'll have to pull him in and get back on my gun quickly."

"Oh, right!" Lydia said, and stepped back. Eric's weary protest reared up in her mind as she disappeared from his sight.

I'm right here! she thought to him. *Seth's going to pull you both in. The pilots said that the fighters are circling around and the harbor guns are still firing, but you're so close...*

"Got him!" Seth shouted into the mic. Sure enough, Lydia watched as he hauled in the limp figure of a man with terrible burns on his face. The port gunner put the man down on his side, and the wounded pilot coughed and spat, then dragged in a great, wheezing gasp of air.

Seth turned back to the door, just in time to grasp his friend's hand and heave his body backwards as the PBY bucked from another explosion. Eric landed half in, half out of the aircraft. He grabbed the bulkhead with both hands and pulled himself forward on his belly until he could scramble up to his knees, and then his feet.

Without bothering to pause for his clothing or boots, he lurched toward his blister, shoved his headset on his wet head and began firing his weapon at the returning Japanese fighters. The light from the punishing South Pacific sun gleamed in the water droplets on his back, shoulders and buttocks, and without even thinking about it, Lydia grabbed her uncle's camera and took the shot.

The PBY rocked again, and Lydia gradually became aware of Seth screaming, "We're in! We're in!" over the intercom as he fired his weapon in tandem with Eric's. She let the camera drop to her chest and dove for the wounded pilot, who was struggling to get to his hands and feet. The moment she touched his skin, his pain and fear came roaring into her mind. She may have screamed out loud, but it was lost in the sound of the PBY's engines as the pilots poured on the power and began hurtling through the choppy water toward the relative safety of the sky.

You're safe! You're safe aboard a US Navy PBY! she shouted into the man's mind. *You're going to be okay! We're taking you to the hospital!*

The man turned his ruined face toward her, made a motion that looked like it was supposed to be a blink, and then promptly slumped back to the deck in unconsciousness, severing the link. Lydia sighed in relief as his agony ceased abrading her mind. She levered her body over from where she'd landed on her knees to sit leaning back against the bulkhead as the PBY pitched up into the sky.

He's still breathing, she sent to Eric as she tipped her head back and let her eyes close. She felt as if she'd been run over by a jeep…or a convoy of jeeps. She'd never used that much power in her life, and it showed. Her stomach gurgled loudly, and a stab of hunger reminded her that she'd need to eat a lot, soon, unless she wanted to follow the unfortunate pilot into unconsciousness.

Good, Eric said, still firing. He didn't say anything else, and Lydia didn't press it. But since he didn't cut the connection between them, neither did she. She could still hear the men of the crew talking over the intercom in her headset, but she said nothing and just let them work to keep her and their other new passenger safe and get them home.

After a while, when the sharp *ka-chunk* of the waist guns fell silent, Eric reached out to her again.

Lydia? Are you sleeping?

No, she said, lifting her head and smiling at him. He wore his trousers and boots once more, though his chest remained bare. *Just trying to stay quiet and out of the way.*

How's he doing? Eric asked.

He's alive, seems to be breathing all right, Lydia thought after a moment's assessment. *That's all I know. It's probably better for him to be unconscious right now. I can't imagine how much he must hurt.*

You don't have to imagine, Eric pointed out.

No, Lydia said, giving him a tired half-grin that she knew didn't reach her eyes. *It's just an expression.*

Thank you, Eric said. *For helping me, before. I wasn't sure I could make it. I'm a strong swimmer, but that…*

I never doubted you, Lydia said.

Well, thanks, he said again. *That was the toughest swim I've ever done. And, you know…if you didn't mean it…about the date…*

Eric Warner, Lydia shot back, putting as much sass as she could summon in her mental tone, *If you think you're backing out of our date now, you've got another think coming, Buster!*

His mental laughter rolled through their connection and wrapped around the contours of her mind like some deliciously silky, furred fabric.

So, you want to go, then? On a date? With me?

Didn't I just say that? she asked, archly. *Of course, I do. Though normally I'm a 'no shirt, no shoes, no service' kind of girl.*

Yeah, Eric said, his smile twisting ruefully. *I ripped it when I took it off in such a hurry. I'm sorry about all of that. I hope I didn't embarrass you.*

Never apologize for what you did today, she said, her tone firm. *You saved a man's life. I may be an unmarried woman, but I hope I've got enough good sense not to let my delicacies get in the way of* that! *You were breathtaking.*

He turned his face toward her, and the light from his blister lit up his irises until they seemed to glow blue.

I couldn't have done any of that without you.

I bet you're wrong, she said.

I bet I'm not, Eric said wearily. Lydia smiled internally and let the discussion go.

You don't think your uncle will mind me taking you out, do you? Eric thought after a few minutes. *I mean, he is an officer, and I'm just a lowly enlisted man.*

After what you did today, you're a hero. You could marry *me and he'd be proud to know you.*

Is that so? Interesting... Eric said, then smiled.

What? Lydia asked, raising an eyebrow.

Nothing.

* * *

"These are good," Uncle Horatio said, pulling one of the newly developed photographs out of the solution. "You captured the intensity on their faces as they're firing. Did you get any of the pilots up front?"

"Ah, no," Lydia said, blushing a bit. Not that he could likely tell, here in the red-lit darkroom. "I got a bit distracted when the rescue call came in, and then they were shooting at us and..."

"Yes, I heard! What a wild ride. Do me a favor and don't tell your mother I sent you out on a combat rescue mission, please.

She'd flay me alive." Uncle Horatio moved with quick assurance to hang the photograph on the line, where it would dry.

"Let's see what else you've got…" he said as he turned back to the developing bath. He trailed off, though, and picked up a pair of tongs to pull one of the other prints closer. "Oh Lydia…"

"Careful, Uncle," Lydia said. "You don't want to bend too close and splash solution on you."

"Who is this?" he asked, as if he hadn't even heard her warning.

"Eric," she said, knowing very well which photograph he'd found. "Aviation Ordnanceman Second Class Eric Warner. He's the one who performed the rescue."

"Why is he naked?"

"Well," Lydia said. "He'd just pulled the downed pilot out of the water, but the enemy fighters and the harbor guns were hammering us, so there wasn't really time for the niceties. He just got back on his weapon so we could get out of there."

Uncle Horatio lifted the print from its bath and held it up, angling it to see better.

"This is a winner, right here," he said. "This is perfect."

"Really, Uncle?" Lydia asked with a grimace. "I'm a little embarrassed I took it. It's hardly proper—"

"Lydia, this is a war. There's nothing proper about it. But this photograph perfectly captures the spirit of the American fighting man. He does whatever it takes, you see. Just like your young man here. Whatever it takes to save his brothers-in-arms, whatever it takes to get his crew home alive. Whatever it takes to complete his mission…whatever it takes to win this damned war. Come hell or high water, he's going to do his job—naked if he has to—and he's going to succeed."

Uncle Horatio turned toward her, his face lost in shadow.

"And *you* caught that, Lydia. That perfect moment. Damn fine work, my girl. *Damn* fine."

"Uncle," Lydia said, panic creeping into her voice. "You can't credit me! I'm not even really supposed to be here, and I absolutely wasn't supposed to be on that mission."

A long moment of silence stretched between them.

"No..." he said slowly. "I suppose you're right. But damn it, it's wrong that you don't get the credit for this beautiful photograph."

"I don't want it," she said. She could hear the high, squeaky fear in her voice. "It was your mission. You would have taken the same shot, had you been there. It's your photograph, uncle, please. I can't...People can't know I was there!"

"All right," he said, reaching out and patting her shoulder softly. "All right, Lydia, it's all right. I'll say it was me, if that's really what you want."

"It is, Uncle. I swear to you, it is. And keep Eric anonymous, too. That way, it will be harder for anyone to trace the photograph back to the flight I was on. Not that I think anyone will care, but..." she trailed off, uncertain what to say.

"Lydia," Uncle Horatio asked, his voice sharpening. "Why is this so important to you? Why are you afraid people will know you were on that plane?"

She swallowed hard and took a deep breath before answering.

"I used my abilities, Uncle. My psychic powers. It was the only way we could find the survivor in the smoke and chaos. Only Eric knows, but if word got out..."

"Ah," her uncle said. "I see. And you trust this young gunner?"

"I do," she said, swallowing hard again and forcing her voice to remain firm. "I trust him with my life."

"It sounds like you already have, if he knows about your abilities."

"His mother was psychic, Uncle. He…we linked up, during the flight. His mind was…"

"What was it, Lydia?" Uncle Horatio prompted, with something like a smile in his tone when she fell silent.

"Delicious," she said, and felt her cheeks heat up.

"Well. I can nearly see you blushing from here," Uncle Horatio teased as he turned back to hang the provocative photograph on the line. "You'd better cool it before you ruin these negatives with all that light coming from your cheeks!"

That surprised her into a laugh. "Uncle!"

"Well, no wonder the photograph is so gorgeous," he went on. "You're half in love with the model!"

"More than half," she muttered. Uncle Horatio's hands went still.

"Ah," he said. "So it's like that?"

"It might be," she admitted. "We're supposed to go out on Friday."

"Go out?"

"Well, go for a walk," she said, "See the morale flick together. Nothing scandalous."

"No more nude photography?"

"Uncle! No, of course not."

Uncle Horatio laughed, and then stepped toward her and wrapped his arms around her in a hug. She clung to him, grateful as always for his unwavering love and support.

"Well, I hope he's worthy of you, my girl," her uncle murmured into her hair. "He's certainly brave, if your photo is any indication."

"*Your* photo," she said, "And yes, he's brave, and kind, and I do think he's worthy."

"Good," Uncle Horatio said. "Bring him by on Friday before your date. I'd like to shake his hand."

*****

Author's Note

This story is based on true events, and an actual photograph taken by renowned Navy photographer Horace Bristol. You can find the photograph and the photographer's account here: https://rarehistoricalphotos.com/naked-gunner-rescue-rabaul-1944/. The author begs Lieutenant Commander Bristol's pardon, and hopes he enjoys her reimagining of the story in her own universe.

* * *

Kacey Ezell Bio

Kacey Ezell is an active duty USAF instructor pilot with 2500+ hours in the UH-1N Huey and Mi-171 helicopters. When not teaching young pilots to beat the air into submission, she writes sci-fi/fantasy/horror/noir/alternate history fiction. Her first novel, *Minds of Men*, was a Dragon Award Finalist for Best Alternate History. She's contributed to multiple Baen Books anthologies and has twice been selected for inclusion in the Year's Best Military and Adventure Science Fiction compilation. In 2018, her story "Family Over Blood" won the Year's Best Military and Adventure Science Fiction Readers' Choice Award. In addition to writing for Baen, she has published several novels and short stories with independent publisher Chris Kennedy Publishing. She is married with two daughters. You can find out more and join her mailing list at www.kaceyezell.net.

\#\#\#\#

Captain Bellamy's War
by Stephen J. Simmons

"That is a splendid galley, my young friend," Henry Jennings called out in greeting. "Quite splendid indeed."

"Why thank you, Governor," Samuel Bellamy replied with a courtly bow before leaping down to the wharf. He waved toward the line of dark-skinned men descending *Whydah's* gangplank. "Her former master sought to deliver these gentlemen to the Carolina coast as slaves, but when I put the question to them, they voted not to keep that appointment. Several opted to join my crew, and the rest wished to accompany me here in search of honest work." He favored his mentor with an overstated wink and made a gesture to take in the Nassau harbor at large. "Though it strikes me that opportunities for honest work may be scarcer than they hoped."

The elder pirate laughed. "They may at that, I suppose." Jennings took a moment more to appreciate the lines of Bellamy's prize, gleaming in the January sun. "I trust the discussion with her former master was as civil as is your custom?"

"Oh, certes, Henry," Bellamy effused. "In fact, we agreed that he should accept my own galley *Sultana* in equal exchange—after I had transferred my crew's treasure and all but her four heaviest guns to *Whydah*, naturally." He sighed theatrically. "I was loath to abandon those thirty-two pounders, but I hadn't the means to transship them. Beside which," he added in a conspiratorial tone, "it would have been wretched of me to leave the man without at least some manner of self-defense. After all, my crewmen have apprised me of scandalous rumors that there may be pirates hereabouts."

"I believe I may have heard similar gossip among my own crew," Jennings decried in a matching whisper.

"But enough foolery." Bellamy sobered and drew a parchment from an inner pocket of his coat. "*Whydah's* former master also carried a thick sheaf of these, to be posted in any port she might call upon."

PROCLAMATION

By Order of His Royal Majesty, King George

Royal Pardon for PIRATES

Be it known that any pirates who shall, on or before the fifth Day of September in the Year of our Lord One thousand seven hundred and eighteen, surrender themselves to one of our Principal Secretaries of State in Great Britain or Ireland, or to any Governor or Deputy Governor on any of our Plantations and Dominions beyond the Seas, shall have our gracious pardon of and for such Piracies as have committed by them before the fifth Day of January.

BOUNTY on PIRATES

Be it also known that we do hereby charge and command all of our Admiralty, Governors, and all other Officers both Civil and Military, to seize any Pirates who shall refuse or neglect to so surrender themselves. Further, any person or persons who discover and seize, or assist Officers in the discovery and seizure of, such pirates shall be paid a bounty:

For any Pirate Captain £100
Any Lieutenant, Boatswain, or Gunner £40
Any Private man £20

Jennings unfurled the parchment, but handed it back after only a cursory glance. "I know, Sam," he replied, his tone matching the younger man's. "I've seen scores of them. In fact, we're to meet in congress tomorrow afternoon to discuss this very matter. Not that I expect much discussion will be needful."

Bellamy shied back from his friend's defeatist tone. Henry's unspoken presumption that they must all defer to the Crown and to faraway wealthy ship owners was anathema to him—in fact, it had been the evils that such monied privilege wrought upon the lives of honest men which had driven Bellamy to the life of a privateer in the first place. To avoid bearding the older pirate on the subject in a public street, he stepped apart to pass orders to his mate and quartermaster concerning reprovisioning the ship and setting a watch to guard their as-yet undivided plunder. That errand settled, he made an effort to recall his earlier jocularity as he returned to Jennings.

"Come Henry, I've a powerful thirst and a hunger for fresh meat. Come with me to the Leaking Bucket and let me buy you dinner, and afterward we can regale the tavern with extravagant tales of our exploits."

* * *

Despite his stated intent, Bellamy spent the meal listening to the talk around them, seeking to plumb the people's thoughts of the supposed royal amnesty. The task needed but scant effort, as the patrons of the tavern spoke of little else. Many were eager to consider it, while many others expressed doubt that the offer could be trusted.

"The king himself proclaimed it, man. How can ye doubt?" asked a voice that rose above the general din.

"Even if I could accept that German pretender as king," came the heated reply, "he sits his throne a thousand leagues away, while the governors are *here*. And *they* want us to swing."

The two captains tarried for another round of ale, but little changed in the talk that flowed about them. Troubled, Bellamy bade his friend a good evening and returned to *Whydah* to seek an early bed.

* * *

The captains began gathering in the square just after their noon meal. The two largest rooms in Nassau were the church and the governor's courtroom, but the consensus among the captains was that either setting might prove prejudicial to the discussion at hand. After a moment's consideration, they agreed upon the common room of the same tavern Bellamy had visited the evening before. Being among the first to arrive, Bellamy claimed a seat near the bar and settled in to listen to what his fellows would have to say.

Henry Jennings led a faction that favored taking the promised royal pardon, while Charles Vane led another that staunchly opposed this course. Some of those siding with Vane favored continuing their piracy unabated, while others favored allying with the Jacobites to depose King George in exchange for pardons from a grateful James Stuart. This latter group included Edward Teach, the man known as Blackbeard, but Teach let Vane carry the bulk of the discussion.

The debate was lively, at times heated, and were it not for the crowding it might have come to blows at a few points. Many variations on the same basic arguments he had heard the night before were repeated, but none present seemed in the least swayed from the positions they held before the meeting began. After more than an hour, Vane gave a cry of disgust and turned to make his way through the throng toward the door, heralding an end to the meeting.

"Tarry a moment longer, friends," Bellamy called out, rising from his seat. He made his way to the center of the floor. "Captain Vane, I beg a moment of your attention. Permit me to divulge my mind, before we retire in disarray and despair."

"Oh, aye," came Vane's sardonic response. "I would be most edified to hear the thoughts of the Prince of Pirates."

"Prince," Bellamy replied earnestly, dismissing the sarcasm. "That title bears most acutely upon my argument." He made an entreating gesture, inviting Vane to stand with him in the small open space at the room's center. After a long moment, Vane acquiesced. Bellamy likewise gestured Jennings and Blackbeard to join him.

"Friends, we have heard many cogent and heartfelt arguments, all generally exhorting us to endorse or reject the positions championed by these three of our most celebrated captains. All three courses have some merit, and are worthy of sober and deliberate reflection. But," his gaze swept the room, gauging the mood to be found there, "before any of you casts his lot irrevocably, I would exhort each of you to consider the possibility of a *fourth* course." His eyes swept the room once more, seeking contact with any eye that met his own. Mutters and murmurs ran about the edges of the gathering, but none dissented openly.

"My old captain—" Bellamy clapped a companionable hand on Jennings' shoulder, "—argues most sensibly that the proffered amnesty represents a grand boon, not to be cast aside lightly. To keep our ships, aye, that and all our spoils beside, and claim the rights of English gentlemen with no man to gainsay us." He faced Jennings squarely, but his voice still addressed the whole room. "If such offer be genuine, I can scarcely fault any man who might seek it. And yet..." his gaze took on a hint of challenge. He scanned the room once again and singled out one of the men who had spoken most openly in support of Jennings' arguments.

"Captain Hale, do you recall the night Calico Jack knifed you in a drunken fury, right here in the Bucket?"

"Aye," the other replied, his tone wary but his eyes alight with remembered ire. "What of it?"

"Do you truly think the two of you could ever live side by side, could ever stand in your door-yard gardens and gossip across the fence, neither harboring any rancorous thoughts harking back to that night?" He turned away without answer, his gaze and gestures taking in the whole room. "Do any of you think you could make your way as 'honest merchant captains' in these waters, doing business with the very traders and towns we have all robbed and plundered?" He turned back to Jennings. "I mean you no insult, my friend, but for myself I cannot credit my fellow man with such saintly capacity to forgive."

The room rumbled with response, but Bellamy raised both hands and bellowed, "Wait! Attend me just a few minutes more. I grant you my oath that I shall be brief." He scanned the room again, this time with a challenging glower. When he sensed that he held them all once again in his hand, he turned to Blackbeard.

"Captain Teach has argued that we might reject the amnesty in favor of casting our lots with those of Queen Anne's heirs, but at its heart, for the likes of *us*, there is little to distinguish his arguments from those of Captain Jennings." He raised a hand to fend off Blackbeard's retort. "*Peace*, Captain," he entreated the larger man. "I mean you no disrespect by this. I merely mean—" he turned to scan the room again, "—that this course also promises us an amnesty, once again pledging to us that the Crown can command the men we have wronged to become angels. I hold no more faith in such a pledge from James than I have for one from George."

The mutters grew loud again, this time coming largely from the men who had backed Vane. Bellamy raised his arms once again, striding to stand between Vane and his adherents.

"Captain Vane called me *Prince of Pirates* a moment ago, a name many among you have ascribed to me." He turned a sorrowful look on Vane. "Can you not see the irony in that sobriquet? I never sought to bear *either* of those titles." He faced Vane and spoke in a voice so low men strained to hear him. "And yet, even as you paint me with both, you miss the underlying truth." He turned back to face the crowd, and his voice cracked with the timbre he used to shout commands to seamen in the rigging.

"*Both of those titles are the SAME*, my friends. Don't you *see*?" He turned back to Vane and grasped both of the man's arms. "A prince is nothing more nor less than a pirate who pardons himself, claiming exclusive right to plunder his fellow man by calling his thievery *taxes*." He turned once again to the throng. "What need have *we* for European kings of *any* House? What need have we for a governor dispatched from London, when we can freely elect one from amongst ourselves?"

The room erupted in confusion. Bellamy scanned the crowd, weighing their mood, just as he had so often gauged the mood of his crews before calling a crucial vote. He could see that they were nearing his position, but he didn't quite have the majority. Yet.

He urged Jennings forward and waved for quiet. "If it's amnesty ye crave, why beg it from some *landlord* when ye can get the same from our own governor?" He waved Teach forward, then turned and laid a hand on Vane's shoulder. "And if it's still the looting ye crave, would it be such a burden to restrict our claim to a moderate ten percent, rather than the whole cargo? Because we could damned well be *collecting* taxes, and using that money right here in New Providence, rather than shipping good money off to enrich King George. I say we should reject not just the Crown's amnesty, but reject the Crown *itself!*"

A stunned silence gripped the room for several heartbeats, followed by bedlam. Bellamy listened, impassive, and judged that he had garnered a strong majority. But it was a fleeting one, to be seized before the tide could turn. Jennings was the first to object.

"But what of the Navy?" he pointed out. "We can't hope to stand against them."

"What of *our* navy?" Bellamy replied. "Look at the harbor, Henry. There are near to thirty armed ships here, and twice that many more who call Nassau their home. Between us, my *Whydah* and *Queen Anne's Revenge* are a match for any British frigate, and none of them could hope to boast so many escorts."

"But the *fleet*," Jennings persisted.

"Their fleet is scattered, while ours is right here." He turned to address the crowd. "Make no mistake—King George *will* send ships here. This island and the others around us are too grand a prize, and he will be loath to surrender the riches he squeezes from us. This new governor, whoever it is to be, will certainly come with several ships at his command. But they will think that they come to *hunt* pirates, one at a time, not to face a navy of our own."

"No, Sam," Jennings said firmly. "I won't sign on for open war against the Royal Navy. I'm for taking the king's pardon, and I'll find myself some land and become one of those rich landlords you disdain. My battles are done." Several of the pirates cursed Jennings, calling him coward. But Bellamy waved them to silence and gripped Henry's hand.

"I understand, Henry. Truly I do." Bellamy turned to the hecklers. "Friends, let us not forget that we have called this man our governor. Upon my oath, Henry is no coward. Whatever else he may have been or may yet become, he is a good captain and an honorable man. And my friend." He released Jennings's hand and turned about, addressing the whole room. "Though I find it not to my personal taste, I own that I can assign no shame to any man who may choose to take the amnesty. If the king's offer be honest and honored, it is a prize beyond price. I would ask only this of those who choose to chart that course:

"Raise not your hand against us who choose else, once your own pardons are secured. We have been brethren here, if only for a brief time. I ask that none of ye should take unto yourselves the Mark of Cain by helping the Crown to ferret out the coves and passages that other pirates may use for concealment. And I would ask one more thing beside.

"If your aim is to retire from pirating and to make a living on land, then sell us your ships before you go. Or failing that, at least sell us your guns." He returned to Jennings, holding his hand out to the older man. "Will you sell me *Bersheba*, Henry? I'll pay a fair price. The money will stand you in good stead when you seek to buy that plantation."

"Aye, lad," Jennings replied after a long moment, taking Bellamy's hand in both of his own. "Aye, that I gladly will. You've the right of the thing."

* * *

It took a week to sort out, but in the end Bellamy bade Jennings farewell as the older man and nearly a third of the pirates boarded a half-score of lightly-armed ships and set sail for Bermuda. Jamaica was closer, and an easier passage, but there were distressing rumors of Governor Hamilton becoming a fugitive on account of a Jacobite relative. That, and the open waters between New Providence and Bermuda were less likely to hold pirates who had not yet received word of Bellamy's rebellion.

And "Bellamy's Rebellion" it had become, to Sam's shock and consternation. He had expected Teach to be Nassau's new governor, having already been elected their magistrate. But even though Bellamy was one of the youngest captains, the men swayed by his tavern-speech insisted that only he saw the problem clearly enough. And Teach, damn his hide, had declined Bellamy's nomination to the post.

"Nay, lad, the men have the right of it," he insisted with a twinkle in his eye. "You do the governing, and I'll be your right honorable Lord of Admiralty. That's the way of it, to my thinking."

That settled, the captains gathered in council to hammer out a plan for defending the city, and to devise stratagems for facing the fleet that the new governor would be bringing.

* * *

"Long guns," Bellamy interjected into the ongoing argument about whether more guns should be unshipped to improve the armament in the fort overlooking the harbor.

"What's that?" Teach asked, startled.

"Long guns," Bellamy repeated. "Nearly half the cannon in the fort are long guns. Nines and twelves, mainly," he went on, referring to the weight of cannonball the guns fired. "But the fort already has the range advantage, because its guns are higher. It should be armed with carronades, not long guns. *Big* ones, by preference."

Blackbeard's eyes lit. He saw that Bellamy was indeed onto something. Because ships of war needed to be narrow in the interest of greater speed, shipboard broadside weapons tended to be seven-foot carronades of varying sizes. Nine-foot "long guns" took up too much space on deck, despite their greater accuracy and nearly a furlong's advantage in range. Also, the longer barrels were perforce much heavier, and weight was always at a premium in any ship. So "long guns" typically only served as bow-or-stern-mounted chase armament, if they were used at all.

The fort had been stripped of its guns when the French overran the Nassau garrison during the wars of the Spanish Succession. When the pirates took the city as the capitol of their makeshift Republic, they had stripped a few guns from prize vessels to re-arm the fort. But no pirate wanted to sacrifice broadside armament, so the guns donated to the fort's rearming had comprised a disproportionate number of chase weapons.

"Go on, Sam," Teach urged. "Finish the thought."

"Most of our fleet are sloops," Bellamy said earnestly. "Faster than the Navy's frigates, nimbler, and gaff-rigged to steer closer to the wind. But speed and maneuverability don't help if we have to get in range of *their* guns to shoot."

"But the sloops haven't the beam to mount long guns a'broadside," Vane argued.

"What about just *one* broadside?" Bellamy countered. "And stagger the gun ports, so the guns don't run back one against the other?

Instead of six heavy guns, your *Lark* could mount four long nines to one side, and three sixteen pounders to the other. With room left for another nine in the heavy-side bow, for chase, since your speed means you're always best to strike from windward. If we can find that many long guns."

Silence gripped the conference table for a moment, then Teach let out a whoop. "I *told* you the men had the right of it!" He shook a finger at Bellamy. "You just keep thinking, lad, and we'll whip those loyalists yet!"

* * *

Captain Benjamin Hornigold's *Ranger* returned in early February, leading a pair of captured Dutch ships, the forty-gun man-o-war *Young Abraham* and a twenty-four gun armed merchant named *Amsterdam*, along with a trio of unarmed prizes laden with plunder. He had been intending to sell his loot in Nassau before proceeding to Port Royal to take the amnesty, but Blackbeard succeeded in swaying him to Bellamy's cause. With Hornigold's three ships anchored alongside *Queen Anne's Revenge*, *Whydah*, and *Bersheba*, Nassau's fleet began to resemble a "line of battle" sufficient to give any Royal Navy admiral pause.

"You should know that King George has named the man he means to be our new governor," Hornigold reported. The other captains all turned to him, eager to hear the news. "Woodes Rogers," he intoned dramatically. "His Majesty seems to think that the privateer who took a Spanish treasure-ship has what it takes to capture us, despite the fact that he ended the adventure in bankruptcy."

"Rogers? The one who wrote the book about rescuing a marooned sailor?" one of the other captains asked.

"Rescue?" Hornigold snorted. "Twas one of Rogers's men who marooned the poor man in the first place. Begged to be put ashore and left behind, because he feared to sail any further under his command."

"When is he coming?" Bellamy asked, drawing the meeting back to matters at hand.

"Rumor says he's outfitting a fleet of ships, to sail sometime after Easter. And that he's been appointed Governor-in-Chief of *all* the Bahamas, not just New Providence."

"Well, then," Blackbeard put in, "after we sink his little fleet, I suppose we'll have to lay claim to all the other islands in his stead then, won't we?"

* * *

"Sails ho!" Lark's lookout called. "Two British ships, just north of east. Two at the least, mayhap more."

Vane acknowledged the report and bellowed commands to reset the rigging to shape a more easterly course. He couldn't see the sails yet from the quarterdeck, but his lookout was a steady man. Just as he began to see what might be mast-heads on the horizon, the man called down again.

"Aye, that looks to be them, Cap'n. Eight ships, all well-armed and flying the Union Jack, and steering just south of west. Bound toward Nassau, sure as certain."

"Very well," Vane replied. "Signal the packets."

For three weeks, Vane and the ships under his command had patrolled the trade routes east of New Providence, searching for news of Rogers' fleet. His twelve sloops were spread north to south along a line over a hundred miles long, spaced just close enough for the lookouts to keep sight of each other. The captains had worked out a number of simple messages that could be passed from ship to ship by means of colored pennants, and his lookout was even now unfurling the paired red and black to indicate the quarry had at last been sighted.

At the center of the line cruised two swift unarmed mail packets. When the signal reached them, one turned west under full sail to bring news to the fleet massed in Nassau. The other, flying a Dutch flag, turned south to rendezvous with *Lark*. After a brief discussion with Vane, the Dutch captain turned his ship as near to the wind as she could steer to close with Rogers's ships. The sloops, meanwhile, began closing up their spacing, the southern half converging on *Lark* while the northern ships, none of which had yet been seen by the enemy, gathered around Stede Bonnet's *Revenge*.

* * *

Captain Anselm van Heusen fought to hide his nerves as he raised the speaking-trumpet to hail the Navy sloop that had maneuvered out of the British formation to meet him. "I bear dispatches for a captain named Woodes Rogers," he called out. "Is he aboard?"

"He commands *Delyssia*," the Navy man shouted back, pointing to one of the larger ships. He turned and shouted orders, signals flashed between ships, and the whole formation slowed enough for van Heusen to launch a boat for the crossing to the impressive thirty-gun man-o-war.

"I am Captain Anselm van Heusen," he announced upon reaching the deck, "of the Dutch mail packet *Koerierstas*." He indicated a leather bag slung crosswise on a long strap. "I was hired to bear dispatches to Captain Woodes Rogers, and to wait for a reply."

"I am Rogers," a splendidly-dressed gentlemen replied. "What manner of dispatches?"

"I know not, sir," the Dutchman replied. "The case was sealed with lead when I received it." He pulled the strap over his head and handed his burden across. Rogers broke the seal to reveal a thick sheaf of parchment.

"Quite a weighty dispatch, it would seem. Come, Captain, let us repair to my cabin for refreshment whilst I examine it."

"*Outrageous*," Rogers bellowed a short while later, startling van Heusen so badly that he nearly dropped his wine. Rogers glared at his guest. "You are no mail packet," he accused. "You are a *pirate*, flying a false flag and pretending to innocence to save your worthless neck."

"No, my lord," van Heusen said, fighting to keep terror from strangling his voice. "I swear, I am nothing more nor less than a simple packet captain out of Sint Maarten, ferrying passengers and mail to make my living. I am no pirate, sir. Never have I raised a hand against any man, not even my own erring crewmen."

"Yet you do business with pirates," Rogers replied, lifting the bundle of parchment.

"I bear mail, Captain," he replied more confidently, back on familiar ground. "Lawfully, and in a manner your own Crown has endorsed, as I am certain you already know. I never know the content, for that is not my business. My business is to ensure delivery. Which I have done." He effected a small bow without rising. "But I was also paid—in advance—to carry back your reply, should you have any." He favored Rogers with a questioning glance.

"You say you don't know the *treason* you were paid to place in my hand? Very well, I shall enlighten you, sir. Not only do these scurrilous knaves refuse to repent of their piracy, they have the *audacity* to declare themselves a sovereign state, independent from the Crown! *This*," he cast the bundle of parchment aside in disgust, "is the draft of a *treaty!* They have the *impudence* to state that," he retrieved the top page from the bundle and read aloud, "*Forasmuch as we have already elected a Sovereign Governor Plenipotentiary from amongst our existing Population, we find it neither needful nor fitting that any Foreign Power should presume to assign us one.*" He snorted in exasperation. "The devils invite me to carry their ridiculous *treaty* proposal to His Majesty, as though I were naught but some mere *messenger*."

The dark look that flitted across his guest's features at this last went unnoticed, and Captain van Heusen swiftly schooled himself to placidity before responding.

"Am I to take it, then, that you do intend to reply, Captain?"

"*Governor!*" Rogers spat, then he reined himself in, but only slightly. "*Yes*, Captain, I have a response for you to carry back." He leaned forward, his eyes aflame. "Tell them that any ship of theirs that sails within range of my guns will be sent to the bottom, with no warning, no mercy, and no quarter. *Tell* them," he stood and glared at the cluster of sails barely visible on the southwestern horizon, "that I shall not rest until every last mother's son among them shall swing from a rope."

"It shall be exactly as you say, Captain," van Heusen replied calmly. "Good day, sir, and I thank you for your hospitality. The wine was most excellent."

* * *

"Thank you, Captain," Vane said sincerely. "You have done very well indeed. I have one more commission for you, if you're willing?"

"So long as it doesn't mean sailing back toward that madman," the Dutchman said bluntly.

"Quite the opposite, Captain," Vane assured him. He pointed west. "There is a large body of ships bound this way from Nassau. Would you be so good as to rendezvous with them and deliver that same message? Tell them also that we should all be in proper position at dawn, two days hence." He tossed van Heusen a golden Spanish coin, then winked. "Tell them I promised payment upon delivery. And then you would be wise to get your ship away to the south and west for a goodly while, I think."

Once *Koerierstas* was away, Vane had his lookout pass the prearranged signal to *Revenge* and then turned *Lark* to the southeast, quickly passing out of sight of the massed British ships. He gathered the other five sloops from the southern half of the line, and together they began tacking to windward, to get behind the enemy. The six northern sloops did the same, taking care that Rogers' ships never saw them.

* * *

The day dawned red and threatening, with the wind swinging around to come from east-southeast and blowing inhospitable clouds before it. Woodes Rogers mounted the quarterdeck to scowl at the unwelcome sky, then jumped at the cry from *Delyssia's* lookout.

"*Sail ho!* East by northeast. I make it six ships, flying black flags."

So, Rogers thought. *Those pirates are still with us. Not that they pose any threat to* this *armada. Let them come. But how did they get around to our north?* "Lieutenant," he called out, gesturing one of his officers closer. "Signal the fleet to shorten sail a bit. Let us see if we can't draw these brigands near enough to force them to action."

"*Sail ho!*" came the cry again. "South by southeast. Two ships, p'raps more. Can't see aught but sails as yet. But one flies a black ensign bearing a skeleton holding a spear."

Blackbeard's flag! Rogers thought. *Has he brought more ships? Or are these the ones we saw before, and the others a new group? Well, it only stands to reason there might be more of the scum. Good, mayhap they'll embolden one another enough to come within range.* He called the lieutenant back. "Come left and steer southwest. Mayhap we can draw these enemies closer together. And shift formation to form the battle line, with *Delyssia* in the lead."

* * *

"*Full sail!*" Vane bellowed as the sun touched the crow's nest, and he made large sweeping arm motions to the ships to either side. The strengthening wind had made him slow his ships during the night so as not to get ahead of the other fleet elements, but the time for such subtleties was past now. The enemy was dead ahead of him, and *Lark* was free to run straight down the wind in pursuit. He called for his gunners to man their stations, and sent the cabin boy to fetch him a pot of rum.

* * *

"*Sail ho!*" came yet a third cry, and Rogers stared up at the crow's nest. "Just south of east, running straight out of the sun," the lookout called, a hint of fear tinging his voice. "Six ships, all under full sail."

Rogers spun to stare to the east, dumbfounded, knowing he would see nothing, but helpless to do otherwise. *Three* groups of pirates? *Preposterous*, he chastised himself, quelling the irrational surge of fear. *Those scum don't collaborate. And even if they did, this is the mightiest armada these waters have ever seen. The more pirates we kill today, the fewer I'll need to hunt down later.*

* * *

"They've turned to the southwest, Cap'n," the lookout called down from the crow's nest of *Queen Anne's Revenge*. "And they seem to have shortened sail a bit, I think."

"Shortened sail?" Blackbeard called back, startled. "You're certain?"

"No doubt of it, Cap'n," the man replied.

He turned to stare northward. *Turned only half-toward us, and* slowed *his fleet?* He wondered. *Does he think to get behind us and run us down from windward? But that only makes sense if we're alone.* "What sign of Vane?" he called up to the lookout.

"Six masts to the northeast," came the reply. "Right where *Lark* should be, and they've piled on every scrap of sail they have. The enemy *must* see them."

"Very well," he acknowledged, still staring northward. *He knows he faces multiple enemies, and yet he steers a course to* help *us converge on him.* He shook his head, dumbfounded. The man must be as inept as Hornigold had claimed. He glanced to port, eying the powerful line of pirate ships that lay below the enemy's horizon. The pirates had hoped merely to weaken the Navy force with this ambush, but Rogers was offering them a chance for a decisive victory instead. And William Teach was certainly not going to complain.

As ridiculous as it seemed, there was actually a chance to try Bellamy's other idea. He waved to his first mate.

"Launch the canoes."

* * *

"What the devil?" Rogers asked, staring in disbelief. A half-dozen lateen-rigged sailing canoes were making their way toward him, coming from the two ships to his south. The canoes could carry more than a score of men, yet each carried only three, just enough to manage their rigging and steerage.

"Ahoy, *Delyssia!*" the man steering the lead canoe called out when he was near enough to be heard. An officer moved to the rail.

"Ahoy, you in the boats," the officer called back, his puzzlement plain.

"Good morrow to you, Lieutenant," the pirate called cheerfully. "We were advised that some of the ships in your company bear settlers, including women and children. Admiral Blackbeard sends his compliments, and begs that you let us carry the innocents out of harm's way before the battle is joined."

"*Admiral* Blackbeard?" Rogers exclaimed, flinging himself down the steps from the quarterdeck and rushing to the rail. "Admiral *Blackbeard?*" He snatched the pistol from the officer's belt and fired it, but the shot went wide.

"*Please*, milord," the pirate called out in what seemed to be genuine concern, "a battle's no place for women and children. If you're intent on making war with us, at *least* let us carry your innocents safely out of harm's way."

"*Reload*," Rogers commanded, thrusting the pistol back at its owner. To the canoe he yelled, "You pirates *dare* to suggest that we might surrender our women and children to be your hostages?" He rounded on the hapless lieutenant. "Run out the guns!" he screamed. "Send these impudent pirates to the bottom of the sea!"

At this the canoes swung their sails and leapt away to the west and out from under *Delyssia's* guns.

* * *

"Range?" Vane asked his gunner, knowing that he should have stayed on the quarterdeck and left the man to his work, but not apologizing for his inability to do so.

"Zat depends, *mon capitaine*," the man said distractedly, his eyes fixed on the enemy. "Ze transport we could hit now," he said, waving a hand at the twenty-gun troopship holding its sheltered position north east of the last ship in the enemy's battle line. "But *Revenge* will range her soon enough, so I thought you might prefer we take ze frigate, instead. She's still a bit far, even for long guns. With zis overtake, we'll have range of her in twenty minutes. Perhaps a bit more."

"You call the shot, Remy," he said, gripping the Frenchman's shoulder. "I trust you." He glared at the enemy a moment longer and turned to make his way back to the quarterdeck.

* * *

"*Now,*" Remy L'ebout cried, lighting the touch-hole just as *Lark* crested the wave, giving his gun maximum elevation. He raised a red pennon and waved it to signal the other five sloops. *Lark*'s bow cannon leapt backward, belching fire, and his crew sprang into action, moving to swab out their gun and reload it before it even came to rest.

* * *

Commodore Peter Chamberlain stood beside *HMS Milford's* helm and wished, not for the first time, that he and his ships had not been placed under the orders of the new governor. Granted, the former privateer was celebrated for his taking of that Spanish treasure-ship, but in that battle he had commanded multiple ships attacking a single target. Rogers had no training for fleet actions, and his inexperience showed. Rather than choosing one of the three enemy formations and closing rapidly to defeat it in detail before the others could come to its aid, the fool was actually *inviting* them to gather and attack his battle line in concert. Chamberlain couldn't imagine what the man was think—

Chamberlain's torso vanished into a cloud of red mist, coating the helmsman in gore. The shockwave of the passing cannonball flung the helmsman against the wheel, cracking his ribs and addling his brains.

* * *

"*Merde!*" L'ebout swore. "Too high. But at least we have the range." He watched *Milford's* stern to see the shots from *Lark*'s sisters arrive. The target's rudder swung sharply, exposing its full surface to their fire, and L'ebout smiled as two of the shots blasted through it and into the hull beyond. The holes their nine-pounders made weren't large, but enough small holes could disable a rudder as effectively as a few big ones. And getting that five hundred ton frigate and her fifty-six twenty-four pound guns out of the fight would make Blackbeard's job a lot easier. He grunted as he helped the crew shove his reloaded gun back to battery and took up his torch once more.

* * *

Lieutenant Armand Hastings stumbled as *HMS Milford* lurched to starboard, her bow swinging to a course that threatened collision with the three hundred ton troop-ship *Willing Mind.* He looked up to the quarterdeck and saw the helmsman hanging from the wheel, coated in blood. Hastings raced up the steps and stopped, staring at the cavalry-style boots beside the helmsman's feet, still glistening with their immaculate parade-ground shine. The boots with the commodore's legs still in them, but ending at the knees.

The world spun about him, and his gorge rose. But Hastings clung to the rail and forced his mind to accept what he saw. He swallowed heavily, twice, and stepped through the carnage. He pried loose the helmsman's convulsive grip on the wheel and shoved the injured man unkindly aside, then brought the ship back to an even keel, swinging the bow away from *Willing Mind.* His voice bellowed commands to the men in the ratlines that his conscious mind never heard, increasing speed to flee the guns threatening her from astern.

* * *

Revenge's gunner touched off his cannon, and her five sisters fired moments later. Three of the six shots went home into *Willing Mind's* stern, but her rudder was pointed almost directly at them, and they did it no damage at all.

* * *

"*Milford*'s closing us up," Captain Brentworth noted on the quarterdeck of *HMS Rose*. "But the commodore hasn't signaled a change."

"The pirates are firing into her stern," Lieutenant Perkins observed. "Perhaps the commodore seeks to evade them?"

"A fourth-rate ship of the line, running from a ragtag handful of pirate sloops?" Brentworth glared at the young officer. "*Commodore Chamberlain*, fleeing an engagement? For your sake, Leftenant, I shall choose not to have heard that ridiculous statement."

The younger man hung his head for a moment, then looked back at *Milford*. "Whatever the reason, sir, she's still closing us up. Oughtn't we to do something about that?"

"Quite right, Leftenant," Brentworth approved. He drew out his spyglass and peered back at *Milford*. "That's odd," he mused, "the commodore doesn't appear to be..." his voice trailed off, and his mouth gaped open. After a long moment, he snapped the glass shut and turned to face Perkins, his face ashen.

"Signal the fleet, commodore's orders," he rasped, spinning to stare at the pirate ships approaching from south and east for a moment before continuing. "Commodore's orders," he repeated. "The battle line shall come left, two points west of south, best possible speed, and engage the two large pirates."

"But sir," Perkins objected, "the commodore hasn't—"

"The commodore is *dead*, Mister Perkins. And so shall we be, if we keep entrusting the fleet to that idiot of a privateer. *Go!*"

* * *

"He ordered *what?*" Rogers demanded. "He doesn't give orders. He *takes* them. From *me*." He glared at the hapless signalman. "I command here, not Commodore Chamberlain." He glared as the helmsman began to turn *Delyssia's* wheel. "*As you were, sailor,*" he snapped. He glanced back along the battle line, and was dismayed to see all seven of the other ships coming about to follow the commodore's orders.

"Get those ships back in line," he bellowed at the unfortunate signalman. "We need to draw those other pirates close enough to force action, or we'll have to chase them across half the ocean."

* * *

"Hard a'port," Vane snapped as the enemy ships turned, grabbing up the red pennon and waving it to alert the other captains. "Hold the range open, and bring the broadside to bear on the frigate." He raised his voice to carry across the deck. "Starboard guns to the ready. Fire when you bear." The range was still long, but the starboard broadside was the one that had been refitted with long guns, like the other sloops in his group. The frigate's maneuver had increased *Lark*'s firepower four times over, while making her rudder an even easier target.

His small force boasted a combined broadside of twenty-two long guns, ten twelve-pounders and a dozen nines. All of those guns hammered *Milford's* stern as fast as they could be reloaded and aimed, and on their third volley the major part of the frigate's rudder splintered and fell away. She staggered out of line, bereft of steerage and left to the mercies of the winds. Moments later, the troopship did the same, crippled by broadsides from *Revenge* and her sisters.

Vane gave no further thought to the crippled *Milford*, turning southwest to close on the stern of the next frigate, *HMS Rose*. Bonnet, caught to the north of the two cripples, turned his formation west to pursue Rogers' four ships.

* * *

"What the *devil* can they be thinking?" Blackbeard asked his helmsman in a conversational tone. The four Navy ships, two fourth-rate frigates, a troopship and a twenty-gun sloop-of-war, had turned straight toward him and piled on full sail. The other four ships, three armed merchants and Rogers' man-o-war *Delyssia*, were still sailing southwest under shortened sails. Did they truly mean to meet him with only half their force, letting the civilian ships stand clear of danger?

It was gallant of them, certainly, but it made no *sense.* With the wind holding strong out of the southeast, the Navy ships were steering almost as near to the wind as they could manage. He could easily shape a northerly course that held his ships to their east, and link up with Vane's force while holding a considerable maneuvering advantage the whole time. He could understand someone like Rogers *giving* such a foolish order, but he couldn't imagine any sane Navy captain *obeying* it.

But if he did that, *Delyssia* and Rogers' other ships would be between him and Nassau, with the wind at their backs and the legs to avoid action. And except for the fort, he and Bellamy had stripped the harbor as naked as a newborn babe to mount this ambush. If Rogers got past them, the war was lost before it was truly begun. And more...he drew out the cameo that hung from the silver chain about his neck, and gazed down at the images of Mary and young William for a long moment.

He raised his eyes to gaze across at *Whydah*, and realized with a start that just as the title "Prince" had changed young Bellamy, the title "Admiral" had changed him. He had donned it purely for sport, but that no longer mattered. These men had taken his orders, had placed their lives, homes, and livelihoods in his care. And by doing so, they had bought him, body and soul. His life belonged to them now, not to himself. And more, his life belonged to his sweet, beautiful Mary, and to their black-haired son. Both of whom would surely die in prison if Rogers took Nassau. He snapped the cameo shut and tucked it carefully away.

"Signal Hornigold and the other captains," he ordered his lieutenant, "to fall into battle line behind us." He turned to the helm and ordered, "Steer northwest, and get us between the two enemy lines."

"North*west*, Cap'n?" the sailor asked. "Not..." he pointed northeast, toward Vane's sloops. "Not northeasterly?"

He stepped close to the helmsman and lowered his voice. "Do you see that ship, lad?" he asked, pointing northwest. "That ship carries Governor Rogers." He waved dismissively at the four Navy ships charging toward them. "These ships can only shoot at us. But *those* ships can destroy us all, even if they never fire a shot today. If *Delyssia* escapes, we lose everything." He pointed northwest. "So get us between their lines, lad, and in range of both. And then pray Hornigold is brave enough to follow us."

* * *

Captain Reginald Burstin gasped as more pirate ships appeared over the southern horizon to line up behind the two he was charging to meet. Three more...no, four...no, *six* new ships streamed into view. And every one of them outmassed and outgunned *HMS Shark*. But the commodore had granted Burstin and *Shark* the honor of leading the line, and he'd be damned if he'd give the Old Man cause to doubt his performance. He kept his voice level and firm as he ordered his starboard gunners to roll out their guns. Then, considering the range, he ordered the rest of his crew to man the starboard rail with muskets and pistols.

Queen Anne's Revenge drew abeam of *Shark*, and Burstin bellowed the order for his crew to fire. The five six-pound guns in his starboard broadside fired as one, scoring four hits and killing a total of three goats—plus the ship's cat—though the shot that caromed through Blackbeard's cabin *did* succeed in smashing a priceless scrimshaw carving to flinders. His musketmen's fire had somewhat more effect, killing one of Blackbeard's master gunners outright and wounding men in four other gun crews enough to make their teams call for replacements before they could reload.

In return, Blackbeard's answering salvo of fifteen twelve-pound cannonballs blasted into *Shark*, turning oaken planking into a deadly hail of splinters that shredded four of *Shark*'s five gun crews, while double loads of grapeshot and chain-shot from the four twenty-four pound guns Blackbeard had claimed from the fort turned *Shark*'s main deck into a charnel house.

Captain Burstin collapsed to the deck in despair, but his one remaining gunner never knew that. Able Seaman Dithers directed his experienced crew calmly, never raising his voice, as though this were just another exercise. Dithers sat directly atop his gun, despite the risk, and sighted along the barrel. He waited for *Shark* to roll down the next wave, lowering the gun's point of aim until...*There!* he thought, and lit the touch-hole.

The recoil flung Dithers off the gun into a cross-beam, and he fell to the deck like a broken toy. But his six-pound cannonball punched through the pirate's hull and into her powder room, and *Queen Anne's Revenge* blew apart with a blinding flash, even as her second volley killed every living thing left aboard *Shark*.

* * *

W*hydah* was next in line, and Bellamy stared at the sinking wreckage of Blackbeard's ship in sick fascination as he passed it. The ten-gun sloop that *Queen Anne's Revenge* had killed seemed unfair payment for her loss, but that could hardly be remedied now. There were men alive in the water, clinging to what flotsam they could find, but Bellamy couldn't spare them attention yet. *Delyssia's* southwesterly course meant that her guns would come to bear on him shortly, and from almost dead ahead. He couldn't turn to engage her without moving closer to the undamaged fourth-rate frigate *HMS Rose*, and the Navy's gunners were likely to be a lot better than the ones Rogers had managed to hire.

The frigate behind *Rose* staggered out of the enemy battle line, clearly not under command. Vane's ships must have succeeded in wrecking her steerage, just as they had been bidden. But their very success might spell disaster for Bellamy. The huge frigate was coming about to the west, in the grip of the wind. Which meant that her port broadside would come to bear on *Whydah* at almost the same moment that *Rose*'s and *Delyssia's* did.

He turned to look back at *Bersheba*, the ship he had bought from Jennings and ceded to Paulsgrave Williams, the friend who had been at his side since before he had embarked on this life, and he summoned a signalman.

"Message to *Bersheba*," he ordered calmly. "Turn west. Keep Rogers out of Nassau." He thought for a moment, then shook his head. "Go. Send that, and then go find a gun." He pushed the signalman away and strode to the helm and nudged the seaman manning it aside.

"*Ready starboard guns*," he bellowed, then spun the wheel to port to open his broadside to bear on *Rose*. After all twenty guns had fired he spun the wheel back, closing the distance to the frigate but staying clear of her guns. The frigate couldn't turn to open her broadside to him, because that would face her into the wind. It wasn't much, but it was all Bellamy had.

* * *

"Sorry, Governor," Williams said softly when the signalman passed him Bellamy's message. "I'm afraid I can't do that." He pushed the man toward the stern rail. "Send the governor's message to *Ranger.* I have promises to keep." He moved to the railing that fronted the quarterdeck.

"*Port guns,*" he bellowed, "*load chain and grape, and fire when you bear! Helm, hard a'starboard.*"

Bersheba swung into the wind, her sails rippling, booming, and then falling slack. But her momentum kept her moving, and she swung far enough east to bring her broadside to bear on *Indomitable's* bow. Twelve sixteen-pound guns roared, and Williams ordered the helmsman to reverse his rudder. "Make for Vane's sails," he told the man. "But stand ready to open the broadside again on my mark."

* * *

Captain Brentworth tasted despair. His commodore was dead, his flagship a drifting wreck. The ship carrying his putative governor was fleeing the battle without having fired a shot. He stared down at the wreckage of what had, until moments earlier, been a King's Ship of the Line. A third of his starboard broadside was destroyed, and the storm of chain-shot had savaged most of his rigging and killed half of his deck crew. The two pirates who had wrought this carnage charged in, maneuvering to strike *Rose* yet again, one from either side this time. And there were still four *more* pirates behind them, plus the raiders who had killed the commodore overtaking from astern.

"Leftenant Perkins," he called out, in a voice so calm it startled him, "would you be so good as to go and strike the colors? And find something to serve as a white flag?"

* * *

"Good afternoon, Captain," Bellamy said cheerfully, as Rogers was escorted into his cabin in chains.

"*Governor*," Rogers spat, his eyes flaming with hate.

"That's right," Teach put in cheerfully, his hand stroking an embroidered waistcoat that was somewhat worse for the hours he'd spent clinging to a scrap of wreckage, "Captain Bellamy here *is* the Governor." The cheer vanished, to be replaced by burnished steel. "And you are *not*. The sooner you come to understand that, the easier life will be for everyone. *Especially* you."

Rogers gaped, and Bellamy waved Teach to a seat. "You see, Captain Rogers, we're not quite certain what to do with you. The Navy men are clearly all prisoners of war, and there are clear conventions for that. But calling you a Navy officer would mean sending you to your death, since by all accounts your ships seemed to be fleeing the battle without having fired a shot." Rogers bristled, and Bellamy raised his eyebrows. "Is there some other interpretation of your actions that we have overlooked, Captain? Please, enlighten us."

Rogers drew in a breath, then held it as he considered the other men. He deflated, staring down at the floor.

"What is it you want from me?" he mumbled at last.

"I want to offer you a choice, Captain," Bellamy said cheerfully. "There must always be a choice." He hefted the leather satchel that had been recovered from Rogers' cabin. "You may deliver my treaty proposal to King George, and return to your estates in Bristol, or...you may walk out that door, a free man, to make your own way among the people you sought to enslave."

Bellamy rose and came around the desk to set the satchel in Rogers' lap.

"The choice is yours, Captain. Choose wisely."

* * * * *

Stephen J. Simmons Bio

Stephen J. Simmons left a teeming metropolis of just over a thousand people in the Catskills to seek his fortune as a nuclear plant operator on Navy submarines. After he retired from the Navy in 2004, he found work helping to build submarines, so that new generations of young men (and now women) could be subjected to the same tortures he had survived. In addition to his SF novel, "The Galileo Syndrome" and the comic-fantasy novella, "Just Grimm And Bear It," he has published several short stories in various genres.

#####

A Safe Wartime Posting by Joelle Presby

Fall 1914, German Port of Doula, Kamerun, West Afrika

"A mined harbor! New fortifications! Wonders of German engineering!" The junior lieutenant with his sand-scuffed boots continued like that while an aide tapped my shoulder and beckoned me out of the governor's office to the wide terrace.

A jungle of thick trees and scrub brush I couldn't recognize covered the steep shore line. But our vantage point, a quarter mile up this foothill of Mount Fako, showed the familiar ocean making a broad harbor for the lonely port city of Doula. It lay undefended, except for the few troops granted by the governor and however many of the local sailors and city dwellers could be convinced to fight on behalf of the foreign colonialists.

My greatest hope was that the young officer under my wing on this war observer assignment got to see nothing at all. Unfortunately, I also spoke no German, so I turned to the man without much hope of conveying my thoughts with any accuracy. The aide scratched a neat brown beard as he regarded me, and I envied him the comfort of his loose cotton civilian clothing.

"That kid," the German said, his English flawless if, well, sounding overly English and not at all American, "is he the cousin or nephew of your President Marshall?"

"Vice President, sir," I corrected immediately. "President Woodrow Wilson is—"

"Yes, of course, of course," the German acknowledged. "Dreadful, just dreadful, the stroke." He shook his head in condolences for a piece of information apparently common knowledge here on the African continent even though the US papers were not printing it. My superior's letters from home indicated the vice president was praying for Mr. Wilson's full recovery, and he considered it a very poor precedent to assume the presidency himself while the man elected for the position lived.

Mr. Wilson's capability remained a question for physicians back home in the States. They were not sharing their thoughts with a navy chief sent to German West Afrika to shepherd a well-connected young officer in need of a position for his last couple years of service. A position, I was made to understand by superiors, that should bolster a future career in politics if it weren't abruptly terminated by an unfortunate twelve-inch artillery shell.

"Sir, Lieutenant Junior Grade Marshall is the son of the vice president's cousin," I said. Let the German make of that what he would.

The man nodded. "I shall let Governor Ebermaier know."

I suppressed a sigh of resignation.

"Come on, Chief!" Lieutenant Marshall called me back into the governor's office.

Piles of work waited on the governor's desk, and his office held few of the luxuries a man in his position could acquire. A bald German manager with a beard too long to be fashionable, he was responsible for a large colony but without the forces to protect it, and I found myself liking him. The governor had also tolerated my superior's excitement at the prospect of war coming here, and I appreciated his patience.

I positioned myself a few steps behind Lieutenant Marshall's shoulder while what seemed to be leave-taking comments were exchanged. A fine oil painting of a gunboat patrolling up the Vuri River with a mixed Afrikan and German crew supervised by the usual white officers hung behind the governor's desk.

My superior, a slight man in his twenties, clean shaven and with an incorrigible gleam in his eyes, switched to English for my benefit as he completed his farewell.

"Thank you so much for your time, Governor." He rendered a flawless salute with casual ease, and he added a smooth nod of his head after his hand returned to his side, which somehow gave the standard military courtesy a touch of extra politeness. The governor's mouth twitched up in unexpected appreciation. I credited the Marshall family political training.

I made my own rough salute to the colonial governor and his military aide, whose name I'd never caught, and followed quickly out of the residence.

We passed through a hall with a cleaning staff hard at work. Clerks in the open offices didn't look up, but the crowd in the visitor's hall examined us with open stares.

They were probably trying to guess which of them should be offended at Lieutenant Marshall being granted an audience in advance of their own time, I thought. I did my best to appear inscrutable and discretely encouraged my lieutenant to keep up the brisk pace of a man with appointments and work ahead, instead of what we were—two Americans abroad with little oversight and more than enough time to have waited in that hall until after all of them had been seen.

Outside, we paused to consider our route. The piers of Port Doula and the nearest beaches beckoned again. My superior had marched along them this morning before our appointment. That walk had destroyed the work of the boot boy I'd given a coin to the evening prior to press our uniforms and apply a fine shine to our shoes. I was for a return to our quarters and a change to my second-best uniform before any more exploring caught my officer's interest.

Lieutenant Marshall turned this way and that examining the buildings around us. Even the colonial government buildings were mostly single story, some brick and plaster, a few painted. Most sat inside a courtyard wall, mirroring the compound style of the older Afrikan buildings in Doula proper. I tapped a finger on the rough brick wall surrounding the governor's compound. Taller than most and with a smooth white plaster, it'd be a challenge for a miscreant to climb, but armed invaders could smash the gate easily enough.

I need to look at the compound around our guest quarters, I thought. There might be a useful spider web of alleyways I could use between the walls. Might even be a route all the way to one or another of the smaller piers where I might find a boat seaworthy enough to brave the open bay at least as far as the nearer Spanish islands. I could imagine messy firefighting going house to house, and some extra cover would be helpful if I needed to drag my charge's unconscious form along a retreat route.

The vice president was said to respect Mr. Wilson deeply of course, but the presidential election of 1916 was only two years away. If the president had recovered sufficiently to run for re-election by then, well and good. If not, my superiors expected me to return a whole and sound young lieutenant to his prominent family in case Mr. Thomas R. Marshall, 28th Vice President of the United States, had an interest in the position of 29th President of the United States.

My orders were clear: I was to ensure a certain young Lieutenant Marshall would be alive and well, so that his family could put him to whatever political purpose most suited that fine ambition.

"Don't let him get himself killed. Don't let him duel. Don't let him eat anything questionable. And by all means, make sure he stays out of gunnery range!" Captain Beach had slapped shut the folder with the printed orders and poked me in the gut with them. "These'll say nice political things about arduous duty abroad and the full faith of the United States Navy and the importance of the young lieutenant's honorable service and on and on. Don't you fall for it. We need more allies in Washington who understand the cost of good strong ships. Keep this kid alive."

I'd replied, "Sir, yes, sir," and here we were.

Doula did boast one larger building. Beyond a flimsy bamboo structure, I considered Port Doula Cathedral, made of solid timber and imported stone, positioned proudly just beyond the governor's mansion. Its steeple stood nice and tall as a quality navigation aid.

I had taken a look at the printed orders themselves which were clearly a copy of the officer's orders. It was just as flowery as Captain

Beach had said. On the final line, a short addendum had been typed in heavy black ink: "Chief Petty Officer Hays assigned to assist."

The large German-built church had enough wood that it could burn, but I doubted the British or French or their Nigerian and Senegalese troops would intentionally raze a holy place.

I suspected no one had told the young officer that he was more valuable in politics than in war and that he was expected to maintain a careful distance from any action. I considered the possibility of dragging him to the sanctuary and sitting on him until any fighting was over.

Priests usually left the doors open back at Saint Mary of Mercy in Pittsburgh, but that might not be the case here.

Lieutenant Marshall interrupted my thoughts by stopping to stare straight up at the narrow bamboo tower. The top swayed in the gentle sea breeze.

"Is this thing a lighthouse?" he asked.

"Um," I temporized.

He circled the structure and found the ladder.

It probably was, but the cement footing around its base seemed insufficient to the task of defending it from wood borers and termites. In daytime, the light above was mercifully out with no chance of it burning down around our ears, but I hoped they paid their caretakers a danger bonus for this swaying terror.

Lieutenant Marshall put his foot on the long ladder and tested it. When the first rung bore his weight, he scampered up as if it were well maintained rigging and not a wobbling tower of death unlikely to hold anyone heavier than a lamp boy. With regret, I scrambled up after him.

The joins and ties were sturdy and frequent, so I had hopes that the thing would at least hold long enough for us to get back down again. My superior clambered all the way to the lookout platform just below the light and leaned on the rail to take in a view of the wide harbor. I tried not to puff too hard as I joined him.

We could see a half dozen similar towers on various little points in the nearer part of the estuary to the south and west. The river Vuri snaked northeast into the dark green horizon behind us.

"What did the charts show? Do you remember?" Lieutenant Marshall asked. "Twenty some miles of bay from the open ocean to the river mouth here at Doula proper?"

That seemed about right. We couldn't see quite so far, but the height did give a fine view of the nearer inlets weaving in fingerlike from the deeper harbor to shallows filled with crab and shrimp boats.

The continent's coastline turned from east-west here to form a near right angle and head south with the mouth of the Vuri river and its estuary tucked into that continental bend. Generations upon generations had traded here, but the Germans had constructed a pair of new railways into the continental interior, making an already prosperous port into the largest in the region.

Fishing trawlers sailed in with full nets, and the larger vessels carrying the wealth of the colony steamed for open ocean. The narrow points of lush greenery between each inlet had appeared impassible from the water, but from above the distance shrank to something a dedicated landing force could hack through if committed enough and led by savvy guides.

The port defenses didn't look like much to me. Doula proper had a deep enough estuary, with dense jungle protecting it from troops landing further south or north and attempting a land assault, but the harbor remained largely clear. I peered again at the ships dotting the waterways.

Steamers puffed in and out of port, most headed just over the horizon to the trade city of Malabo on the neutral Spanish island of Fernando Po. Tiny fishing vessels darted this way and that with a carefree navigation that made me doubt the officers in charge of Kamerun's defenses had placed any mines at all.

"Our quarters are down there near the harbor, sir." I pointed. "Not as fine as they could be but there's another one of these observation posts just beyond there."

"Excellent, Chief!" he said. "I shall have to climb that one for a better view of the sea."

I made a noncommittal noise of acknowledgement. We probably would be climbing it regularly now that I'd pointed it out. More importantly, if the observers at the much more solidly built lighthouse at the Point of Suellaba saw an attacking squadron headed our way, the warning would flash from bamboo tower to bamboo tower right to our doorstep. We might hear of an attack even before the governor did.

My officer studied the nearer inlets once more and snorted.

"Not enough mines." Lieutenant Marshall frowned at the shining bay. "How many steamers do you suppose the governor can use for defense?"

I shrugged. "All of them."

My superior goggled at me, and I only lifted my shoulders again.

"They fly German flags, sir," I explained. "Probably belong to the colony already. Though if the war doesn't come here, might be tough to explain to higher authorities why good seaworthy vessels were commandeered and sunk to constrict a fine commercial harbor."

The lieutenant suppressed a laugh at the idea.

"They haven't got enough mines to protect everything. They'll need to sink a dozen ships at least to narrow the waterway for a proper defense," he said. Lieutenant Marshall paused to consider the port again, turning to look out towards the ocean and then tracing the darker blue of deep channel up to the river mouth with Bonaberi town on the north shore and greater Doula on our side to the south.

Shouting from directly below drew our attention to tiny faces, white and black, looking up at us from the safety of the ground. I took one last look to memorize the waterways as well as I could and followed my boss down the ladder.

I missed the first of the introductions when I paused to catch my breath halfway down. As soon as my boots touched solid ground, I brushed my uniform off and studied the gold braid to guess the ranks of the two men in front of us.

"This is Major Zimmermann, commandant of the defensive forces here in the Kameruns," said Lieutenant Marshall, identifying the easy one, and I saluted. "Sir," he added, "please meet my chief, Johnny Hays."

The man returned my salute but hardly glanced at me. "Of course, Lieutenant," he said. "I understand you arrived with just the one staffer, but we can supply you with a few more. Allow me to introduce," the German nodded to the local in an immaculately pressed suit and his English fumbled as he searched for the right word, "His Excellen—?"

"It's Ntsama Atangana, or Karl if that's easier." The black man smiled and held out a hand to my boss who reached out and shook it.

"An honor, sir." Lieutenant Marshall said.

"Not at all," Atangana replied. "An honor for me to meet an American prince come all the way to my homeland."

"Um, well, certainly not a prince." My boss blushed.

"Of course." Atangana gave him a nod. "You don't use those terms. My people don't either. I'm a chief of chiefs technically. And this continent has plenty of other actual kings and princes as well. But you are the cousin to the most important man in America."

I opened my mouth to try to explain again Mr. Wilson's continued presidency, when my boss stepped firmly on my foot.

The major examined the termite mound near the bamboo lighthouse dubiously and looked up the ladder as if he thought he should climb it himself, but absolutely did not want to.

"Could you see the British cruiser from up there?" the major asked.

My jaw dropped.

"Ah, no sir." Lieutenant Marshall replied. "There were no military vessels in sight, though it seemed you have a good dozen steamers in port and perhaps some smaller launches you may have equipped as gunboats? Might I suggest deploying a few more mines if you've got them?"

"Excellent!" Atangana agreed.

The major nodded with an expression of resignation. "I've given orders to deploy as many as the workshops can turn out. And," he added brightening a little bit, "since we have a dignitary of your status with us, the governor has authorized a message by telegraph calling for reinforcements."

"And he's finally allowing our people to fight for their homes," Atangana put in.

"Why would he not?" I forgot myself and actually asked the question out loud. "Um, Your Excellency," I added quickly.

"Karl," Atangana repeated again with another brilliant smile. "Here in the West Afrikas, the kingdoms and the tribes disagree from time to time with trade agreements and taxes for the roads and railways. Not as much within the Kameruns, but for the English or French, and especially for the Belgians, if they bring troops to steal this protectorate from the Kaiser, they'll return to fewer colonies than they thought they had. They may find no workers left on their cocoa plantations and palm oil groves. Maybe they'll find new tribal leaders no longer in accord with past arrangements. Perhaps both."

"There's no profit in an Afrikan campaign." Major Zimmermann shook his head. "We'll need to destroy the telegraph station of course, but as I've told the governor, I can protect his family and withdraw everyone up the longer rail line towards Ngaundere or march still further north to make a stand at Garua."

I tried to follow the geography in my head but gave up as Major Zimmermann continued, "We could have a fine land battle with defensive support from the interior. The locals can harry the troops from the jungle all along the route if the Nigerian conscripts and whatever forces the British can spare choose to follow us inland."

"But the sea!" My lieutenant looked aghast at the German army man. "You must defend the port!"

"We can try, I suppose." The major looked doubtfully towards the harbor. "Or I could get you passage across to Fernando Po."

Yes! I thought. But I could see my boss's face growing red.

"The Spanish are neutral yet," he continued. "And they could see you back to your home country if you feel this conflict exceeds, um—" He fumbled with a way to suggest my boss leave on the eve of a battle while my officer's back stiffened.

"I shall certainly stay, sir!"

"Well then." Atangana clapped my lieutenant on the shoulder. "Let's see to the defenses. I have runners out everywhere to bring us news. At present we face only a cruiser, her launches, and a gunboat towed in. Three converted steamers hold some troops but not so many as to give us trouble if they have to fight through our jungle to reach us. If we hold the harbor, we hold the city."

"We must keep Doula," my lieutenant said.

"Yes," even I had to agree.

* * *

My boss reveled in a flurry of activity as the cruiser, now identified as HMS *Cumberland*, requested Governor Ebermaier's surrender and was refused.

Most of Major Zimmermann's sixteen hundred soldiers were stationed further in the interior of Kamerun or on the other side of British held Nigeria in Togoland, but 1st Company, with its artillery and three fine maschinengewehr 08s and their crews, were in Doula.

I followed behind on the inspection of the machine guns. They didn't seem too great a change from Hiram Maxim's gun, but Major Zimmermann's pride in having the firepower required I keep my thoughts to myself. All three only had the slower Schloss 08 firing assemblies but with a limited stockpile of the 250-round ammunition belts, I figured it was probably for the best. Major Zimmermann boasted a nearly 3,900-yard range, but a quiet word with the lead gunner confirmed closer to two thousand yards would be better if we hoped the current somewhat out-of-practice gun crews would hit their targets.

Atangana listened closely to everything, and, when we left, a half dozen locals arrived with tools.

"We may be able to make use of the spent cartridges to make reloads for the rifles, if not for the machine guns themselves," the Afrikan suggested.

My lieutenant wished loudly for a decent gunboat of our own or the time to find a way to install one of the machine guns on a larger fishing vessel and secure it well enough to allow decent targeting. I inquired after the gunboat in the governor's painting, and was rewarded with a number of stories of previous small battles it had won along the Vuri River. After briefly lifting my hopes, our guides concluded the discussion with the news that *that* gunboat also currently sat upriver in Yabassi undergoing major repairs to the hull.

The major refused my lieutenant's schemes for installing the maschinengewehr 08s on boats. So instead we had to make do with finding appropriate placements for the guns along the shore line and installing discrete floats in the water to act as range markers.

Atangana grumbled when the governor declined to pull 7th and 8th companies south from Garua and Ngaundere, but he returned with additional strong young men. With my superior's hearty support, he convinced Major Zimmermann to mix his sharpshooters in with the Germans and supply with rifles any local vouched for by Atangana who proved able to hit a target at forty paces.

We sank a full dozen steamers in the port to leave only a narrow, mined approach to Doula. The mine men's wires ran only so long, leaving wet and cold soldiers crouched on the beaches with the detonators, but Lieutenant Marshall ran up and down the beach himself with a spyglass, and Atangana ensured the spotters had food and regular relief while we waited for the first wave of attacks.

My officer spent hours with Atangana scheming ways invaders could be confused, to include constructing portable lighthouses and having teams of porters carry them to and fro on the beach while lit to mislead nighttime attackers.

I appealed to Governor Ebermaier through his aide, Hans, whose name I'd finally gathered. One of the German government steamers was kept back from the harbor blocking effort. She boasted only ten knots and was singled screwed, but Zimmermann christened her *Nachtigal* and produced for her one five-centimeter gun and one 3.7-centimeter revolving gun. She couldn't match the British gunboat, *Dwarf,* a *Bramble*-class vessel equipped with two four-inch guns, four twelve-pounders, and four Maxim guns. And with *Dwarf*'s twin screws and reported 13.5 knot max speed, she couldn't even outrun her. But Lieutenant Marshall brightened at having at least one armed vessel in what he liked to call, "the Bamboo Squadron."

Out in deeper waters, the *Cumberland* began a blockade of Doula and the shipping stopped, leaving the docks oddly quiet for a port city. Nothing much of use could be done with the cocoa filling up the warehouses, but the palm oil delighted both Zimmermann and my lieutenant. They put their heads together imagining situations where an extra-long burning fire might be of some military benefit.

Hans shook his head and begged Atangana and me to consider that the governor might need to have some resources left to bring in an income for the colony after all the fighting was done. Atangana sent the aide back up to the governor's mansion with encouraging words, but I thought the Kaiser would be very unreasonable indeed if he begrudged the use of a few warehouses of oil when he'd chosen to give the governor so little in the way of naval defenses.

The first day, *Dwarf* oversaw a few small skiffs poking at the edges of our defenses and withdrew back to safety at dusk. We left the lighthouses dark that night and watched the waters by moonlight and saw nothing.

Lieutenant Marshall spotted empty British launches on the beach of a nearby inlet when he made his dawn climb. He clambered down and called a warning to an alarmed Major Zimmermann.

A pleased band of locals reported back that the remains of the exhausted and hopelessly lost British cutting out party had been found and had given their parole to some Kamerun tribesmen in exchange for directions back out of the jungle. A compound on the inland side of Doula was converted to hold the prisoners. Hans spoke hopefully of the blockade being broken soon, but even Atangana didn't have the boldness to pretend the capture of a few men from the greater blockading force would do much to save Doula.

For a solid week, British skiffs ground back our mines bit by bit. A few times the mine could be detonated before the wire was cut or mishandling on the side of the clearing crews bloodied the British, but they had too many lives to spend, and there were too few mines in the harbor. And with the powerful *Dwarf* in the shallows, the Kamerun crews couldn't directly attack the mine clearing boats without being sunk. We'd risked the small boats we had in abundance, but we held *Nachtigal* back.

Atangana, Zimmermann, and my lieutenant considered and rejected a dozen schemes. They attempted the moving of lighthouses, but *Dwarf* didn't need to continue work at night with our harbor so close to being cleared. And the carrying of even lightweight bamboo in quantity enough to form a full lighthouse required exhausting a dozen men who might be needed to support an armed retreat if the next day proved to be the day Doula fell. So, the three gave up on bamboo and turned to palm oil and explosives.

The next night, we lit the lighthouses dimly for our own counterattacks, and several fishing crews gave their lives in desperate struggles with the British mine clearing boats. Too many wires were cut and *Cumberland* again sent forward the gunboat *Dwarf* to cover the last of their mine clearing boats, which made our little skiffs unable to hold their own.

Our machine guns on the shore turned a few invading sailors on overly eager small boats into hamburger, but at nightfall it became clear that by the following day, the harbor would be all but cleared. It might take the British a few additional days to realize the fact as Atangana's men had sewed the waterways with plenty of makeshift non-explosive devices to help confuse the mine clearers, but with no response yet to the wireless telegraph and no word by radio, Doula had to assume any reinforcements would arrive too late.

Hans did share encouraging word of tribal uprisings in both French Afrika and British Afrika, but if our attackers knew, they didn't withdraw.

Atangana and Lieutenant Marshall went to Major Zimmermann with a plan to use *Nachtigal* to attack *Dwarf* and afterwards reseed the harbor with more mines improvised by the artillery company. Zimmermann allowed it reluctantly, but held back a core of German troops at the telegraph station and began his plans for evacuating the governor and the other most important officials.

Under cover of dark again, with all light struck, we loaded a barge with explosives and oil barrels and attached poles to the front of a small launch to push it. *Nachtigal* steamed alongside ready to take on any boat patrols we might encounter on our way to *Dwarf*'s anchorage. The plan was simple: use the launch to get the barge full of explosives close to *Dwarf* and detonate them. Then pray we'd didn't get killed by our own bomb.

The locals nearly mutinied when Atangana attempted to captain the little launch. With great reluctance and palpable anger, he was left on shore, and he sent a cousin along instead to aid with navigation. The original master of the steamer maintained command of *Nachtigal*, and additional crew from Zimmermann's 1st Company manned the guns.

From the bleak look on the *Nachtigal* captain's face, I could tell he didn't expect to survive the night, but preferred not to be left behind if his vessel were to be sunk. A respectable choice, but I'd rather he had the stamina to pretend to more confidence. He had crew to think of, after all.

The soft splash of waves against hull did little to calm me. Of course, the lieutenant had to be "at the decisive point," as he'd said. In the launch. Which meant I was also observing this bit of the Great War from a far closer vantage point than I suspect our superiors intended.

"Sir, my orders preclude—" I'd tried in a fast whispered conversation on the shoreline to keep him off the barge. But Lieutenant Marshall had given me a pitying look.

"Some aunt or uncle of mine tried to order you to keep me safe did they?" His grin had been infectious. "I take my orders from the Navy, thankfully, and not from them. Don't worry, they like to think they have influence, but it doesn't extend to inside the service." He had given me a one-armed hug, over in a moment, and had climbed aboard.

I would have liked to have had a good crowd of Americans in Port Doula that night to insist on Lieutenant Marshall's importance and to get him put safely ashore with Atangana, but all I'd managed after climbing in after him was to move him to the seat furthest from the barge of explosives. He settled in at the rear of our little pusher boat next to the coxswain.

I crouched at the prow watching our approach. A trembling young German from the artillery company sat next to me, and the cousin of Atangana's directing all the sailors aboard sat on my other side, grinning like a madman. We pushed the barge of explosives and had one remaining mine with a wire running back to me for detonation.

The white-faced German to my left had been supposed to be the one to press that lever, but I snatched it from him at the first sandbar when a small bump of the barge panicked him into reaching for the detonator with us still too close and *Dwarf* well out of range.

Jutting narrow triangles of peninsula from the south made dark treed shadows in the starry skies. A few boats of Atangana's brave men had made their way along that coastline to flank *Dwarf*. If we failed, they might make a desperate attempt at a night boarding.

Nachtigal steamed too loud in the soft night some quarter mile ahead. Our little boat had only so much power and we had the whole weight of the barge ahead to push. I wondered if the *Nachtigal* had already given up and hoped to surrender to *Dwarf*, but six of the crew on that steamer were Atangana's handpicked sailors, and I doubted the German gunners would support such cowardice either.

A lookout's cry over the waves ahead of us made me fear we'd been spotted and *Dwarf's* guns would soon ensure Lieutenant Marshall never had a political career, when firing instead ranged out towards the south and small bonfires erupted on the coastline.

It wasn't a picket boat and *Nachtigal's* dark shape slid on with no returning fire ahead or to the north.

"The chief of chiefs!" came the too loud whisper, almost a cheer, quickly shushed. Rather than wait for us to fail, Atangana had staged a diversion for us.

British cries echoed clearly over the water. I made out orders to guard the anchor and directions to fire toward the south.

I cursed. We didn't need an alarmed gunboat with lookouts wary of attackers. Lights from the deck of *Dwarf* swept this way at that over the water towards the nearer beaches to the south. Worse, our planned course would soon take us between those near shores and the British gunboat where the bonfires would silhouette us very nicely for *Dwarf's* gunners.

My lieutenant, smart boy, saw the problem immediately, and we slowed, letting the shape of *Nachtigal* slide even further out of protective range. Gradually, ever so gradually, we moved our little vessel about to turn our barge and begin another approach towards *Dwarf*.

This time we came not from the direction of Doula, where faint flickers of the city light might give us away, not from the nearer little peninsulas where Atangana's men made their desperate attacks, and not even from the far coastline to the north where a prudent British commander might expect another flurry of small craft to venture another attack. We came from behind, from the pitch-black ocean side.

In the clarity of the echoing commands from *Dwarf*, we could hear the British contempt for what appeared to be pitiful, barely armed boats whose former crews now swam hard for the safety of the shore with bonfires provided to help them find their way.

More gunfire roared as spotters on *Dwarf* finally noticed *Nachtigal*. The horrible sound of large enemy guns being answered by smaller friendly guns rang out over the waves. The captain of *Nachtigal* turned the steamer to flee, but the *Dwarf's* guns had too great a range. The *Nachtigal* fell silent.

I made an inaudible prayer for the men already in the water, and our barge glided up to the looming shape of the British gunboat. Giving up silence for speed, we reversed our course and surged back with all the power our small craft could muster.

The wire tightened, and at last, I slammed down the detonator.

Fire fountained over the waves, hot against my back and unbearably bright even with my whole body crouched and turned away. The barge boomed, and all sound vanished into the single bellowing *kaboom.*

A heavy wave lapped over the prow of our vessel, and Atangana's cousin with silent open mouth and clear gestures ordered the crew to bail and pressed a bucket into my hands. My lieutenant found another bucket as we fought to keep our boat seaworthy long enough to reach a shore.

Fire and roaring still filled the sky. The British gunboat sank with burning oil spreading over the waves. All sound blanketed to nothingness still, but as the brightness dimmed to dull flames, *Nachtigal* appeared out of the graying night.

The least injured of the sailors pulled us from the damaged launch onto the bloodied deck of the steamer, and Doula's only naval vessel powered for homeport.

We two crews limped up the sandy beach to join with the survivors of Atangana's diversionary attack. The blast from the barge had been seen from our bamboo towers, and we were greeted by a triumphant cheering crowd of Germans and locals.

* * *

By day, we could see *Dwarf's* ruin now joined the dozen sunken steamers helping to guard our harbor. Our own small boats, with assistance from the newly eager *Nachtigal*, sank the small craft *Cumberland* attempted to send into the shallows.

Hans congratulated us all and encouraged us to come on up to the mansion for a celebratory toast.

The chief of chiefs clapped my lieutenant on the back and asked for the next plan.

With *Dwarf* sunk and new mining well begun, our port would hold. But *Cumberland* still blockaded the shipping routes and the spotters now reported that four converted troop transports flying British and French flags waited offshore.

"Four transports you said?" Major Zimmermann asked with an expression of interest he'd not shown since being ordered to conduct a naval defense.

The local who'd just reported it to Atangana confirmed again and supplied a guess at the total number of troops embarked.

Zimmermann grinned and turned to Atangana. "How would your fighters like to try a proper land campaign?"

I rubbed my ears, convinced that my hearing loss had been more permanent than I'd thought.

"With that many troops waiting uselessly off at sea, the whole of Nigeria is open. We only need get there. And I have inland troops to redeploy if only we can convince Governor Ebermaier that the Kaiser ought to have a larger set of protectorates in the West Afrikas."

"But the cost!" The governor's aide stammered. "The palm oil supplies can be explained, but we still can't ship out our cocoa yet, and we'd lose the whole season's harvest if you took enough men to take and hold the whole of Nigeria!"

"Not to mention the joys of a march through Afrikan jungle," I added, but I kept my voice down and thought only my lieutenant heard me.

"The northern railway goes far enough to reach the grasslands, and it's prairie land all the way west into Nigeria at that latitude," Atangana explained. "But with, of course, enough scorpions, grass vipers, and burning sun to make a man long for a decent bit of rain-forest."

Zimmermann shook his finger at the chief of chiefs. "Don't you go backing down now. It's not thousands of Londoners out on those steamers waiting to sack this city."

"Of course, Major. Of course." Atangana made a bow of acknowledgement. "Their forces are mostly hired from my brother chiefs in Senegal and Nigeria, as I believe German mercenaries have also fought in other nation's wars from time to time. But more of their brothers are trying out independence wars. Wait a few more months, and you might have Nigeria and even Senegal for the Kaiser by treaty without a war at all."

"Treaties." Major Zimmermann threw up his hands. "Always with you it's treaties and a new road for that chief and a bridge for this other one. Most of the interior of this territory wasn't fought over at all!"

"It is the more profitable choice," Hans observed.

The German major clamped his mouth shut, but favored the aide with a dark glare that implied the only things he considered more beneath a fighting man's dignity than preemptive peace treaties were the profit motives that drove a bureaucrat to accept them.

Just then hoots of joy came from the bamboo tower, and separately a runner came from the wireless station.

"News! News from the Americas!"

My lieutenant and I started bolt upright.

"The South Americas," the junior German messenger added with a nod towards us. "Some weeks ago, our very own Vice-Admiral Graf Maximilian von Spee, who once commanded a gunboat out of this very port, met the British Navy at sea off the coast of Coronel, Chile, and defeated a squadron, destroying two cruisers!" He paused in his recitation to add to his superior, "Sir, the British Navy can be bested!"

"Of course, they can be bested." Major Zimmermann glared at the man before him with deep affront. "The refitted *Nachtigal* sank *Dwarf* just this morning, and *Nachtigal* outgunned by eight times too, I'll thank you to remember!"

And we did it by stealth with great barrels full of luck and some eighteen dead of the Chief of Chief Karl Atangana's people, not to mention the two dead and six injured on *Nachtigal.* But I held my tongue and let Major Zimmermann remind the crowd of listening local fighters and German soldiers of our recent victory.

Hans stood up and clapped his hands loudly. "To the Kaiser! To von Spee! To victory!"

Celebration spilled out into the streets, and the aide turned to us. "Please, Gentlemen, you must come consult with the governor. He may finally have news of the reinforcements."

"Ah yes," Atangana and Major Zimmermann agreed, but from the expressions, I suspected they were each hoping for a different kind of reinforcement and directly opposite orders on how those forces were to be used.

The men in the governor's waiting hall—who by now I recognized as overseers and grove managers from cocoa and palm plantations, factors from other farms further off, a few of Atangana's junior chiefs, and the men from the railway—all looked as we entered. They not only made no complaint as we brushed past them, disrupting the governor's morning appointments, but first a few and then all stood and clapped for us as we went by.

I ducked my head, but my lieutenant brandished a wide politician's smile and gave them all a big wave of greeting as we passed. Major Zimmermann's spine straightened into stiff march as if he were on a parade field, and his cheeks went pink at the praise. Atangana gave a regal nod and exchanged some words of thanks to those of his chiefs present.

But there was little time before Hans hurried us all into Governor Ebermaier's office and closed everyone else firmly out. The man in charge looked to have aged three years in the weeks since the blockade began.

He'd not had significant hair on the top of his head to start, but his beard had more gray in it now than I recalled from our last meeting. The lines around his eyes and shadows under them certainly sank deeper.

Major Zimmermann drew himself up and gave the crispest salute I believe I'd ever seen a man give a superior.

"Thank you, Major," the governor said. "Thank you for your excellent defense of the colony. If you would, please sit, all of you."

Noting three chairs besides the one behind the governor's desk, I helped myself to an unobtrusive spot against the back wall where Hans joined me. Atangana, Zimmermann, and my lieutenant sat with the governor.

"We've had word finally from Togoland," he said. And the despair in his tone made clear than no good news would be coming. "It fell to the combined British and French assault before our blockade here even began."

"We will take it back!" Major Zimmermann stood and pounded a fist on his chest.

Governor Ebermaier rubbed the bare patch of skin on top of his head. "Perhaps." He turned to my lieutenant. "How long can we keep Doula? There's a second armored cruiser out there now, HMS *Challenger*, and a total of four converted steamers packed with mixed French and British troops, and of course Nigerian and Senegalese support—porters and fighters both."

"But no more gunboats, Governor? Or at least not of the *Bramble*-class?" Lieutenant Marshall confirmed.

"Not as yet. The Zaians are fighting the French in North Afrika. The Senussi in Egypt are making threats against the British there, but may not yet fight. The Dervish are making attacks on the British in Somaliland with no sign of stopping." The governor shook his head. "I thought it'd be foolish to bring the war from Europe to this continent at all, but it's now quite clear General Dobell and his French allies disagree."

"Togoland has fallen," Major Zimmermann repeated dully. "Then why did they not land at Victoria and march their forces to Doula with none of this bother with mines and fighting at sea?"

"The rain," Atangana said quietly. "Rainy season makes that route impassible for another two months. A barefoot hunting party with spears could do it. But the mud would swallow whole any artillery pieces they tried to move."

"Just so," the governor agreed.

He pointed a fat finger and circled it around the three men in front of him. "In 1884, at the Berlin Conference," he said, "all these governors swore to one another that on this continent we would keep the peace with one another even if war broke out at home."

"But even with our neutral observer, and not just any officer but the very cousin of the American Vice President here." Governor Ebermaier nodded to Lieutenant Marshall and stood as though the frustration were too much to stay still. He started to pace.

"Even with an American watching," he repeated, "the British and French governors violated their sworn word. The first opportunity! The very first and the promises they made on behalf of their nations are forgotten! They stole Togoland before news could be sent out, but we have not been silent. For weeks now, the message has gone out. The British and French should be ashamed."

He held up his hands. "So be it, we are also reporting by wireless and by radio the location of two armed but small cruisers staying confined to one small bit of ocean. The British Navy is not invincible. A German admiral has sunk two such vessels quite recently with the loss of only three German lives.

"They have two months to wait here before their land forces have a chance of breaking through. Perhaps they think they can keep up a blockade for that long. I think Germany has a Navy too."

He smiled at Major Zimmermann. "Give me two more months, and I'll approve your transfer to command a fighting unit engaged in this Great War back on the continent. Two more months, less even! And go with my blessing. I strongly suspect that before that time is up we shall see some German flagged ships come over the horizon and you can return to Berlin in the company of our own officers."

"And you, Lieutenant." Governor Ebermaier saluted my officer who shot to his feet to return the courtesy, for once surprised. "When you go tell your cousin in Washington what happened here, you shall do it wearing an Iron Cross."

The governor returned to his chair and sat. "That will be all gentlemen."

We filed out.

I glanced at Atangana. "He didn't promise you anything."

The chief of chiefs raised an eyebrow in response. "I have a country under the protection of a Kaiser who recently unified his own tribes. A ruler who understands small powers combining to be a large power instead of merely being swallowed up in Englishness or Frenchness or," he shuddered, "having to watch the Belgians do to the Kameruns what has been done in the Congo. I have my chiefs and my chiefs have their people. What more could he give me?"

I looked at him and whispered softly enough that I was absolutely certain no one else at all could hear: "Freedom?"

Atangana winked. "When my Beti people are strong enough. Not yet. And not while we're better in this kingdom than out of it. I do like to honor treaties, you may have heard."

He smiled again, and I went looking for my officer, convinced that of all the fine politicians I'd met while sheltering my lieutenant, the toughest and most capable was the quiet black man in the pressed German suit still grinning at my back.

I found Lieutenant Marshall outside the governor's compound, with one hand on the bamboo lighthouse and the harbor with the wreck of the gunboat *Dwarf* over his shoulder. A man with photography apparatus scrambled about to set up the shot while a reporter nodded encouragingly and scribbled as fast as his little pencil could move.

"Of course, you must understand I'm only a war observer here," Lieutenant Marshall was saying, "and as such my role has been quite limited. As I'm sure you're aware, President Wilson greatly values American lives and would not waste our sons' blood in someone else's fight. Germany has sunk some shipping, it's true. But in these last weeks, I personally saw Britain and France, the supposed allies, break a treaty without diplomatic warning. And the German forces held them off, of course.

"It leaves me to wonder, if the American people were one day to enter this war, would we really want to do it on the side that breaks treaties and includes a nation that once burned our capital?"

* * * * *

Joelle Presby Bio

Joelle Presby is a former U.S. naval officer who grew up in the former German Kamerun. She did not serve during the Great War. She co-wrote The Road to Hell, in the Multiverse series, with David Weber. She has also published short stories in universes of her own creation, Charles E. Gannon's Terran Republic, and David Weber's Honor Harrington universe. Updates and releases are shared on her website, joellepresby.com, and on social media through Facebook, LinkedIn, and Twitter.

# # # # #

Beatty's Folly
by Philip Wohlrab

Chapter 1

26 August 1915
The North Sea

Vice Admiral David Beatty contemplated the sight before him. From the bridge of HMS *Lion,* he could observe three obsolescent American battleships of the *Virginia* class, their distinctive stacked turret design giving them away. The three ships were steaming forward of the convoy that Beatty was ordered to intercept. As the distance fell below eight thousand yards Beatty turned away from watching the American ships.

"Signal the commander of the American fleet to turn around at once," Beatty ordered his signals officer. "Tell them that this will be their only warning before we open fire."

Flags leapt up the lines to either side of HMS *Lion's* forward mast, giving the warning to the American ships. In reply, a series of flags appeared on the forward mast of USS *Virginia,* that to put it succinctly, told the British, "Go to Hell!"

Beatty snorted a chuckle, reading the answering flags before his signals officer could report what they said. Turning to his flag captain he said, "Well, at least they are a bunch of spirited fellows. Won't do them much good, though. We might be in range of their guns, but they are poor things compared to ours. You may shoot when ready, Captain."

HMS *Lion*, *Queen Mary*, *Princess Royal*, and *Tiger* open fire with their main batteries of 13.5-inch guns. In answer, the USS *Virginia*, *Georgia*, and *New Jersey* replied with their smaller 12-inch guns. The fight was mismatched from the beginning as the four modern British battlecruisers tore through the smaller, obsolete American battleships. After repeated hits, the USS *Virginia* capsized and sank abruptly from an explosion in a coal bunker that blew out her port side. She took Admiral Sims, who was in charge of Convoy G214, with her. *Virginia* was quickly followed by *New Jersey*, which blew up from a hit to her forward magazines.

The USS *Georgia* started to turn away from the fight, but a torpedo from Beatty's accompanying destroyers blew the ship's bow off. Her aft guns still firing, the USS *Georgia* sank bow first, the Stars and Stripes fluttering from her foremast. The remainder of the American escort, two old cruisers and ten destroyers, died swiftly under the weight of the Battlecruiser Squadron's superior firepower.

Vice Admiral David Beatty had just handed the US Navy its worst defeat. British cruisers and destroyers raced ahead of his battlecruisers to complete the scattering convoy's destruction. In all that day, the British took 18 prizes, in addition to destroying the three old American battleships and their escorts.

* * *

27 August 1915

The Admiralty, London

"Well that's done it," said First Sea Lord Jackie Fisher. "The Americans are in the war now officially. But what is it going to mean for us?"

"Well sir, the American President, that cowboy Teddy Roosevelt, has been in office a long time. He has been a staunch proponent of their naval power, and a firm disciple of the teachings of their theorist Mahan," replied the Deputy Chief of Naval Operations David Keiths.

"Their fleet is respectable, but still a third-rate fleet. I mean look at the terrible gunnery that was shown by the American escorts," replied Fisher. "Why, they only managed a few hits on *Princess Royal* and *Lion*."

"Yes sir, but what about the reports of the construction in their yards?" Keiths pressed. "If it is to be believed, they have some very large ships under construction. In light of that, my Lord, I think we need to reactivate the Third Fleet, and bring most of our pre-dreadnought battleships home from the Med," stated DCSNO Keiths.

"I think you may be right, but we cannot split up the Grand Fleet, not with the High Seas Fleet looking for any chance to break out."

"What are we to do about American shipping that wasn't part of their last convoy?" asked the DCSNO.

"Snap it up, of course," Fisher replied. "It isn't like we can anger the Americans any more than we already have. Issue an order service-wide to begin operations against American merchantmen and warships where found."

"Understood, sir. Also…" said Keiths in a worried tone.

"Also what?" snapped Fisher.

"Well sir, I, and the lads in planning, are worried about the US naval construction. As I said a few moments ago, they have several bloody great awful brutes under construction," replied Keiths. "Intelligence states that one may have 18-inch guns."

Fisher snorted but did not interrupt as the DCSNO continued.

"I don't know that that particular monster will be ready any time soon, but several of their new dreadnoughts mount 15- and 16-inch guns. I don't believe their fire control is up to our standards, but they are going to outrange pretty much everything we have except the *Queen Elizabeth* class."

"I don't believe they can get those 18-inch guns working, at least not any time soon," replied Fisher in a somewhat animated voice. "As to the rest, think how much trouble we had with the 15-inch guns in development before we got it right. I don't think that will be any easier for the Americans trying to get *two* different gun types into service."

Fisher sat back in his chair after making his point. Still, privately he was extremely worried about US naval construction.

The Americans, while not up to Royal Navy standards, have a lot more yard space then we do, he thought.

Fisher absently scratched his nose as he regarded the framed painting of HMS *Royal Sovereign* hanging on the wall. Battlecruisers had been one of his many ideas to modernize the Royal Navy, and he was quite proud of his new ships.

But will they be a match against the Americans, he mused.

* * *

31 August 1915
The Capitol Building
Washington D.C.

"Remember the *Virginia!* Remember the *New Jersey!* Remember the *Georgia!* Remember all of our slain sailors," roared President Theodore Roosevelt from the Speaker's Rostrum before a joint session of Congress.

With each cry for remembrance, Roosevelt banged his fist down on the Rostrum to the thunderous applause of Congress. These men were furious. Like a previous Congress before them, that had had to deal with foreign interference in American policy, they were ready to repay the British for their hostility. But not just the British; no, Teddy Roosevelt had come to them with a declaration of war against Britain, France, and Russia. France was particularly hated by America for its interference in the US Civil War which had dragged it out to 1867. Congress roared its approval; the US was now at war.

President Roosevelt, however, wasn't done with Congress just yet. Newspapers had run with lurid accounts of the short battle, to include fanciful prints of USS *Georgia* going down still fighting, since news first reached the United States. Teddy Roosevelt was going to use that to his advantage. Project S-584 had started construction, despite much hemming and hawing by both Congress and the US Navy. It was planned that the super-dreadnought battleship would be the largest in the world once completed. The target date for completion, however, had continuously slipped as Congress took every opportunity to slow construction on the behemoth. With a fully aroused public at his back, Roosevelt intended to fix *that* particular issue immediately.

"Further, I move that in response to this treachery by Great Britain and France, that Senator Tillman's project S-584 battleship be completed with all due haste, and the ship named for the heroic USS *Georgia*! Let her be the spear point with which we use to thrust into the treacherous British, and once and for all end their mastery of the sea!"

Congress roared its approval for a second time. Roosevelt had his war, and his battleship.

Retribution may take time, but it will be *certain*, Roosevelt thought grimly. *But first, to Canada.*

* * *

Chapter 2

15 May 1917
Off of Wexford, Ireland

This isn't a fight; this is a goddamn massacre, thought Lieutenant Commander Fitz Walker. His cool grey eyes watched as the 15-inch shells from the guns of USS *Nevada* straddled the British pre-dreadnought battleship HMS *Mars*. The *Mars* couldn't range on *Nevada* yet and, like the other ships in the British Third Fleet, it was struggling to come to grips with the US Atlantic Fleet. But all for naught.

On Walker's fourth salvo, he saw what he was looking for—solid hits to the hull of HMS *Mars*. Gouts of flame and debris marked where three shells from *Nevada's* broadside of ten 15-inch guns had found their mark. Walker ordered a few adjustments to his guns and then…

"Fire for effect!"

On salvos five, six, and seven, taking just five minutes to fire, HMS *Mars* took several more hits. One of the shells plunged through nonexistent topside armor on *Mars* and found the powder magazine under her forward turret. The turret exploded upward with tremendous force, and fire raced the length of HMS *Mars*. No one had time to escape the burning inferno that erupted out of the stricken battleship.

Lt. Commander Walker stepped away from his rangefinder, a grim, satisfied smile playing across his lips for just a minute.

It would have been far better if that were a French warship, what with what they did to America during the US Civil War, but these British bastards will have to do for now, he thought.

Aloud he said, "A small repayment to the king, Gentlemen!"

"Aye sir, it surely is," answered Chief Petty Officer Harper. The big, burly man's voice still held some of the brogue of his native Ireland. "I had a friend on the old *Georgia*. I hope the Everlasting allows them to see what we are doing here today."

At the mention of the old *Georgia*, Walker glanced over to the new USS *Georgia*, smoke wreathing her from the firing of her great guns. He lifted his fine Zeiss binoculars to his face, and peered out in the direction of where USS *Georgia* was firing. Finding his target he focused the binoculars until the features of what looked like either HMS *Lord Nelson*, or HMS *Agamemnon* resolved into some clarity. The ship's upper works were afire from multiple hits from *Georgia*, and one of her masts had collapsed. He could also see that the enemy ship's guns were out of action. Walker swept the sea to starboard, and all he could see were burning British ships or those settling deeper into the water. The American fleet managed to pin the old and tired vessels of the British Third Fleet against the coastline of southern Ireland and were now turning them into so much scrap iron and dead men.

"A mess of sailors are drowning or burning today, sir," Chief Harper remarked. The man didn't have the fine binoculars that Walker had, but he cast his gaze to starboard using an old fashioned telescope to watch the dying British ships. Both men's gaze followed the American destroyers steaming past the *Nevada* at high speed. These smaller vessels raced in to make torpedo attacks, delivering the coup de grace to the crippled and burning British ships.

Behind USS *Nevada*, 4,000 yards to stern, the USS *Arizona* let loose another broadside, but this time not at enemy warships. The *Arizona*' guns were targeting suspected British positions on Curracloe Beach, just outside of Wexford, Ireland. It was here that the US commanders had decided to put ashore Lieutenant General George Windle Read's IVth Corps as the spearhead of the invasion of the British Isles. Already troops from the 29th Infantry Division were boarding boats to begin the assault.

Walker didn't see those boats yet, but he didn't need to see them for his next part. He worked his figures in a notebook, and, using his distance finder, he calculated at what angle the guns needed to be to strike shore positions. Orders hadn't been telegraphed from the bridge yet, but he wanted to be prepared for when they were. No one expected the British fleet to be so soundly beaten, so no thought had been given to the entire battleline being used for shore bombardment beforehand. Walker's calculations were rewarded when orders were passed up to his position from the bridge, tasking him with attacking shore positions.

"God bless Teddy's insistence on bigger guns for our warships," Walker said aloud in an almost prayerful tone.

"Aye, aye, sir," replied Chief Petty Officer Harper.

As the two men were talking, the battleships *South Carolina*, *Delaware*, and *Florida* maneuvered closer in to shore so that their smaller 12-inch guns could join the bombardment. Though Walker and Harper couldn't see it, the men of the British Territorials, 2nd Northumbrian, and 52nd Lowland Division, as well as the Royal Irish Fusiliers, hunkered down into their trenches. Despite the impressive explosions and amount of dirt tossed in the air, the well-constructed fortifications were serving to keep the casualties among the British troops relatively low.

Walker's ears perked up as he heard the distant booms of field guns coming from the Irish shoreline. He was amazed that the sound carried all the way out to him.

Must be an off-shore wind, he thought, stepping over to *Nevada*' rangefinder. Scanning the shore, Walker could see that one of the firing batteries was within range of his guns.

"Report enemy field guns are within range of our main battery and request permission for us to open fire," he instructed his talker.

"Aye, aye, sir," the talker replied. The young man passed on Walker's request. He listened for a minute then turned to Walker and said, "Sir, permission is granted."

Walker made the calculations necessary for firing and passed them on to the gun directors and fire control stations. Two minutes later, the main gun turrets swung out to train on the distant shore. The *Nevada* class' unique main battery set up had her No. 1 and No. 4 turrets being triple-mounts while her No. 2 and No. 3 wielded two guns in a super firing arrangement. This gave Walker ten of the new 15-inch naval guns with which to target the enemy battery. Confirming the range and azimuth, he pressed the button to fire the battleship's full broadside. The *Nevada* seemed to leap sideways as the first shells fired. Watching through his powerful range-finding scope, Walker watched as gouts of earth and flame erupted 800 yards behind the enemy field guns.

Dammit.

In answer to this massive salvo impacting behind them, the British guns went to rapid fire at whatever their target was, rather than displacing.

Brave bastards, Walker thought. *They must know they don't have much time left.* The second broadside fell roughly four hundred meters short, and Walker saw guns, horses, and men cut down by fragments. The *Nevada*' third salvo finally hit something important, as a great gout of flame and smoke erupted immediately behind the breast-works housing the guns. The explosion touched off others, and the British guns from the position fell silent. Through his rangefinder Walker watched as other British gun positions were silenced by fire either from the American battleships or the cruisers which had moved in close to shore to provide close fire support for American troops landing on the beach.

"God Save Ireland," intoned Chief Harper, "and see the British in Hell!"

* * *

18 May 1917
Admiralty House, London

The door to Admiral Jackie Fisher's office flew open, the door knob splintering the wall paneling behind it. Fisher looked up at the disturbance in time to see the red, florid features of Field Marshal Lord Herbert Kitchener as he strode through the door, a protesting yeoman calling desperately after him.

"*What in the bloody hell do we have a Navy for if all it's going to do is sit in Scapa Flow?*" roared Kitchener as he stalked menacingly toward Fisher's desk.

"That will be all, Terrence," said Fisher in a mild tone to the yeoman who had come through the door behind Lord Kitchener. The yeoman nodded, his face skeptical at leaving Fisher alone with the furious Kitchener. Fisher pointedly waited until the door fully latched.

"Now, my Lord, if you wouldn't mind having a seat, we can discuss this like civilized men."

For his part, Field Marshal Kitchener wasn't about to be mollified just yet. The news of Third Fleet's defeat had been one thing, but news that Ireland had risen in fresh rebellion was straining him. Adding to this strain was the fresh news that Russia, now under Alexander Kerensky's provisional government rather than the Tsar, was vacillating on whether to continue the war.

"Look here, Fisher, we have got to stop the Americans cold, and right now they control the Irish Sea. What is the Navy going to do about that?" asked Kitchener, still standing over Fisher's desk without having taken a seat.

Jackie Fisher lost his patience. "By God man, sit down! I am the First Sea Lord; I will not be shouted at like I were some midshipman!"

Kitchener harrumphed, but then he took his seat.

"Now then, you ask what the Navy is going to do about this," Fisher began, his tone sharp. "Well what would you have us do more? My fleet is stretched trying to protect the lifeblood of the Empire—protecting our convoys from India, our African Colonies, and South America. Fortunately, it appears the Americans have relegated their older ships to the Pacific, which means we can get supplies from Australia and New Zealand, but the Japanese have announced that they will not make war against the Americans, and they are apparently in talks to give Formosa back to Germany! It appears they think we are going to lose this war, and with what is going on in France, it certainly makes it appear that way."

Kitchener sat back in his chair as Fisher grew more animated in his explanation. He knew Fisher was right; the war was going very badly. The loss of Canadian forces in 1916 had hurt and had caused the British Army to effectively cease fighting in the Middle East, as those forces were shifted to the Western Front. The American Army had attacked across Lake Ontario and across Lake Erie, and so far, the only thing that seemed to be holding them at bay had been lack of enough troops to complete their conquest of Canada. Ontario, Winnipeg, and Montreal had fallen, while there was fierce fighting around Vancouver.

"Now, what I could do is send the Grand Fleet after the Americans. God knows we outnumber them in ships almost two to one, while in smaller ships even more so. But, and this is a very large but, the High Seas Fleet will sail while we are trying to deal with the Americans, and I don't know a good way to prevent the Fleet from being caught between two forces that would have an advantage over us in heavy ships if we did so. Worse, with Italy switching sides again, that means the Kaiser could land a couple of his free divisions in the North. Then where would we be?" Fisher rose from his own seat and planted his first firmly on his desktop, fixing Lord Kitchener with a basilisk gaze. Then a thoughtful expression crossed his face. Sitting back down, he looked back over to Kitchener.

"I apologize. We are both under a great deal of pressure, and I shouldn't have taken it out on you. I think I have an idea that might be worth pursuing."

"Oh, pray tell," Kitchener replied.

"I think we may detach Vice Admiral Beatty's battlecruisers and some of our armored cruisers. Use their speed to get in among the Americans and disrupt their operations in the Irish Sea. That way Jellicoe can keep the High Seas Fleet bottled up with a show of force, while Beatty deals with the Americans."

* * *

21 May 1917
Irish Sea

Captain Robert Ledford, Commanding Officer, USS *Nevada*, sat at the head of a long table around which he had gathered his senior officers. Ledford was a stocky, barrel-chested man with prematurely white hair. Walker had served under Ledford before when he had been a midshipman on his summer cruise aboard the old battleship USS *Ohio*. Ledford was then the *Ohio's* Gunnery Officer, and he had impressed upon Walker the importance of delivering accurate fire. But that was ten years ago, and now Lieutenant Commander Walker served Captain Robert Ledford as *Nevada's* Gunnery Officer.

"Gentlemen, it is now time to reveal to you a secret that has been closely held by the Office of Naval Intelligence for just this time. We have broken the British Naval Code and have been reading their messages for a year now."

A murmur shot around the table at this news, with the various officers looking at each other in some excitement. Ledford continued on once everyone quieted down.

"We and German Naval Intelligence have ensured that nothing we have done will alert the British to that feather in our cap. In fact, we and the Germans have known now for about a year that Britain was reading Germany's messages, and it is because of that that the High Seas Fleet has had a couple of major operations blown. The Germans have continued to allow the British to read their messages and to lull them into thinking they have the upper hand."

"So why are they telling us now?" inquired the ship's executive officer.

"The Grand Fleet is splitting up," replied Ledford simply.

The table erupted into buzzing excitement.

"Alright gentlemen, alright, quiet down. I know we are all excited about this prospect. As such, Admiral Knight has devised a trap for the British. They are detaching nine of their battlecruisers and several lighter ships to attack us here in the Irish Sea. In the meantime, the rest of the Grand Fleet plans to sortie to impress upon the Germans that they are in fact still blockaded in Wilhelmshaven."

"Sir, what will be our part of the plan?" Walker asked, the excitement in his voice clear to the rest of the men around the table.

"I am glad you asked, Mr. Walker. What we are going to do is present the British with what appears to be a juicy target. The battlescouts *Lexington* and *Concord* are going to range to the north of the squadron, along with a screen of scout cruisers and destroyers. We suspect the battlecruisers *Courageous* and *Glorious* will be their lead ships; both are extremely fast. It is our intention that *Lexington* and *Concord* will exchange a few shots, and then using their superior speed, lead the enemy squadrons into a trap consisting of the battleship line, headed by *Georgia*, and then us. We plan to smash as many of their ships as possible, and then we will proceed up the west coast of Scotland, round Scotland, and try to cut the rest of the Grand Fleet off from returning to Scapa Flow, while the High Seas Fleet comes out to meet them in the North Sea."

The sheer scale of the plan is audacious, thought Walker, *but can we pull it off?*

* * *

Chapter 3

21 May 1917
Rosyth, Scotland

Vice Admiral David Beatty knew trouble was brewing when his adjutant informed him that Sir John Jellicoe, Admiral, Commander in Chief, Grand Fleet, was coming aboard. Jellicoe had rarely come down to Rosyth from the Grand Fleet's base at Scapa Flow. His doing so now indicated the senior officer had something of great importance he wished to impart to Beatty which he didn't trust to be communicated via telegraph.

Beatty impatiently took a stroll about the bridge of HMS *Lion* as he awaited the arrival of Jellicoe, vainly trying to contain his excitement at finally being let loose to hunt the Americans. As if summoned by his thoughts, Admiral Jellicoe appeared on the battlecruiser's bridge with his aide…and ominously, with no staff.

"Ah, there you are, Beatty. Say, will you come down on deck with me? I wish to go over some things before you depart."

"Certainly, Sir John," Beatty replied cautiously, gesturing for the Grand Fleet's commander to lead the way. The two men descended the ladder from the bridge and proceeded past the forward gun turrets. Jellicoe led Beatty to a quiet section of the deck and away from listening ears; what he wanted to say was for Beatty's ears alone.

"Look here. I know they have detached you to hunt the Americans, but I don't like it. I have protested the loss of all my battlecruisers to the First Sea Lord, but Fisher has told me to buck up and do my duty. I want to stress on you, David, that we cannot lose your force. Do not become decisively engaged without having a way out. Your ships are fast and your crews well trained, but let us face facts here; they are sending you against a superior force," Jellicoe's worry was plain on his face.

"Understood, sir, but we have got to break up the American force before they stage further landings. Bad enough that they have landed troops in Ireland, and those rebels sure did rise up awfully fast," replied Beatty, who for the moment was taking everything in stride. Jellicoe's eyes narrowed, but Beatty pressed on, "The other thing to consider is that with the Irish in full rebellion, Kitchener is worried that the Americans will dash across the Irish Sea and land on the Welsh coast. Our submarines have proved completely ineffective in doing the Americans any real harm, as have our torpedo boats."

Jellicoe grunted at that. He too was disappointed at how poorly British submarines had performed. Worse for the Royal Navy, a few German torpedo boats had managed to stage daring raids on the ports located at the mouth of the Thames and Portsmouth, itself.

"Yes, well, as I have said, do not allow yourself to be decisively engaged by the Americans. Get in, get your licks in, and get out. I have also decided to send *Queen Elizabeth* with you." Mention of that perked Beatty up; his battlecruisers had frequently worked with the super-dreadnoughts of the *Queen Elizabeth* class. "This will stiffen your line and give you some umpf if you need to break away. Also, given the number of large ships, I am hoping that the Americans will decide they cannot risk losing too many of their ships and turn for home. That is the best case."

"Yes sir," replied Beatty.

With fifteen capital ships to the American's sixteen, that should certainly give an American commander pause, Beatty mused. *Especially as they know our ships are better.*

"I will be getting underway once the tide favors us, sir, and I will rendezvous with your battleships off Scapa Flow. Has intelligence given us any idea what the Germans are doing?"

"Apparently, they are sitting still," Jellicoe replied. "Intelligence hasn't picked up on any new signals other than routine traffic to their fleet."

"Well sir, if that is the case, I think we can be out and back before the Huns are any the wiser," quipped Beatty, a boyish grin lighting his face.

* * *

26 May 1917, 0900 Hours
North of the Isle of Man, Irish Sea

Lt. Commander Fitz Walker paced his gunnery platform, trying hard to hide his anxiousness. The sound of heavy guns sounded in the distance, carrying over the *Nevada*' normal noises. Even with the auditory reports, the Royal Navy's battleline still wasn't in sight. From the signals being passed back by *Lexington* and *Concord*, they had managed to score a few hits on the enemy before reversing out of range. The two battle-scouts, unique American designs that were as fast as a light cruiser, but carried large guns like a battleship, would pass to the west of the Isle of Man and then into the Manx Sea, an area that was just 37 miles across.

It's going to be an unpleasant surprise when they pass the Isle of Man, Walker mused while baring his teeth. The American battleship line sat just eight miles off the Point of Ayre on the northernmost tip of the Isle of Man, just over thirty miles away from the British fleet's last sighted position. The trap was set and, as Admiral Knight had predicted, Vice Admiral David Beatty was falling into it. Admiral Knight's battleships were going to cross behind Beatty's battlecruisers and pin them between Ireland and the Isle of Man. At the southernmost portion of the Manx Sea, most of the American destroyers and cruisers lay in wait, planning to make torpedo runs once the British battlecruisers tried to escape the trap.

"I can't believe they are doing it sir, I mean, where the hell are their screens?" asked Chief Gunners Mate Harper. His expression showed true puzzlement. Like Walker, Harper was raised in a service that viewed the Royal Navy as the gold standard of naval services. Yet, here the Royal Navy was committing to something monumentally stupid.

"Well Chief Harper, all I can think is that it is like the matador and the bull," Walker stated. "Admiral Knight presented Beatty with what he wants to see, and just like the bull charging the cape, Beatty has taken off after the decoy. Still, it isn't one sided," stated Walker matter-of-factly.

"No sir I guess not, those poor bastards on the *St. Louis*. Those ships don't have much use in this fight."

"You're right, Chief, too old and too slow for this fight, but we needed them to make the British think they were after our scout force."

As the two men conversed in their fighting position, they could feel the sway as the USS *Nevada* picked up speed. She accelerated from a stately five knots to 18 knots, and black smoke poured from the single stack behind her forward superstructure. Ahead of her, the USS *Georgia* did the same, and behind her the USS *Arizona* and the rest of the battleline increased their speed. Peering to starboard, Walker and Harper could just make out four American battleships moving to plug the North Channel that connected the Irish Sea to the Atlantic. These were the battleships *South Carolina*, *Michigan*, *Delaware*, and *North Dakota*. Being the oldest of the dreadnought battleships in Admiral Knight's force, it was decided that they were too slow for the chase of Beatty's battlecruisers and would instead serve as a third blocking force to prevent any from escaping back to the

North Atlantic. With them steamed twelve destroyers of the *O'Brien* and *Sampson* classes.

* * *

HMS Lion
1100 Hours

Admiral Beatty was in his element. He stepped out onto the bridge wing to feel the air rushing past his face as HMS *Lion* poured on speed at 28 knots. It was a glorious midmorning with not a cloud in the sky. His mood was only slightly dampened due to the damage that had been done to HMS *Courageous*. The enemy ships had knocked several holes in her thin armor, and she had been forced to reduce speed. Still, Beatty's battlecruisers were pursuing what must be American battle-scouts given their speed.

Too bad for them their cruisers were not as swift, Beatty thought with a predatory smile. His squadron had drawn first blood that morning, killing a lagging American armored cruiser. Speed, speed was of the essence, and that is why Beatty had made the decision to leave the *Queen Elizabeth* class dreadnoughts behind when he spotted these American ships. He had to get them to grips before they could give accurate details of his force.

HMS *Lion* was the third ship back in the line; *Glorious* led the squadron, followed by *Renown*, then *Lion*, and finally the newer *Repulse*. The old battlecruisers *Inflexible* and *Invincible* lagged behind their newer sisters by roughly 3,000 yards, their weary engines gradually losing ground. Even so, as Beatty watched, his guns fired another salvo at the enemy battle-scouts, and the British admiral was confident the older vessels would close up once his force had crippled the two Americans. He didn't think they would really hit given the speeds and maneuvering that the ships were doing, but rapid course changes were causing the distance to close with the American ships. If he could just get them to 10,000 yards as doctrine demanded…

"Sir, signal from *Inflexible*! She is under attack!"

"What?" asked Admiral Beatty in astonishment.

The signals officer glanced down at his message form and then back up at the Vice Admiral. "Sir, *Inflexible* says she is under attack from a strong force of battleships."

Beatty stepped out onto the bridge wing, ready to furiously inquire as to what his staff was talking about, and then he looked for himself. He raised his binoculars just in time to see a forest of shell splashes surround *Inflexible*, their height telling him the battlecruiser's captain was quite accurate in his report.

"Damn," muttered Beatty, feeling a momentary stab of panic before he regained his composure and sought to save his force.

"Make signal, all ships to fall back on HMS *Inflexible*. Also raise the *Queen Elizabeth* and have Rear Admiral Evan-Thomas get his ships up here as fast as possible. Perhaps we can catch the Americans between us and destroy them."

Beatty was putting on a good face, and everyone on the bridge of HMS *Lion* knew it. Since the Battle of Trafalgar, the axiom that, "No captain can do very wrong if he places his ship alongside that of the enemy," had held sway. Turning to engage American battleships with his battlecruisers was a very dangerous proposition.

And can anyone blame us after the Troubridge affair? Beatty thought as he looked at the plot. *Churchill's instructions regarding the court martial sent a clear message; you will engage the enemy or else.*

As HMS *Lion* completed her nearly 180-degree turn, two things seemed to happen simultaneously. First, HMS *Glorious* staggered in the water from multiple hits. Her aftermost 15-inch gun turret exploded, rendering half her guns out of action. The resultant spall and flooding below the waterline also rendered the battlecruiser a near cripple, her speed dropping below 10 knots.

The second arrived in the form of a wireless message from HMS *Invincible*. An ashen-faced rating burst onto the bridge and hurried over to the signals officer. That man read the message form, and Beatty watched as all the blood drained from the officer's face. Turning to Beatty, the man's mouth worked briefly.

"Out with it!" Beatty snapped.

"Sir, message from *Invincible*; *Inflexible* has blown up!" the man exclaimed in a disbelieving tone.

Beatty rushed out to the bridge wing and trained his binoculars back to the horizon. What he saw almost made him vomit; he could just make out the flaming wreckage that was *Inflexible* sinking beneath the sea. Of the Americans, all he could see was dark smudges against the distant horizon, smoke from their engines and their guns. Splashes were soon being thrown up around HMS *Lion*, and Beatty looked to the stern of the ship to see that the American battle-scouts had turned back and were now directing fire at his ship and HMS *Glorious*.

They've certainly found their backbone, Beatty thought bitterly. *We'll see how long that lasts when Evan-Thomas gets here.*

Beatty grew angry as he watched *Glorious* fall further behind. The battlecruiser staggered once again as an American shell found its mark. Her stern was aflame from her aft turret back, and this shell impacted just behind her funnel. A great gout of flame followed by plumes of black smoke showed where the shell had exploded in *Glorious'* engine room. Her speed dropped to nothing.

"Bloody hell," Beatty swore helplessly. There was nothing to be done for *Glorious* now; Captain Farthing would have to fight his ship as he saw fit. Beatty could see more columns of smoke were beginning to show in his rear.

"Damn, what is back there?" he asked aloud.

* * *

1130 Hours

Lt. Commander Fitz Walker peered through his ranging scopes at HMS *Invincible*, the *Nevada's* first target in this battle. USS *Georgia* had engaged HMS *Inflexible*. Much to everyone's surprise, on *Georgia's* seventh salvo from her forward guns, the *Inflexible* had blown up.

Georgia must have gotten that British battlecruiser's magazines, Walker thought. *My God, those guns are ship killers.*

Walker directed his guns to fire a ladder to bracket the enemy warship. What this meant was that each gun turret fired at a point that spaced out every 400 yards, the idea being that one should hit close enough, or on target, to give him the data he needed to hit his targets. As the British closed the range, the *Nevada* turned to present her full broadside to the oncoming British warships. Although this made the battleship a larger target for the British guns, it also allowed Walker the use of his full main broadside and secondaries. The range between the lead British ships and his ship had fallen to 13,000 yards.

Looking up from his rangefinder Walker could see a blizzard of British shells fall around USS *Georgia*. The lack of explosions told him that the shells failed to penetrate, but had likely splintered on impact.

Probably quite lively on deck, but that beats having something explode in the innards, he thought. *Just ask that Brit crew.* Walker was just glad it appeared the British were concentrating their fire on *Georgia*. It was a poor tactical decision, as it gave every other USN battleship a chance to fire freely. Behind the *Nevada,* the USS *Arizona* and USS *Pennsylva-*

nia were next in line. They swung out their dozen apiece 16-inch guns and hammered away at HMS *Tiger* and HMS *Queen Mary*.

"Damn sir, what a sight from up here," opined Harper, his voice betraying his awe. Harper held a portable rangefinder to his face, the smaller device used in case something was to happen to the main rangefinder that Walker currently peered through.

The rangefinders, both fixed and handheld, were odd looking pieces of equipment. They looked like periscopes laid on their side, with two peering scopes at either end joined to a set of viewing scopes in the center. The stereoscopic view was supposed to help spotters with both the fall of the shot and getting an initial fix on the range. The *Nevada's* various rangefinders, like all US battleships currently in service, were the same Zeiss optics found aboard German warships. These, like the Krupp homogeneous armor, were fruits of the close relationship developed between the US and Germany since the Prussians had helped a war-weary America kick France out of Mexico in 1872.

The cage mast swayed again and again, each time a volley issued forth from the main guns. But now Walker had the range on *Invincible*, and he was moving all his guns to rapid fire. The 5-inch secondaries cracked at a rate below their maximum, Walker having told the gun chiefs to expect a long fight and to conserve ammunition in case the British light forces managed to join the battle. The main turrets, on the other hand, were ripping out a teeth-jarring broadside every two minutes.

It must be hell down there on the guns, Walker thought. A fighting turret was a din of noise in a cauldron choked with dust. Many of the men would suffer permanent hearing damage this day.

Still, as he looked through the spotting scope, he knew things could be far worse. The secondaries scored hit after hit on the *Invincible*, tearing up her upper works. For a moment, he considered what it must be like on the battlecruiser's bridge. No sooner had he finished the thought when he observed a large shell entering into the structure. The ship lost control and staggered out of line for a few long seconds, then started to correct as the auxiliary helm took over.

Well, it looks like we just made a whole bunch of work for the Admiralty, Walker thought.

"Sir, we have trouble coming up," pointed out Harper.

"Which ship do you make her out to be Chief?"

"Looks like it's either *Indefatigable* or *New Zealand*. She seems to be coming right for us."

"Well until we deal with *Invincible*, she is *New Mexico's* problem."

"Aye sir," replied Harper.

Sure enough as the two men discussed the new threat, shells from *New Mexico* and *Idaho* splashed around the hull of the sleek-looking British ship. Meanwhile, the *Georgia* had switched targets and was now joining the assault on *Invincible*. The bigger 16-inch shells plunged right through *Invincible's* armor as if it weren't there. Walker was mildly irritated that *Georgia* was getting in on his kill, but even as he thought this, his irritation vanished. *Invincible* seemed to just come apart when two of *Nevada's* 15-inch shells penetrated her A turret barbette. Walker watched as the *Invincible*'s A turret rocketed into the air on a geyser of smoke and flame, as if it were made of wood and not steel. The forward tripod mast violently lurched backwards, then sheared off as the explosion spread, lifting the forward superstructure into the air. What had been HMS *Invincible* snapped in two just forward of her second funnel, then turned turtle and sank rapidly.

Walker and Harper were stunned silent for a moment. They had seen the destruction of *Inflexible*, but that ship's death had been mostly obscured by thick smoke clouds. On the other hand, *Invincible*, and the poor souls that made up her crew, died fully in their sight. The men both simultaneously exhaled, neither realizing they were holding their breath throughout the vessel's annihilation. Once the shock passed, the men of the fighting top searched for their next target. To their surprise, HMS *New Zealand*—they could now tell it was her based on slight differences between her and her sister ship HMS *Indefatigable*—had turned away from the US battleline. Walker laid his rangefinder on the ship and looked through it to see that *New Zealand* seemed to have serious damage to her stern.

New Mexico must have jammed her rudders, he thought. *Won't be long for her now.*

* * *

1500 Hours

Vice Admiral David Beatty knew he had screwed up by the numbers. He felt like falling to his knees and praying for divine mercy and raging against the Almighty at the same time, but he could only blame himself for his predicament. His force was being hammered from two sides. Worse, he could now make out American destroyers, their small, sleek silhouettes knifing toward the remainder of his ship like sharks on a bleeding carcass.

Glorious was out of action. To his dismay, the battlecruiser had surrendered when American cruisers had come upon her in the wake of the American battle-scouts. *Invincible*, *Inflexible*, and now *Indefatigable*, had exploded under American shell fire. *New Zealand* was out of control after her steering gear had been wrecked by the only hit she had received so far. Remarkably no one had been killed aboard her when it happened. HMS *Courageous* had rolled over on her side, her crew abandoning her, after repeated hits had caused her to lay over. In all, six of his thirteen battlecruisers were either sunk or out of action, and he was trapped between two American forces that were both well within range of him.

Beatty was tossed forward into the front bulkhead of *Lion's* bridge when the ship was tossed about by another large shell hit. The stink of ozone and cordite filled the bridge. It had been there since the beginning of the engagement. Now a new smell added itself, that of burning metals, woods, and rubber. Beatty pulled himself upright and walked out onto the port bridge wing to look over the ship. To his horror, the X turret aft burned furiously, the aft funnel had been shot away, and the aft mast had fallen across his amidships Q turret. Beatty observed sailors working furiously with torches to cut away the damaged mast so that they could get the Q turret back in action. Hoses had also been rigged to fight the numerous fires on deck, though no one was going near the burning X turret. That it hadn't destroyed the ship when it blew up was a miracle in itself.

"Flood the magazines to the Q turret, fires are out of control below decks, and I don't want to lose the ship," ordered a far-too-calm Captain Wright. His steady voice and controlled demeanor worked to calm other members of the bridge crew on HMS *Lion*. "Give the men time to get out of there and then flood them."

Captain Wright stepped out onto the bridge wing with Vice Admiral Beatty, surveyed the damage, and then brought his binoculars up to glass the distant shoreline of the Isle of Man.

"Sir, two of my main turrets are out, the engine room is a shambles, and I have had to reduce our speed to seven knots. Fires are out of control below decks and on our stern. I am going to deliberately beach *Lion* so that she doesn't sink."

"Do what you must, Captain Wright," Beatty stated, and then he quipped, "There appears to be a problem with our ships, they keep blowing up."

As if to punctuate that statement, a series of shells impacted HMS *Lion* in her A turret from the USS *Texas*. The 14-inch, armor-piercing shells impacted at an angle just at the base of the A turret, then slanted their way into the barbette and exploded inside the handling room. The blast and hot fragments touched off the stacked bags of cordite that were on their way up into the main turret. British warships had hatches in place to prevent an explosion in the handling room from flashing into the magazine, but one of the practices put in place in the battlecruiser fleet by Vice Admiral David Beatty was to jam those doors open to allow for faster passage of powder and shells to the guns. This came back to bite HMS *Lion* as the explosions in the handling room flashed back through the turret in a roiling, sailor-immolating conflagration. The fire licked down into the ship's forward 13.5-inch gun magazine, and thermodynamics far outraced mortal attempts to flood the structure. Vice Admiral David Beatty, Captain Jonathan Wright, and the 1,100 men of HMS *Lion* died violently when the flagship became the last battlecruiser to blow up in the Battle of the Irish Sea.

* * *

1745 Hours

The fight wasn't entirely one sided. USS *Arkansas* was forced to beach herself on the Isle of Man when several hits and near misses opened great rents in her hull. Despite counter-flooding to try to offset the damage, progressive flooding threatened the vessel's engine and fire rooms, so her captain decided to beach her while he still had power. The American battleship came to rest not far from where HMS *New Zealand* had, and the latter's crew decided to strike her colors rather than be hammered to death at close range.

The worst losses for the US Navy, however, were the destruction of USS *South Carolina*, and USS *Delaware* at the hands of HMS *Barham*, *Warspite*, and *Valiant*. These three modern *Queen Elizabeth*-class dreadnoughts were the lead ships of the second British force that came south through the North Channel that separated the Irish Sea from the Atlantic. Even though they had been bottled up in the channel, their modern 15-inch guns made a hash of *South Carolina* and *Delaware*. The two American battleships made for the Irish coast, intent on beaching themselves, but sank in relatively shallow water. Their cage masts and upper works stuck up from the Irish Sea like grave markers.

But the British dreadnoughts didn't get off unscathed. HMS *Barham* took three torpedoes from US destroyers, and she turned over on her side. British sailors were scrambling up onto her side when some internal fire found a magazine. HMS *Barham* blew up, taking many of her crew with her. HMS *Warspite* took two torpedoes forward and, taking on water, managed to wreck herself on the Scottish coast, just 6 miles from where she had been torpedoed. HMS *Valiant* turned herself around and joined the rest of the British dreadnought force entering the Firth of Clyde to make for Scapa Flow.

Conspicuously absent from Rosyth was the remainder of the British battlecruisers, trapped with no hope of escape under the USN's heavy guns. With HMS *Lion*'s destruction, command fell to HMS *Tiger*' captain. Realizing the doomed situation, the officer tearfully ordered the remaining ships to deliberately beach themselves on the Isle of Man. He hoped that by doing this, they could later be recovered once the Americans were seen off by Admiral Jellicoe and the rest of the Grand Fleet. Unfortunately for him and the crews of these ship, American Marines were put ashore, and they proceeded to capture the British ships, who surrendered without firing another shot.

Lt. Commander Walker considered all of this from the comfort of an easy chair in the officers' wardroom aboard USS *Nevada*. That ship, along with the battleships, *Georgia*, *New Mexico*, *Idaho*, *Mississippi*,

Pennsylvania, *Wyoming*, *New York*, *Texas*, and *Oklahoma*, were even now steaming into the North Sea. With them were the battle-scouts *Lexington* and *Concord*, and twenty-two destroyers. Admiral Knight had made the decision to leave three battleships and the rest of the cruisers and destroyers to continue to support the four Army divisions ashore in Ireland. In a few hours the US Navy was going to attack the British Grand Fleet from the north as the High Seas Fleet hit it from the east in the Skagerrak. The British knew this place as Jutland...

* * *

3 June 1917
Admiralty House, London

Admiral of the Fleet John "Jackie" Fisher, 1st Baron Fisher, and First Sea Lord, sat at his desk. His features showed every one of his considerable years. Spread out on the desk before him were his favorite newspapers. Their headlines all spoke of disaster, but even that word was an understatement. The Grand Fleet had not just been decisively beaten, but its survivors had been forced to inter themselves in Danish ports. Of the twenty-one dreadnoughts that Jellicoe went to sea with, eight had been sunk outright. A further six were so badly damaged that they were scuttled rather than face capture by the Germans and Americans. The rest, cut off from ports in England, had sailed to the Danish coast to inter themselves rather than surrender as they ran out of coal. Admiral Jellicoe had died fighting aboard his flagship, the *Iron Duke*. Fisher's own beloved HMS *Dreadnought*, the revolutionary ship that had redefined warship construction for a generation, now lay at the bottom of the North Sea.

It had been several hours since Admiral Fisher had called for anything, and Yeoman 1st Class Terrence Howard was beginning to get worried. Getting up from his desk he walked over to Fisher's door and gently knocked on it. Getting no answer, the Yeoman knocked again, more loudly. Still there was no answer. Yeoman Howard opened the door to Admiral Fisher's office.

"My Lord," he called out, his accent harkening to the Midlands, "is everything alright?"

Not hearing an answer, Howard stepped all the way through into Fisher's office. The sight that met him shocked him to his core. Still sitting behind his desk, Admiral Jackie Fisher's features had taken on the mask of death, his skin grey with lack of perfusion. The shock of Jutland had been too much, and Jackie Fisher's heart had quite literally broken.

*****

Philip Wohlrab Bio

Philip Wohlrab has been a medic with the Army for over 12 years, and he has served his time in the sandbox. He currently trains the next generation of Combat Medics, and runs a schoolhouse medical section. When he isn't doing Army things he can be found at various Sci-Fi Cons, and writing his first full length novel in the Squidverse! You can find him on Facebook at https://www.facebook.com/DocFather6/.

#####

Martha Coston and the Farragut Curse by Day Al-Mohamed

"My signals will prove a valuable auxiliary for the Navy, and the night would lose half its terrors at sea, when in the darkness and through the storm ships could talk to each other."

Martha Coston would have regretted those words if she had not believed them to be true. She didn't bother with field glasses as she gazed up at the night sky. Faint shimmers of light reflected off smoke as they floated downwards, remnants of what had been her pyrotechnic display. Martha's lips were set in a tense line. She was grateful that none of the other observers noticed the expression on her face in the darkness. Tonight had been a success. No, the truth was, tonight should have been a success. The darkness had been illuminated by the explosion of dozens of signal flares. Fired high above the waters of the Potomac in Washington City, they had burned a brilliant clear green for at least ten seconds. The first Coston Night Signal.

However, rather than exclaim at her success, Martha heard the men from the Navy examination board mutter misgivings and doubts and questions. Of course, none of the officers aimed any of the questions at her. She was, after all, only a woman. Granted, she was the woman who had created the flares, but they found that fact inconvenient. Even in this dreadful time of war, with the very nation divided against itself, and urgency, like a dog nipping at their heels, they were unwilling to alter their preconceptions. It didn't matter that the Secretary of the Navy had invited her to be present when the board tested the signals. All that mattered was that she was a woman and therefore anything she did was suspect.

Martha retreated back to her lab at the Potomac Yards with their words echoing in her ears. It wasn't really a lab. The Navy hadn't been convinced enough to give her an actual lab. She worked in a tiny shed not far from the waterfront. No assistants, no chemists, it was just her, on her own, every day. It had taken her more than ten years to perfect the plans and produce a finished product. But that was meaningless unless she was able to sell her night signaling system. Martha had invested every cent she had, and several she didn't, into this project. She sighed and leaned against the rough wooden wall. It creaked ominously. Perhaps she should go to Europe and find out if the British or French would be willing to invest in her Coston flares.

She tucked an errant strand of hair that had escaped her bun back behind her ear and rolled up her sleeves. The Aldens had agreed to keep her sons for the evening so she might as well take advantage of the extra time. Besides, she had an idea for a new additive to her signals. Martha walked over to the small desk crammed into the corner of the room. Papers and books were neatly stacked on and around it. There was a clear sense of order. Martha sighed again. Her husband would have had them tumbling in piles with crumpled and stained pages all over the lab. She missed him desperately, and, as her two boys grew older, she missed him even more.

Martha narrowed her gaze and her attention. She flipped open a journal and skimmed down until she found her latest notes. It would be a long night. She had a new recipe for her flares. These would burn hotter and brighter, and, if her calculations were correct, they might even be unquenchable by water. She would show those vazey bantams. She would create something so remarkable that they couldn't ignore her. Step one, calcium.

"Mrs. Martha Coston?"

Martha looked up from where she was putting large cow bones into a vat. A naval officer stood at the entrance to her lab. She nodded, not stopping what she was doing.

"How can I help you?" Her words were curt.

She knew she was being rude, but right now she didn't feel like being polite in the face of potentially more ridicule.

The older man removed his hat and ducked his head to enter, "You may not remember me, but you were a friend of my wife's, Susan Marchant?" He wrinkled his nose and added without thought, "What is that smell?"

Martha stopped what she was doing. Ignoring his question, she wiped her hands off on her apron and answered him with a question of her own. "Mr. David Farragut?"

"Yes, Ma'am," he said.

Martha stoked the fire under the vat. As the slurry heated, the smell that rose was indeed terrible. She used the few moments to gather her thoughts. Martha knew all about Flag Officer David Farragut. The entire country knew about Farragut. He had failed in an attack on New Orleans. It had destroyed almost the entire Union fleet and resulted in the death of his foster brother, Captain David Porter. In fact, every military endeavor he attempted during the last three years of the war to preserve the Union had ended in failure. Some even whispered that he was cursed.

"Susan was a very good friend," Martha responded cautiously. "I am sorry I could not attend her funeral."

She ducked her head, unable to meet his gaze. The truth of the matter was that she had been unable to afford the journey to New York. Through her own ignorance and "the duplicity of others," what savings she had as a widow had been taken from her. As it was, she was currently living with friends and reliant on their charity for both herself and her boys.

Martha swallowed back tears. She wasn't sure if they were for herself or for Susan. "I'm sure it was very beautiful."

Farragut gave her a small sad smile. "You are kind. I am here to ask for your help."

Martha gestured to a bench, the only seating other than the chair at her desk. "The boiling will take some time. Please sit."

Farragut shook his head. "I prefer to stand."

He paced back and forth as if readying himself, and the words began to flow. "The West Gulf Blockading Squadron is tasked primarily with preventing Confederate ships from supplying troops. These blockade runners are often coming in from neutral ports such as Nassau and Cuba. Outbound ships carry cotton, tobacco, and other goods for trade, and inbound ships are bringing in guns and other ordnance."

Martha exhaled slowly, hiding her impatience. She was well aware of General Winfield Scott's Anaconda plan. The Union navy was to create a blockade to extend along the Atlantic and the Gulf of Mexico coastlines and up into the lower Mississippi River. The newspapers reported often on its failures.

Martha sat down in the chair and watched him pace. "And you need my help how?" she prompted.

Farragut kept talking as if he hadn't heard her question. Martha pursed her lips, her irritation rising.

He continued, "We are failing in our task. With 3,600 miles of coast and more than 200 river mouths, inlets, bays, and channels, it is impossible to stop all maritime trade. But the fact that these blockade runners can fly past us in the dead of night outside of major trading ports is an embarrassment."

Farragut stopped pacing. "I need something to tip the balance."

He took her hands in his, and his fingers felt warm against her cold skin. He glanced down, and she could see him taking in the white scars that decorated her knuckles and the backs of her hands. She pulled her hands away and yanked down her sleeves.

He took a step back, his back stiff and his words formal. "I'm sorry, Mrs. Coston."

She gave him a rueful look, "When working with incendiaries, one will get burned. It is not a matter of 'if' but 'when' and 'how badly.'" She flexed her hands, feeling the tightness against her skin.

"Surely you have men to do the research?"

She shook her head dismissively. "We hear much of the chivalry of men towards women, but it vanishes like dew before the summer sun when one of us comes into competition with the manly sex." She paused and smiled to take the sting out of her words before continuing, "I am perfectly capable of running my own lab, Mr. Farragut."

"My apologies. I did not intend to offend. I have the utmost faith in your abilities, and I saw your accomplishments just this night. That is why I am here...asking for your help."

She felt her annoyance dissipate. All that remained was a hollow feeling in the pit of her stomach.

"To me, it was a most bitter thing to find in that lofty institution, the Navy," she said, "men so small-minded that they begrudged a woman her success."

"Then you understand. Mrs. Coston, we need each other. I need the success that your signals will give my squadron and you need a real world success for your invention."

"Mr. Farragut—"

"Don't give me your answer tonight. Just please, consider it. We can discuss it further tomorrow afternoon."

* * *

Time flew over the next three months. Farragut had asked for 400 flares, but that had been just the beginning. Martha had been hard pressed to complete the task, but she had found a manufacturer, procured the necessary ingredients, and begun production of the Coston Signal Flare. And since that time, Farragut's squadron had achieved unprecedented success. Her pyrotechnic night signal flare and code system allowed Farragut's navy vessels to communicate quickly and easily with each other by night, and firing the flares in the path of the blockade-runners made it easy to track and then trap them. Three months expanded to six months, then eight, then ten. And then things started to go wrong.

"I need to come onto your ship." Martha was abrupt and to the point.

She glared at Farragut as he, once again in her tiny lab, paced back and forth, his steps heavy with worry.

Farragut reeled backward as if he'd been struck. "Absolutely not."

Martha didn't flinch. "I have examined the signals at the design phase. I have checked with my manufacturer in New York. I pulled some of the signal flares off the railcar delivering them to you. The only place I have not tested their efficacy is when you are underway."

"I cannot allow—"

"Because I'm a woman?" Martha cut him off.

"You know that's not true," Farragut snapped.

"Don't lie to me. It is very true."

At the stubborn expression on his face, Martha sighed and softened her tone, "In the last ten months, you have intercepted more than 300 blockade runners. Mobile, Alabama, was the largest cotton port in the world, and the last large Confederate port, and you successfully stopped all maritime commerce. That made you a hero."

"Yes," he said through gritted teeth. "Some fool hero."

"And now?" Martha prodded, like the way her younger son would play with a loose tooth. "Tell me again. Tell me what is happening."

Martha knew she had to get him to say the words out loud, or he would continue to try and ignore what had become an increasing problem of the last few weeks.

"And now, they aren't working. Some of the signals fizzle; some don't even light." Farragut started pacing again, his steps faster and faster. "You know all this. Blockade runners are getting through because my ships cannot communicate to each other."

"Which means we have to do something," she finished. Her words fell like stones into water, their import rippling out in a way that felt almost physical.

Farragut ran a hand over his face. "The men are right. I am cursed." The words were muffled but understandable.

"You're not cursed, David." Martha said. "But we do need to understand what is happening, and, regardless of propriety, I am the only one who knows the recipes concerning how to mix the chemical compounds to create the bright burning signals. I need to board *Hartford.* I need to test the flares."

"War is no place for a woman," he snapped.

"War is no place for anyone," she countered. "David, let me discover what is wrong."

Farragut growled in concession. "Do we have a choice?"

Pregnant silence was his only answer.

* * *

Martha Coston walked across the spar deck towards the small room where the flares were stored. Thankfully she didn't have far to go. The USS *Hartford* had dropped anchor for a few hours before their final approach to the mouth of the river just outside Mobile, Alabama. Martha considered herself lucky they'd stopped. She'd wanted to take advantage of the opportunity to check her signal flares one last time.

Martha pulled her cap farther down over her head and kept her face averted from the faint light emanating from her shuttered lantern. She was dressed like a navy officer, but it would not take much for anyone to discover the ruse. She shifted the heavy leather bag containing her testing kit onto her shoulder. Inside, there was the faint clink of glass as the vials of chemicals jostled each other.

On her right, in the shadows, squatted a row of 9" Dahlgren smoothbores. Each required a crew of sixteen and a powderman to fire. She couldn't help but note the shape of the powerful guns. It really was a brilliant design. The smooth curves equalized strain and concentrated more weight of the metal in the gun breech where the greatest pressure of expanding propellant gases was. The result was a strong, maneuverable cannon that was much less likely to explode from pressure. Martha reached out to touch one of the guns, but pulled her hand back and gave herself a mental shake. This was a distraction; she needed to focus on her mission.

The sounds of water splashing against the sides of the ship and the snapping of the lines against the mast seemed to fill the air. For a full ship, the night was eerily devoid of human sound. *Hartford* was a sloop-of-war with a full complement of 302 officers and sailors, but tonight, she'd seen fewer than half a dozen men. And so Martha only barely stifled a very feminine shriek when a voice rasped out of the darkness.

"You should know the ship well enough to not be using that lantern."

Martha squinted through the dim light to better see the speaker, but she recognized him immediately. There were only a few black men who served on *Hartford*. It was Landsman John Lawson. She remembered him from her frantic half-hidden days on the ship. Regardless of the worn and frayed state of his naval uniform, he always seemed to carry himself with a confidence that made him memorable.

"It's bad luck," he added in a hushed voice.

She nodded, ducking her head lower as she passed. So many things were bad luck on a ship.

His eyes narrowed. "My apologies, but I do not recognize you, Sailor."

Martha felt the air on her neck go icy. "Checking...for the admiral...important." She mumbled thickly so her words were almost unintelligible. Her pace increased as she sped across the deck and away from Lawson. The whole time she could feel his gaze on her retreating back. She would have to be quick before Landsman Lawson thought too much about what he had seen.

Of course, Farragut had no idea of Martha's current whereabouts, nor did the captain of *Hartford*, Captain Drayton, nor Farragut's own chief of staff, Captain Jenkins of *Oneida*. Martha rolled her eyes at the thought. Captain Jenkins was a pompous little man who was very much like the naval officers she remembered from that night so many months ago in Washington. He would have had a fit if he knew she was aboard the ship, dressed as a man. Even Farragut—David, she corrected...sometimes it still felt awkward calling him by his Christian name—was still trying to persuade her to leave. The only reason he wasn't with her now was because he thought she was "resting" in his cabin until she could be returned safely to Union territory.

She knew David and his officers were likely poring over maps and determining how best to maneuver their ships to address the incoming wave of blockade runners. It would be especially difficult if they did not have any working signal flares. They had become the cornerstone of their strategy. At the thought, Martha felt her teeth come together and grind in anger. Even before getting on the ship, she had checked and rechecked her formula. It was perfect. All the tests over the Potomac those months earlier had just reinforced her feelings. She knew they worked.

She'd even pulled a few flares from the last batch of kits to be delivered to *Hartford*. Red, white, and green; three colors allowed the Navy to have a full code. Every single one had burst brightly over the water, flared to life, and then drifted down. So what had happened? Why weren't the flares working anymore on Farragut's squadron? Was it water? The fuses?

Martha opened the storage room door, frowning at its unlocked state. It needed to stay locked, or any fool with a flame could blow them all sky high. She slipped inside the storage room and closed the door behind her. Martha felt secure enough to lift the cover on the lantern granting greater illumination in the cramped storage room. Shadows warped and danced and under her feet, and she could feel the thrum of *Hartford's* engines as she idled.

In the last week alone, at least a dozen blockade runners had made their way through to Mobile and no doubt more were doing the same for Wilmington and Galveston. Even with Farragut's success of the last few months, the cities remained central ports of call with ships arriving every day from Great Britain providing arms and supplies by way of Cuba.

Martha wound through the various crates and boxes. Finding the crate she was looking for, she set down her bag and firmly grasped the lid. She lifted and slid it off, grunting in exertion. Maybe she should have asked for assistance from Landsman Lawson or simply had Farragut bring her a box of flares for testing in the comfort of the cabin. Doing this on her own was not only ridiculous, it was dangerous. She yelped as a nail caught her hand, dragging through the flesh of the underside of her palm. Martha glared at the offending nail. She pulled out her handkerchief and awkwardly tied it around her left hand. While the cut wasn't deep, it bled messily. It would have to wait, though; her thoughts were already on the signal flares.

The testing had to be done in secret. Martha had decided that someone had to be purposefully damaging the flares. She did not want to risk the possibility that whoever was sabotaging Farragut would suspect that she was on their trail. She paused and rolled her eyes at the thought. Perhaps "On their trail" was a bit much. Martha felt melodramatic—like one of the heroines in a Victorian novel—for entertaining the idea. But she had to examine every possibility. Farragut had agreed to use the flares. Like he'd said, they needed each other. They would only succeed if they both succeeded. He wouldn't sabotage himself. But he also wasn't a popular man, especially after his failure to take New Orleans and the loss of so many ships with so many lives. And of course, there was the Farragut Curse.

Martha leaned into the crate, this time much more cautious of wayward nails, and brushed aside the loose straw. Dust rose and she stifled a cough. Below was a smaller wooden box. She lifted it out and set it on the ground. Retrieving the lantern, she set it down beside her, careful to keep it well clear of the box and any errant straw.

Pulling a small knife from her pocket she pried open the box lid. Inside was a full set of colored flares. Red. White. Green. All carefully labelled. She picked one up and examined the strip of tape and paper that wrapped the flare. In the flickering light it was difficult to see clearly but she thought she could detect marks on the tape.

She peeled back the casing to better view the multiple layers of gunpowder, the chemicals in between that added the various colors, the central fuse, and the incombustible layers in between that kept the signals separate. She shifted to get better light, careful to keep the combustible ingredients well away from the heat and flame of the lantern.

What was that? Martha frowned and used the knife point to pry out one of the incombustible layers. It was clearly damaged. The gunpowder and chemicals would all ignite together. She didn't need her testing kit to see the damage. It was clearly visible. This collection of chemicals wouldn't hurtle into the night sky as a flare. It would explode.

Suddenly, Martha didn't feel like a silly Victorian heroine anymore. She had proof of a saboteur. "No, that can't be right." She reached into the wood box for another flare. She had to be sure.

Martha started pulling at the tape, engrossed in her examination. Strontium nitrate for color, potassium perchlorate for a rapid burn, magnesium…She only looked up when a burst of air came through and her lantern flickered.

"You! Halt!" The voice was low and threatening.

Martha froze.

"You move, and I'll put a bullet in you."

Martha didn't even dare breathe. She heard the sound of boots getting closer. Boots. That meant it had to be an officer.

"I can explain." She said breathlessly, turning. "I just need to see Flag Officer F—"

A large hand wrapped itself around her upper arm and yanked her to her feet. "What a surprise! Mrs. Coston." Another set of fingers wrapped around her hand holding the knife and squeezed.

Martha's gaze travelled up and up. "Captain Drayton?" Martha's tone was a whistle of air. He was big man, not only tall, but graced with broad shoulders and a barrel chest. She tried to remember everything she knew about Drayton. He had been with Farragut since the war began and was the well-respected, if not well-loved, captain of *Hartford.*

Martha tried to pull her hand free but Drayton's grip tightened even more. Martha let out a soft cry as pain shot through her hand, and the knife fell to the floor with a dull thump.

"Let go of me!" She hated hearing the bite of fear in her voice.

Drayton released her hand, reached down, and picked up the knife, slipping it into his boot. He paused and picked up the opened flare. Powder spilled across the floor.

"Careful!" Martha hissed, her eyes going to where the lantern sat. "If you do not care for the lives of the sailors on this ship, at least have care for your own."

Martha stilled as she realized Drayton had addressed her by name. A chill wrapped itself around her heart, and her throat tightened. She licked her lips that had suddenly gone dry.

"Ah, Martha. I can call you Martha, can't I? Yes, I know all about you and your new invention." His voice was liquid, completely unconcerned, as if he were telling a story rather than talking about actual lives.

Drayton tossed the half-opened flare into the far corner of the room. "I was there that night. I saw your test, and I knew what it would mean for the war. Did you know I was Superintendent of Ordnance at the New York Navy Yard? I—"

"How did you do it?" Martha interrupted, her words sharp.

She didn't want to hear his story about his past. How he had almost destroyed her project. She wanted to know about the present. "I checked on the signal flares every step of the way. From the mixing and manufacture all the way to their delivery into the holds of each ship. "

"And here you are."

"Where else would I be? You are ruining my work!" Martha's voice rose as she renewed her struggle.

Drayton's hand was like a vice. Outside the storage room, a board creaked as someone passed. Was it Lawson?

"Keep your voice down." Drayton snarled.

He yanked her close. She could smell his breath—tobacco and onions.

His lips brushed her ear. "Don't you know? Having a woman on board is bad luck."

"I'll scream," Martha said, desperation edging her words.

Drayton's smile widened. "That's bad luck too."

He raised his hand, a pistol in it. Martha opened her mouth to scream. He brought it down and everything went black.

* * *

Martha woke slowly. Her head ached, and she had the urge to retch. There was a rocking motion and water lapped against wood. She exhaled slowly. She tried to put a hand to her head but discovered they were tied in front of her. She blinked. She was in a small rowboat. There was a dull scraping sound that caused Martha to wince in pain as it ran aground.

"Good evening, Mrs. Coston," Captain Drayton said as he hauled her to her feet.

This time Martha did vomit. She wasn't sure if she was more embarrassed at the action or more satisfied to see Drayton leap backwards to avoid it.

She stumbled as he jerked her out of the boat. Water and mud swirled thick around her ankles. She could smell the brackish water. No doubt they were at one of the many small inlets or coves that dotted the coastline.

Drayton walked at a quick pace, half dragging her behind him. She dared a quick glance back over her shoulder. She could see nothing out in the water but she could hear *Hartford* just faintly and smell the coal from her furnaces. Ahead of them was nothing but the dim outlines of beach and grasses and scrub forest.

She blinked slowly, her vision was fuzzy and blood pounded in her head. "Why didn't you kill me?" The words seemed to rebound in her head, and she winced, stumbling again.

Drayton didn't slow his pace. "I am not a monster."

"You're a spy."

"No, madam. I am a saboteur."

They reached the building, a small wooden affair just out of sight of the water. Drayton opened the door and stepped inside. He threw Martha forward into the blackness. She grunted as her shins came in contact with a hard wooden frame and, unable to catch herself, she fell forward onto the mattress of a bed. Martha coughed at the flurry of dust and dirt that rose around her. The world spinning around her elicited a groan, and she fought down another bout of nausea.

Silhouetted by the faint light of the crescent moon in the doorway, Drayton lit the candle on a pocket lantern. Martha could now see the details of the tiny one-room cabin. It had a dirt floor, the bed she was on, a couple of chairs, a table and little else. She noted a lack of windows.

"You'll be safe here."

She squinted up into the light. "And how will you explain my absence?"

At that, Drayton laughed. "A better question might be, how will Farragut explain your presence?"

He shrugged. "A woman with delusions of adequacy. She fell overboard."

Drayton hung the lantern on a hook by the door and set down a bag by the door. It clinked as bottles inside it shifted. "Provisions. I'll send someone in a few days."

Martha wanted to respond with something clever and scathing, or perhaps just launch a physical attack and win past Drayton, but her thoughts felt as heavy as her winter woolen dresses, and the blackness at the edges of her vision warned against sudden movement.

He turned hard eyes on her. "This is not your fight. This is not your place."

Drayton closed the door behind him, and the wooden bar across the outside slammed home with a finality that unnerved Martha. She drifted in and out for some minutes. She couldn't sleep. She knew that would be disaster. With effort, she sat upright and leaned against the wall. Her stomach rebelled at the movement. Perhaps women truly were not cut out for war.

She'd heard variations of that phrase so much over the last year. Even from David. And now he would fail. And her signals would fail. And she would lie here—maybe even die—miles away from her sons. Martha choked on a sob. Her thoughts tasted like copper and acid on her tongue.

It is my own fault I didn't suggest sabotage to begin with, Martha thought wretchedly. She took a couple of slow deep breaths, trying to ignore the pain shooting through her skull. She paused and then took a few more.

"I am not going to die here. I am not going to let that odious man win."

Martha's words were barely audible over the sound waves and water, but just saying them aloud made her feel better. Gathering her legs under her, Martha stood. The room swam and, unbalanced, she promptly fell back onto the bed. Martha cursed inwardly.

Maybe if her hands were free? Martha struggled with the rope that bound her wrists, attempting to work the complex knots, but her movement was limited. She flexed and straightened her fingers, feeling every scar and burn. She put her teeth to it and bit down over and over, chewing like a dog with a bone, to no avail. It was just too tight.

She sighed and leaned back. She needed something to cut the rope. Martha half laughed as she remembered the bag Drayton had left—a bag of food and water, a bag with bottles. Not trusting herself to stand again, Martha slid from the bed and scooted across the dirt floor. With her hands in front of her, it was easy to open the bag and pull out one of the bottles. She eyed the deep olive figural bottle. Drayton had given her a bottle of whiskey. Yes, it would do nicely.

She said a quick prayer of thanks that Drayton had not just given her water in a standard Union-issue canteen.

Using one of the chairs for balance, Martha levered herself up to a standing position. She wobbled for a second but remained upright. Lifting her leg, she brought her boot down on one of the bottles, smashing it. Dropping to her knees she picked up the largest piece of glass and started sawing away on the rope.

Her hopes buoyed as she felt the cords fray and release, and Martha next turned her thoughts to the door. She ran her hands over the frame, testing its strength.

"I just have to figure a way out."

She leaned against the thin wooden door and pushed. It creaked and swayed but didn't give. Maybe a little more force? Martha took a deep breath and launched herself at the door. She hit it with all her weight and immediately she saw sparks dance in front of her eyes. She fell to the ground retching, hands clasped on her head. Oh, that was very much a poor idea.

Minutes passed, and as the pain receded, Martha stood and readied herself to try again. She took several steps back and, dropping her shoulder, ran at the door. She closed her eyes tightly and waited for the impact. It didn't come.

The door swung open, and Martha staggered and would have fallen if two strong arms had not caught her and set her back on her feet. She squinted into the darkness. With almost no moon, it was nearly impossible to see.

"Landsman Lawson?"

"Yes, ma'am," he said, giving her a half-salute.

"I don't think you need to do that," Martha said. "I'm not an officer, and you're the one rescuing me."

He hesitated and then grinned.

"I reckon that's about right," he said, handing her a bloody handkerchief. "I found this and thought you might like it back."

Martha took the small square of cloth and stared at it dumbly. It was just a faint piece of white in the dark.

"You knew?"

Lawson shook his head.

"No. But I did know you weren't a sailor," he said, then offered her his arm. "If I may? You look like you might need some assistance."

The man nodded back towards the shore.

"I've a boat anchored up by the point," Lawson told her.

Landsman Lawson's words swirled in Martha's mind as she tried to put together the pieces.

"I don't understand. How did you find me?" she asked.

"I followed."

They tread carefully towards the water. Martha's limbs were slow to obey her, and she leaned heavily on Lawson. Out in the bay, the engines of *Hartford* still thumped gently in the night.

She frowned. "Why would you follow Captain Drayton?"

"I was following *you*," he said, his voice low. After a moment he continued, his voice dropping even lower. "I'm with the Black Dispatches."

Martha's head snapped up. She immediately regretted the sudden movement as Lawson seemed to appear as two separate men. She closed her eyes and counted to ten.

"You're a spy," she said with conviction.

"I am a spy," he repeated amiably.

"So you know Captain Drayton was a saboteur."

"No. We thought Flag Officer Farragut was the traitor," Lawson said. "He was born and raised in Virginia. His wife was from Virginia. He had too many ties to the Confederates, and too many losses in battle for us to ignore."

Martha opened her eyes, grateful that now she was facing only a single Lawson.

"And Captain Drayton?" she asked.

At the question, Martha thought she saw the corner of Lawson's lips twitch upward.

"Captain Drayton, you discovered," he said. "I knew he had a brother in the Confederate army. Now we know he is working with the Rebels. But what I do not know, and what I very much want to find out, is—who are you? And what are you doing aboard *Hartford?*"

* * *

"It's unbelievable." Captain Jenkins said, pouring himself a glass of amber liquid. The alcohol sloshed around in the glass, catching the light.

"And yet it is true." Martha replied.

She herself felt the need for some liquid fortification but didn't ask. It wasn't appropriate for a lady. Then again, none of this was appropriate for a lady. Of course, she'd already destroyed a full bottle of similar liquor. Martha squelched the urge to laugh. She did not want to be seen as a hysterical female.

"I'd best go see to Captain Drayton," Lawson said. "I have no doubt some of my superiors in Washington City will have many pointed questions for him."

He slipped out of the cabin, leaving Martha with Farragut and Captain Jenkins. The silence grew long.

"Drayton has no doubt sent a message notifying the blockade runners." Martha said, looking for something to break the silence.

Farragut had been at his desk staring at the maps.

"You are correct," the admiral said.

More silence.

"And we will not wait nor try to stop them," he said slowly, drawing out each word. "We're going to take Mobile."

Captain Jenkins choked on his drink.

"What?" the man asked.

Farragut rubbed his hands together.

"Oh yes, Captain Jenkins. Call together the other captains of the Squadron. We have many plans to make and very little time to make them in."

"Yes, Sir," Captain Jenkins said, springing to his feet immediately.

"So what should I do?" Martha asked.

"Find a dress?" suggested Captain Jenkins at the door to the cabin.

Martha glared at him.

He shrugged in response.

Farragut was pulling out another map.

"You've done your part, Mrs. Coston. You discovered the source of the Farragut Curse. Rest well and tomorrow, God willing, you will see us victorious."

Martha prickled slightly at the dismissal, but it wasn't like battle plans were her strength.

"Thank you. Goodnight, Mr. Farragut."

"Goodnight, Mrs. Coston."

Martha yawned and headed back to her cabin, but she had no plans to rest. She'd ask Landsman Lawson to bring her signal kit and powders. Perhaps there was something she could do that might make a difference. She'd also have Lawson see if the ship's cook had any bones.

* * *

The sun rose sluggishly over the Mobile Bay as the Union fleet moved in from the Gulf of Mexico. The ironclad monitors sailed parallel to the wooden ships. They would take the brunt of the fire from Fort Morgan. Martha winced as the sound of cannon fire exacerbated her headache, but, rather than wait in the cabin, she dressed and came out onto the deck. She'd even, as suggested by Captain Jenkins, put on a dress.

Martha had expected some animosity from the crew at her presence but their attention was elsewhere. They were all looking out towards an ironclad that seemed to be pulling away from the rest. Faster and faster. The ship was flying across the water. It was the USS *Tecumseh*. Her smokestack belched large black clouds of smoke as she left the rest of the squadron behind. Martha hefted the leather bag that held her testing kit on her shoulder more securely and walked to where Farragut and Captain Jenkins stood.

"What the hell is Commander Craven doing?" Farragut's words were low and fierce.

Martha followed his gaze to the ironclad USS *Tecumseh*. The ship was steaming forward to attack the Confederate CSS *Tennessee*. However, now Martha could see why the sailors had all stopped in their duties to stare. Even to Martha's untrained eye, she could tell the

Union ironclad was headed directly across the massive minefield that blocked the entrance to Mobile bay.

The air was heavy, as if the whole world was holding its breath. Could they make it through? There was a muffled boom and water, wood, and other detritus sprayed high in the air. A torpedo had gone off under her hull.

Martha watched in horror as the water surrounding the ship bubbled, and the large ship quickly sank. It took only two minutes. She could hear the sailors as they talked to each other softly, desperately scanning the water for men, but only bodies floated up from the wreckage. She put a hand to her throat at the horrific image. There were no survivors. The murmuring from the crew of *Hartford* grew louder, matching their fear. The Farragut Curse had struck again.

Martha looked back at Farragut. He was ashen under his tan.

Captain Jenkins growled, "We have to pull back."

The Confederate cannons of Fort Morgan and Fort Gaines at the entrance to the bay boomed, like an ominous thunder. There was a crash as one of their shells slammed into the wooden sloop USS *Brooklyn* that was now unprotected without *Tecumseh* to block the fire.

Martha felt *Hartford* leap forward as the coalmen added on more fuel. Smoke from the ship's stacks and from the Dahlgren guns filled the air as the Union ships answered the vicious fire.

"We can't pull back," Farragut replied.

"You need to go forward," Martha said, walking up to both men.

"What?" The question came from both men. One was incredulous, and one was questioning.

Captain Jenkins' nose wrinkled. He leaned toward her and sniffed.

"What is that stench? Animal fat? Bone?" he asked, aghast.

Martha ignored him. Her attention was on Farragut.

"*You* need to be first. *Hartford* needs to be the first ship through the torpedoes. You have to prove to them that the Farragut Curse is no more."

Farragut stared at her as if she had gone mad.

"I think I can help us get cross the minefield," Martha said.

Martha looked out over the bow of the ship. Dark water swirled ominously. She pulled out a flare from her pocket.

"Calcium. From the boiling bones," she said, as if it explained everything.

"What good is that going to do us? A signal flare won't work during the day. If you are so desperate to prove the worth of your flares, wait until night," Captain Jenkins said with exasperation.

She locked the brand new calcium phosphide flare into the pistol and took a deep breath. It really did stink. This had to work. She looked at Farragut.

"Let me help. Trust me."

He nodded once and took a position beside her.

"You're both mad," Captain Jenkins murmured.

"Be ready," Farragut said over his shoulder to Captain Jenkins.

The captain stomped back to the helm and took the wheel of *Hartford.*

"Ready!" he said, with the air of a man doomed to death.

Martha took aim and fired the flare into the water in front of *Hartford.* There was a hissing and bright light bloomed ahead of them. The water shone bright blue and everything below the surface was visible.

"There! And there!" Farragut pointed. "Torpedoes!"

Farragut called for changes in direction. The ship turned, cutting neatly through the water, slipping past the deadly incendiaries.

"How many more of those do you have?"

Martha's expression was tense. "Enough."

Farragut looked at her as if he wanted to ask a question but then stopped himself. He turned back. "Captain Jenkins, order the men to signal the squadron. Follow me!"

As *Hartford* steamed ahead, Martha saw her incandescent signals blazing below the water, highlighting the underwater bombs. This was it. This was her moment, her success. One by one by one, the other fourteen ships followed *Hartford* through the mine field.

"Damn the torpedoes! Full speed ahead."

* * * * *

Day Al-Mohamed Bio

Day Al-Mohamed is author of the YA novel Baba Ali and the Clockwork Djinn, editor of the anthology, Trust & Treachery, and a regular host on Idobi Radio's Geek Girl Riot. Her latest novella will be out in 2019 from Falstaff Books. In addition to fiction, she also works in comics and film. She is a Docs in Progress Fellowship alumna and a graduate of the VONA/Voices Writing Workshop. A disability policy executive with more than fifteen years of experience, she presents often on the representation of disability in media, most recently for the National Bar Association, at New York Comic Con, and at SXSW. She lives in Washington, DC, with her wife, N.R. Brown. Visit her online at DayAlMohamed.com and on Twitter @DayAlMohamed.

# # # # #

The Blue and the Red: Palmerston's Ironclads by William Stroock

"But Freddie!" Emmy cried.

Emmy put her head in her hands and sobbed. I reached out for her hand but she slapped mine away.

"But it will only be for six months," I said.

"Nooo!" Emmy stood and stormed out of the drawing room. "How could you do this to me!" she shouted as she ran upstairs.

I took a deep breath and stood.

"She'll be all right, son," said Mr. Herridge. I turned to my future father-in-law, who stood at the drawing room doorway, poking his pipe with a filter. "You know how she can be." No one knew the temperamental Emmy like her own father.

I replied, "I am sorry to upset her like this, sir."

Mr. Herridge came forward and patted my shoulder. "Don't worry at all, Freddie. A man must do what he feels is best. Even if his spoilt love doesn't understand that." He nodded toward the stairs that Emmy just ran up.

"Sir, I really don't think..."

"Please, lad. I know. When her mother left us, I spoilt her rotten." Mr. Herridge looked off to the distance. I sensed he was thinking about expensive tutors, horseback riding lessons, seasonal theatre tickets, trips to the Continent. Emmy had an education and upbringing to rival any princess. For the millionth time, I wondered how I would keep her in the life style she expected on my reporter's salary.

Mr. Herridge said, "Don't worry, lad. I'll give her a talking to later. Explain the way things have to be."

"I am grateful, sir."

"And I want you to know you undertake this job with my blessing." Mr. Herridge smiled. "Tell the English people how we punished the Yankees."

My future father-in-law shook my hand and said, "Off you go."

Off I went. In those days, I was a young correspondent, much in demand after my reports on the plight of coal miners in Wales and my work on East End sweatshops. I was renowned for my attention to detail, for making the suffering of working wretches come to life, for being truthful. In short, for reporting the facts as they stood, without embellishment. I was a newspaperman.

As the American crisis unfolded in the wake of the Yankees' impetuous interception of *Trent*, the editors of *The Times* contacted me and asked if I would sign on as their special correspondent with the great squadron then assembling at the North American Station. I agreed right away. What a story! Mr. Herridge actively encouraged me, perhaps thinking of Emmy's long-term interests, and he said, "You can make a first rate book out of it." He was right.

Days before my tearful argument with Emmy, I sat in the House of Commons and watched the Parliamentary debate. It is hard to believe now, with the ensuing war making such an imprint on the history of the Anglo-Saxon world, but there was a time when Parliament's vote seemed in doubt. The Moralist man wondered why Great Britain, a nation that spends so much to stop the evil slave trade, would make common cause with the slavers of the Confederacy. The Middle Class man fretted about sending his sons to die in North America. The Historical Man remembered the previous two wars with the Americans from which Britain profited little and wondered what good could come of a third such conflict. The Paranoid Man worried about the ever-scheming French, or Russian designs on India's Northwest Frontier. The Pacifist Man asked after the Crimea and the Mutiny, did Britain really need another war?

In answer to these questions, Palmerston, the Great Man, walked into the house and took his seat on the front bench. Then he rose and came to the rostrum. I am no Tory or lover of "Pam," but on this day, he was magnificent.

"Civis Britainus sum!" Palmerston thundered from the floor. "An Englishman must know that wherever he goes, Her Majesty's government goes with him and, if need be, the full might of her armed forces. So the Roman went in the ancient world, so the Englishman shall go in the modern!"

At that point, the issue was never in doubt. The Loyal Opposition knew when it was rhetorically out-maneuvered. By that afternoon, Parliament chose war with the Americans. Her Majesty's government acted accordingly.

After my tearful parting with Emmy, I took a train from London down to the great Royal Navy base at Portsmouth. I was to travel aboard HMS *Himalaya*, recently returned from Admiral Donlop's Mexican Expedition, to the Royal Naval base at Halifax, Nova Scotia. She was transporting the 9th Regiment of Foot. Under steam power, our trip to Halifax took eleven days. During the journey, the ship's skipper, Commander H.I Hilsely, invited me to dine with him in the evenings. Hilsely was an old naval hand, his weathered face protected by a great beard of bushy whiskers, which made a mockery of my pencil mustache. Hilsely came of age listening to his own father's tales of Abukir Bay, Copenhagen, and Trafalgar, and he had enlisted in the navy at fifteen. He was kind enough to educate me on naval affairs and the general situation in North America. At just twenty-four years of age, I knew little of either subject, though I became expert in the Great War to follow.

"You see," Hilsely said over a dinner of lamb and port, "our border there with the Americans is thousands of miles long. We can never defend it, even if the bulk of our army were there."

"Oh dear."

"In fact, we are extremely vulnerable on the Great Lakes, and I suspect that when we arrive in Halifax, we shall learn of several American successes there."

"Really?"

"The Americans can take the Canadas whenever they choose to do so."

I asked, "So why don't they?"

"I am a navy man, see, not an army man. But certain things are obvious. In the southern states, Mr. Lee has tied up the Union Army. It will be some time before Mr. Lincoln can marshal sufficient resources to invade the Canadas."

"Good for us then," commented I.

"Most certainly." Captain Hilsely took a bite of lamb and wiped his mouth. "Secondly, as the border is vulnerable, so is the American coast, from Maine down to Virginia. And that plays to our strengths."

"The Royal Navy," I said.

"Quite right, my boy." Hilsely smiled. "Further in our favor is the American public."

"How so?"

"They remember well our own burning of Washington in 1814. The Americans should be quite concerned about that now. Imagine if we were to go to war with France, and French raiders appeared off Portsmouth." He waved a hand most animatedly. "Or at the mouth of the Thames as De Ruyter did in the 1660s?"

"De Ruyter?" I asked.

"A Dutch Admiral."

"Ah."

"Why, if the French burned even a few small towns, the public outcry at home would be enormous. You're a newspaper man; don't you think so?"

I nodded. "Indeed it would." I sipped my port. "I would go so far as to say it would bring down the Palmerston Ministry."

"And you yourself would stoke that outcry."

Taking umbrage at that, I was about to rise to the defense of my profession but the captain said, "I jest, my boy."

But Captain Hilsely was right. Even then, as great fleets gathered for battle in North America, the Admiralty kept several of our best ships in the Channel Squadron to keep an eye on the French, and right it was to do so. One can never be too careful as regards to the French.

Below decks, the Norfolk men of the 9th Royal Foot Regiment were in good spirits. These men were named for their home county on the northeast coast, an entity considered a bit out of the way where little happened. The soldiers spoke in a clipped, shortened accent with many strange idioms. They seemed to enjoy using them in my presence, so as to confound a proper Englishman like myself. The younger men were eager to "whip the Yankees," the exact words one used with me. Older men, who were at Crimea, were more circumspect about the prospect of battle. All were now sympathetic to the Southern cause. *Himalaya's* crew felt likewise and had even decorated the bulkheads and passages with makeshift Confederate flags.

In this manner, we crossed the Atlantic, arriving at Halifax eleven days after we left Portsmouth. The harbor seemed well defended. At the entrance lay York Redoubt, a small position of some dozen guns. At the entrance to the harbor, a stone fortress stood watch on Georges Island. On the mainland, another fortress lay on the high shore line, 150 feet above the water, her guns capable of delivering devastating plunging fire to any ship that attempted to force. One day they would do so. The wooden steamers HMS *Hydra* and HMS *Orlando* patrolled the entrance.

Past these defenses, Halifax was choked with ships. Here were colliers packed with coal from the great Canadian mine at Cape Breton. Several warships lay at anchor. Most impressively waited the most modern and powerful ship of the Royal Navy, HMS *Warrior,* one of the new steam-powered ironclad warships. She was a three master, with two engine funnels and a single deck of two dozen 68-pounder guns and ten massive 100-pound Armstrong rifles. Those same decks were ringed with four and a half inches of armor plating. This protection would be strong enough, it was hoped, to repel shot and shell from all but the largest caliber guns. *Warrior* carried 800 tons of Welsh coal in her belly and could make almost 15 knots.

Next to *Warrior* lay the ironclad steam-rams, HMS *Defence*, HMS *Resistance*, and HMS *Black Prince*, each armed with bulkhead shattering 7-inch rifles. As I gazed upon the mighty ships of war, representing the very best in Anglo-Saxon engineering and technology, a gritty seaman walked past me.

"Aye, ye can practically smell the fresh paint," he said after a dramatic, sardonic inhale. Indeed all three of the steam-rams were rushed to completion as the American crisis festered.

At dock with these architypes of modern British excellence, lay two older such examples, the two-deck wooden steamer *Trafalgar* and the three-decker *Duke of Wellington*. Both grand ships had tall masts and powerful steam engines. They may not have been ironclads, but they were mighty warships in their own right.

Upon arrival, we learned of great tidings from all across the North American Station. The Royal Navy was at war. Admiral Milne had sent his squadron out from Bermuda and attacked the American blockade. To the south, Commodore Hugh Dunlop set out from Havana with a four-ship squadron and routed the Americans sailing off the Confederate port of Mobile. At the same time, Commodore Nowel Salmon, who had captured the American adventurer Walker in Central America the previous year, led his own squadron north from Jamaica and sent the Americans running from their Florida Station.

Sadly, Captain Hilsely was right about the Great Lakes. American steamers had raided far across the Canadian border, burning all they saw and even landing troops to occupy a few lakeshore towns. Even then it was feared that an American army would gather there and invade Ontario proper.

When I set foot ashore, I was surprised by the bleakness of the North American winter. The air was so crisp as to bite the lungs. The shore was brown, except for the occasional stand of evergreens. The sky gray, seemingly promising bad tidings ahead.

I was anxious to get to sea so that I might tell the story to *The Times'* readers. I presented my credentials to a Colonel Felt, aide-de-camp to General Hastings Doyle, the Army's commander in the Maritimes.

I asked, "When does this squadron set sail?"

"We are waiting for Admiral Milne, who is right now aboard a steamer from Bermuda."

"He's coming to Halifax?"

"Yes, to sail with the squadron gathering here."

"Do you suppose I could get passage on one of the ships?"

Colonel Felt, annoyed at the general having pawned me off on him, replied, "Oh, I suppose you want passage aboard HMS *Duke of Wellington.* A seat by the captain, do you?"

I played along. "Yes, actually."

"Why I…" Colonel Felt replied. He looked at me, admiring my nerve, I like to think, and smiled. "Yes, well."

And so Colonel Felt wrote out a writ, asking *Duke of Wellington's* captain to accommodate myself, a very important journalist from *The Times.* Indeed, when I showed the writ to Captain John Secombe, he agreed right away. Even the most powerful, hard-willed men wilt at the prospect of getting their name in the paper. Secombe good naturedly accommodated me, giving me my own small cabin. I put my things away and sat down at the cabin's small desk and wrote a letter to my Emmy, telling her of the great things happening here. I had gone on for three pages when there was a knock upon my door. I opened and saw a small, broad shouldered man.

"Afternoon sir, I'm Williams." I knew from his accent that Williams was a Welshman. "Captain Secombe has assigned me to escort you during your stay aboard *Duke of Wellington*."

"Oh, well, that is good of him," said I.

"Aye, sir. The captain says I'm to take ye around decks and show you the ship."

"That would be wonderful, thank you."

Duke of Wellington was big. So large that wags had estimated she required the clearing of 76 acres of trees to construct. She boasted three decks of guns, 131 smoothbores in various calibers, mostly 32-pounders. She had a crew of more than three hundred and a complement of Royal Marines for shore parties and boarding actions. *Duke of Wellington* had rightly been the fleet's flagship in the Crimea.

Later that evening, Admiral Milne arrived in Halifax aboard HMS *Nile*. I met him only once, very briefly. He had little time for me. Who can blame him? Milne came from a naval family, with extensive service in North America and other environs. Williams proudly told me that when skippering HMS *Snake*, Milne had captured a pair of slave ships. That Milne was now technically fighting in support of slavery I did not point out. He was also something of a reformer, Williams told me, and the force behind the creating of a good conduct badge for British sailors.

One thing I learned that night, Milne was not a man to wait. All through the darkest hours, the ships took on provisions, food, water, and precious coal for the trek south to American shores. As the sun poked over the horizon, a harbor pilot guided us out of Halifax and into the open Atlantic.

And so the squadron set out for war. Canadians waved from the docks and the shoreline, people made nervous by the prospect of American invasion, relieved to see that the mother country was coming to their defense. Indeed, the Royal Navy was coming to the best defense possible by going on the offensive. Eight ships in all, four of the new ironclads and *Duke of Wellington, Trafalgar*, Admiral Milne's own *Nile*, and *Himalaya* carrying the 9th Regiment of Foot.

For two days, we steamed southwest, then due west toward Portland. Several times, we spied smoke plumes and masts in the distance. These were Yankees ships keeping an eye on us as we sailed. At one point, I asked Williams if the Union Fleet would give battle before Portland, but he gave a shrug. "Aye, I couldn't say either way. I'm not a Yankee commodore." As it turned out the American navy was then in no condition to offer battle and was in fact gathering well south of Portland. At least initially, Britannia truly did rule the waves.

Admiral Milne was not eager to attack Portland, nor was the Duke of Somerset at the Admiralty. In cabinet session, the Duke pointed out to Palmerston the difficulty of reducing shore defenses from sea, and he brought up the specter of the long siege of Sevastopol. In response, Palmerston slammed his open hand upon the table and demanded to know why the ministry was spending thousands of pounds on state-of-the-art ironclads only to have them remain safely in port. Admiral Milne, was in effect, ordered by Palmerston to attack hardened American ports at great risk to the best ships in Her Majesties' fleet.

On the third day out of Halifax, our squadron sailed north into the channel that lead northeast toward the city. Williams took me to *Duke of Wellington's* fo'c'sle, from where I was to view the battle. A thousand yards toward shore, I saw onlookers staring in awe at the mighty British squadron steaming past them. People pointed and shook fists. Young boys ran along the shore trying to keep up with us, their inquisitive minds seemingly captured by the four ironclads sailing north.

Our first target was Fort Preble, an old, stone, hexagonal fortress dug into the earth. Rock stone, brick-faced, Fort Preble had two dozen gun portals. To the northeast, a thousand yards or so off the entrance to Portland harbor was House Island, upon which stood Fort Scammell. Admiral Milne sent *Warrior* ahead with *Def*[illegible] following three hundred yards behind. The two steamed tow[illegible] Prebble. My stomach tightened in anticipation of a gr[illegible] conflagration. But then *Warrior* broke northeast toward House Island and Fort Scammel.

It was at that point, sensing that he was about to be outmaneuvered, that the American commander in Fort Prebble opened fire. The fort's guns let lose a great torrent of shell and in moments was obscured by cannon smoke. *Warrior* was well within range of Fort Prebble's guns, but, as she was turning north, the American guns had a terrible angle on the ironclad. Perhaps a shot hit *Warrior*; I don't know. *Warrior*'s captain quickly brought her to starboard and *Defence* followed. Both captains held their fire. Now the Fort Scammel battery opened fire. As *Warrior* was showing most of her portside to the fort, two 32-pound shells hit with an almost comical *klaaaang* echoing throughout the harbor. If the shells did any damage I did not see it. All of a sudden, *Warrior* and *Defense* let lose a terrible volley of 68-pound smooth bore and hundred-pound rifle shells. Great geysers of water, dirt, smoke, and fire spouted up around Fort Scammell. The gunners in the fort seemed dazed and did not return fire before Her

Majesties' two ironclads let lose another volley. More geysers of destruction pierced the air. So enthralled was I, that I did not notice our own *Duke of Wellington* and *Trafalgar* were coming to starboard and presenting their portside guns to the fortress.

Williams smiled and said, "Get ready, boyo."

Someone shouted fire and both wooden steamers belched out a massive volley. The deck beneath my feet shook, and I felt the gun's concussion reverberating through my body. It was at once terrifying and exhilarating. The noise was terrific, and in vain I clasped my hands over my ears. I choked against the gun smoke, and my eyes watered. Williams handed me a kerchief and over the noise motioned for me to dunk it in a nearby bucket of water and tie it over my face. I did so.

A moment later *Warrior* and *Defence* fired again, and then so did we and *Trafalgar*.

Duke of Wellington held her course. Fort Scammel was falling in the distance now, but no relief was coming to those within as *Black Prince* and *Defence* tacked starboard, slowed and maintained their barrage.

For the next hour, we looped around House Island and then west toward Portland, all while the ironclads hammered Fort Scammel. This put us within 1,500 yards of Fort Prebble, well within the range of *Duke of Wellington's* 32-pounders. Three of the ironclads moved into position, forming a crescent before Fort Prebble, and *Black Prince* led our own *Duke of Wellington* past the fort toward Portland. *Trafalgar*, *Nile*, and *Himalaya* remained with the other ironclads and hammered away at Fort Prebble.

Before us was the city of Portland. Along the shore were dozens of docks and several ships. People on the docks and waterfront stared at us in awe. Did they not realize what was about to happen? I heard Captain Secombe ask the same question. He ordered a couple of blank charges fired to scare off onlookers. These did the trick and people ran back into the town, for all the good it would do them. Then Captain Secombe calmly said, "Open fire." Three decks of smoothbore guns sent forth a torrent of shell at the docks. Instantly the ships there buckled, their masts snapped, paddle wheels smashed. *Black Prince* followed with her own volley, and eleven Armstrong rifles sent 100-pound shells slamming into the docks. A second volley of 68-pound smoothbores followed; these smashed into the buildings and warehouses dockside. By then, *Duke of Wellington's* gun crews had reloaded and let lose another volley. This left the docks and ships in ruins. But our ships didn't stop firing, and the deluge continued until the town was choked in smoke. After a time, I saw flames piercing the smoke, and I felt the heat. Then *Black Prince* slowly came about. Duke *of Wellington* followed so that both ships showed their port side guns to the town. These too roared as the ships passed at five knots.

By the time we exited the harbor, the other three ironclads had reduced Fort Prebble to rubble. As I watched, the flames in Portland grew higher. We left a flaming Portland and her defenses behind. On Admiral Milne's orders, the squadron let lose a great celebratory bellows from the stacks, drowning out all other noise aboard or around the ships.

After that, the squadron steamed towards and then anchored off of Cushing Island's south cape, just over a nautical mile south of Fort Prebble. I retired to my cabin in awe of the destruction I witnessed. I closed my eyes, but all I saw was Portland in flames. My ears rang from the day's deluge. Sleep proved impossible so I wrote my first dispatch for *The Times* and then a letter to my dear Emmy. The act of creation tired me just enough for a few hours of sleep, and I drifted off wondering what the next day held.

At dawn, the squadron made steam and got underway, heading south-southwest. Admiral Milne kept the American coast just on the horizon. From my vantage point, I could make out little more than a dim line of winter-laden coast. Americans landside could not really see us, but surely they spied the smoke plumes made by our great steam engines. I supposed that Union officers were telegraphing our every movement to authorities in Washington.

Indeed they had, for about one in the afternoon, lookouts reported smoke columns ahead. At that time *Defence* was at the squadron fore, and she built up steam and went ahead to have look. She signaled back that a column of US Navy ships was making their way toward the squadron. Admiral Milne ordered *Defence* back and made ready for battle.

Aboard *Duke of Wellington,* Captain Secombe shouted, "The Americans are coming out for a fight!"

On and below decks, the crew gave a great cheer and made ready for battle. As the squadron deployed, *Himalaya* dropped back, and Milne detached *Trafalgar* to escort. This left our four ironclads, which Milne arrayed in column, *Defence, Black Prince, Warrior,* and *Resistance.* Following three hundred yards behind came *Duke of Wellington* and *Nile.* As the crew made ready, Williams and I took our position at the fo'c'sle

The battle line steamed for the enemy at six knots.

This American squadron was a motley collection of converted merchantmen, and only a few ships were actual naval vessels. These ships were ill-equipped for battle but crewed by undeniably brave men. Did they suspect what was about to happen to them? If so, the Americans did not care. They steamed toward us in line. At about two thousand yards, the line of American ships turned. One vessel broke left while another broke right.

"What are they doing?" I asked Williams

"They are attempting to broadside us," Williams replied.

"What will we do?"

"I'm not the admiral."

Here's what we did. Admiral Milne kept the squadron in line, steaming ahead. At a thousand or so yards I saw muzzle flashes, and a puff of smoke and then the fearsome sound of American guns. A moment later *Defence* disappeared in a flurry of geysers and smoke. When the smoke cleared she steamed ahead, seemingly unaffected by the American cannonade.

"Ha-haaa!" Williams shouted. "You blasted Yankees!"

Another volley belched forth from the American line but did nothing to *Defence*. I could actually hear the American cannon shells clanging off of her iron platting. The Yankees fired another blast but the ironclads came on until *Defence* passed between both halves of the American line.

"Yes, go!" Williams shouted.

"What I…" I began, not understanding what was about to happen.

Then *Defence*'s smoothbores and Armstrong Rifles let loose a great volley. At three hundred yards, shot and shell shattered the American steamers' fore and tore through bulkheads and beams. A great blast emanated from the American steamer on *Defence*'s starboard.

"They must have hit a powder keg!" William shouted.

Then the steamer exploded. Wood and debris flew into the air and cascaded down to the water.

I looked on in awe.

"Aye, look at that!" Williams pointed to *Black Prince*. Rather than follow *Defence* she broke to port toward the next nearest American steamer.

"What is she doing?" I asked.

"Those are steam-rams, boy," replied an annoyed Williams.

At five knots, *Black Prince* made for the next American steamer in line, a mid-sized merchantmen hastily armed with some 32-pounders. The ship got off a volley at point blank range, but this affected *Black Prince* not at all. I closed my eyes at the impending collision. *Black Prince* slammed into the steamer just foreword of her screws. The impact jarred both vessels, and *Black Prince's* foremast came crashing down.

"Ooof!" William said, appalled at the shoddy seamanship of a mast coming down.

Black Prince kept her steam up and cleared the American ship. The sight she left behind her was almost comical. The steamer's aft was shorn from the rest of the hull and the decks within exposed. She was taking on water and the fore was already rising out of the water.

Williams shook his head. "It's a shame."

Black Prince let lose a volley. "What!?" I shouted over the fusillade.

"The men on that American ship…damn."

Black Prince made five knots, her guns blazing away as she steamed toward her next victim. By the time *Black Prince* was finished, the American ship's rigging was knocked to the deck and she was aflame.

Another American steamer had come about and crossed *Black Prince's* "T."

"That's no converted steamer," Williams said. "Thar is a navy frigate."

The American frigate let lose a volley and for a moment *Black Prince* disappeared in a hail of shell and smoke. But all this seemed to do was make *Black Prince's* skipper angry.

"Ho, boy she's gaining steam!" Williams shouted.

The cloud from *Black Prince's* stacks came faster and thicker.

"Go! Go!" Williams shouted. He shook his fist at the Yankees.

My stomach leapt into my throat as *Black Prince* landed a blow on the frigate amidships, and her armored prow pushed into the frigate's hull. The Yankee ship shook with the impact, and wooden beams popped out from the hull and up from the deck, then her middle mast came crashing down into the water. This time, *Black Prince* backed water, and the act of pulling the prow free tore a great gash in the frigate's side. The Yankee ship rapidly capsized.

"By God, those men will not have time get off…" Williams said. He crossed himself and uttered the Lords' Prayer.

By the time Williams was finished, the frigate's fore and aft were gone, leaving nothing but the flotsam and jetsam of a sunk ship in her wake.

And so the squadron went. Led by the ironclads, we made quick work of those Yankee ships that stood and fought. Gallantly they did so, I admit, their guns blazing away at the ironclads coming for their destruction. But it was a massacre. As we watched, Williams actually shed tears. "Those men, those brave, determined men..." he choked.

We sunk three more Yankee ships before they finally had enough and came about, running southwest as fast as they could. Later I learned that the ironclad skippers had their blood up and wanted to pursue, but Admiral Milne wisely reigned them in and ordered the mighty ships to resume formation.

Duke of Wellington sailed through the detritus of the doomed Yankee ships. Wreckage was everywhere—masts, barrels, tables, mattresses, cups, plates—everything one might imagine to be aboard ship. We saw bodies too, and here and there destitute American sailors clung to wreckage. In the name of Christian decency, Captain Secombe slowed to a knot and deployed lifeboats to pick up these poor souls. *Trafalgar* and *Himalaya* did the same. We took aboard a few dozen besotted, waterlogged Yanks. They were a pathetic lot, their clothes ripped, torn, burnt, doused. *Duke of Wellington*'s marines stood guard, though the Americans were too stunned to do anything other than sit on the deck and dry off. After a time, the marines led them below decks to the mess for hot food and tea.

Boston was less than sixty nautical miles ahead. Admiral Milne determined the squadron was to sail there straight away, and we pressed on to through the night. The men of *Duke of Wellington* were in high spirits, and I heard much talk of the battle and their awe at the destruction wrought by the ironclads. Though prideful of their own ship, many a man expressed admiration and even a wish to be aboard one of the mighty modern monsters. It was understandable. I expressed a similar feeling to Williams who said, "Aye, you fool lad."

"I'm sorry?" I replied.

"The men on those ships must have gotten rattled around like a mouse in a tin can trap. Why I bet the sound of those Yankee shells bouncing off the iron plating has left their ears ringing."

"I see," I replied.

Williams looked askance at me and said, "Why don't you write that girl yer always talking about?"

Sage advice indeed. I spent the next hour composing a long letter to Emmy on the day's extraordinary events, and also on how much I loved and missed her. After that I composed my second dispatch.

Though the seas were calm, I slept little, invigorated from the day's sea and excited as I was for the looming confrontation at Boston.

At dawn, Williams rousted me out of bed and led me to the fo'c'sle. We walked past crewmen cleaning their guns and replenishing ammunition stocks in preparation for another naval engagement. The sun rose, its rays of light cutting through the mist, and suddenly there lay Boston Harbor. I saw several islands, Boston Peninsula, and the city itself. American vessels were absent. Would anyone dare confront the ironclads after Milne's great naval victory?

There were, however, the harbor islands with which to contend. Admiral Milne had good information about the harbor's defenses collected by British officers before the war. Three of the islands had forts. Fort Warren lay at the harbor entrance, Fort Winthrop north of Boston, and just before the city, Fort Independence. Milne could not be sure what kind of guns lay within these forts, though he suspected they were armed with 10 and 15-pound Rodmans; rifled guns with a range approaching 5,000 yards. Even after the two great victories about Portland, Admiral Milne was wise to be cautious.

I watched from *Duke of Wellington's* fo'c'sle. At five knots, *Warrior* steamed toward Boston Peninsula and Fort Warren. *Defence* followed two hundred yards behind. Gradually *Warrior* broke east and *Defence* west. A thousand yards behind was *Black Prince*, her mast repaired since yesterday's battle.

"Aye, they're going to take the fort from three sides," said Williams.

I nodded. Then I saw a flash from Fort Warren. It was a lantern signal. *Warrior* signaled back, and a small boat came out from Fort Warren and met *Warrior*. A few minutes later the boat returned. *Warrior* then signaled Admiral Milne. I was not then privy to what was happening but learned later as word spread throughout the squadron. It seems Fort Warren was home to several hundred Confederate prisoners and Federal authorities asked if Admiral Milne would consent to keeping the fortress neutral in the coming battle in the interests of humanity. Being a Christian, Admiral Milne agreed right off, but warned his American counterpart that if one gun fired, he would blast Fort Warren to bits. After the destruction of Fort Prebble and Fort Scammel, the Federal commander at Fort Warren needed no further persuasion.

So Boston's main fortress was neutralized for the battle ahead. Milne sent *Warrior* and *Defence* into Boston Harbor past Independence Island and Point Charley. Fort Independence lay directly ahead, Point Dewey to the north and Specter Island due south. I wondered, would Fort Independence wave a flag of truce too? We steamed closer and closer, and I waited for the Yankee barrage to begin. I looked toward Boston, perhaps a mile away. It was then that I saw smoke plumes rising from the city, thicker and stronger than normal chimney plumes.

"What is that?" I asked.

"Aye, it looks as if there are fires in Boston," said Williams.

"Why?" I asked.

"I canna say."

Then Fort Independence signaled *Warrior*. Another boat came out to *Warrior*, and soon her captain signaled Admiral Milne aboard *Nile*. It seems that Fort Independence too had Confederate prisoners and requested, in the name of humanity, that we not fire upon it.

"Aye, they do not want to fight."

"Why?" I asked.

By that evening we knew why. It seems the destruction of Portland had terrified the citizens of Boston. It broke them into three camps, those who didn't want to see their city burned to the ground, the Irish who didn't want to die for slaves in the South, and those Irish who hadn't fled Ireland only to fight and die against indestructible British ironclads. This left the Union commander in a predicament. He had orders to defend Boston, but could not do so as the population was dead set against fighting. He tried to impose martial law, which led to huge riots, not just by the Irish, but native-born Bostonians as well.

And so our squadron lay at rest in Boston Harbor as the riots gradually engulfed the city, doing the job Admiral Milne had set out to do. By nightfall, the docks and waterfront were in flames. The entire municipal government had broken down, and Union troops were occupied trying to quell the riots. As such, there were no fire brigades available to fight the fire. The flames fanned inward until all I saw from the harbor was a great, glowing sheet of red, yellow, and orange. Heat reached out across the water, warming us against the winter cold. I removed my coat but still I continually wiped sweat from my brow, both from the intensity of the heat and the moment. Eventually over half of the city burnt to the ground. As the hour approached midnight, Admiral Milne sent a message boat over to

Fort Warren and demanded a pilot to guide us out of the harbor under penalty of bombardment. The weak-kneed commander acceded immediately, and by dawn, we had cleared the harbor islands and were back in the Atlantic proper.

"Revenge for Bunker Hill," said I.

"Aye it is."

"Are you not disappointed that we didn't do the deed ourselves?"

Williams looked at me as if he wanted to throw me overboard and raised a great bushy eyebrow. "God Almighty, you better hope that lass of yours doesn't come to her senses."

"Sorry?"

"I have been in a cannonade, boy," he said bitterly. "And it is no pleasure cruise like the one you are enjoying now."

Williams turned and left me on the fo'c'sle.

From there, Admiral Milne considered his options. He could take the squadron to Providence, and from there through Long Island Sound, assailing the State of Connecticut as it went. But he decided that Providence and Connecticut were ancillary to the task at hand. The squadron could steam back the way it came and deal with them as needed. New York City, its great harbor, port, and naval dock awaited.

So we steamed south-southwest, with the American coast just over the horizon, "So as to add uncertainty," Williams said. There was much idle speculation below decks, with some positing that the squadron would sail right past New York and make for Washington. But in the darkest hours, the fleet steamed west and then turned north. As the morning sun rose, we sailed past Sandy Hook and the Verrazano Narrows and into New York Harbor. It is a truly impressive anchorage, even more so than London, with a massive dockyard running up the west and east sides of Manhattan and Brooklyn Navy Yard across the East River. Winter landscape surrounded us on all sides.

There was some hope among the officers aboard *Duke of Wellington* that New York would follow Boston's example and capitulate without a fight. It was not to be. We learned later that Federal authorities, fearing that William Tweed and his political machine would surrender, flooded the city with troops. Smart officers arrested Tweed and dozens of prominent Irish rabble rousers, so that as our squadron sailed into New York Harbor, Federal authorities had the city under their thumb.

The city boasted formidable defensive works. The harbor was protected by two island forts. On the right, at the entrance to the East River, lay Governor's Island and Fort Columbus. On the left, Bedloe Island and Fort Gibson defended the Hudson River. Behind them on the tip of Manhattan was Castle Garden and the Battery. This was a devil's triangle of massive guns. Later, we learned that the ordnance native to these fortifications was reinforced by a dozen batteries of Federal Artillery. No naval expert was I, but even I could see that sailing into that triangle would mean certain destruction for our squadron.

"Aye, we should be most concerned with that island on the right. Look, it has that fortification and the castle," William said to me. He pointed.

I saw a fortress on the island center, and on its north end, a round, casemated fortification stood almost like a duke or lord's castle.

The four ironclads steamed directly for Bedloe Island at the entrance to the Hudson. All of a sudden, Fort Columbus' guns opened fire. After the first volley, the batteries on Governor's island joined the fusillade. For a moment, the ironclads disappeared in the haze and water. Then the ironclads fired a volley back. One could actually hear the shells streaking through the air. The volley slammed into Fort Gibson on Governor's Island and sent geysers of debris flying into the air. Then they fired on Fort Columbus. In this way the four ironclads steamed around to the west side of Bedloe Island so that they put Fort Gibson between themselves and Governor's Island. Several batteries fired on the ironclads from the other side of the river, but these were just 12-pounder Napoleon guns. The Americans might as well have thrown rocks.

There followed a long cannonade of almost unimaginable force. Fort Gibson wilted before the onslaught; masonry, ramparts, and guns all blew to pieces. As the ironclads blazed away at Fort Gibson, *Trafalgar* and *Nile* followed in their wake. We stayed back and guarded *Himalaya.* When Admiral Milne decided that Fort Gibson had had enough, he signaled the four ironclads to steam east-southeast. Gradually, the battle-line snaked around Bedloe Island. As it did so, guns from Manhattan's Battery opened fire at 2,000 yards. Fort Columbus' guns joined in. The ironclads closed with Governor's Island, as did *Trafalgar* and *Nile.* As they did so, *Duke of Wellington* built up steam and went north-northeast toward Governor's Island's west side and the East River.

The deck beneath me shook as *Duke of Wellington's* 32-pounders opened fire by sections. *Bam-bam-bam-bam-bam-bam*, went the guns so that by the time the final gun had fired the first was reloaded. And so our cannonade went for several volleys. The entire squadron kept Governor's Island under fire. Suddenly I felt something passing close by me, an imperceptible whizzing sound through the air. Above me rigging snapped and a long piece of the foremast fell to the deck just next to me, and I dove to my left. Then I felt water cascading down upon me, and incredibly, several fish flopped on the deck about my person. The Yankees were firing back! I expressed my astonishment to Williams who laughed at me above the deluge.

As I lay on the deck, *Duke of Wellington* picked up steam and let loose another clapboard rattling volley. There was a blast, and then I heard a scream. I sat up and saw a sailor standing perhaps ten yards down the deck, his arm missing. Then a wave of water splashed across the deck, and when it dissipated, the sailor was gone. *Duke of Wellington* let lose yet another volley. I looked out to the harbor and saw Governor's Island receding. Williams stood and offered me a hand. He pulled me to my feet, and there I stood, soaking wet. I looked ahead. We were steaming northeast now, past Manhattan's Battery and into the East River. On our right lay Brooklyn. We were steaming for the Brooklyn Navy Yard.

Behind us the furious cannonade continued. I saw the never-ending flashes of guns, both ours and theirs, and water geysers spouting up around our ships. Fires dotted Governor's Island now and the battlements of Fort Columbus showed great damage. I wondered how much more the garrison there could take. Guns at Manhattan's Battery fired in support of Fort Columbus, and a few took pot shots at us, but their angle was no good, and they missed.

We steamed northeast and then due east up the East River. Our port guns opened fire on the eastside Manhattan docks, splitting wooden boards and pylons, and starting several fires. Ahead loomed a point of land in the river marking the west end of the Brooklyn Navy Yard. It was then that we spied a strange ship lurking in the water. Lookouts reported her, and Captain Secombe came to the fore to see. He put a telescope to his eye and asked, "What is that?"

The strange vessel was low in the water, with a steam funnel and a circular structure at its center. She made smoke and was steaming toward us. Several small wooden paddle steamers were following behind. This was *Monitor*, virtually unknown then, though infamous in the Royal Navy now.

"I…." before I could finish, the vessel flashed. I heard a great boom and suddenly *Duke of Wellington's* bow shattered. Planks and rigging fell all around me. Men screamed. There was another boom, and I no longer stood on *Duke of Wellington's* fo'c'sle. I felt a tremendous blast and then, somehow, I was underwater. I looked around but saw only black, but then I burst out of the depths and gasped. I was on the surface. I splashed and flailed about until I grabbed hold of something. It was a sailor, and he didn't move. I swam away from the corpse and was overwhelmed by a wave which washed over me and pushed me down back into the murk. I was aware of a large object passing me. Desperately I kicked my way to the surface and saw a great, black ship steaming by, no more than a few yards from me. Great guns bellowed again and their shock wave sent me back under. I furiously kicked myself back up to the surface.

Monitor steamed past. Then I saw *Duke of Wellington*. I did not believe my eyes. Moments before, I had stood on the deck of a great ship. Now I saw a shattered wreck. *Duke of Wellington's* rigging was gone, and her fore was sinking into the water. *Monitor* steamed past and fired a volley at point blank range. I did not see the result of the blast because another ship's wake pushed me back under. By the time I got myself to the surface, I saw several paddle steamers following behind the American ship. She fired again, but at what I did not know.

Around me was the detritus of the once-mighty *Duke of Wellington.* A body floated past me face down in the water. I saw a bit of debris floating in the water and swam to it, a door as it turned out. I climbed aboard and clung to the sides and tried to catch my breath. Then I heard a great crashing sound; it was *Duke of Wellington* capsizing. She came crashing down to the water and sank. I looked on in shock as *Duke of Wellington* broiled beneath the waves and disappeared.

Monitor steamed ahead. Her great guns boomed, at which of our ships I did not know. Then I heard one of our own rolling cannonades. As the Yankees shells bounced off our own ironclads, so our shells bounced off *Monitor.* She pressed on, as did the half dozen steamers following behind her. They stood no chance against even a wooden steamer, much less an ironclad, so what were they doing?

A moment later I found out. Two of the lead steamers were suddenly afire. *Monitor* slowed. As her guns fired once more the two flaming steamers passed and pressed toward our own battle line. I watched in shock and then I heard a great crash and suddenly more flames shot into the air. The flames gradually engulfed a ship—it was one of our ironclads, though I could not tell which one. Monitor turned to port. Silhouetted against the flames I saw her two guns within fire I could not see what the deadly little ship was firing at, *Black Prince* I learned later. She made directly for *Monitor,* and I realized her captain intended to ram. *Monitor* let lose a point-blank cannonade that smashed the ironclad's bowsprit and jib boom, but she kept coming and took the Yankee ship just aft of the turret. With her steam engines pushing her, *Black Prince's* fore came out of the water and ran across *Monitor's* deck. The entire river heard the screech of metal on metal. *Black Prince's* four thousand tons were too much for *Monitor* to take. Her iron deck bent and gave way as *Black Prince* settled upon the ship, pushing her down into the river and swamping her. *Monitor's* stern lifted out of the water as she sank.

Then an eardrum-shattering explosion snapped *Monitor* in two and lifted *Black Prince* out of the water. *Black Prince's* fore snapped off and the ship began to sink. The shock hurled me into the air. I landed in the water, the force of the blow knocked the wind out of me, and desperately I gasped for breath. Then something hit me and everything went black.

I came to floating face up in the water. I righted myself, kicked, and flailed until I found a barrel to hold onto. At first I thought I was in hell. How could I think differently? The tide had taken me further up the East River. I became conscious of a great blast of heat on my right. I looked and saw Brooklyn Navy Yard. Docks, warehouses, ships—all were engulfed by a terrible sheet of orange-red flame. To my right, Manhattan's east side was smashed. Docks were shattered, and behind them the waterfront buildings and warehouses burned. Later, I learned that a vengeful *Warrior* simply made full steam and tore them apart with her bow ram while her port side guns delivered volley after volley into the city. *Defence* laid waste to the navy yard.

Up ahead, *Monitor* and *Black Prince* lay in a smoldering embrace. The water around the dead ships broiled. Past them I saw one of our ironclads steaming out of the East River and into New York Harbor. It was then that I realized to my horror that the squadron was leaving me. With no other choice, I swam for Brooklyn. Waterlogged, I pulled myself onto the shore and turned onto my back. Here I lay for several minutes, just trying to catch my breath and get hold of myself.

I thought of the horror I'd witnessed that day and sobbed. "Emmy, oh Emmy!" I fell to the ground in exhaustion.

After a time I heard a child's voice. "Hey, Mister…" a girl said.

I turned onto my stomach and pushed myself up.

"Are you alright, Mister?"

"Yes, thank you," I said.

"You talk funny," she said.

"I'm an Englishman," said I.

The girl went white with horror, screamed, and ran down the street. "The English are here!" she shouted.

At these words, I saw several blue-clad men running toward me. I stood up strait and held up my hands. They lowered the rifles to their hips—I saw bayonets—and walked toward me.

"Who are you?" a small, bearded soldier asked.

"I am Frederick Hart."

"You English?"

I nodded.

He punched me in the stomach with the butt of his rifle. I collapsed in a heap. Two men picked me up by the elbows and dragged me away to an artillery battery. They dropped me on the ground, and the little bearded man said, "Captain George. We have a prisoner!"

They stood me up. This Captain George walked over to me and asked, "You one of those bastards who did this?"

"My name is Frederick Hart, special correspondent to *The London Times*."

"*The London Times?*"

"Yes."

"You are a newspapermen?"

"I am."

This put Captain George in something of a quandary. I was a not a soldier or sailor but a reporter, and therefore not his responsibility. He had more important things to worry about, so he put me aboard a wagon and took me down to the Hamilton Avenue Ferry which would take me to Manhattan, where I could find the good offices of the *New York Times.* We passed terrified people, rushing soldiers, fire companies, ambulances and people standing about listlessly watching the waterfront burn. The Yankee soldiers put me aboard a Navy paddle steamer ferrying a fire engine to Manhattan. Nobody had any time for an English journalist.

We went across the harbor. The docks of Manhattan smoldered, as did most of the southern tip of the island, including the great battery. Fort Columbus and Fort Gipson burned as well. The Ferry on Manhattan was reduced to wreckage so we sailed past the Battery. Out beyond the islands, I spied our squadron, less two ships now. I wondered what Milne would do next.

We steamed into the Hudson River and docked on the east side, near city hall. I came ashore with the engine and made my own way. Having no idea where I was, I saw a livery cab standing idle by some artillery caissons and asked him to take me to the *New York Times.* Only when we arrived at "newspaper row" opposite city hall did I realize I had nothing with which to pay him. He took one look at me, wet, sooty, and exhausted, and said, "That's alright friend."

"Thank you." I nodded.

Not knowing what else to do, I went to the *New York Times* building. A doorman held up his hand. I stepped forward and said,

"I am Frederick Hart of *The London Times,* and I would like to speak to an editor."

The doorman looked at me skeptically and said, "I've heard enough Englishman in my time; you sound like one alright. *The London Times* you say?"

I nodded.

"Wait here."

A minute later, the doorman came back with a bedraggled man, his suit jacket gone, sleeves rolled up, and ink smeared across his face.

"You supposed to be this fellow from *The London Times*?"

"Yes, sir."

"I find that hard to believe."

I told the Timesman how I came to stand at his newspaper's door. "Incredible," he said. "Come in, right away."

He led me up to the newsroom, which was crowded with people trying to write copy for the next morning's edition. The editor called several reporters over. "Now, Mr. Hart, tell us your story…"

And so I did, crisply, quickly, with all the details and only the facts. We were not Englishmen and American, but newsmen. I wrote an article on my experiences aboard *Duke of Wellington*, for which the *New York Times* paid more than enough to assuage my worries about providing for Emmy. After that I wrote my own dispatch which the *New York Times* kindly sent across the Atlantic. Within ten days my words were splashed across the front page of *The London Times*—the Burning of Portland, the sack of Boston, and the Battle of New York. In that time Admiral Milne had steamed up the Hudson River and burned many a town—Yonkers, Peekskill, and Poughkeepsie, until he reached Albany and linked up with Wolsley's flying column of ten thousand sent down from Montreal. From there I took the train to Portland, where Her Majesty's forces then waited. The Union Jack has flown there ever since.

* * * * *

William Stroock Bio

William Stroock lives in Northern New Jersey with his wife and three daughters. He is the author of several alternate history novels including the World War 1990 series and The Austrian Painter: What if Germany won the Great War? He is a former teacher and adjunct professor of history at Raritan Valley Community College. He blogs at williamstroock.blogspot.com and invites fans and enthusiasts to look him up on Facebook.

# # # # #

Far Better to Dare
by Rob Howell

The Flying Squadron rounded Punta Maisi, daring the Spanish fleet in Santiago de Cuba to come out and face it. The squadron's sailors stayed close to their posts, eager for the call to general quarters. The Caribbean danced under the bright morning sun, mirroring their excitement.

No sign of that excitement appeared on Captain Arthur Crenshaw's face, but, like many of the sailors, he had hoped to fight this battle a decade ago.

But maybe this is the right time. The Bulgarians broke free of the Ottomans a month ago. The Austrians overextended themselves in Bosnia. And of course, Theodore Roosevelt finally won. Yes, this will be the morning, and maybe 1908 will be remembered as when the monarchies of Europe finally start to die.

"Captain," said an ensign as he pulled a stadimeter down from his eye, "range to *Texas* 420 yards."

"Thank you, Mr. Thompson. Mr. Aitken, please be so good as to ask the engine room to give me another turn on the propellers."

"Aye, sir," responded the helmsman. He twisted the crank on the engine order telegraph.

This was not the first time Crenshaw had made that order. He loved this ship, but she was the oldest in the squadron and often struggled to keep her station, even when following her sister ship.

He peered through his binoculars. USS *Connecticut* led the squadron, where Rear Admiral Robley D. Evans flew his flag. Behind "Fighting Bob's" flagship steamed *Kansas*, sister to *Connecticut*, and *Texas* trailed her. Crenshaw's command was the last of the capital ships. However, two armored cruisers trailed her, *Pennsylvania* and *West Virginia*, as did the refrigerated supply ship *Culgoa*. Three divisions of torpedo boats escorted that line, with one in front and one to each flank.

"Signal from Flag," reported Lieutenant Pope Washington, the signal officer.

"Yes, Mr. Washington?"

"*Delong* has sighted the Spanish fleet, bearing two points to starboard at 27,000 yards. Admiral Evans' compliments to all and the squadron is to increase speed to twelve knots and proceed in line on a heading of 200."

Crenshaw nodded. *Good, we can pin the Spanish against the Cuban shore.*

"Thank you, Mr. Washington. Acknowledge."

He turned to the helm.

"Mr. Aitken, please increase to twelve knots and stay on station behind *Texas* on a heading of 200."

"Increase to twelve knots, aye. Continuing to stay in line with *Texas* on a heading of 200, aye."

The ship shook uncomfortably as it followed its sister. Even these moderate seas hampered both of them. The two battleships ahead of them sliced through the waves and wind with a smooth, quiet grace, despite each displacing more than twice Crenshaw's command. The *Connecticut*-class battleships were the pride of the U.S. Navy, but Crenshaw was exactly where he wanted to be. She might wallow under him, but he had loved this ship since the first time he had boarded her as shiny new cadet.

Crenshaw patted the steel of the bridge armor. *The girl that stole my heart. She's been waiting for this dance, too, especially now that she's adorned with the new, longer six-inch guns added in last winter's refit.*

"Sound general quarters."

"Bosun," continued Crenshaw.

"Aye, captain?"

"Note the contact time and date in the log."

"Aye, sir. 9:47AM, December 8th, 1908, contact reported by torpedo boat *Delong*."

The older man's phlegmatic response eased Crenshaw's tension. Nielson had been a coxswain on this ship during Crenshaw's first cruise, and he had followed the midshipman after that eventful trip.

I've never asked why he wanted to stay with me, mused Crenshaw, *but I'm damn glad he did.* He blinked back to the moment and looked at his executive officer.

"Mr. Bronson, be so good as to order the main and intermediate batteries loaded with armor-piercing shells."

"Aye, aye." Commander Amon Bronson, leaned down to the voice tubes.

"Signal from Flag direct to us, sir," added Washington.

"Yes?"

"The admiral would like to know our maximum speed in current conditions."

Crenshaw glanced over to Bronson, but decided to give a nervous midshipman fidgeting on his bridge something to do. "Mr. Howell. Would you be so kind as to consult with Commander Morris? I need to know how much more speed our lady will give us, should we need."

The midshipman, son of Crenshaw's first section commander, nodded and ran off. The captain glanced at Nielson, who smiled slightly.

"Captain, another signal from Flag. *Delong* reports two *Espana*-class battleships, three armored cruisers, and six smaller vessels."

"That matches our reports of the entire Santiago de Cuba squadron, sir," added Bronson.

"Thank you, Commander. Nice of them to join us, don't you think?"

"Yes, sir. They must have laid a patch when someone saw us." Bronson's beloved handlebar mustache quirked above his smile.

Lieutenant Washington continued, "The admiral's compliments, and we are to focus on the armored cruisers along with *Texas* and *Pennsylvania. West Virginia* and *Culgoa* are to slow and stay out of range."

Crenshaw's eyes narrowed. Connecticut *and* Kansas *were built to fight ships like the* Espanas, *but so were we, at least at one point. The Spanish are supposed to have more ships in the Caribbean, including two more* Espanas. *If we have to fight the rest of the Spanish fleet before we can repair the* Connecticuts *from any damage they take today, we're going to wish people had listened to President-Elect Roosevelt's call for a bigger stick these past ten years. It would certainly be nice to have* Minnesota *and* New Hampshire *here instead of half-built in their shipyards. Or if the Spanish hadn't sold their Pacific possessions to the Germans so they could afford their Fleet Plan of 1903.*

He looked out from his bridge impassively. *But none of that matters now.* "Acknowledge the order."

Midshipman Howell rushed up and saluted.

"Commander Morris's compliments, sir. He believes he can give you four more knots, maybe even six, though if you wish to remain at that speed for long he requests the release of all backup coalers from their other duties."

"Thank you, Mr. Howell." Crenshaw turned to the signals officer. "Mr. Washington, please inform Admiral Evans we can guarantee him sixteen knots." Then he turned to the bosun. "Mr. Nielson. Would you please assemble parties to serve as coalers?"

"Aye, Captain." He blew a complicated pattern on his pipes, and trumpets echoed throughout the ship in response.

"Thank you." Crenshaw turned back to the midshipman. "Mr. Howell. Now be so good as to see if Lieutenant Boyd has all that he needs."

Howell turned but before he could run off, Crenshaw spoke mildly. "Mr. Howell."

"Huh?" The boy turned.

"Mr. Howell, what are you supposed to do when receiving an order?"

Howell's eyes widened. "Uh, acknowledge it."

"Now." Crenshaw paused. "Would you be so good to speak with Lieutenant Boyd and see if he requires anything?"

"Aye, captain," the midshipman saluted and hustled from the bridge, his cheeks burning. Crenshaw could forgive the boy failing to acknowledge one order properly as he went into battle for the first time, but not two. Now Nielson's face held a grin.

Crenshaw stared back with twinkling eyes as he remembered the bosun beating Cadet Crenshaw over this ship's original six-inch guns for exactly the same offense.

I think he went easy on me. He sure didn't beat me like he did the two idiots I stopped from lighting their recently "acquired" Cuban cigars near the coal bunkers when we were moored in Havana. Lit cigars near coal dust? I think I'd rather one of the Spanish battleships hit my ship with a full broadside.

His humor faded as *Texas* relayed more signals.

"Flag to Torpedo Boat Division Two. Advance and make ready for a run. Torpedo Boat Division One is to move a point south and cover our left," reported Washington.

Crenshaw nodded. *Makes sense. Admiral Evans will undoubtedly send Division One in later, but he's smart enough to make sure we don't get any nasty surprises. On that topic…*

"Mr. Washington, would you be so good as to detail a yeoman to monitor Torpedo Boat Division One? I want to know immediately if they signal anything."

"Aye, aye, captain."

The spotter in the crow's nest called down. "Enemy in sight! Sailing at bearing 285, approximately fourteen thousand yards."

"Bosun, be so good as to note that in the log. Please also note which lookout spotted them first."

"Aye, aye sir." Mr. Nielson added the note as Midshipman Howell rushed back in.

"Mr. Boyd's compliments, sir, and he requests you make more speed so his gunners can open fire sooner."

The bridge crew chuckled.

"Very good, Mr. Howell. I'll do my best to oblige him."

As Crenshaw and Bronson trained their binoculars westerly, straining to see the Spaniards with their own eyes, a series of booms wafted over the sea.

"The Spanish have opened fire, sir," commented Mr. Bronson.

"Already, sir?" blurted Midshipman Howell.

Crenshaw raised an eyebrow at him.

He blushed and stammered, "I, er..., I mean, it seems a long way away."

Crenshaw nodded. "It does, Mr. Howell. However, the Spaniards designed the *Espanas* to fight at longer range than our *Connecticuts.* Their twelve-inch guns can reach well over twenty thousand yards—"

"Twenty thousand!"

"Yes, Mr. Howell."

"But, sir, even the twelve-inchers on *Connecticut* and *Kansas* can only get to—" the midshipman paused "—nineteen thousand, I think."

"You're correct, Mr. Howell. And that's about the farthest our ten-inchers can reach as well. I shouldn't fret though. Have any of their shots connected?"

The midshipman glanced out the window. "No sir."

"It's deucedly hard to hit a target at that range, and I doubt Spanish gunnery is as good as ours. Fighting Bob knows what he's doing.

I doubt he'll order us to open fire before we get to ten thousand yards or so."

"Sir, word from the spotters," said Commander Bronson. "Two of the armored cruisers are *Princess de Asturias* class. The last has three stacks."

"*Reina Regente*?" asked Crenshaw.

"Probably."

"Who are their cruisers firing at?"

"Looks like *Kansas*."

As if to answer a large splash rose near the *Kansas*. She sailed through it, ignoring it as if it were but a pleasant, light rain on a summer day.

"A clean miss, sir."

"We'll focus on the *Asturias*. They're older designs but *Regente* only has 5.5-inchers instead of the 9.4s on the *Asturias.*"

"Aren't they supposed to have torpedo tubes?"

"So do we, Mr. Bronson. So do we. I assume they're loaded if I need them?" Crenshaw smiled slightly.

"They are, captain." Bronson returned the smile. "And, of course, all guns report ready and loaded with armor piercing."

"Excellent. Our ship is a credit to her captain." *A stupid joke, but every little bit helps.*

"That she is, sir." Bronson's mustache quirked again. "That she is."

Lieutenant Washington reported, "Captain, orders from the Flag to the main body. All ships, make sixteen knots."

"Acknowledge." He turned to the helmsman. "All ahead full, Mr. Aitken. Our lady's wanted this fight since she was commissioned. Let's not dawdle."

"Aye, aye sir," answered the helmsman with a grin.

"Range to the lead *Asturias*?"

"Ten thousand yards," replied the executive officer.

"Lay in the main batteries and the starboard six-inchers."

"Aye, aye." He hesitated. "Captain…"

"I'm aware the six-inchers will be at their maximum range, but we'll close that soon enough."

"That's true." Bronson agreed.

"Signal from flag. Open fire at nine thousand yards."

"Acknowledge." Crenshaw stared at the lead *Asturias* intently through his binoculars as the squadrons closed on each other.

"Range to lead *Asturias* nine thousand yards," reported Ensign Thompson.

"Thank you, Ensig,n. Commander Bronson?"

"Yes, Captain?"

"You may open fire. Alternate single fire with the main batteries, if you please."

The executive officer passed on the order, and the four ten-inch guns, set *en echelon* in dual fore and aft turrets fired sequentially. Staggering their fire meant the main guns fired a shot every six seconds or so. The ship shuddered from each shot's recoil, but not as much as if all four fired at the same time. The three six-inchers on the starboard side joined in, sounding sharp and tinny in comparison to the ten-inchers.

Crenshaw stared at the results. "Looks like the forward battery went high and the aft battery missed to their starboard."

"Agreed, sir."

The second round of fire was much better. Crenshaw might have the oldest ship in this squadron, but her sailors shared his love for her.

Best trained crew in the Navy.

And it resulted in a shell taking off a mast of the *Asturias.*

No real damage, but that'll make them think, especially coming on only our second shot.

"Signal from Flag to Torpedo Boat Divisions Two and Three. They're to advance to flank and run at the *Espanas.*"

"At the *Espanas*? What is Fighting Bob, thinking, sir?" asked Bronson.

The Bliss-Leavitt Mark 2 torpedoes the torpedo boat destroyers carried had a maximum effective range of 3,500 yards. However, their warheads were much more effective against smaller ships like the armored cruisers, not the battleships.

"Apparently Admiral Evans believes those reports about the light armor on the *Espanas*, especially below the waterline." Crenshaw nodded to himself. *And now our orders make more sense.*

The five smaller ships of Torpedo Boat Division Two swooped in under the twelve and thirteen-inch projectiles from the battleships. Evans had timed their run perfectly. The Spanish torpedo boats changed course to meet them, but the Spanish battleships and cruisers had already aimed their secondary batteries on the American capital ships. Shifting aim would take time, allowing the torpedo boat destroyers to get closer before taking fire.

The lookout's cry broke Crenshaw's contemplation. "Sir! *Kansas!*"

Crenshaw turned his glasses ahead. A Spanish shell had taken off the rear mast on *Kansas.* The loss did not impair her in this fight, though, and in return, one of her twelve-inch rounds took off the aft turret of the lead *Espana.* The Spanish ship trailed smoke, but she responded from her fore turret and splashed two more rounds on either side of *Kansas.*

In the meantime, Crenshaw's gunners had found the range and begun pounding the lead *Asturias.* They landed at least three hits on her, including one that took a chunk off from her bow.

"That's it, lads!" cried the bosun.

"Mr. Nielson, I'd appreciate if you would keep your attention on your duties."

Nielson grinned back. "Aye, Captain."

"Mr. Bronson. Please pass on to Lieutenant Boyd my compliments. Inform him Chief Boatswain's Mate Nielson approves of their accuracy, but that I think they can do better."

Bronson smiled broadly as he opened the voice pipe. "Aye, aye, sir!"

Two Spanish shells exploded alongside them in quick succession and wiped the smiles off their faces.

"It seems that *Asturias* would like us to pay attention to her."

"Indeed, Captain."

Nielson turned from his speaking tubes.

"Damage, Mr. Nielson?" asked Crenshaw.

"We've lost two of the starboard lifeboats. The two marines on the one-pounder between them were killed. Sergeant McDermott is sending replacements to see if they can put the gun back into action."

"Thank you." Crenshaw lifted his binoculars. Smoke surrounded *Reina*, but the second *Asturias* had found the range on *Texas.*

"It looks like *Texas* decided that *Reina* was the greater threat."

"Yes, Mr. Bronson, and she's paying for that decision."

"It's not like Captain Blandin to make a mistake like that."

"He didn't make a mistake, Commander." Crenshaw's eyes turned frosty. "*Reina* is not as much a threat to us, but she could have hammered Torpedo Boat Division Two. He took a chance."

Crenshaw hid his wince as a 9.4-inch shell landed on *Texas. Right on the bridge. He paid for that decision with his life.*

"Mr. Bronson, please be so good as to shift fire to the second *Asturias.*"

"Sir, the first one is still firing at us."

The captain turned his binoculars to her. "Yes, she is, but only from the forward turret, and I think the *Pennsylvania* can deal with her. Besides, the second *Asturias* clearly has better gunners, don't you think?"

Bronson nodded and passed on the order. Firing the main batteries sequentially instead of as a salvo not only kept the ship more stable, it allowed the gunners to shift their aim while barely losing their rhythm. Crenshaw estimated they lost only about fifteen seconds.

They were fifteen seconds well spent, too, as the first shot from the forward turret landed only ten yards ahead of the second *Asturias*, making it shudder and slow from the concussion.

"Mr. Neilson, is Chief Williams still the fire captain on Turret One?"

"He is, Captain."

"Please pass on my compliments to him and his crew. That was a fine first shot."

"Aye, aye Captain."

Crenshaw turned his binoculars to *Connecticut* and *Kansas*. Both looked to have taken more damage, but neither seemed hampered. They still comfortably made sixteen knots and all of their main batteries continued to fire.

And doing a fine job. Both of the *Espanas* trailed smoke, though they looked mostly operational.

He then returned to the torpedo boats. Division Three found itself in a melee with the Spanish torpedo boats, and they swirled around each other. As for Division Two, its third ship had taken several hits and was sinking at the stern. However, the other four had a clear path and looked to be about ready to launch their fish.

Yes! The Caribbean is an American sea, not some damn European monarch's fiefdom.

His ship punctuated that thought with another round from the forward main battery. Crenshaw watched its flight, and kept his face impassive when the round hit directly above the waterline amidships of the Spanish cruiser. It opened a hole in the cruiser, and the cruiser listed almost immediately.

The rest of the bridge was not so restrained. That was why it took a moment for him to realize Lieutenant Washington was yelling at him.

"Sir! Sir!" Washington waved a hand. "Captain Crenshaw! Signal from Torpedo Boat Division One."

Crenshaw lowered his binoculars. "Yes, Mr. Washington?"

"Another Spanish squadron in sight bearing 170. About twenty thousand yards from the torpedo boats. Several larger ships, though no confirmation of classes."

"Acknowledge and pass that on to the Flag."

"I believe the Flag has seen the notice, sir."

"If Admiral Evans wishes to chastise me for redundancy while I ensure he knows of an enemy fleet, he is welcome to do so, Mr. Washington."

"Aye, sir."

"What do you think the admiral will do, Captain?"

"Well, Mr. Bronson, it's a pickle, there's no doubt. We've got the Santiago squadron on the ropes, but we need time to finish them off. We can't do that with another squadron engaged with us."

As if to confirm Crenshaw, a torpedo exploded against the lead *Espana*. It staggered out of line. However, the other *Espana*, for the first time, landed a solid hit immediately aft of the rear turret on *Kansas*. She did not fall out of line, but the twelve-inch shell had clearly damaged her engines, and she slowed.

"Flag to Torpedo Boat Division One. They are to do their best to keep the southern Spanish squadron at bay."

"The division acknowledged," reported Washington. The signals officer paused. "Sir, they report two more *Espanas* and at least two more armored cruisers, along with another division of torpedo boats."

Crenshaw nodded.

At that moment, two 9.4-inch shells hit *Texas* in quick succession, one amidships and one on the stern. She immediately starting listing as a huge plume of black smoke mushroomed over her.

"Bosun, get the life..." Crenshaw's eyes narrowed, and he swiveled his binoculars from *Texas* to Torpedo Boat Division One. He hesitated.

"Sir?"

"Yes, Mr. Bronson?" He glanced over at his executive officer, who was staring at the two *Asturias*.

"Looks like *Pennsylvania* has found the range. She's hit that *Asturias* at least twice."

"Excellent." Crenshaw nodded firmly. "Mr. Nielson, be so good as to get the lifeboats launched. All of them. Use all the ensigns and midshipmen. This is a good opportunity for them to get some experience."

"All of the boats, sir?"

"*All* of them. Make sure they're fully crewed. Use the cooks and carpenters and whoever we can spare. Take every person not manning a crucial post or serving as a backup coaler." He hesitated. "And captain one yourself."

"But—"

"Nielson! Do as I say. Get those boats launched and save all you can from the *Texas*."

The older man narrowed his eyes.

Crenshaw pounded a railing. "Mr. Nielson, I'll thank you to carry out my orders. Unless, of course, you'd rather me to prefer charges of insubordination?"

"No, sir." He snapped. "I'll carry out your orders. Sir."

"Thank you, Mr. Nielson."

The bosun twittered his pipes, then stomped off the bridge, dragging Midshipman Howell and Ensign Thompson with him.

"What are you planning, sir? We'll likely need some of those boats ourselves," asked Commander Bronson after Nielson had left with the cadets.

Crenshaw glanced at his executive officer. "Let me know the moment the boats are clear. In the meantime, why don't you take the signals station? While I think Mr. Nielson is perfectly capable, I think we should at least have a junior lieutenant in charge. Don't you agree?"

Bronson cocked his head and glanced south at the torpedo boat squadron, who had accelerated and turned towards the new arrivals. "Aye, sir. I do agree." He went to the signals station. "Mr. Washington, I relieve you."

"Mr. Washington," added Crenshaw.

"Sir?"

"You'll be the ranking officer of all the lifeboats. However, I urge you to do as Mr. Nielson suggests. The Bosun helped me immensely over the years, and I hope he will do the same for you."

"Uh, yes, sir!" The bewildered young man left the bridge.

Crenshaw stared out at the battle, responding curtly when needed but saying nothing else for the next ten minutes.

"Sir, the boats are clear," announced Bronson.

"Thank you, Mr. Bronson."

"Second Spanish squadron sighted," reported the lookout. "Range approximately fourteen thousand yards."

"Excellent." He turned to the helm. "Mr. Aitken, bring us about on a heading of 170."

"What?" asked the startled helmsman.

"Bring us about, lad," said Crenshaw gently. "The torpedo boats would like some company. Smartly now, let's not waste time."

Aitken glanced at Bronson, but the executive officer merely glanced back blandly. He turned the wheel.

* * *

"What the hell is Crenshaw doing, sir?" snapped Lieutenant Holden.

"What do you mean, Mr. Holden?" Admiral Evans looked over.

"I don't think he's taken a hit, but he's turned his ship to the south."

Evans whipped up his binoculars and studied the situation. "Please send my compliments to him and request his status. Has he taken any damage?"

"Crenshaw reports no significant damage."

"In that case, please inform him that he should return to station immediately."

"Aye, aye, sir."

* * *

"Sir, message from Flag," reported Bronson.

"That was quick. Fighting Bob's people are paying attention."

Bronson smiled. "His compliments, and he requests our status. Have we taken damage?"

"Let him know we have taken no significant damage."

After a moment, "In that case, he requests we return to station immediately."

Crenshaw turned his glasses to *Connecticut* and smiled. *Fighting Bob's probably looking right at me at this very moment.*

"Sir, how would you like to respond?"

"Hmmm. What was that quote by Teddy after he won?" Crenshaw thought for a moment. "Ah, yes. Send back, 'Far better is it to dare mighty things, to win glorious triumphs, even though checkered by failure than to rank with those poor spirits who neither enjoy nor suffer much, because they live in a gray twilight that knows not victory nor defeat.'"

Bronson chuckled. "I haven't been a signals officer in several years, sir, but I'll give it a go."

"I have complete faith in you, Mr. Bronson."

"And if he makes a mistake, I'll help the commander out," snapped Nielson from the hatch as he entered the bridge.

Crenshaw turned, startled. "Mr. Nielson, what are you doing here? I ordered you off my ship."

"She was my ship years before you came aboard, sir." He stood before the captain, chin thrust out and eyes narrowed.

Crenshaw stared at the man for a long moment. "That she was, Bosun. That she was. You're right, as usual." He motioned. "Take your place, then."

"Aye, Captain!"

* * *

"Are you thinking what I think you're thinking, lad?" mused Evans.

"What was that, sir?" asked Holden.

"Nothing, Lieutenant. Has he responded?"

"He's starting to, but it's apparently a long signal and his signals officer is surprisingly slow."

"Indeed?"

"Sir, he sends back, 'Far better is it to dare mighty things…" Holden paused. "Sir, he sent back the opening to President-Elect Roosevelt's victory speech."

"Damn him," whispered Evans.

"What shall I send back, sir?"

"Damn him," repeated Evans.

"You want me to send back *that*?" Holden's eyes widened.

"No, Lieutenant." Fighting Bob thought for a moment. "Tell him, 'Congratulations on finding your Fort Fisher. Sign it, 'Gimpy.'"

"Gimpy, sir?"

"You don't think I know what the boys call me? And I earned that limp over forty years ago. I'm proud of it." His frosty eyes glared at the Lieutenant. "I said, 'Gimpy,' and I meant it."

"Very well, sir."

* * *

"Signal from flag, sir."

"Well, Mr. Bronson."

The executive officer smiled. "He says, 'Congratulations on finding your Fort Fisher,' and signed it, 'Gimpy.'"

Those on the bridge chuckled, then sobered as they remembered just what Fighting Bob had gone through in that battle. That his leg had not been amputated had been a miracle, though he never walked right again.

"Mr. Bronson, send to Evans, "Non sibi sed patriae."

* * *

Evans did not hear the response as he had turned his eyes back to the Santiago de Cuba squadron. The damage to *Connecticut* was not superficial, but she was still in the fight. Two twelve-inch rounds landed in quick sequence on her target, and the *Espana* started to smoke heavily and list to starboard. Evans could see crewman start to jump off the side and boats getting lowered.

"Please ask Captain Osterhaus to switch fire to the other *Espana.* Let's finish her off, quick as we can, then eliminate the armored cruisers."

"Aye, sir."

"Sir, *Texas* is starting to settle."

"I see that, Mr. Holden. Looks like they got most of the crew off her, though."

"Aye. And she put paid to *Reina Regente.*"

"Yes."

The Santiago de Cuba squadron had been defeated, but with the other squadron here Evans had to annihilate it or have them at his back while he fought the new ships.

Which Crenshaw knew.

* * *

"Heading 170, sir," reported Aitken.

"Excellent. Make all speed possible directly at the Spanish line."

"Aye, aye sir."

Crenshaw turned to Nielson. "Be so good as to inform Lieutenant Boyd to cease firing with our main batteries. He may continue firing with any intermediates that can range the Santiago squadron."

"Aye, sir." Nielson's eyes turned wary, as he wanted to ask why send someone for an order that could be communicated via the voice tubes.

Then the captain continued, "Also, you are to have him turn the rear battery forward. Then prepare all relevant stations for firing both turrets forward."

Nielson eyes cleared with understanding. He snapped to attention, saluted, and went off.

"Both batteries forward, sir?" asked Bronson.

"It's what our lady was designed for, is that not correct?"

"Well, yes, but the concussion caused by firing ten-inch guns will cause immense damage amidships."

"I know, Mr. Bronson. I was a cadet in '99 when we tried it the last time."

"Then—" He thought about it. "Of course, sir."

A shell exploded a hundred yards to port.

"It seems the Spanish of the second squadron have noticed us."

"That they have, sir."

"What's our range to the lead *Espana*?"

"Eleven thousand yards, sir."

"Let me know when we are ten thousand yards away."

A sudden relative silence filled the ship as the last of the rear intermediary guns stopped firing.

Nielson returned. "All set, sir."

Crenshaw nodded. "Thank you." He turned his glasses to the scattered remains of Torpedo Boat Division One. Only one of its five ships remained intact, and, judging by its position, it had already launched its torpedoes. Of the rest, one had turned over, and two others listed heavily, belching smoke. Another wallowed as its crew abandoned ship. It looked that all they had accomplished was to put a torpedo into one of the Spanish armored cruisers. It had fallen out of line, but that left the two *Espanas* and the rest of that squadron.

"Range to lead *Espana* ten thousand yards, sir." More shells exploded, rocking the ship.

"Gentlemen, we're about to lose our hearing. Make such decisions as you see fit conforming to helping our lady attack the Spanish."

"Aye, sir."

"Mr. Bronson, please retire to the port torpedo battery. Fire at the first available target."

"But sir—"

"The time for signals has passed, Mr. Bronson, and it's unlikely anyone either here or there will hear me order the launch. Be so good as to make sure you use them well."

"Aye, aye sir."

"Mr. Boyd," ordered Crenshaw through the voice pipe. "Open fire. Continue sequential fire from the main batteries."

The gunnery officer's response came in the form of the fore turret firing.

Everyone on the bridge anticipated the aft turret's shot, but even so, the concussion and sound was far greater than they expected.

Crenshaw shook his head to clear it. As he did so, he could sense his ship protesting at the strain. *She doesn't feel right!*

Nielson jumped over to the helm, where Aitken had barely kept control of the wheel. He pushed the helmsman out of the way and corrected the ship's course, just before the aft turret fired again. He twisted her back again, and again on the next shot. Crenshaw raised his binoculars to watch their shots fly at the Spanish.

Without the aft turret, we'll be little threat, but if I turn to open my broadside, I'll be a much easier target.

Another shot landed far to the port of the Spanish battleship.

* * *

"But we're still outnumbered, if the reports from Torpedo Boat Division One are correct," muttered Evans.

"It seems so, sir. The Spanish have essentially destroyed that division. Only one of the ships seems unhurt, and it has already launched its torpedoes."

"Any damage?"

"Maybe a hit on one of the *Asturias*."

"Any little bit helps." Evans sighed. He turned his glasses to Crenshaw's ship. "He's firing both turrets directly forward."

"I thought they determined that did too much damage to the ship with the concussion amidships? And doesn't it hurt her range some?"

"Crenshaw seems unconcerned with the prospect."

A shell landed on *Connecticut*, but fortunately it was four-incher and it bounced off the armor. Still, it drew Evans back to the fight in front of him.

* * *

Crenshaw watched as the first eight shots went wide, left or right, as Nielson struggled to get control. Then, however, he got a feel for the effect as the concussion torqued the seven thousand-ton warship in a way her shipbuilders had not properly accounted for. Each correction took less as he anticipated the shot.

And that steadied the batteries.

The ninth shot hit immediately in front of an *Espana*. It ripped a small hole in the bow, which enlarged as the Spanish battleship slammed forward at eighteen knots.

The Spanish captain turned the *Espana* out of the line, not only limiting damage to her bow, but exposing three of its main turrets at Crenshaw. His ship might be damaged, but she still could bring six twelve-inch and ten four-inch guns to bear.

Boyd's crew put two six-inch shells into her side as she turned, but that did not prevent the *Espana* from unleashing a broadside at Crenshaw's ship.

A four-inch shell went through the starboard midships six-inch gun casemate. Another four-inch shell went straight through the aft funnel.

Worse was the twelve-inch shell that went through the casemate of the forward starboard six-incher. It completely destroyed the gun, sending the barrel flipping over the remains of the bow. It lifted the entire foredeck in a storm of teak and steel that showered the bridge as the ship drove straight through the cloud of debris at almost seventeen knots.

One chunk of steel shattered the bridge window and a shard of glass ripped through Crenshaw's thigh. He screamed, but then pulled out a handkerchief and wrapped it around the wound. *I guess I'll be the next 'Gimpy.'"*

He put his binoculars up again just in time to see a ten-inch round land on the port midships turret of the *Espana*. It exploded in a gout of flame, and the *Espana* turned away.

"Shift fire to the next *Espana*, Lieutenant Boyd," he shouted into the voice pipe. He yelled the order several times until he could see the turrets swivel.

More shots exploded around his ship. The two *Asturias* had pulled out of line to expose their 9.4-inch guns, and their shots landed all around him.

Good, at the very least we've managed to get them out of formation. And we're only about three thousand yards away now. Maybe we can give them something else to think about.

"Mr. Nielson, turn to heading 200, please." As Nielson turned the wheel, Crenshaw yelled the course change into the voice tube to Lieutenant Boyd.

The turrets swiveled to match their targets as they turned, and Crenshaw watched intently. *Now!*

There was a double thump in the ship as Bronson launched two torpedoes at one of the *Asturias.* The midships and aft port six-inchers, heretofore without targets, also let loose. At least one struck the *Asturias.*

Unfortunately, the Spanish cruiser's crew was just as sharp. A 9.4-inch exploded along the port side of the ship. It did not fully penetrate, but struck right where the port torpedo tubes had been.

Goodbye, Commander Bronson, thought Crenshaw. He saw another six-inch land in the corresponding spot on the *Asturias* and refocused on the battle.

Now if we can just score a hit or two on that other Espana.

As if by request, he watched as a ten-inch shell landed on its second turret. When the smoke cleared, one of the two twelve-inch guns it contained pointed up at an odd angle and smoke came from it.

But smoke also came from the forward turret, which had not been hit. Two twelve-inch shells rose in his direction.

He watched impassively. *One's going to miss to our port. But the other...*

His lady had been incredibly innovative in her time. She had been a place where American shipbuilders had honed their craft. Lessons learned building her would make every other American battleship better, including *Connecticut* and *Kansas.*

Among those lessons was the need for heavier topside and main deck armor.

* * *

C*renshaw's done some damage*, Evans thought. *And they're out of formation. He's given us at least a half-hour.*

At that point, the twelve-inch shell landed on Crenshaw's ship. A bolt of fire stretched up from her. A secondary explosion rocked her. Then a third one snapped her in half, cracking the superstructure and flinging the bridge away. Seven thousand tons of steel and flesh sank into the clear, perfect blue of the Caribbean almost in the blink of an eye.

All but one person on the bridge gasped as Crenshaw and his lady died almost in an instant.

But not Evans. He had already turned back to the Santiago squadron. Both *Espanas* were now clearly out of the fight. The only ship with any fight in it was an *Asturias* armored cruiser, but that ended soon enough as two shots from *Pennsylvania* detonated her aft magazine in an explosion that ripped off her stern.

"Good." He muttered. "Lieutenant Holden. Be so good as to make signal to all units. Reform. Report best available speed. Please order the *West Virginia* to take up station behind the *Pennsylvania.* Any ships that cannot keep to at least twelve knots are to rendezvous with the *Culgoa.*"

That took time. Fortunately, thanks to Crenshaw, the Flying Squadron had the time. The Spanish squadron had also reformed, and they slightly outgunned Evans's ships, but that made no matter.

"Lieutenant Holden, signal all ships." He paused. He rubbed the ancient wound on his thigh and remembered charging Fort Fisher.

This will be my last fight, I bet. Let's make it count.

Fighting Bob straightened and nodded fiercely. "Send this: Crenshaw and his crew died to give us this chance. We're going to kick the Spanish out of the Caribbean forever, and it'll be because of that ship, captain, and crew. Gentlemen, fire as you bear and…"

"And what, sir?" asked Holden.

"Remember the *Maine!*"

*****

Cast of Characters

All characters in *Far Better to Dare* served on the USS *Maine* at the time of its explosion in Havana Harbor except Seaman Aitken, Midshipman Howell, Ensign Thompson, and Admiral Evans. The first three are fictional sons of men who served on the *Maine* during the explosion. The fourth, Fighting Bob, was one of the U.S. Navy's great admirals of the time.

- Aitken, James, Jr. (son of James Aitken, Boatswain's Mate, First Class, USS *Maine*, 1898)
- Blandin, John (Lieutenant, j.g., USS *Maine*, 1898)
- Boyd, David, Jr. (Naval Cadet, USS *Maine*, 1898)
- Bronson, Amon (Naval Cadet, USS *Maine*, 1898)
- Crenshaw, Arthur (Naval Cadet, USS *Maine*, 1898)
- Evans, Robley "Fighting Bob" (Commander of Great White Fleet, 1908)
- Holden, Jonas (Naval Cadet, USS *Maine*, 1898)
- Howell, Charles, Jr. (son of Charles P. Howell, Chief Engineer, USS *Maine*, 1898)
- McDermott, John (Marine Private, USS *Maine*, 1898)
- Morris, John (Assistant Engineer, USS *Maine*, 1898)

- Nielsen, Sophus (Coxswain, USS *Maine*, 1898)
- Thompson, George, Jr. (son of George Thompson, Landsman, USS *Maine*, 1898)
- Washington, Pope (Naval Cadet, USS *Maine*, 1898)
- Williams James (Gunner's Mate, Third Class, USS *Maine*, 1898)

*****

Rob Howell Bio

Rob Howell is a reformed medieval academic, a former IT professional, and a retired soda jerk who uses that experience in his writing. As a child, his parents discovered books were the only way to keep him quiet. Without books, either he or his parents would not have survived. Possibly both. You can find him at www.robhowell.org, @Rhodri2112 on Twitter, and www.facebook.org/robhowell.org on Facebook. Book one of his epic fantasy series set in Shijuren, *I Am a Wondrous Thing*, is at https://www.amazon.com/gp/product/099612599X/.

#####

Off Long Island: 1928
by Doug Dandridge

Admiral Lord Charles Edward Madden stood on the bridge wing of HMS *Rodney*, his flagship, looking back at the smoke rising in the air over Boston. The city was well over the horizon, the only sign of it the five columns of smoke, all that could be seen of the strike his fleet had performed on the city this morning. The admiral had felt bad about bombarding a civilian target, arcing the fifteen-inch shells of his older battleships into the business district of the city, retaining his eighteen-inch ordnance for battling other ships. Of course, he had also worked over the naval yards, but there had really been nothing of interest there.

Damn Colonials, thought the baron, shaking his head after he lowered the binoculars. If only they hadn't insisted on the naval buildup. If only they hadn't played the dangerous game of naval chicken off the coast of Ireland. No one was sure who actually had fired the first shot, since both destroyers had gone to the bottom with all hands. The only thing they knew was that shots had been fired, torpedoes launched, and two ships, along with over five hundred sailors, had been destroyed.

War had followed, both governments rushing through declarations. Neither thinking of the consequences. The navies were the only real option for strikes against the other, but the last year had passed with nothing more than a few feints, some submarine attacks on anchorages that amounted to nothing much, and some raids on commercial shipping. Cruisers blasting merchant ships out of the water, leaving liners alone for the most part. Since the United States didn't require merchant shipping to survive, while Great Britain did, this type of warfare was in the favor of the colonials.

And why in the hell did we have to bomb Buffalo? thought the admiral, closing his eyes and gritting his teeth. The Americans had seemed well disposed to leaving the Dominion of Canada alone, until the Royal Air Force had launched a raid with twelve Handley Page H. P. 24 bombers. The squadron had dropped a total of six and half tons of bombs on the city, nothing more than a nuisance raid, and had lost five aircraft before crossing the border to American fighters. The next day the Americans were no longer well-disposed to leaving Canada alone, and the troops had marched across the border.

It had been insanity. The United States had deployed over a million men to France in 1918, and that was less than half of their army. Canada didn't have a chance, though as usual they fought hard. And the mother country was obligated to reinforce them.

Madden had been there when the reinforcement convoy, escorted by his battle fleet, had landed troops at Halifax harbor. Thirty thousand men, artillery, even forty of the ungainly armored vehicles called tanks. He would have sent them to Quebec to bolster the defense. Instead, the prime minister, in his infinite wisdom, had order them to attack into Northern Maine. As far as he knew that was a wilderness, not the easiest place to supply an army. By the time it reached the southern part of the territory, where anything of importance was located, American logistics would be well sited to supply their force, while the British Expeditionary force would be starving on the end of a long line.

"I hope she makes it," said Captain Smythe, stepping up next to his admiral. The captain nodded, indicating the armored cruiser that was breaking away from the fleet and curving to the north, trailing black smoke.

"I give her better than even odds," said Madden. The cruiser *Sheffield*, one of the most modern in the fleet, had been the only casualty of the American air attack on his fleet. Everyone knew that aircraft were not a threat to a fleet. Almost all of the bombs dropped by the biplanes had missed. Those that hit had done little damage to the heavily armored ships, though one destroyer had taken some superstructure damage. One torpedo bomber had gotten lucky, coming in under the pom poms and putting a fish right into the cruiser. Engine room flooding had cut her speed to half, and *Sheffield's* crew hadn't been able to correct the resultant list. She wasn't in danger of sinking, but she also couldn't keep up with the fleet. The choice was either to scuttle one of the most powerful cruisers of the fleet, or to send her home. He couldn't afford to send any escorts with her, so she was on her own.

"I don't like the next target, sir," said the captain, looking forward from the bridge wing. "You know they're going to go all out to protect that city."

"That's what the Admiralty is hoping," said the admiral, again closing his eyes. "We're not here to lob shells into cities and kill businessmen and workers. Our mission is to meet and destroy the American fleet."

"In their waters?" asked the captain, raising an eyebrow. "They will have air support, you know."

"And so do we," said the admiral, pointing at the closest of their two aircraft carriers, *Glorious*.

Her sister, *Courageous*, was on the other side of the fleet. As they watched, a biplane fighter fell off the end of the flight deck, dropping for ten feet before starting her climb. They had a constant air patrol up. If anything spotted them it would be splashed quickly.

"Captain, we have our orders. We have the most powerful fleet the British Empire has ever sent into foreign waters. And we will destroy the United States Atlantic Fleet."

* * *

Admiral William V. Pratt stood on the flag deck of his command ship, *South Dakota*. The forty-eight-thousand-ton battleship was the deadliest vessel in the American fleet, and some would say in the world. She carried twelve of the sixteen-inch guns that were as good as any ship mounted. While not as large as the eighteen inchers of the Royal Navy, they outranged the larger weapons by almost five thousand yards, three miles. The twelve weapons, with a shell weight of twenty-seven hundred pounds, could throw thirty-two thousand four hundred pounds, versus the twenty-nine thousand eight hundred pounds of the large British battleships. He outclassed them in most respects, and would have felt very comfortable pursuing battle except for two factors. He doubted he would be able to target them at maximum range, bringing his distance to about the same as the eighteen-inch guns. And not all of his battleships were *South Dakota* class. True, he had *Indiana* and *North Carolina*, but the three other sisters were still in the Pacific. Two were working their way to the Panama Canal, but they might as well be on another planet for the good they did him now.

Of his other battleships, at least *Colorado* and *West Virginia* had the same guns as his more modern ships. What they lacked, in their thirty-three thousand-ton hulls, was the armor protection of his larger vessels. That and the speed, since they were capable of at most twenty-four knots, compared to the thirty-three of the larger ships. If he needed to disengage, those vessels might be left behind to be overwhelmed. At least they were better armed than his old ships, *California*, *Pennsylvania,* and *Arizona.* They carried antiquated fourteen-inch guns, twelve of them, behind old-fashioned armor protection. They could at least keep up with the older sixteen-inch gunships, if not his newer ones.

His two battlecruisers, *Constellation* and *United States*, had armor protection as good as the old battleships, and at forty-five thousand tons were stable gun platforms for their nine sixteen-inch guns. He still didn't see the need for the ships, and if it had been up to him he would have finished the four of the class as battleships. Especially since they only crammed one knot greater speed into their hulls. It hadn't been up to him. He also would have finished the two aircraft carriers as at least battlecruisers, if not battleships. The flattops were useless as far as he was concerned. He could have used the float planes from his capital ships to recon and left the vulnerable vessels in port. Command had ordered that he take them along, though, since they were anxious to prove their worth. Since aircraft weren't much of a threat to ships at sea, he thought their worth would be minimal.

Two of the new scout cruisers, *Baltimore* and *Dallas*, were ahead, searching for the enemy fleet. Both were powerful ships, seventeen thousand tons, with a maximum speed of thirty-three knots. The problem with them was their armor protection wouldn't hold up to battleship fire, and the most they could get out of their nine eleven-inch guns was minor damage to the enemy capital ships, who would have the cruisers well with their range. The rest of his fleet consisted of seven heavy cruisers, thirteen thousand tons each with eight ten-inch guns, five light cruisers with six-inch batteries, and eighteen destroyers. His fleet was a match for what the British had on paper. Only on paper didn't always translate into what happened in battle.

Pratt, a tall, silver-haired officer, had always wished for a battle fleet assignment. As far as he knew, he was to be soon up for the position of Chief of Naval Operations, and would never walk the deck of a warship again. Fortunately for him, this war had come along.

But why did it have to be the Limey's? he thought. He had no problem with the Brits. As far as he was concerned, this war was a misunderstanding, a great tragedy. There were many more countries he would rather be fighting, like Japan. Unfortunately, this was the war he had, and his orders were to find the British fleet and send it to the bottom.

"We're receiving a wireless transmission from *Dallas*," reported an ensign, holding out a piece of paper for the admiral to read.

"HAVE SIGHTED SMOKE FROM ENEMY FORCE, FIFTEEN DEGREES NORTH-NORTHWEST ON A HEADING DUE SOUTH."

"Order them to not engage, but to shadow the enemy force. Transmit order to all ships in the fleet to make best speed to the enemy position."

The ensign saluted and ran off, heading for the radio shack where he would pass on the message to a rating. The admiral walked back into the flag bridge, looking at the map on the wall. His own force was located thirty miles due south of Montauk Point, Long Island. The enemy was located twenty miles south-southeast of Nantucket Island, heading his way. It was still early morning, and at his current speed and heading he would meet the enemy in three hours, early afternoon.

"Commodore Stephens is asking if you want him to launch?" asked the ensign, pounding up the ladder from below.

"Tell him to launch a couple of scouts to shadow the enemy force. Otherwise, he is to hang back with his escorts and avoid battle." He didn't see the use in exposing those ships to fire. While the two flattops had decent armor and carried batteries of eight-inch guns, they were not made to battle it out in the line. "Tell him to prepare a couple of flights of fighters, in case we need to drive enemy aerial scouts off."

As long as he could keep those ships behind him they should be safe. They were fast ships, capable of thirty-three knots, and could outrun anything the enemy had if it came to that.

"I want *Colorado* and *West Virgini*a behind *Indiana* in the battle line, with *California*, *Pennsylvania* and *Arizona* further behind." He hoped he could screen the older ships until they got within their range. He wished he could exclude them from the line, but he thought he would need all the firepower he could muster.

"*Constellation* and *United States* are to stay to our starboard. I want them ready to cut off anything that might try to work around our flank. And get the escorts up here to screen us. I don't want them putting a couple of spreads of torpedoes into us."

The ensign turned and ran back down the ladder to give the message to the radioman. The admiral wished he had some submarines. Unfortunately, none were within range to come to his aid. They were slow and ungainly vessels, but in ambush they could tilt the odds. He considered for a moment not engaging until he could set up an ambush situation.

And if they shell Brooklyn, they'll be hell to pay. No, the enemy was ahead, he was ready for battle, and the fight had to be joined.

* * *

"Lord Charles," called the lookout over the speaking tube. "We've spotted smoke to the port. Two ships, probably cruisers. Estimated range, thirty-eight thousand yards."

"Just within our maximum range," said the admiral after clearing his throat. "Captain Smythe. You are to take those ships under fire."

"We're not likely to get a hit at this range," said the captain through the speaking tube.

"Then get some tracker aircraft up over them. But open fire as soon as the guns bear."

Rodney, and her sisters *Nelson* and *Anson*, were the newest design of British battleship, carrying eight eighteen-inch guns in four double turrets. They were the strength of his fleet, weighing fifty-one thousand tons and capable of turning thirty-one knots. Along with them he had the battleships *Malaya* and *Barnham*, thirty-five thousand tons, and the older ships *Royal Oak* and *Resolution*, thirty-three thousand tons, all carrying eight fifteen-inch guns. His battlecruisers included the new ships *Repulse*, *Iron Duke,* and *Prince of Wales*, forty-four thousand tons and carrying eight sixteen-inch guns, along with the older battlecruiser *Hood*, forty-five thousand tons and armed with eight fifteen-inch weapons. Along with them he had four heavy cruisers of three different classes, five light cruisers, and fifteen destroyers.

The forward turrets started swiveling to port, lining up for the shot. With a thunderous roar the four eighteen-inch guns spoke, sending thirty-three hundred-pound messengers of death on a high arc over the horizon. They would spend over a minute and a half in flight before coming down on targets the battleship couldn't see. Four shells gone from the eight hundred and sixty-four shells the ship carried.

Our guns outrange our vision, thought the admiral, wondering if they would ever develop anything that allowed them to track targets at such distances. There was nothing on the horizon, so they would have to do it the old-fashioned way.

Two Westland Walrus biplanes flew over on their way to the American cruisers. The radio equipment aircraft would be able to call fire, adjusting the shots. Of course the enemy ships would try to shoot the aircraft down, but if they kept their distance they should be able to accomplish their mission and stay in the air.

Thirty-five seconds after the first salvo, the second was in the air. Moments later, *Anson* added her forward guns to the fire.

"Recon Alpha three is reporting enemy ships sixty miles ahead," called out the rating in the radio room. "Looks to be ten capital ships, along with thirty-odd cruisers and destroyers."

Madden felt a shiver run down his back. There was the enemy, and they knew where he was. For a moment he was tempted to turn around and run. His more modern ships would be able to stay ahead of them. But it would mean leaving behind his four older battleships, which would be easy meat for the newer American capital ships. He cursed again the high command who had burdened him with those ships.

They should have only sent fast ships with this force. That was what he had argued from the start. Only ships capable of thirty knots or more, hit and run. The Admiralty had wanted to teach the Colonials a lesson, and so here he was, committed to battle against a force probably the equal of his own.

"We have enemy aircraft overhead, sir. They look to be Corsairs."

The admiral walked out on the bridge walk and trained his binoculars to the sky. The American aircraft, like all of theirs, had much greater range than his, and a somewhat better turn of speed. The result of being developed by a large continent power, when even a flight from one province to another was longer than one across the length of England and Scotland.

"Launch Flycatchers and bring them down."

Moments later a flight of four of the small biplane fighters, Fairy Flycatchers, was in the air and climbing toward the U.S. Navy recon aircraft. Surely they had already radioed the position of the British force, but Madden was unwilling to let them continue.

* * *

"D*allas* and *Baltimore* are under fire, sir," came the voice from the speaking tube coming up from the radio shack.

William V. Pratt had moved to the armored flag deck just above the bridge, where he could listen to commentary from both speaking tubes and the loudspeaker coming up from the radio room, letting him listen in to the words from his scout ships.

"Put it over the speakers."

"*Baltimore* was just hit," called out the excited voice over the radio. "Her stern turret is gone, and she's putting out black smoke."

The radioman was silent for a moment, while in the background the heavy boom of guns could be heard.

"We're making smoke and pulling away at flank speed. *Baltimore* is slowed. She's hit again. Flames are shooting up from the stern stack."

I should have scouted with my battlecruisers, thought the admiral, then second-guessed himself again. The two battlecruisers would have also been outclassed. They might have been able to hit back harder, but he still might have lost one, if not both. It was better to have them with the main fleet, where they could add their fire.

"Sir," called out the radioman over the tube. "Our recon aircraft are under attack by fighters."

"Send an order to Stephens to send a couple of flights of F4Bs to support our scouts." The naval fighters, a Boeing biplane, was much faster than the Brit bird, one hundred and eight-nine MPH to one thirty-three, almost double the range, and similarly armed. He thought they could knock the Brit planes out of the air.

"We have scouting aircraft to port. Approximately two miles, at ten thousand feet."

"Okay. Order the first flight of fighters to go after those aircraft. The other can go rescue our scouts."

The aircraft were almost more of a hindrance than a benefit. For every benefit so far, there had been a hindrance. He could scout, but so could the enemy.

"Commodore Stephens wants to know if he can launch some torpedo bombers?"

"Not yet. He can get them ready, but he is not to launch until I give the order."

They could possibly hit an enemy ship, or they could get in the way of his shellfire.

"*Baltimore* is listing to starboard. *Dallas* is requesting orders."

"*Dallas* is to get its ass out of there," yelled the admiral, closing his eyes, then gritting his teeth. It looked like he had already lost one very expensive scout cruiser. He didn't want to lose another. And the men would be going into the cold waters of the North Atlantic in winter, putting them at risk from death by hyperthermia.

He looked up at the clock on the bulkhead above the front view-ports. It was just after noon, which meant they would be within range in just over an hour. Men were at their battle stations, all guns manned. On the five-inch mounts, double turrets along the side, guns were elevated. Even the twenty-millimeter weapons were partially manned. Men were still getting their hot meal before battle, a tradition carried over from the British navy.

"Maybe some outbreak of sanity will occur," said the admiral under his breath.

He didn't want to fight this battle, not against this opponent. Pratt knew many of the men on the other side. He had served beside them in the last war, the one against the Germans. He liked most of them. And their nation had been next to bankrupted by that war, not able to sustain the naval buildup that the flush with cash United States had embarked on. Even many of the electorate in the United States had not been in favor of the buildup. Enough had, though, and the president had been able to force the bills through congress.

On his last visit to the UK, the reality of the situation had been thrust into his face. The shipbuilding business had been doing well, the only thing in the country that had. Everything else had been in decline as taxes had risen. Many of the colonies had been put under a greater tax burden, and the Army had to be expanded to keep them under control. It was a bad situation, and all that had been needed was for the US to sign the treaty. Pratt had not wanted that, since his country was willing to increase the size of the fleet that he loved. Now, on the verge of the battle that the rejection of that treaty had made inevitable, he was wishing it had been signed.

"Sir. We've lost contact with our recon aircraft."

So, they've been shot down, he thought, looking out the windows to see the churning waters of the ocean. He hoped those crews would come out of this alright, but that was never a given in cold waters like these.

"Send an order to Stephens. He is to launch another pair of scout aircraft. This time I want fighter escorts."

The acknowledgement came back. The admiral put his binoculars to his eyes, scanning the horizon ahead. There was nothing to see, but he couldn't stop himself from looking.

"The commodore is reporting that his planes have shot down the enemy recon aircraft," came the call from the radio room.

"Make sure we have some destroyers out searching for their air-crews."

"Yes, sir."

A steward appeared at the side of the admiral, a cup of coffee on a tray alongside a hot Danish from the galley.

"Thank you, Renato," said the admiral, giving the Filipino steward a quick smile.

He had forgotten about getting some food for himself, not thinking about anything but the upcoming fight. The rumbling in his stomach indicated he was hungry, and when the battle started he wouldn't have time. He grabbed the Danish and took a large bite, following it with the good coffee the steward brewed for his admiral. Then he had no more time for the man, who he rarely even thought of until he needed something from him.

"*Dallas* is reporting that *Baltimore* is sinking."

Pratt almost spit up his coffee. He had been expecting that transmission, but it still hit like a punch in the stomach.

"Thanks, Renato," he said to the steward, putting the remainder of the pastry on the tray and waving the man away. What appetite he had was now gone, with the thought of hundreds of men going into the water. With a looming battle, it was unlikely he would be able to fish them out before most had died.

* * *

"Enemy ships. Twenty-five degrees off the port bow. Range, forty-nine thousand yards."

Lord Charles brought his glasses to his eyes and stared into the distance off the port bow. The black smoke of oil-fired boilers rose over the horizon. That would be all they would see for some time, even after they were within range of the guns.

Guns suddenly began going off, their sharp cracks disturbing the quiet. The secondaries, their largest antiaircraft weapons at six inches, were firing high, trying to shoot something down.

"We have more American aircraft overhead, sir," called the captain from the bridge. "About a dozen of them."

And I'm sure this time they sent fighters along, he thought, walking out onto the wing and turning his glasses up to focus on the area where shells were bursting in black puffs. He spotted the planes, flying over at high altitude, getting a good look at his fleet. There were at least two types up there. The larger had to be the recon birds, the smaller their escorting fighters.

"Get more of our planes up there," he ordered, knowing that this was a game he could not win.

He had two carriers, and as far as he knew so did the Americans. Their pilots had to be as good as his, and all of their aircraft classes were faster and longer ranged. But his carriers only carried about half the aircraft the Americans did, so even if he shot them down at the rate of two to one he would still run out of scouting aircraft. He doubted he could get such an exchange rate, which meant he would be out of spotter aircraft long before his enemy. As long as the enemy kept putting up spotter planes, and he had the aircraft to match them, though, he had to keep anteing up.

"Orders, Admiral," came the voice of the captain through the speaking tube.

"As soon as they are within range, concentrate all fire on the lead ship. I'll assess the fire plan after that."

The tactics that would be pursued by both sides were clear. The capital ships would try to get the enemy within the firing arcs of their broadsides, where all of their heavy artillery would bear. Unfortunately, while on approach, they would only be able to fire with their forward batteries. And not all of his ships would be in range at the same time. Unless.

"Captain Smythe. Reduce speed and prepare to turn to starboard on my command. Radio room. Transmit orders for all ships to assume formation Omega Seven."

Within fifteen minutes, all of his ships would be in an even line, equidistant from the enemy, prepared to make a turn that would bring all of their broadsides to bear. If the enemy didn't react, they would continue in, taking maximum fire while only able to respond with half their artillery. It was a reverse of Trafalgar, with his fleet playing the part of the Spanish. Of course, the US commander could make his own changes to his formation to counter it, but Lord Charles was hoping he would get some minutes where all his artillery was on target while theirs wasn't.

The forward turrets started to swing to port while the barrels elevated, then locked into place.

"Range, forty thousand yards."

That was the maximum range for the eighteen-inch guns. They were unlikely to hit at that range, but they would definitely not hit if they didn't fire. They had one hundred and eight volleys for each gun, less what they had used to sink the scout cruiser. That was well over an hour's continuous fire at the best rate they could manage.

The guns fired, the shock wave of their blast washing over the front of the ship. Madden had opened his mouth while he put his fingers in his ears, protecting himself from the worst of the shock wave.

In the turrets, the crews were going to work with best speed. New shells were raised up on the hoists, followed by powder bags, as men in flash protection clothing sweated to get everything into place. Forty seconds after the shot, the guns were elevating again. A moment after they locked into place the guns went off, sending another six thirty-three hundred-pound shells on their minute and a half journey.

His two remaining eighteen-inch gunships had moved up, one to either side of the flagship. They both opened fire within seconds of each other, and every ship he had that could reach out to that range was now in the battle. It would take minutes for the enemy to come within range of his sixteen-inch gunships, and another minute for the fifteen-inch battleships to be able to respond.

Water rose in spouts ahead. He estimated three thousand yards; the enemy ships were testing the range. It wouldn't be long before they were dropping shells among his ships. Soon after that he would begin his maneuver to bring his broadsides to bear.

* * *

Six large spouts of water rose into the air as massive shells hit the ocean. Admiral Pratt cringed slightly, even though the shells were in a spread that missed his flagship by a good thousand yards.

I didn't think they had that range, he thought, realizing that he was going to be under fire for six thousand yards before he could return accurate fire. However, he could start sending shells at them already.

"Captain Willis. Return fire."

"They're not within our effective range, sir."

"And I don't think we're within theirs. But they're putting down fire on us, and I want to return the favor."

The two forward turrets on *South Dakota* began to turn to port, aligning on the enemy force. Six sixteen-inch guns began to rise into the air, coming to a stop at the maximum elevation. A moment later they fired, huge blasts of flame and smoke the visual markers of the twenty-seven hundred-pound shells starting their journey to their targets. Beside the flagship, *North Carolina* opened fire as well. The rest of the sixteen-inch gun ships were moving up, while the fourteen-inch vessels moved up behind them. There was no use letting those older vessels take fire they couldn't respond to.

Thirty seconds after the first volley, the second set of shells were on their way. The first volley still had a minute's travel time when the second set arced into the air. Another volley from the enemy had already come in, this time twelve shells, still way off target.

Pratt watched as a squadron of destroyers maneuvered in front of the battle line. They were weaving, trying to make themselves the hardest targets to hit. The admiral could understand the thoughts of their captains. But right now everything coming in was random, and they could be steaming straight ahead and still have the same chance of being hit. They needed to be in front of his capital ships, though, ready to take on the destroyers of the enemy if they raced ahead to launch spreads of torpedoes. To do the same to the enemy if ordered. One torpedo was unlikely to sink a battleship, especially the newer ones with anti-torpedo bulges. A lucky hit could flood boiler rooms and reduce the speed of a ship considerably. Multiple hits could cause a list that crippled a ship. Which was why all the capital ships had secondary armament. Five-inch guns in double turrets in the case of the newer battleships and battlecruisers, open mounts for the older warships.

Another flurry of spouts formed, still to the front of the American ships, this time eighteen of them. Until they turned into broadside configurations the most modern ships would not be bringing all their guns to bear. The British, with two thirds of their guns on the front deck, were not as inconvenienced as the *South Dakota* class, which carried half of their main armament on the stern.

A fourth volley came in, seventeen misses. And one that hit the bow of a destroyer and exploded into an enormous fireball that rose into the sky. The destroyer, now pushing through the water with a third of its bow missing, slowed considerably and was passed by many of the other ships of the fleet.

Pratt wondered how many men had just died on that ship. The blast had to have impacted further back than was evident from the outside. The ship had over two hundred crew, and had to have sustained at least forty casualties. Still, it was better a ship like that than a cruiser or larger.

The next volley was even more of a disaster. Six rounds straddled *North Carolina*, one hitting the command deck in a blast of fury and killing everyone on the bridge. The ship continued on, a large column of smoke rising into the air. Her guns rose, locked into place, and she fired again, sending more rounds back in retaliation.

* * *

"Our scout planes are reporting a hit on a destroyer, Lord Charles," reported the voice from the radio room. "She's slowing, putting out smoke."

Madden scanned the distance, spotting the rising plume of smoke. Then another, this one tinged with fire.

"A hit on one of their battleships. It's taken out their bridge superstructure." The radioman paused to catch a breath before speaking again. "They report they are under attack by fighters."

"Launch more spotters, and give them fighter cover," ordered the admiral.

His ships opened up again with antiaircraft, puffs of smoke blooming high in the sky. Numerous dots of biplanes moved through, more than he had in the air.

"The carriers are reporting they only have one spotter plane left."

The admiral grimaced. Only the spotter planes had radios. The others didn't have space for the devices. Still, each of his capital ships had a pair of spotter plains on catapults.

"Launch all shipborne spotters," he ordered, wondering if he had doomed those men. They were floatplanes, slow and unmaneuverable, and would have to land on the water to be recovered. That might be a problem in the middle of an engagement. But Madden needed eyes in the sky, no matter the cost to the aircrews.

More spouts rose out of the water, these much closer than the last, obviously called in by the US spotters. Another volley, and two hits on the bow of *Nelson*, one on the turret, raising another ball of fire.

"Get a report from *Nelson*," Madden ordered, his breath caught in his throat at the thought of losing so much firepower. The turret that had been hit rotated onto target, its guns rose, and two of them spoke, the third remaining silent.

"They're reporting damage to the B turret. One gun out."

"Can they repair it?"

"Unknown at this time. They have people working on it, but it would be easier if they could shut down the turret."

Not in the middle of an action, Madden thought. So most probably he had lost one of his heaviest artillery pieces for the duration.

"We are in effective range, Admiral," came the call up from the bridge, where they had been receiving the information from the fire directors up high.

"Prepare to turn the line on my command."

More shells dropped in on high arcs, these raising water spouts around four of his ships. *Malaya* took a hit, the sixteen-inch shell, more than two tons, blasting through her deck armor. Hatches blew off the old ship, fire shot into the air, and a column of black smoke rose into the air. The ship had been hurt, but seemed to still be in the fight, ready to fire now that they were moving within her maximum range.

"Turn the line. All ships are to fire broadsides into the American line as soon as the stern turrets can bear."

The deck heeled underneath as *Rodney* leaned into the tight turn. The forward turrets rotated back at the same time as the stern turret moved. All nine guns rose, locked into place, and fired. The ship heeled in the opposite direction due to the recoil, and quickly rolled back into position. In the rest of the Fleet seventeen more eighteen-inch guns were joined by the fire of twenty-four sixteen-inch guns and forty fifteen-inchers, arcing shells into the air toward the American force. Though still over thirty thousand yards away, the top masts of the enemy ships were now visible over the horizon.

If we can see them, they can finally see us, Madden thought grimly. Shots from both sides were starting to come in with much more accuracy. Even as that thought went through his mind, *Malaya* was hit again. Two shells, plunging down into the other forward turret, piercing the armor and exploding inside, just as new shells had been plunged into the breech and bags of powder were on the way up.

There was a flash, then a deafening explosion that lifted the turret out of its rings to fly into the air and fall into the water. The ship rocked in the water but continued to make way. The guns on the stern spoke, sending their quartet of fifteen-inch shells into the air, while the remaining forward turret remained silent.

"The Americans are turning their line, Lord Charles."

So now it would be broadside to broadside, both lines running parallel as they slowly continued to close the distance.

* * *

Colorado was hammered by a double volley from the British line, fifteen and sixteen inchers coming in at high arcs, plunging fire to the deck. Three fifteen and two sixteen-inch rounds struck, hitting the forward deck, B turret, and the stack right behind the bridge. Three of the sixteen-inch guns were put out of action. The ship slowed, and the next in line was forced to adjust course. *Arizona* still scraped sides with *Colorado*, trading paint and firing as she passed.

More rounds came in, splashing water, some getting hits. Not even Jutland had seen this volume of fire. More guns, bigger calibers, countered by heavier armor. As the fight raged more ships were hit. *West Virginia* was struck in the stern, slowing until she was barely making way. *North Carolina* was hit by a half dozen fifteen-inch shells that couldn't penetrate her vital areas thanks to her all or nothing armor plan. Still, men were cut down by shrapnel flying across the deck, while smaller antiaircraft guns were dismounted and flung into the sea. A destroyer blew up, a heavy shell smashing through its thin deck into the magazine below, the center of the ship erupting into the air, the hull settling back to quickly sink, taking all hands with it.

Pratt stood on the flag deck, watching as shells landed all around. A dozen ships were burning, firing away with everything they had. A heavy cruiser took a couple of large shells and started to list, while a smaller ship just behind it launched a turret into the air after a strike.

The armored shutters were down over the windows, allowing at most a cursory glimpse of the area. The wisdom of this decision was reinforced moments later when a small piece of shrapnel flew through the slit after shattering the glass and sliced into the admiral's arm.

"Goddammit!" Pratt gritted out, clapping his hand to the limb. He was glad to see it was only a superficial wound, albeit one that would require stitches if he survived the action.

South Dakota fired again, twelve guns sending their shells into the sky, the shock wave washing over the ship. The guns were no longer at maximum elevation. Still at a high arc, but getting closer to the deck with each shot.

More rounds flew in. The British were no longer sending in organized multi-ship volleys. Now it was every gun that could bear as soon as they were ready. Pratt could say the same for his fleet. The ships were doing everything they could, sending the greatest weight of shells they could on the most accurate firing arcs possible. Both fleets were doing that, the only thing under their control. The rest was a matter of luck, trying to hit maneuvering ships that were sometimes in the right place to intercept a shell, sometimes not.

More shells were getting hits as the distance closed, though more than three quarters were still hitting the water. Pratt had always wanted to be a part of a battle like this, big gun against big gun. Now that he was in it he was terrified, not just for himself, but for the people he had led here. A ball of fire blossomed on the bow of the *South Dakota*, the shock wave rolling over the deck, the shuddering plates under his feet almost dropping Pratt to the deck.

"Are we still getting information from our spotters?" he shouted into the speaking tube that connecting him to the radio room.

"Still coming in loud and clear sir," answered the anxious voice of the rating.

Pratt was sure the man wanted to know what was going on outside his cubicle, but had enough discipline to stay on task.

"They're reporting our fighters dogfighting with the Limeys, but we have more aircraft, so it's going our way."

"Keep transmitting the adjustments to the gunnery departments of the ships," Pratt ordered. That might be their only advantage, if they still had planes in the air, and the Brits didn't. Now he was starting to feel happy about having the flattops along. Another shell hit his ship, out of his sight, felt through the deck. Having the spotters might be of great help with his gunnery, but they wouldn't win the battle by themselves. He still needed to overwhelm the enemy fleet, disable its ships, or send enough of them to the bottom that they would surrender. There was still a fight, and *South Dakota* shuddering again pushed forward the point.

* * *

Good old *Hood*, the pride of the British fleet and one-time largest warship in the world, was the first to die. She was straddled by a volley from *North Carolina*, the twelve guns of her working turrets arcing shells down from above. Three shells struck the thin deck armor and burst through into the lower decks before exploding. One detonated in a forward magazine. The deck bulged out for a moment, then exploded outward. In seconds the entire ship blew apart, taking all but a quartet of lucky seamen to the bottom, almost all dead before she went under.

Madden recoiled as the sound of the blast rolled over the fleet. He looked out the side hatch of the flag deck in time to see a huge ball of fire ascending to the heavens while the hull of the ship settled into the water before taking the final plunge.

"My God," he blurted, not able to believe his eyes. It was like Jutland all over again, when the British battlecruisers blew up under the fire of German battleships. Only this time he wasn't a squadron commander, but the admiral in charge of the entire force. *Hood* had been a mistake to take along, despite her speed. His other battle-cruisers were much better armored. Of course, none of his ships were invulnerable.

Rodney shook as twin balls of fire blossomed over the forward deck, while huge spouts rose into the air on either side, splashing water across the deck. The nine guns of the battleship spoke again. *Nelson* was hit next, fireballs rising over the superstructure of the ship. When the balls had risen high enough to allow the damage to show, the forward superstructure, with the bridge and fire direction finder emplacements, were gone.

Royal Oak took hits, three large shells landing on the stern, a huge ball of fire rising from one of the turrets. *Resolution* was straddled by a flurry of shells, escaping damage for the moment. Every ship that could was still firing with everything they had. Even the secondaries were starting to join in the battle, sending six and five-inch shells toward the enemy. They probably wouldn't do major damage to any of the enemy heavy units, but they could do their part hitting the enemy secondaries, their fire direction centers, and their viewing platforms.

Shells were also coming in from the enemy secondaries, mostly five-inch as well, with some six-inch from the newer ships. Cruisers were adding their own six and ten-inch shells to the mix. It was hell on the water, as it started to fill with debris, flaming oil, and people trying to get to life rafts or anything they could grab onto. A heavy cruiser blew up, the victim of a half-dozen large shells. Nearby, a light cruiser slowed to a dead stop as she settled low in the water by the stern. A destroyer slid into the water in two halves, broken by a sixteen-inch shell.

Looking through his binoculars, Lord Charles could see the enemy was catching hell as well. A couple of battleships were burning, one older ship slowing to a near stop. The air was filled with smoke, and it was becoming difficult to see anything but the most obvious of damage. There could be a dozen smaller ships sinking over there and they wouldn't know it until after the battle was over, and the tally counted. All he could tell was that the enemy was taking damage, and that it could be heavier than what his force was absorbing. Or it could be less.

I need some more spotter planes, he thought. But there were no more. He could send some bombers or torpedo planes over, escorted by the few Flycatchers. But the enemy obviously had more planes, probably from a couple of their larger carriers. Anything he sent would most likely be splashed in the frigid water, but what other choice did he have. He needed to know what they were doing to the enemy, even if the aircraft couldn't call in fire.

"I want all of our bombers and torpedo planes in the air," he called down to the radio room over the tube. "They are to scout and attack the enemy ships. Whatever fighters we have left are to engage the enemy aircraft overhead."

"Yes, sir."

"And I want all of our destroyers to move toward the enemy and engage them with torpedoes." He wasn't sure if his torpedo and dive bombers would do much against the enemy. Destroyers, on the other hand, were a proven weapon to use in the confusion of battle. They were fragile, likely to be blown out of the water, but every torpedo hit they got would cause major damage.

Madden raised his binoculars to his eyes once again. Another American battleship had slowed. He thought it one of the older ships. Then it exploded, the entire center section rising up into the air, large pieces arcing through the air, trailing smoke, to splash into the water. A second explosion followed the first, larger, fiercer, taking out a hundred feet of superstructure to either side of the primary blast. The ship stopped dead in the water, then started on the way down. *Hood* had been avenged, though the admiral wished it had been one of the *South Dakota*-class ships that had gone down.

* * *

Pratt was looking right at the *Arizona* when the ship exploded, then blew again from the secondary detonations of its forward magazine. The blast resounded across the water, deafening, drowning out all of the other explosions echoing across the nautical battlefield.

It had to be over a thousand people, Pratt thought in shock, trying to pop his eardrums out. The ship had carried over fifteen hundred people, and he couldn't see many of them getting away from something like that.

"Report from one of our spotters, Admiral. Half of the enemy ships are on fire, but they're still in action. One capital ship has gone down. And..."

"Well, what is it?"

"Enemy destroyers are on their way toward us."

"All ships are to prepare for a torpedo run. And I want our destroyers to intercept."

He was sending his lightest warships into a death match between the jaws of the two fleets. Not only would they have to deal with the enemy destroyers. They would also be in the line of fire of every secondary battery the enemy possessed, weapons designed to kill torpedo launching ships. In the line of fire of his own as well.

It's really going to piss Debbie off if Thomas gets himself killed, he thought, seeing his sister-in-law and his nephew's mother in his mind. Unfortunately, he couldn't hold back a ship from the line just because someone he cared about was aboard.

* * *

"Right ten degrees," ordered Commander Thomas Pratt, standing on the bridge of the destroyer *Lawrence Murphy*. She was a new ship, a vessel to be proud of for someone with the rank that would not allow command of anything larger. Two thousand tons, she was the largest destroyer in the American inventory. Five hundred tons more than the largest British destroyer, with six five-inch guns and six twenty-one-inch torpedo tubes, she should have been more than a match for any of the enemy ships. Still, like all destroyers, she had no armor, so anything that hit would penetrate. She depended on her speed and maneuverability to survive, but those qualities might not be enough in this caldron.

The air was filled with smoke from cannon fire and burning ships. There was burning oil on the water ahead, and behind. Continuous flashes shone through the obscuring atmosphere, the huge guns of battleship sending shells at their opponents. Suddenly another series of flashes erupted to life, and spouts of water rose in between the squadrons of tin cans. The enemy had spotted them, and was opening up with their secondaries to try and take them out.

And where in the hell are their destroyers? Commander Pratt wondered. They had been sent out to stop those ships and had yet to catch sight of them. *I'd hate to find out we're only out here so the Limey's can get target practice.* Pratt wasn't sure of the other captains, but the first clear look he got at the enemy battle lines, the *Murphy* was going to turn and launch her full spread of torpedoes. In that mass he was sure to get a hit.

"Sir," cried one of the lookouts from the bridge walk to port. "Ships coming through the smoke."

The commander swung his glasses to the port, to see the bows of a pair of Brit destroyers coming through the obscuring smoke.

"Helm, twenty degrees to port. All guns, open fire on the closest enemy ship."

The destroyer turned to bring all of her guns to bear, two double turrets on the bow, one on the stern. The guns opened fire, sending rounds on almost flat trajectories at the target ship. Three rounds hit, three missed, and both enemy ships returned fire.

The *Murphy* shook from a pair of hits. She fired again ten seconds after the first volley, again concentrating on the one ship. Shells exploded on the second vessel, and the commander knew that one of the other ships in the squadron had opened fire.

"Torpedoes in the water," called out another lookout.

The commander looked at the water near one of the Brit destroyers, one that had made a turn to unmask its tubes. The tracks of two fish were in the water, and it was obvious that the *Murphy* was the target.

"Helm. Fifteen degrees to starboard."

The other ships were too close for any other kind of maneuver. All he could hope was that they could comb the torpedoes, slipping between them. The destroyer almost made it. The torpedo to port was a clean miss, heading on, where it would now endanger the battleships. The one to starboard hit the stern of the ship, a blast that shook the destroyer and threw everyone on the bridge to the deck.

"Radio room. Send a signal back to the battleships. Let them know that we have fish in the water heading their way."

"We're taking on water in the forward boiler room," came the voice of the engineer.

"Can you control the flooding?"

"I don't think so."

"Helm. Forty degrees to port. Prepare to launch all tubes."

Rounds blasted across *Murphy* from the secondaries of the capital ships. One hit the bridge, killing Thomas and everyone else in the structure. An instant later, the torpedo tubes released all of their fish. In minutes some of those capital ships would receive a surprise.

* * *

Pratt watched through his glasses as one of his destroyers flew apart from multiple hits. The explosions were too powerful to be five-inch. Probably eight-inch rounds from a cruiser. A little further away, a Brit destroyer came apart under multiple hits.

"We have torpedoes in the water, heading right for us, sir."

"All ships are to turn toward those torpedoes," he ordered. Of course, he would be taking his stern weapons out of the battle. Looking through the glasses he saw that the Brit ships were doing the same, trying to avoid the weapons launched by his destroyers.

Now both fleets were approaching each other straight away again. Ships were still firing away, but now the rounds were on shallow arcs, hitting before the next volley was ready to go. The ships were pounding each other at close range, blasting holes in each other. The more modern British battleships were also armored on the all or none plan. Shells hitting the protected areas either bounced away or exploded with little effect. Anyplace else and they blew through. The older vessels were mostly wrecks by now, barely making way, firing with the few guns they had left. Some only had their secondaries, but were still in the battle, at least taking some of the enemy attention away from the fully capable ships.

Explosions were going off on the side of ships, below the waterline, torpedoes striking targets by luck. A few ships were listing heavily. Crews were below fighting the flooding, trying to stop the water, fighting fires, in many cases counter-flooding to keep the ship from listing too heavily. A few ships were so heavy by the stern that water was washing over the decks.

The *South Dakotas* and the *Rodneys* were still slugging it out, concentrating on each other, firing as fast as they could. Both forces' premier ships were now turned broadside to broadside again, sending shells into each other, raining hell.

"We're down to less than twenty percent of our primary ammunition, sir," shouted a messenger who had just run up the outer ladder.

How is that possible? Pratt thought. That was something none of the wargamers had thought of. *Ships so tough that both sides run out of ammo before sinking one another would have been denounced as lunacy before today.*

South Dakota shook again, more rounds striking her. Another of the old battleships, Pratt wasn't sure which, blew up and went down.

Even the *Colorado* class, carrying basically the same weapons as the *South Dakotas*, didn't have the armor to stand up to this kind of fight.

A massive fireball rose over one of the older Brit battleships. It started to list to the port, the angle growing by the moment, until it rolled over and turned turtle. Their older ships were not holding up any better. Unfortunately, their new battlecruisers seemed to be just as tough as their battleships, which gave them an advantage, six modern ships to three.

One of those battlecruisers went up in a ball of flame, not as tough as it had seemed. Or else a lucky round had hit a weak point and drove through to the magazine.

California had also developed a severe list, and it looked like it might be touch and go. It still had working turrets, and sent six of its fourteen-inch shells on a shallow arc into another of the enemy battlecruisers. It was hammered back by the sixteen-inch rounds of that ship.

Where in the hell are Constellation *and* United States*?* thought Pratt. He had sent them out earlier in the fight, and they should have worked their way around to be ready to fire. But still no sign of them.

South Dakota shook again, and the admiral could tell the deck under his feet was at a significant angle. He wasn't sure how long they would remain afloat. Her guns fired again, and he was overwhelmed with pride in his flagship and her people. Even if she went down, she had acquitted herself well.

* * *

"I think we're going to win this thing," said Lord Charles under his breath. Of course, there was winning, and there was a Pyrrhic victory. The latter seemed to be the direction they were going. He had five ships that would be leaving this battle with enough capability to possibly retreat back to Britain. His five surviving modern ships. A couple might be able to make a full speed run. The others would be slowed considerably. Not as much as his surviving older ships. They would be lucky to get away from the modern enemy battleships. Which meant he needed to pound them into scrap before he disengaged, so that his older ships might have a chance.

"We're down to fifteen percent of our eighteen-inch shells, Lord Charles," called an officer from gunnery over a speaking tube.

"Continue hitting them. We must sink or disable those battleships."

The ships were now so close that they were firing almost flat trajectory, shells flying into enemy vessels that they could no longer miss. The armor was tough, but not tough enough to withstand this kind of fire. Turrets were crushed, side armor pierced, crew trapped in flooding compartments.

Rodney shook from more flat trajectory hits, then shuddered as shells came down in plunging fire.

"Where is that coming from?" he shouted, unable to get a view in that direction.

"Two American capital ships are approaching on our stern. Range, thirty thousand yards."

Lord Charles wasn't sure what they were, but he was betting on the American battlecruisers. That would give them eighteen sixteen-inch guns, firing on him while they closed. There was no way he could engage them and the ships to his front at the same time with any kind of success.

"Turn into those battlecruisers. We have to push through them and get out of here."

He wasn't sure if that would work, but he had to do something, and retreat seemed like the only option. But the enemy behind him would continue to fire, and he would be lucky to get anything away from this fight.

* * *

"Enemy vessels are starting to turn away, sir. At least all that can."

"Heading?"

"For our battlecruisers."

"Order those ships to keep the range open and continue to fire."

The battlecruisers had full magazines, so in a running fight they could keep up their fire. He didn't want them getting into the close-in fight that had occurred between the Brits and his main force. But if they could keep their distance and keep them under fire, they could possibly cripple the enemy ships.

"Commodore Stephens is asking for permission to let his aircraft strike, sir."

Stephens was one of the new class of aircraft proponents in the fleet. The fools actually thought that the carrier would be the new capital ship, the future of the fleet, and not just a recon platform. He had torpedo and dive bombers. They were an untested weapon, though they had hit targets in maneuvers. Unmoving targets without antiaircraft weapons. There was still a chance five of the British capital ships, their best, could get away. So it was worth a shot.

"Tell him he's free to attack those ships. But make sure that he knows we have battlecruisers out there, and where they are located." He didn't want the overanxious aircrews proving their worth by sinking one of his ships.

* * *

"We have enemy aircraft attacking, Lord Charles," called out the voice from one of the remaining observation tubs.

Madden felt his stomach flip over. No one attacked ships with aircraft. Not in the middle of a gun duel. Sure, many naval powers had aircraft that could theoretically strike at ships, but no one had ever actually tried it. Most admiralties had agreed to the carriers and aircraft when they were forced on them. But now…

Lord Charles ran out on the bridge walk, turning his glasses toward the oncoming aircraft. A dozen biplanes, flying low and slow toward his flagship. Flak blossomed nearby the biplanes, his ship trying to blast them from the sky before they could launch whatever they were carrying. He spotted the objects hanging underneath, torpedoes. One of the planes was hit, folding up and splashing into the water. Another, then a third, into the water. He was beginning to think that they might survive this one when five torpedoes fell into the water and started toward the *Rodney*. Four more were in the water a moment later, and the aircraft started their turns to get away.

Something hit the water to the side of the ship, and the admiral looked up to see more aircraft coming out of the sun. Dive-bombers, dropping their small loads onto the ships. Not large enough to cause much damage, but enough to catch the attention of the AA gunners.

Rodney shook as a pair of torpedoes struck, then three more. The ship started to list, then went dead in the water. Lord Charles landed on the deck, agony shooting through his arm as it broke. The admiral heard the captain yelling over a speaker to abandon ship, and he wondered if this battle had been the last between big gun ships, and if the fragile flying craft would rule the seas in the future.

The admiral struggled to his feet, a couple of seamen coming to his aid and steadying him.

"We need to get you in a life preserver, my Lord," said a petty officer, strapping the device onto the admiral.

Only those who can get into a lifeboat, he thought, thinking that most of those would have been reduced to kindling, *or a raft are going to make it, unless the battle ends.*

As he made his way with the petty officer to the side of the ship and the long drop into the water, he regretted that he had not been able to order his remaining ships to surrender. The thunder of shells going off all around told him that the battle was still ongoing, even though his fleet had lost.

* * *

Admiral Pratt stared out over the carnage through his binoculars, getting a clear glimpse here and there through the heavy smoke put out by burning oil. His fleet had been hit hard, though it seemed that the enemy force had taken a bigger beating. Still, there were ships still afloat over there, some still firing on his vessels.

Why the hell isn't that fool over there giving it up, he thought, cringing as another shell, this from a secondary gun, hit the stern of his flagship.

"The captain reports that she'll make it, sir," said a young ensign who was acting as messenger now that the intercoms and speaking tubes were out.

The young man looked like he might make it too, though the bloody bandage on his head indicated he had been banged up.

We've all been banged up, Pratt thought, looking out over what was left of his fleet. Every surviving capital ship, with the exception of his two battlecruisers, would have a date with the dry docks. At least they would be repaired, while the British ships, those still afloat, would become prizes of war. A short war, devoid of glory, that would poison the relationship between the two countries for decades to come.

No matter, we've won today.

*****

Doug Dandridge Bio

Doug Dandridge was born in Venice Florida in 1957, the son of a Florida native and a Mother of French Canadian descent. An avid writer, Doug has written over thirty-five novels and has been a full time writer for the last seven years. He has military experience in the Army (Infantry), and academic experience at the Florida State University and the University of Alabama, receiving a MA in Clinical Psychology. Doug writes in the genres of science fiction, fantasy and steampunk, and has plans for a post apocalypse series and several alternate histories. His first traditionally published novel, Kinship War: Contact, is due out in June through Arc Manor Press.

# # # # #

For Want of a Pin
by Sarah Hoyt

December 5 1807, aboard the *Principe Real*

Dear Albina,

I write to you not knowing if my letter will ever reach you, though I suppose I can send it back with the part of our English escort that will be going back before we reach Madeira.

However, the reason I write is to relieve my feelings. Truth be told I might as well be writing in a diary, but I feel as though I left our conversation incomplete on November 15 when I rushed to you to procure a pin to secure my hem which had torn.

It was the most absurd fix, since Mama had already had all our household packed, and who knew where the pins might be, and we were supposed to tell no one we were leaving or where, even though everyone must have seen we were packing.

What a ridiculous time.

Of course, as I told you then, the purpose of it all was to get us aboard these fifteen ships, which among them will transfer the entire royal court to Brazil.

This sea travel business is not as much fun as you'd imagine. The ships smell of fish and unwashed clothes and never stop swaying. And we're piled in like cattle.

I know Papa isn't a nobleman. But as one of the secretaries of the regent, charged with his highness's correspondence, you'd think Papa would have secured better berthing for his family. No. I'm in a cabin which I share with five other girls, and the whole cabin smaller than my dressing room at home, and the whole smelling strongly of salted cod. Mama is lodged similarly, and I know not where father eats or sleeps, or if he does. It seems every time we see him he's either running after His Majesty, jotting down things in sheaves of paper, or else being rowed away in one of the boats, to take a message to someone, usually one of the English captains in the ships escorting us. This makes sense I suppose, since Papa speaks fluent English, learned from his English mother, but all the same, it's very painful not seeing him at all. It's as though I've lost, at one moment Lisbon and my whole family. And when I ask him when we'll get to Rio de Janeiro, or how we'll live there, all he does is shake his head at me.

* * *

Her name was Maria Francisca Joana dos Santos e Leal, but her whole life she'd been called Joaninha or, more often, "a menina" since she was the only girl born in the family in many a year, and the only daughter of her parents.

She was named after her English grandmother—well, almost, as her grandmother had been Frances—from whom she'd inherited the blue eyes, and a dimple on her left cheek when she smiled.

Her eyes were such an unusual color in Portugal that even without the dimple she would have been considered beautiful. Since she also had considerable natural beauty, her whole life, she'd been used to having people defer to her, or go out of her way to make her happy.

Only now it had all gone wrong. People wouldn't listen to her or stop behaving in the most absurd ways.

It had started early in November. She'd heard the conversation at first, not knowing what it meant. Oh, she understood the language well enough. Her grandmother had ensured she knew English almost as well as Portuguese. It was the content that made no sense.

The gentleman in the study with Papa was an Englishman she recognized, a tall man with the reddish tan of a fair man who spent much time in the sun. He was dressed in a uniform that Joaninha didn't recognize, and people called him "Commander" or "Milord." To include Papa, even though it sounded like they were friends, and Joana could hear the clinking of port wine glasses.

"Is there nothing we can do to convince him to take action, instead of this vile, revolting submission?" Milord asked.

"Nothing if we can't convince him that the French mean to depose him," Papa said.

"But does he not care for his country?" Milord asked, his voice sounding shocked in the way British people spoke when they found something outrageous. "Does he not care for the kingdom of his ancestors and the people who are his responsibility? Does he not care if they're making French subjects and kept under the boot of the beast?"

"I used to think he did," Papa said. "Now, I'm not so sure. I've started to suspect the regent cares for the country only as a possession. And as a possession, meant to add to his glory, he doesn't want it taken from him. Nothing else matters, nor what conditions are put upon that possession."

Papa walked to the window.

"The sad thing is that the regent will do anything rather than risk losing power and the chance to be John VI one day," he continued. "And besides, what precisely can we do? And what does it matter to you if Portugal falls with the king in it or not? Is it not bad enough that we fall, with no plan to defend ourselves from the French? That the French will add us to their empire and resources?"

"It would be bad enough," Milord said, and again there was the clinking of the port decanter being opened, before he continued, "But the thing is the French will get their real objective, which is your fleet. With your fleet, Bonaparte can make true his plans for invading the British Isles, which have been out of reach since Trafalgar."

"But I don't understand how the king can prevent their doing that. Soult has been marching towards us since the king's first tender of surrender, and he will be on us too soon for—"

"No," Milord said. "Listen, Leal, if we can but convince him to escape, ahead of the French, on all of the Portuguese fleet, or at least all that's currently seaworthy, to Brazil, and establish his capital in Rio, it will not only—"

"Brazil! A wilderness, halfway around the world?"

"Yes, listen, it will put the entire fleet out of the reach of Bonaparte, and it will—from the prince's perspective—allow him to keep the crown of the kingdom. Even should Bonaparte crown one of his puppets to rule over Portugal, the prince will have a chance of recovering the kingdom someday." He paused a second. "Particularly since we, English, can then be supplied from Rio and continue the fight. Now what we need to understand is how to make him agree to this."

Joaninha hadn't been, exactly, listening in. Well, not precisely. She'd been walking from the music room to the parlor and on passing Papa's study had walked very slowly and caught that much.

Yes, she knew it was bad manners to listen in, but the fact was that she was fourteen and bored. Yes, there was war, and everyone said Soult would come to Lisbon and kill everyone. It was said he had done very horrible things in Spain as he marched his way through. There were stories of villages pillaged and entire nunneries "disturbed," though Joaninha got a feeling that meant more than that the nuns had been told horrific tales.

But there had been war since she'd been aware of the talk of adults, and of worried whispers in the corners of drawing rooms and parlors. It was normal, and therefore boring. Sometimes news came of some city taken, of people killed, of many dead.

Mama or Eufemia, Joaninha's Nurse, would exclaim and cross themselves, and Mama or her nurse made her pray for the safety of some city or other, but Joaninha never saw war, never saw anything distressing.

Life in Lisbon was interesting, and sometimes enlivened by uniforms, both Portuguese and foreign, but she was protected, kept inside, made to learn her needlework and say endless prayers. It was boring. Thus, she didn't understand what Papa's visitors were talking about, but still it was interesting to listen to them.

Milord's words stayed with her, and she reasoned that if the king went to Brazil, her father, as one of the royal secretaries, would also go. She'd heard of Brazil mostly in shops. Cacao which made the sweet chocolate that Joaninha drank for breakfast every morning came from Brazil, as came the dark, rich coffee Papa drank. Pineapples came from Brazil, too. And her friend, Albina, had a very funny pet monkey that an old uncle had brought from Brazil. It wore red shorts, and could dance when Albina played her piano.

The idea of living in a land of such wonders colored her dreams. Meanwhile Papa looked more worried and harassed every day, and it was three days before Joaninha found herself alone with him, in the parlor before dinner, and ventured to ask, "Papa, if we go to Brazil, may I have a pet monkey?"

Papa had gone white. "Who told you we might go to Brazil? Who said anything?"

"I don't know," she said. "I heard something. I just thought I'd like to have a monkey and—"

"You must not, under any circumstances, speak of going to Brazil, Joaninha." The indulgent smile that Papa normally gave her when she was vague and silly didn't materialize. Instead Papa looked as stern as Joaninha's confessor did when she told him of overhearing things or sneaking a sweet from the kitchen. "Don't speak of Brazil. Don't even think of Brazil. You could ruin us all. Amelia, Amelia, come and tend to your daughter. She could destroy us all."

Mama had come, all alarmed, and even she wouldn't be kind to Joaninha, or allow her to explain that she'd just been talking of Brazil because she might have dreamed—

Instead Mama had been as stern as Papa or Joaninha's confessor and told her it would be a sin to say anything about Brazil, even in other contexts. She'd ended by yelling, "Brazil doesn't exist," and locking Joaninha in her room, which Joaninha thought very odd.

Then things had gotten stranger.

Two days later, Joaninha woke up to a house full of relatives. Normally, she lived with Papa and Mama, Eufemia, her Nurse, Mama's maid and Papa's valet and any number of servitors and drudges she barely noticed.

Oh, she had family enough around, beyond those people. Her aunts lived in the next street, grandmama and grandpapa—on Papa's side—next door to the aunts, and there were other relatives and cousins all over Lisbon.

She liked some, didn't like others, and was usually amenable to being taken to visit them on Sundays or for long summer weeks. There were really no cousins her age, and all the cousins were boys, so her society didn't vary much while visiting. But the aunts gave her sweets, and her grandparents petted her much.

There had never been an occasion—at least not in her remembered lifetime—that the entire family came to the house. Her two maiden aunts, Eugenia and Miranda, her married uncle Miguel, and his wife and their two infant sons whom she could never tell apart, and her widowed uncle Manuel and his sister-in-law Mariana who helped him look after his three sons, Rui, João and Joaquim, ranging in age from fourteen to three, and all very naughty, Joaninha thought.

But they were there when Joaninha woke. She was already alarmed she'd woken on her own, and not been woken by Eufemia with a tray of hot chocolate and toast.

She'd dressed herself anyhow, and caught back her curly hair, before opening the door to her room to what seemed to be an impossible scene.

The house was full of relatives and luggage.

No one had noticed Joaninha. She'd stumbled around, amid people arguing and talking, and she gathered they'd been there all night, since shortly after Joaninha had gone to bed, and they'd brought with them baskets and bags and some very large travel trunks called Baus de Porão. Joaninha had always thought them very romantic, since their whole name indicated they were built to travel in the hold of a ship. But it was bewildering to be barely able to move for the press of them.

What was stranger was that all the house servants, and most of the family, were packing. Taking everything they could reach and stuffing it willy-nilly into more of those hold-trunks. Mama, who never did any housework for herself, was wandering around distractedly and picking up anything small enough—a clock, a candlestick, a piece of unfinished embroidery—and putting it in an open trunk.

She was talking to Papa, who stood by, "Very generous of you, I'm sure, to include my brother," she said. Her brother was Widowed Uncle Manuel.

"Look," Papa said, sounding just a little exasperated. "We were told we could bring twenty people. They might have to make themselves useful, but the regent is not so cruel as to expect us to leave family behind."

"My sister in Coimbra…"

"Ah, no, Amelia, don't you see, that's impossible. We could send word to our family in Lisbon and have them all come in the dead of night. No one need know outside the house. But your sister would have to have known earlier, and to travel—"

"Yes, I know. Poor Almerinda. I shall pray for her."

Joaninha wasn't sure of understanding this, but then she didn't understand any of it. Not only was everything being packed, it wasn't as they'd packed before when they went to Sintra for the summer. No. Things were packed without rhyme or reason.

She'd wandered to the kitchen, unnoticed, to find the cook, Maria, being besieged by Joaninha's two evil cousins, João and Joaquim.

"Maria, if you please," Joaninha said, overwhelmed by the strangeness of the morning, and trying to speak loud enough to be heard over the brats, "Maria, I would like some breakfast."

Papa had once said the cook was "as large and majestic as a galleon under sail." Though Mama had rebuked him, and he'd said he'd never say it where Maria could hear him, Joaninha could never forget it, and had always thought of Maria that way. She looked more like a galleon now, with the two boys, one attached on either side, each yelling "Biscuits, biscuits, biscuits." As she turned, the boys holding on to her skirts turned with her, like lifeboats on a galleon. "Oh, Menina," Maria said. "Let me get you something. These two brats—we all forgot, didn't we?"

And like that, cook had gotten chocolate and toast for Joaninha.

Which was the beginning of the problem. Because João and Joaquim had been upset. "Why do you get her things but not for us?"

While Joaninha ate, they'd thrown themselves, time and again, at Maria's skirts and apron, while the cook ignored them and...well, she seemed to be packing hard-baked goods and jams into a trunk, so the madness continued even here.

Just as Joaninha got up, Joaquim threw himself at her, grabbing her skirt and screaming, "Make her give us biscuits."

Joaninha went over against the wall with the impact of the boy, and heard her skirt tear.

She hadn't cried in years, but suddenly she found herself crying, "Oh, oh, oh, my skirt."

The cook had emerged from her labors only long enough to scold the boys, but it was obvious she'd do nothing about the tear.

Holding the tear closed, Joaninha ran to find Eufemia. When she couldn't find her, she tried to tell Mama she needed a needle or a pin to fix her skirt. Mama paid no attention, and Joaninha ran down the hallway to her room, but all her other dresses had been packed, and she couldn't find either needle or pin.

Taking a deep breath, unable to get anyone's attention, she decided she'd go to Albina for a pin. Sure, she'd caught the implication that no one was to leave the house. But Albina was just two houses away. If Joaninha ran quickly, down the back garden and over the wall, no one would see her go and detect her coming.

Whatever was happening—and she suspected it was the trip to Brazil, she couldn't be expected to travel with a torn skirt. It wasn't decent.

And she was right, and went and returned with no issues, to find the house in the same uproar.

Joaninha was sure they'd be going to Brazil after all, even if Papa didn't seem too sure and said things like, "We'll be unpacking it all again in a week, and then watching all of it getting seized, robbed, and destroyed by the French." She'd told Albina all of it, and also how Mama had said they'd have to leave Lisbon anyway, because otherwise Mama and Joaninha might get killed or worse.

Joaninha had heard this before. When she'd gone to Albina she'd tried to make a joke of the worse, which was just the sort of thing Mama said, but Albina said, "It is not funny. You know Etienne, and you know the stories he tells."

She knew Etienne, or that is to say, Joaninha had seen him once or twice from a distance. His family was French, and they'd escaped the revolution. And she knew Albina loved him. Or at least, Joaninha thought that explained why they had somehow arranged to exchange notes by hiding them in between two stones in the garden where the two friends often walked.

The notes were the stuff of high tragedy and undying love, and Joaninha had enjoyed immensely hearing them read and envied Albina—three years older—her grand love affair. But this was real. The house being packed up was real. Fearing the "worst" was real. Things being so confused that Joaninha couldn't find a pin was real. Things being so confused no one prepared her meals or listened to her was real. And her possibly having to leave everything behind to go to Brazil or staying in Lisbon and enduring whatever it was the French would do was real.

Whether the stories Etienne told were real or not was open to discussion. After all, he'd been born in Portugal, and Joaninha knew he'd never even been to France, much less remembered the revolution. And besides, "Where did he ever tell you any stories?"

"Oh, we meet sometimes. I go to mass, and he goes to mass, and we sit way at the back, where we can talk."

The conversation had thereafter turned to this exciting intrigue, and Joaninha forgot all about Brazil. Until of course, they embarked.

It hadn't been too bad at first. It was new, at least. Her relatives had been dispersed among the boats, with other people of scant importance. And it was a relief to get away from Uncle Manuel's bratty sons.

The thing was that no one was paying her any attention. The girls she roomed with were all older and two of them were married. They talked and laughed in ways that made no sense to her, and often she thought they might as well be speaking a foreign language. Which was why she had started the letter to Albina. But finding a place to write in peace was difficult, and she didn't want anyone reading over her shoulder. Besides, she found she really didn't have much to say to Albina other than describing her intolerable situation, which in turn seemed to make it more intolerable.

So she'd folded the letter inside her missal, which was one of the few things she'd been allowed to carry with her, and instead had gone up on deck. One of the good things about this disturbed situation and Papa and Mama not being anywhere near nor paying any attention to her, was that she could wander about at will.

She was sure if Mama were aware, she would tell her the ship wasn't safe, and that on deck she'd meet rough seamen who might take liberties. No one had, though, and she couldn't spend her life confined with other people. On deck, there were many people, sure, mostly seamen putting sails up and pulling them down, and doing who knew what. However, as long as she stayed out of their way, she could walk and look out at the sea. On deck, no one bothered her or tried to ask her questions, or made jokes over her head and laughed in an irritating manner.

She was walking on deck, inhaling lungfuls of the clean sea air that didn't smell of fish and human misery, like the confined spaces downstairs, when she heard Papa's voice, "Joana! What are you doing here? And alone?"

"Just walking, I—" She was so shocked at being called Joana and not Joaninha she couldn't find her words.

"Never mind that, girl," Papa said. "Go find your Mama and your nurse. We're moving to the *Marlborough*."

"The British ship?" she said, turning around enough just to catch a glimpse of the frigate, a flutter of sails to the west, tinted by the setting sun.

"Yes. Mister Graham and I have some things to discuss, some plans to make, and he's offered to lodge my family and myself. At least your mother and nurse, and Leticia, your mother's maid, will be able to look after you."

* * *

Traveling between the ships was exciting. They all piled into a little rowboat, like the boats the fishermen rowed in the villages around Lisbon. Joana sat with her Mama, with her nurse and Leticia following in the next boat. After them came a train of other servants, and enough of her luggage that Joaninha wouldn't be living with two dresses and only a missal for reading material.

"Now, Joana," her father had told her. "You must remember we'll be the only family onboard, and that many of these sailors haven't seen any women or girls in months. You must remember that you're a good and religious girl, and you must not give your mother and I any worries."

Now, thinking about it as the boat tied up to the much bigger ship, and she was helped up a rope ladder to emerge onto a deck filled with young men in uniform, Joaninha didn't know whether to laugh or cry. Laugh because it was utterly ridiculous. It was Albina, not Joaninha who'd exchanged notes with a boy! Boys had never even noticed Joaninha, other than smiling at her. And besides, she would be too shy to even talk to one of these young men, who all looked so grown up and busy.

She had an impression of tallness, of hair that sparked in the sun, of beards and of amused light-colored eyes. She'd never be able to talk to one of these young men. Even if Mama or Nurse gave her a moment alone to do so. And they wouldn't. Besides, why would any of these young men want to talk to her?

* * *

His name was Jonathan Winter. She didn't remember how they'd started talking. It had started with smiles, proceeding to casual greetings, proceeding to comments about the weather and when they'd arrive. And somehow it had become normal, within a week, for them to find a corner of the busy deck, where—because others were busy and intent on their work—they could go unnoticed and talk.

There was no grand passion of the kind that Etienne had talked about to Albina, mind. They weren't that sort. And even had they been, what future could they have, being of different countries and aboard a ship headed to a distant land of coffee and monkeys.

"I've heard it's very savage," Jonathan said. "Little more than farmers in a vast wilderness."

"I wonder how we'll survive!" Joaninha said, picturing herself as a farmer's daughter, digging for onions and milking cows.

Jonathan laughed, as though he knew what was on her mind. "Well enough," he said. "I wager. With the entire court and the Portuguese king present? They will arrange things to be comfortable for you and those with you. It just won't be like Lisbon."

"You'll be there?" she asked. "You'll go, too?"

"Only for a day or two, while we unload," he said. "Half the English ships will turn back next week, with Admiral Sir Sydney

Smith. Mr. Graham will command the rest of the way. They reckon there isn't much danger when we are so near Madeira and out of the sphere of influence of the continent. It's unlikely the French will catch us."

Joaninha felt a pang. "Perhaps," she said. "Lisbon is captured and utterly burned, now." She wondered, even if she ever finished the letter to Albina, whether Albina would receive it, or even if Albina was alive.

"I doubt it is burned," Jonathan said. "Sacked probably." He paused. "All the same, I'd give something to see the look in Marechal Soult's eyes when he saw that the Portuguese fleet evaded him, and the king was gone."

* * *

The majority of the British ships had turned back to supply the English troops on the peninsula and to try to win back Lisbon. To the last minute, as men were being transferred between ships, and much communication was going on by lifting flags on masts and poles, with each new pennant hoisted making people aboard another ship rush about, Joaninha feared that Jonathan might leave with Sir Sidney Smith, after all.

It was good having someone to talk to, someone who appraised her of what was really going on. Many things that she had heard from Papa in his study now made sense. Jonathan told her, for instance, that the regent had hesitated before making the decision to move the whole court to Brazil. Before that he'd tried to surrender to France, and had ordered his troops to pose no resistance. It was only when Sir Sidney Smith—whom Joaninha had identified as "Milord" who had talked to Papa in his study—had shown him a copy of a

French gazette that talked of the deposition of the Portuguese monarchy that the regent had made up his mind to move the whole court.

"He's not a very brave man, your regent," Jonathan had said. "But perhaps no man is, when his whole family and kingdom are threatened."

It made Joaninha feel very grown up to understand what was going on at last. It made her calmer at the prospect of sailing into the strange tropical land that awaited them. So she watched the ships turn back, relieved that Jonathan was on deck and not going back with them. Of course, she didn't expect anything to happen between them. Certainly not a romantic relationship or even a lasting friendship, but for now he was an anchor of sanity in a world gone mad. Because Father was still very worried, still going between ships, or closeting himself with Mister Graham late into the night and discussing who knew what.

"We'll be in Madeira in a week," Jonathan said. "We'll make port and resupply. I think until we pass it, your father won't be wholly calm. I mean, it is still possible for the French to catch us. I don't think they will, mind you. Napoleon is no sailor, and his navy is incompetent, which is why we've trounced them again and again, but it is remotely possible the French will catch us, or perhaps ambush us, before we're past Madeira. After that it's very unlikely. It is too far for them to sail at venture, trying to catch us.

"Mind you, I think this is too far and so did Sir Sidney Smith. Or he'd not have left. But I think your father is one of nature's worriers. He worries about everything that the regent should worry about and doesn't."

"Yes. He was always like that," Joaninha said, with a little pride at her hardworking, conscientious Papa, even if she had an inkling it wasn't the best way to be.

* * *

The knock came in the middle of the night, in the cabin she had—gloriously—all to herself. That it seemed luxury even though it consisted of a sleeping berth and barely enough space to sleep in, told her how cramped she'd been in the other ship.

"Miss! Miss Leal!"

She was sure it was Jonathan's voice, and she wondered what he was doing knocking on her door in the middle of the night. He'd said his father was a clergyman. And surely, he knew that Joaninha's father would kill him if he tried any gross impropriety such as entering her room while she was alone.

But she got up and opened the door a crack, positioning her foot so he couldn't push his way in, and she could scream the ship down if needed.

But Jonathan was very pale and seemed not to see her, even while staring at her, "Miss, there are ships sighed. They came from Madeira. We think they are French."

She clutched at her nightgown. "They are? Are you sure?"

"Not yet, but we'd like you to remain below decks. Your father wants every one of our guests to stay below decks. Perhaps they don't know who we are. Perhaps they won't try to give chase."

The truth is, Joaninha thought, *fifteen Portuguese ships-of-the line of and four English ships will have little chance of being mistaken for anything but the Portuguese fleet carrying the royal family and escaping the French.*

She wanted to ask Jonathan if there were more French ships than the combined Portuguese and English force, but he'd already left. She heard his feet clamber up the steps to the deck.

"Menina," Nurse's voice called, and Joaninha saw her, a bulky woman in a nightgown and wrapped in a dark shawl. "Menina, your mother says to come to her cabin to pray."

* * *

Mama's cabin was crowded, and as Mama called the rosary, the three of them repeated the prayers mindlessly. Or at least Joaninha repeated them mindlessly, while she tried to hear for sounds from above. Was that a boom as of a cannon firing?

She knew it probably wasn't, but she couldn't help hearing every creak as a scream, and every clack as a boom. Aboard ship, that meant she was in continuous alarm.

Through the night and into the morning they prayed, until Joaninha must have fallen asleep while praying.

She woke up alone in Mama's cabin. Scrambling down the narrow corridor to her cabin she encountered no one and heard no sounds. All the sounds—other than the ship's ubiquitous noises—came from above. Was everyone on deck?

Dressing quickly, she ran up the stairs to the deck, where indeed everyone was.

Mama and Papa stood together. Papa was looking through binoculars and sometimes saying something to Mama. Nurse and Leticia were just behind them, looking worried, and sometimes talking to each other.

"Miss Leal," Jonathan said, coming up from behind her. "I wouldn't worry. There's only ten of them."

"But they're French."

"Yes, they're French, but they're far fewer than us."

He'd gone away, then, because there were message flags to hoist and to interpret, and orders to be relayed. As she watched him move astern rapidly, Joaninha thought that perhaps he was right, but perhaps not. Sure the Portuguese fleet alone was fifteen ships, and there were four English escort ships. But she doubted very much the Portuguese ships were armed. She'd once read that sometimes when they were being chased, ships would throw cannon balls overboard, because the balls weighed too much. She doubted the ships loaded down with courtiers had the ability to carry also the cannon balls. She very much doubted it.

She stood by her parents, staring out and trying to pray.

I fear it will fall on deaf ears, she thought.

"How could they have known we were coming early enough to plan and send out an ambush?" her father said. "After all, they have a small navy, and they couldn't have moved it that fast."

But none of it seemed to matter, as someone shouted, "They're hoisting flags demanding our immediate surrender, our handing over of the ships and the Royal Family."

"And what do we do?" someone else shouted.

"We fight by God," said a voice she thought was Mr. Graham's.

* * *

It was both very fast and agonizing slow, the ships approaching, gliding over the water, wind impelled.

"We can't really run," Jonathan said, in one of the few

moments he managed to stop by her. "We can't run without leaving the Portuguese fleet and the royal family utterly unprotected. To run is to surrender. And they can't run, the ships loaded down as they are."

The French ships circled the fleet. The English ships fired, the noise horrible and confusing. Powder and smoke were everywhere. Joaninha thought that it was silly firing at the French ships, because all the men were visible, and they'd all climbed the masts, where the cannonballs couldn't injure them, unless a mast itself was brought down.

And then the French ships returned fire, and hell on Earth erupted. Amid the smoke and the smell of gunpowder, there was now the sudden cracks and explosions of cannon balls, or worse of charges shaped like bars with a bulge at each end that whirled through, cutting things or breaking things.

Someone shouted the ship was taking in water. She realized she was huddled against coils of rope on the deck, and couldn't see Papa and Mama, much less Jonathan through the smoke. There were screams of people, and she wondered if any of them had been hit and were, perhaps, dying just inches from her. But she couldn't see them, and every instinct told her to make herself small and unobtrusive, like a hunted creature.

She wondered, as shouts redoubled and the ship listed, if she'd go down into the cold dark waters, and die like that, forgotten.

It seemed to go on forever, before it stopped. It stopped very suddenly, without warning.

Now there were shouts, but they were close at hand, and she opened her eyes enough to see that the ship was full of fighting. French sailors had boarded. There were sword fights everywhere, and suddenly, out of the smoke and the confusion, Jonathan emerged. "Get up, Miss. Your Papa has one of the boats, and he's going to try to make land in Madeira."

It was a mad scheme. Joaninha wondered at it. After all, Papa was no sailor, and she didn't remember his ever having rowed a boat, not even a pleasure boat on the lake in the park. And the island of Madeira was no more than a nebulous grey streak in the distance.

"Come, miss."

"We'll never make it," she said. "And Papa—"

"Come."

He half guided her, half pulled her through the deck. She slipped a couple of times, and realized she was slipping on blood. She tripped over the bodies of men who she was sure were dead. It was a scene she wouldn't have believed outside her nightmares.

Nor would she have believed being lowered onto a boat with a rope under her arms, while all around her battle still raged, as some ships—she couldn't even tell which, as night had fallen—still fired on each other, in flashes of sudden illumination. It seemed to her even the water was angry, tossing the little boat around while she and Mama and Papa and Leticia and nurse huddled together in the cold and damp.

Papa rowed. But the land seemed no closer. They did get away from the battle.

It was sheer luck a fisherman's sailboat rescued them. He took them to the house of a local gentleman, and it was days—mostly sleeping, taking trays in her bed—before Joaninha could get up and find her family.

The house was large and what she could see of the gardens and the isle was a riot of flowers.

Mama and Papa were sitting outside in a sort of terrace. They both looked pale, and Papa was saying "The Kingdom of Portugal is no more. The north has been offered to the former regent as a fiefdom of his family, the Braganzas. The central part is given to Spain. And the South goes to France, giving them good ports from which to sail. And of course, the fleet."

"But—" Mama said. "How did they know where and when to ambush the escaping fleet?"

"Some damnable spy in Lisbon. Etienne something or other. He got word of the escape, or possible escape two weeks before we left. Family had escaped the revolution, but they were still French you know?" He saw Joaninha then. "Hello, Joaninha. Don't worry too much. The French will need a man who can speak many languages and write in them." He smiled, a pale smile. "We'll probably go to England when the French invade. Not much chance of England holding out now."

But Joaninha did not, could not move. She'd gone very cold.

For want of a pin.

*****

Sarah Hoyt Bio

Sarah A. Hoyt was born in Portugal and lives in Colorado. Along the way she's published over 32 books (around there anyway. She keeps forgetting some every time she counts) she admits to and a round dozen she doesn't. She also managed to raise two sons, and a countless number of cats. When not writing at speed, she does furniture refinishing or reads history. She was a finalist for the Mythopoeic award with her first book, and has won the Prometheus and the Dragon. To learn more about Sarah and read samples of her work, visit http://sarahahoyt.com.

#####

Nothing Can Be Said Sufficient to Describe It

by Meriah Crawford

2303 Worcester Ln.
Ashburne, Virginia
NA1 A21 4AJ

25 October 2018

Dear Lauren,

Your mum told me yesterday that you're studying history in college now. How wonderful! I studied history for a time during my years at Fairfax College, but my father—your great grandfather Harvey—forbade me to continue. You see, he felt it was a waste of time, since I was destined for a low-level management position in the family business (Harrison's Hats and Co.) as soon as I graduated. He was right, I suppose, though I always regretted leaving Henry Winstanley behind. It's been such a joy to start looking into his life more now that I'm retired.

I don't know whether seventeenth century England is of interest to you, but I always found inspiration in Winstanley's determination, innovation, and passion for his work. His accomplishments are positively breathtaking. During his long career, you see, Henry was an artist, an engraver, a clerk of the works at two royal palaces, a designer and builder of no less than three lighthouses, and an apparent influencer of significant changes in ship design and naval tactics, though to what extent is unclear.

In addition to all this, he designed and built many bizarre contrivances in his own home (like trick mechanical chairs and rooms that rotated), for which he charged admission, and built a waterworks theatre in London, which was a popular attraction for decades. (Both of them helped finance his lighthouses, which he built largely at his own expense!) I spent many hours as a first-year undergrad wondering how he dreamed up his creations, and how he dared to take on such tremendous tasks.

It's the lighthouses that are of greatest interest to me, though. They were greatly in need at the time. As far back as 1637, King Charles wrote:

Whereas we have beene lately informed, by severall Certificates of diverse of our chiefe Officers of our Navie Royall, and of ancient Sea Captaines, that frequent and lamentable Shipwrackes, have from time to time beene, and doe continue...to the great losse of many of our Subjects and Strangers their lives and goods which have beene occasioned by want of Light houses and lights...it is very convenient and necessary that light houses should be erected.

(I love the old spellings! They add such wonderful colour to the writing, and they practically give off the scent of ancient wisdom.) The problem of treacherous seas became more serious over time, as commerce increased dramatically. According to the *Encyclopedia Britannica*, "English shipping nearly doubled in tonnage between 1666 and 1688."

As for Eddystone specifically, a traveler named Richard Warner wrote in 1808: "The horrors of Eddystone had long been a subject of alarm to all the navigators of this part of the British channel; and innumerable accidents pointed out the necessity of taking some measures to remedy an evil, which, as commerce increased, became every day of greater magnitude." Yet, building a lighthouse at the Eddystone Rocks, about 14 miles SSE of Plymouth, was hardly considered possible for some time. But the losses were so great that, at last, King William and Queen Mary (for whom your college was named) gave orders in 1694 for a lighthouse to be built there. It was Henry who, within a few short years, obliged—though not without great difficulty.

As you'll see in the image I'm sending you, history has preserved an engraving of the delightfully absurd and elaborate design for his first lighthouse. The shape will seem odd to you, as it lacks the curving conical taper of his final construction, but that was a considerable innovation when he accomplished it. Hard to imagine now, isn't it? That shape for a lighthouse seems so obvious—but some of the best designs are like that: obvious once complete.

The area of the Eddystone Rocks has always been a stormy one, and the reef beneath the water seems all but designed for massive, punishing waves. And Winstanley actually built his lighthouses on a tiny, slanted chunk of rock that was completely underwater at times. Can you imagine? I suppose the man must have been a bit of a nutter.

Well, my dear, I hope you enjoy these fragments from my past studies. Perhaps you can put them to good use in your own work. Do let me know how college is going! As always, your grandmother and I miss you, and we look forward to seeing you when you're home for Christmas.

Love,

Granddad

3 November 2018

Dear Lauren,

I am so delighted that you've taken an interest in Henry. I've looked through more of the material I've gathered. I collected an astonishing number of references in college, considering I already knew I was destined to work for Harrison's and couldn't finish my major—and there's far more to the story than you'd imagine. Do you know, poor Winstanley was actually taken captive by privateers at one point?

In 1698, the French and the English weren't at war at the time, at least technically, though they often were in those days. But France had experienced dreadful famine in 1693-4 and faced an enormous deficit during this period. They vastly overspent on building up their army, engaging in war, and building ships for their navy, but then couldn't afford to fully outfit or man the ships. So, instead, they rented many of their ships out to privateers. These men operated under the sanction of the government (this being the distinction between a pirate and a privateer) to harass, sink, or (ideally) capture mostly merchant vessels, taking their ships and cargo as prizes, if they could. Usually the privateers had smaller, less powerful craft, but these French privateers had, in some cases, large and powerful ships, along with a powerful reputation as skilled, determined, and bloodthirsty.

In any event, in 1698, Winstanley had been working on constructing his lighthouse for two years, or three summers. The work was quite difficult—his descriptions of the conditions are harrowing at times. (I'm including a part of his own narrative below.) Because of the increased privateer activity, Trinity House (who were in charge of lighthouses, among other responsibilities) assigned a ship to guard them while they worked. The ship, HMS *Terrible*, was a 26-gun "fifth rate" fireship, launched in 1694. It was a fairly small sailing warship, designed to be capable of being set fire to and run into enemy ships in battle, though apparently few of them were actually used for that purpose. Henry had little to say about the ship or her crew, except for this. (Part of a letter written by Henry Winstanley in 1698, to be sent to Trinity House):

I receiv'd Word upon landing in Plymouth that our guardians, HMS Terrible *and her fine crew, were to be withdrawn. I am writing to urge you not to permit this. In the last week alone, we have sighted no less than four Ships which we believe to be French Privateers. As you know, given the Conditions in which we work, we can have but few workers on the Rocks, and each must do his part to complete as much Work as we may during the brief intervals in which we are able to work on our sea-batter'd Light house. We spend a part of that time awash in the waves that crash upon this bit of Granite, our attentions focus'd on holding fast to both our Tools and the work itself, lest we be wash'd away. Our Progress will be impeded even further if we must continually keep watch against attack—and we simply have no means to defend ourselves. Furthermore, it is the opinion, I know, of* Terrible's *captain that the Privateers are merely awaiting an opportune moment to attack. If they do, I fear greatly for the Outcome. At the least, our work would be delay'd. More likely, our achingly slow and hard-won Progress would be destroy'd and, in all likelihood, the lives of myself and my intrepid workmen would be lost.*

There's no clear indication of whether the letter was sent, or received, or responded to, but it's a fact that the *Terrible* was withdrawn, and a trio of privateers took advantage of the opportunity to swoop in, destroy poor Henry's hard work, and abscond with—well, with whom?

I found one source claiming that Henry and all of his workers were taken; another claimed that only Henry was taken and the men sent off in their boat; and still another that claimed the men were stripped naked and set adrift! I suspect the second is most accurate. There's no way to be certain, except the last possibility seems like mere sensationalism, and only Winstanley can have been considered worth a decent sum as ransom. (Clearly they couldn't simply be left behind, considering what the privateers did to the lighthouse!)

The privateer, incidentally, was an infamous rogue named René Duguay-Trouin. He set sail on his first ship when he was just 17, and his family gave him his own vessel to command a mere two years later. Ridiculous! Mind you, he was quite successful while he lived, so I have to give him credit for that, I suppose. Does it make me a hypocrite that I think less of him that his family gave him so much? Yes, I expect it does.

Do you know, there's a saying that the third generation in a family business is often the last? The reasoning is this: the first generation, of course, works hard and builds up a business (or if he or she doesn't, there's no second or third generation to discuss); the second generation likely grew up in lean times and/or saw how much trouble their parent or parents went to in order to be successful, and manages to be competent and focused much of the time; the third generation, meanwhile, grew up with success. He (or she) doesn't know what hard times or struggle look like, and therefore doesn't know how to appreciate it. And worse, that third generation is often *given* too much, because the parents—and often the grandparents as well—want to give the young'uns all the benefits and experiences and gewgaws they didn't have growing up. All of the advantages they wished they'd had, you see? Except they forget to make sure the little darlings value it and have to work for their successes, and the kids end up entitled, lazy, and incompetent. Sometimes it's the fourth generation, of course, but it's really quite common. If you're lucky, one of your kids grows up OK. Maybe two. (But you and I are both only children, so our parents had to make do. They were luckier than they know, as I'm sure you will agree.)

As for privateer René, I have no idea what generation he was, or how talented, but he was presumably able to make men work for him. No—strike that. He was on a small ship, and he was successful. A bunch of crusty seamen wouldn't have worked hard for him if he wasn't either worthy—or, I suppose, a very successful SOB. Sometimes—especially in past times—being nasty and angry could be just as effective as being a good, charismatic leader, as long as you're willing to follow up the nastiness with punishment. And on the open seas, you certainly didn't just walk out on your job.

I suppose you know the punishment for mutiny is still death, even now. Of course, there's more room for extenuating circumstances these days, and I imagine it's been a very long time since the sentence has been carried out for that crime. Treason is the only other crime punishable by death now, though activists are always working on changing that. I cheered as loud as anyone when that law was passed in parliament (eliminating the death penalty for all but those two crimes), but I admit I'd do little more than sign a petition—and that only half-heartedly—to end it for treason.

Anyway, as for me, I was actually the *fifth* generation, about which there seems to be no clever saying. Perhaps my passion for studying history was evidence of my being over-coddled and inclined to laziness? My dear father certainly suggested as much. But I gave my all for the company: sacrificing, working long hours, racking my brains for ways to save "the old Co.," as your great grandfather called it. I don't know how much your mum has told you about Harrison's Hat Co., but my goodness, are there stories to tell. So many of them. Do you know, every governor general for most of the life of our company wore a Harrison's hat? However, the biggest story is, I'm sorry to say, the saddest: *The Decline and Fall of the Old Co.* In my defense, the Co.—and the entire business of selling hats to men—was well into its terminal decline when I climbed aboard. But that never stopped the old man—my father—from blaming me, at least in part.

Oh dear, I suppose I sound a bit bitter, don't I? Well, I oughtn't to be. It was a good life, and a good business to be in, however harrowing it was once the end appeared on the horizon. *Respected* and *respectable*, as my father and my grandfather always emphasized. I may have shrugged at that when I was your age, but I was proud of it, too—and all the more so as time passed and our sales steadily declined. But, that's a long story—and one for another day.

More soon, my dear. And tell us all about school! Your grandmother and I are eager to hear.

Love,

Your long-winded grandfather

8 November 2018

Sweet and patient and much-wronged Lauren:

Yes indeed, you're quite right, and I apologize. Sending my letter with the best and most dramatic parts of the story of Henry's abduction by privateers left out was no less than cruel, and it was wrong of me. Your grandmother rolled her eyes when I read her your emailed response, and she told me to immediately commence writing my story while she drives to the store. I don't know for sure, but I suspect this letter will be accompanied by her famous almond-raspberry thumbprint cookies, and maybe some scones, too, by way of apology. Hopefully you will be more than compensated for my oversight.

Well then: it was a chilly morning in August of 1698, and Winstanley and his men were hard at work. They were nearly done with version one of his grand tower. The men had just finished using their block and tackle to shift to the rocks their construction materials and supplies for a week's work on the rock. Since the tower was so advanced, they'd taken to staying in it for several days at a time, though not without some difficulties. (More on that in my next letter.)

Part of the trouble is that the men were working inside mostly at this time. They saw the *Terrible* was gone, but hoped that it had simply sailed into port to collect supplies and would be back shortly. And so, they focused on their work, as good, solid, perhaps unimaginative workers. Winstanley, meanwhile, was a bit more of a visionary—or more of a sightseer, at any rate, as he tells the tale. He'd climbed the many steps up to the absurd porch-like area between the living area and the light itself, which was still being constructed, took a deep breath of the brisk sea air and gave a good stretch (so I always imagine him doing—we have no historical record, I confess) and gazed around him.

Poor Henry. Imagine his thoughts upon seeing not one—not two—but *three* stout ships sailing toward him. Imagine the thud of his chest as he whipped out his spyglass. Were they friend or foe? He suspected the latter—and indeed, it appeared they were. The ships were French and the flag they flew was a modified French flag, though they couldn't legally use it after the peace treaty signed in 1696.

Winstanley reported that he led his men to the lowest chamber in the base to await their fate, though one can easily imagine much running and shouting, rather than the cool-headed, orderly procession he seems to imply. Seeing no resistance, the privateers boarded the rock and the lighthouse on it, and forced the unarmed men out at gunpoint. They then took—well, just Winstanley, let us say—and let the men take to their small boat and row vigorously away. While being brought aboard the captain's ship, Winstanley reported that he remonstrated vehemently with the privateers, but to no avail.

Before they departed, with Winstanley locked up and under guard, the three ships took out their bitterness against the English by using poor Winstanley's lighthouse for target practice. The three ships, though they had only 38 guns between them, managed to demolish it down to the iron rods holding the lowest course of blocks in place on the slanted bit of rock. Volley after volley rocked the ship, the bellows of the lead ship's captain calling "Fire!" and "Look lively, men! Hop to, hop to!" or words to that effect (but in French, of course) ringing out in between the crash of the cannon.

This firing was punctuated by the crash and splash of tumbling rocks, and the following cheers of the men. One can only imagine the deep moral suffering of dear Henry, who no doubt realized that the long-anticipated completion of his tower would now never come, and that he was a prisoner at the mercy of men who could commit such a grave and horrible act.

What did he think, our Henry, when the guns finally fell silent and the ship came about and headed south toward France? What fears filled his thoughts? What terrors caused his hands to shake and his heart to ache in his chest? And how did he feel when he learned that his captor was none other than the infamous René Duguay-Trouin? Assuming he knew of the man at all. Mustn't he, though? Perhaps you can find evidence of it in your searches!

Well, of course, we know next to nothing of what comes next. Henry was either locked in a prison with his workers in St. Malo, Duguay-Trouin's hometown and base of operations; or he was locked up there alone; or he was in Paris, led before Louis IV himself when the king learned of Winstanley's capture; or perhaps some other scenario I haven't heard of. It's quite amazing to me Winstanley didn't write the whole dramatic tale himself, but he was far more of a builder and inventor than a storyteller, clearly. Or perhaps the banality and boredom and small humiliations of imprisonment didn't seem like a fitting tale to tell?

In any event, once Winstanley had arrived wherever he did, and René announced his grand success to the king by whatever means he did, the king's opinion of the kidnapping of Winstanley and the destruction of the nearly-completed lighthouse soon became clear. Whatever Duguay-Trouin expected, it wasn't what he received—which, depending on who you believe, was either to be thrown in irons himself for his audacity (rubbish!), or a rude insult, or perhaps a stern scolding. We don't really know, except that the king was clearly not pleased, and René certainly did not receive the reward he might have expected.

As for Winstanley, he was either lauded by the king and sent home with gifts, or offered a job with the French government, or simply sent on his way. I found several different versions of a statement, supposedly by the king, about his release of Winstanley—that the French were at war with England and not with humanity—meaning, of course, that he respected the work Winstanley was doing, saw its necessity for commercial shipping (though the Eddystone Rocks were also quite lethal to warships over the years), and wished for him to continue his work.

As with so much else, the precise truth will never be known. Even the fact that this statement is replicated so many times proves nothing, except that it sounds lovely and dramatic, and like the sort of thing one wishes the king might have said.

What we do know for sure is that Henry soon found himself home again. He first flew to the arms of his loving wife, Elizabeth (or so I tell myself, as history has left no record) at their home in Littlebury. However, Henry very soon returned to his favorite inn at Plymouth.

You can imagine the amazement of the townspeople when Henry appeared again, alive and well. Do you know, during the earthquake several years ago in Virginia, electronic messages from there reached New York City before the tremors did? Almost unimaginable. In the 17th century, meanwhile, Winstanley would likely have reached Plymouth long before formal newspaper reports of his miraculous survival did and, whatever rumors may have flown during that time, they surely would have been stunned to set eyes on him again, in one piece.

While answering questions and reassuring the townspeople that he was not, in fact, a ghost, Henry waited impatiently until the weather permitted travel, then hired a boat and a few seasoned fishermen to man the oars, and went to see what was left of his lighthouse.

Just imagine, then, Henry's feelings upon seeing what few shattered rocks and bits of twisted iron remained of his work, which took two years, an enormous amount of effort and money and materials, and likely the lives of a few of his workmen. (History, you know, rarely records the names, let alone the lives or the deaths, of the men and women who do the actual work—only those of the people who possess the power and the wealth to set them in motion.) And not just the bulk of the tower, but the reportedly lavish, ornate interior, fitted out at his own expense, to his taste, with a sort of luxury that was unheard of at the time for a lighthouse, was all now sunk in the ocean. One could easily excuse our hero if he looked upon those works and despaired—but, no! Not our Henry. Not this ingenious, buffeted, thwarted man. He was not to be stopped. Instead, he penned the following note to his wife:

My dearest Elizabeth,

As I fear'd, my Light-house has been consign'd to the sea, and nearly every block of Stone with it. It wounds me to see so much of my labours all for naught.

Still, at least now I know for sure. I do believe it was the uncertainty that drove me nearly to Distraction. Now, with a belly full of the inn's excellent pigeon pie and a fine glass or two of wine besides, with my feet dry and warm by the Fire and my heart content in knowing you are Safe and Well, I can at last look to the future—and the future appears thus: Providence has seen fit to wipe the Rock clean and force me to start again. I must do so, only with greater Care and a stronger Design.

Oh—I know. There is no Tower I could design that would withstand the might of a trio of ships (or even a single one!) when once the Guns commence to fire. Yet already, even without the final board nail'd into place—already, I had begun to find Fault and to see ways to make an even better Beacon on that ocean batter'd Rock. Indeed, the damages caus'd by the storms of the previous winter brought home to me the desirability of such a course. Yes—though I deplore the Cause, though I detest the rapacious criminals who were the Instrument, still I will embrace the Task before me and build again, only better. Broader, better anchor'd, taller by far, and with perhaps a bit less ornamentation. Thus the privateers will perhaps, in sailing these waters again, see that I—that we, England—continue on Undaunted—Undeterr'd by their casual viciousness. Better, in fact, than before!

Alas, building can, of course, not begin again until I have had time for completing my new Design, for having new stones prepared for an even larger Base, and new iron Anchors made to my specifications, and so forth. I shall, therefore, be home with you again very soon, I am pleas'd to report. Until then, my dear, I remain,

Your loving husband,

Henry

The months that intervened are little documented, though there is one event that stands out: the sinking of the *Hermes*, with nearly 100 sailors and passengers on board, along with a rich cargo. Cruel to have survived the long voyage from North Carolina only to be dashed upon the rocks with their destination in sight. And the ship's loss meant a dreadful financial disappointment to a man known to Winstanley. Whether this new tragedy accelerated Henry's efforts or not, the man went to work with speed and enthusiasm. With the wisdom he gained from building his first structure, he was able to work longer, smarter, and with better preparation for the grim conditions. The weather also seems to have been more cooperative than previously, as he noted, according to a magazine article about his second tower: "*My Prayers were often answer'd, and the men and I were able to land more frequently and with less Difficulty than before. Providence, I do believe, sought to reward me for my Faith amidst so many Obstacles.*"

The overall design of this structure featured a wider, thicker base, more thoroughly anchored into the rock. The tower was taller, though the top half, approximately, was still of an octagonal wood construction. He eliminated the open area beneath the "lanthorn," though there were large windows that could be swung open—or protected with heavy shutters. The interior was still lavish, though more restrained. Overall similar in appearance, but more sturdy and serious. Completed in 1701, the lighthouse was hailed as another marvelous feat of engineering (though not by all!) and ships once again were safe from the devastating reefs.

In the ensuing couple of years, Eddystone Lighthouse stood tall amidst the waves, though many tales of harrowing storms in the tower were apparently passed around. For example, one keeper (Elias Worth) wrote to his brother:

Tis a lonely spot, and a passing Violent one at times. When I was carried here by Mr. Winstanly himself, it wasn't so bad, though the looks of Pitye on the faces of his men as Winstanly assured me of the structures safety showed I might have some surprises in store. Yet nothing could ever have Prepared me for the jarring of the Waves when the wind and tides carried them in Full Force against the Walls of my narrow home. At times, I have learned I must hold tight to my Dinner lest I find it tumbling to the floor. And it's more than one night I've been forc'd to lash myself to my bed, calling upon the Almighty to preserve me.

Yet, aside from occasional repairs and frequent re-provisioning, all was well on the rocks—for a time.

On that ominous note, I will close. I am pleased as punch, by the way, that your program requires study abroad. Outstanding idea! Where are you thinking of going?

Be well, my dear.

Much love,

Granddad

20 November 2018

Dear Lauren,

Your grandmother is delighted to hear that you and your roommates enjoyed your box of treats. She promises to send you back after Christmas with more to share, as well, if you promise to tell us more about this new young man you've met. We're both looking forward to meeting him next month—and your grandmother has made me promise not to talk both of your ears off about ships and lighthouses and hats.

Now, my dear, your questions about the area around the rocks are far from "ridiculous"—at least until you understand just what Winstanley and his men had to cope with. It helps, I think, to learn that as late as 1940, with the use of a motorboat, an approach to the lighthouse was still quite perilous, even to the point of being lethal. I found this in an article I think you'll find enlightening. According to the *Record and Mail*, from Saturday, January 13, 1940:

An accident occurred off the Eddystone Lighthouse yesterday morning, as a result of which an officer and six men belonging to the Trinity House lighthouse tender, Vestal, *were lost.*

The Vestal *had gone to the Eddystone Lighthouse to deliver gear. The weather conditions were suitable for the operation, and following the usual routine, the motor boat was lowered close to the lighthouse…*

The anchor line of the motor boat was laid out and the lighthouse approached safely, but, while the ropes thrown by the keepers were being made fast, an unexpected sea broke over the boat, putting the engine out of action….

The Vestal *sent another boat immediately to her assistance, but before it could get up to her, the motor boat had disappeared, and only one member of the crew was picked up, nothing being seen of the motor boat or the other occupants.*

On a less dramatic note, Richard Warner wrote in 1808 of his failed attempt to visit the lighthouse during a trip through the area: "the wind got to the south-west in the night, and we were informed any attempt to reach it would be unsuccessful; as it requires both that the wind should be *in*, or northerly, and blow lightly, to render a landing practicable."

Winstanley found that high tides, which submerged the rocks completely, as well as high winds and rough seas—which were exceptionally rough around the rocks because of their structure—prevented them from not only working on the rocks but, at times, from even attempting to approach them. Winstanley wrote that even in summer,

The weather would at times prove so bad that for ten or fourteen days together the Sea would be so Raging about these Rocks, caused by out-Winds and the running of the ground Seas coming from the main ocean, that although the weather should seem and be most Calm in other Places, yet here it would mount and fly more than two hundred feet, as has been so found since there was lodgment on the Place, and therefore all our Works were constantly buried at those times, and exposed to the Mercy of the Seas.

And winter was typically impossible, given the danger of becoming soaked (or worse, submerged) when the water was that cold. It takes a distressingly short period of time to die from hypothermia during the cold months. In fact, his working season might, at times, be as brief as two to three months during the summer, depending on the weather and the stage of construction. This is why Winstanley worked to make the structure inhabitable as quickly as possible, though during the building of the first lighthouse, he was considerably too optimistic on that front on one occasion. As he reported shortly before the privateers attacked:

We ventured to lodge there [in the lighthouse] soon after Midsummer, for the greater despatch of the Work. But the first Night the weather came bad, and so continued that it was eleven days before any Boat could come near us again, and not being acquainted with the height of the sea's rising, we were almost all the time drowned with wet, and our Provisions in as bad a condition, though we worked night and day as much as possible, to make shelter for ourselves. In the storm we lost some of our Materials, although we did what we could to save them.

But the Boat returning, we all left the House to be refreshed on shore.

With regard to the rocks themselves, you must understand two things. First, that the two rocks upon which lighthouses have been built since 1696 are just two of a large number of rocks, all part of a series of reefs, much of which is underwater but still well within reach of the wooden hulls of ships of that day. They would be nearly as damaging to the metal hulls of today, in fact. For this reason, the lighthouse continues to shine (as well as many others) even with the existence of GPS devices on most boats of any significant size.

And second, they didn't have access to anything like the explosives we have today, and none of the explosives they did have were compatible with water. Even if it were wise to attempt it, the task would simply be too large, and essentially impossible without powerful modern explosives and high tech SCUBA gear. (Incidentally, my dear, remind me to tell you about the time we took your mother snorkeling for her sixteenth birthday. It's a wonderful story—but you mustn't let her know I told you! She's still quite embarrassed by it. She shouldn't be, though. Anyone could have mistaken that tarpon for a shark.)

As for the rough seas and the extent of the rocks, a biographer of the rocks themselves, Fred Majdalany, wrote:

This red reef, which is called Eddystone, is part of an isolated underwater rock mass six hundred yards long, and rising steeply from the Channel bed. Because of its position and configuration, the waters around it are nearly always rough, even when the sea beyond it is calm. . . . In the course of time, the Atlantic has worn down their western sides to a gradual upward slope of about thirty degrees, so that even in a moderate westerly sea the waves pile up to a great height as they roll up this runway to break over the edge. . . . An easterly swell, striking in rapid succession three broken walls of rock, creates immense curtains of spray and an effect of violence out of all proportion to its true power.

So: too huge by far to move or remove, or otherwise tame than with a lighthouse. And so ill placed that it put an outstanding harbor in danger of losing relevance as a sea port. Brave Henry to take it on!

More soon, I must dash. Your grandmother and I are off to dinner and cards, apparently, with some of our neighbors.

Much love,

Grandad

1 December 2018

Dear Lauren,

Your grandmother is off with her friends this afternoon, for lunch and a long gab, so I have time to continue my story. I'm not sure if you know, but Mary is still close with many of the people she worked with at the Ministry of Natural Resources. I'm quite jealous of them sometimes. Not that they never had any drama, but they always came together, through the years to help each other.

Things at the Co., on the other hand, were so grim near the end. My father was angry at the change of times, and that we simply hadn't been able to change along with them. But his decision to diversify into suits was too little, too late, as the saying goes. I was against it, really, but I had nothing better to offer, to my eternal regret. My ideas were too small, too limited, and too much like what we'd tried before. We had such a fine brand, but nothing worthy to attach it to. And the suits he designed, in concert with what meager staff we still had, were out of fashion before they were made.

I remember, back when I was 27 or 28, looking around myself one day at work and noticing how old everyone was. Not that there's anything wrong with being old—I have a greater appreciation for elders every day (haha)—but if a business doesn't have any young people, it's a sign of a business on the decline.

Mind you, I did point out the problem with the cut of the suits, but father merely grunted and carried on. I once, in a fit of pique, suggested we start manufacturing barrels or bespoke shoes. Both of those, of course, were industries that had died before ours. My father stood up, walked out, and went home. The next day, he sent me a note saying he thought we might consider selling the company, since there was clearly no future in it—by "it" he meant me—but then he returned to work the following day and said nothing more about it. Typical, I suppose, of the both of us. Your poor mother didn't have the most even tempered or communicative of fathers, I'm sorry to say, though I always prided myself on being a better father to her than mine was to me.

Well, anyway, you know (I think?) that we finally shut the old Co. down in 1987. Much later than we should have, probably, but there was no doubt by then that it was time. Mary was contributing much more than I was to the household at that stage—in more ways than one. (I blame "the times" for some of that, but even then, I suppose

I knew better. But she hardly ever complained, except through one of her looks—I'm sure you know what I mean. She is more of a woman than I ever deserved.)

But, back to Henry. The biggest and most dramatic part of the tale—even more momentous than the adventure of the privateers—came in November, 1703. As Majdalany wrote, "It was not just a storm. It was The Storm." Winstanley had been planning to visit the lighthouse to spend several days so they could make some repairs before the worst of winter weather hit. He'd gathered materials and his workmen and waited only for suitable weather to embark on the trip to the rocks. The weather, however, had been terrible for two weeks. As the justifiably famous author Daniel Defoe, who wrote his first book about the storm, noted:

Several Stacks of Chimnies were blown down, and several Ships were lost, and the Tiles in many Places were blown off from the Houses; and the nearer it came to the fatal 26th of November, the Tempestuousness of the Weather encreas'd.

At last, however, on Friday, the 26th of November, the winds and seas finally calmed, and Winstanley's men and supplies and his boat were all at the ready—but Winstanley didn't join them. Instead, the men went to the lighthouse on their own, bringing food and other goods to the lighthouse keeper and his family, and commenced the repairs.

Late that night, when most were long abed, the winds kicked up again. Defoe reports:

About One, or at least by Two a Clock, 'tis suppos'd, few People, that were capable of any Sense of Danger, were so hardy as to lie in Bed. And the Fury of the Tempest encreased to such a Degree, that as the Editor of this Account being in London, and conversing with the People the next Days, understood, most People expected the Fall of their Houses.

And the violence of the storm only increased:

From Two of the Clock the Storm continued, and encreased till Five in the Morning; and from Five, to half an Hour after Six, it blew with the greatest Violence: the Fury of it was so exceeding great for that particular Hour and half, that if it had not abated as it did, nothing could have stood its Violence much longer.

In this last Part of the Time the greatest Part of the Damage was done: Several Ships that rode it out till now, gave up all; for no Anchor could hold…the Damage done on that Account was incredible.

And, if you can imagine it, terrible storms and additional damage continued for some days afterward, until (Defoe reports) about 4pm on Wednesday, December 2nd, "Thus ended the Greatest and the Longest Storm that ever the World saw."

As for the aftermath, Defoe noted:

The next Day or Two was almost entirely spent in the Curiosity of the People, in viewing the Havock the Storm had made, which was so universal in London, and especially in the Out-Parts, that nothing can be said sufficient to describe it.

More precisely, with regard to the seas (or as precisely as the records can tell us), many ships had been blown into port by the stiff winds leading up to the great storm, and many more were unable to depart, *So that when the Great Storm came, our Ports round the Sea-Coast of England were exceeding full of Ships of all sorts.*

Defoe says the *Paris Gazetteer* reported 30,000 dead and 300 ships destroyed of all types: merchant ships, men of war, tenders, victuallers, East India men, West India men, vessels of the Russian and Dutch fleets, and more. Though, he also reckons these numbers are inflated. (Majdalany claims about 150 ships destroyed and 8,000 dead: grim numbers, still.)

Defoe reports on damages at length, down to specifics at times, including hundreds of smaller boats and barges destroyed and a great many thousands of livestock drowned. He also lists 12 Royal Navy ships destroyed, some with their captains, and adds that "The damage done to the Ships that were sav'd, is past our Power to compute." It's a fascinating, though grim read. Take a look, if you're of a mind to know more.

More to our point, when the sun came up on the morning of Saturday, November 27th, 1703, the Eddystone Lighthouse was simply gone. As Defoe wrote:

The loss of the Light-House, call'd the Eddystone at Plymouth, is another Article, of which we never heard any particulars other than this; that at Night it was standing, and in the Morning all the upper part from the Gallery was blown down, and all the People in it perished...The loss of that Light-House is...a considerable Damage, as 'tis very doubtful whether it will be ever attempted again, and as it was a great Security to the Sailors, many a good Ship having been lost there in former Times.

Henry had often, with his critics in mind (many thought him a fool for even attempting to build on the Eddystone Rocks, and condemned his designs besides), declared that he hoped he would be inside the lighthouse when the greatest storm ever known hit England. And he clearly intended to go there: to be inside it, and—as it turns out—to meet his doom there. So, the question one must ask is: Why wasn't he? Why did he stay in Plymouth in spite of his declared intent to oversee the repairs himself?

Some accused Henry of having known the storm was coming (the morning the ship left for the lighthouse, he was warned of foul weather) and avoiding the lighthouse for that reason. But that hardly seems likely given what we know of the man—and however much of a genius he was, the science of weather forecasting was neither an interest of his (as far as we know) nor particularly advanced at that time.

Henry countered, apparently, that he'd fallen ill due to mutton stew gone bad from an inn a short distance from the docks. The inn, apparently a reputable one, expressed their concern for their reputation by swearing Winstanley was lying. Whether true or not, the view of the public seemed against him, perhaps influenced by the deaths that had already attended his works. It was apparently murmured that he was a coward or a fool. Whatever the case, Winstanley's response to the storm and this adversity was to renew his commitment to providing a lighthouse at Eddystone, contrary to Defoe's prediction, rather than to retire from public life, as many *lesser* men would have done.

He thus begins almost immediately to plan a replacement for the building. Though he seems not to have retained copies of his letters or of the responses, we know he sent many to men of science and engineering backgrounds around the region in the aftermath of the storm, asking them for their thoughts on the best approach to building a better lighthouse in that most difficult of locations. More than one correspondent urged him to give it up, as he would surely fail, and even likely die in the attempt. Another told him that any sufficiently tall and sturdy tower, once properly affixed to the rock beneath it "even supposing that were possible" would tear the rock apart, thus causing the tower to collapse anyway. We know of these responses because of his letters to his wife, Elizabeth, in which he (amongst other topics) spent no small amount of time ridiculing or lambasting his correspondents, depending on his mood.

Interestingly, Winstanley seems to have found his inspiration for his third lighthouse largely through a mix of observation and discussions with John Evelyn and an unknown shipwright, whom he met at the inn that was his base of operations (not the one where he consumed the fateful mutton stew) while he worked on his grand projects.

The observations were largely completed in the immediate aftermath of the great storm: Winstanley was horrified by the destruction around him and felt tortured by the view of the sea that was his usual fare on days he didn't travel to the rocks. He turned inland, instead, and found views that were no less destructive, but that proved *instructive* instead. One parson found Winstanley climbing on and around a range of downed trees around the parsonage, and struck up a conversation with him. In a letter to his sister, the parson (John Marshall) said he initially took Winstanley for a madman, obsessed with talking to the trees, before coming to understand that Winstanley simply sought to understand why some trees fell and others stood through the violent storms. Marshall led him around to various trees, pointing out areas where some of the fallen were damaged by lightning or insect activity, or in some cases had too dense a canopy, while others of all sizes (with no apparent correlation to size or height) still stood, in spite of winds that had torn down sheds, cottages, and steeples alike.

Soon after, Winstanley wrote to John Evelyn, author of *Sylva, or A Discourse of Forest-Trees and the Propagation of Timber in His Majesty's Dominions*, and asked for his thoughts. Evelyn (who was a fan of Winstanley's Waterworkes, Henry's very successful London show) had given great thought to the effects of the hurricane on trees, as can be seen in later editions of the book. For example, he wrote: "But for the Oak, Elm, Wall-nut, Firs, and the taller Timber-Trees, let the dismal Effects of the late Hurricane (never to be forgotten) caution you never to plant them too near the Mansion, (or indeed any other House) that so if such Accident happen, their Fall and Ruin may not reach them."

Evelyn also writes of staking, grouping trees, and so forth, but such notions don't particularly apply to lighthouses. What Evelyn did have to offer in his letters was the idea that the tapering of trees—with the bulk of the weight and mass at the bottom—helped them stay upright in a gale. Evelyn also pointed out to Winstanley that the sides aren't a straight cone, but that they curve inward from the base, with tremendous roots holding them in place. Winstanley used both notions—albeit in a limited manner with respect to the roots—in his final design. Evelyn also, incidentally, noted that older trees tended to succumb to the greatest winds; he believed this was because of fading vigor and strength as much as because of great size. This may have influenced Winstanley as well: he no longer made grandiose claims for the strength or the longevity of his creation—though he most certainly did ensure he was present in the lighthouse, once complete, when the annual storms rolled through.

In short, Winstanley's explorations and discussions led him to believe that attaching the various parts of the structure together more securely—including the very base to the rock itself—would be essential, while also helping him to appreciate the concept of wind (and water) resistance, and the need for a smooth surface. This latter notion, along with close examination of ship hull design with his shipwright friend, led him to decide that a tapering, smooth, and closed surface would be least vulnerable. (These conversations clearly helped launch him into the next stage of his career, as well.)

His initial two designs were (in my modern view) absurdly ornate. These design decisions, while in some ways adding to the comfort of the occupants, also made the lighthouse far more subject to the force of the incoming wind and waves. And oh dear, this is getting long!

Well, I have little to add about the building of the third lighthouse, except that he included next to no ornament other than several mottoes on the outside: Glory be to God, Vires in Bello (strength in war), and Post Tenebris Lux (after darkness, light). That and the fact that this lighthouse lasted far longer, though it was never tested by a storm like The Great Storm. This tower stood until 1787, when the base was shown to have begun to be dangerously undermined.

Sometime after his third and final lighthouse was built, Winstanley began working for the Royal Navy. During that time, before his death in 1715 of apoplexy (stroke), he was part of a group working to improve ship designs (those of the larger ships designed and commissioned by the Navy). They made some intriguing changes: the ships grew longer and somewhat narrower in relation to their length. Those new ships carried more sail and thus moved faster, though they were slightly less maneuverable in battle. This led to some enhancements in steering. And they also carried more guns, more ammunition, and more supplies to feed the men, which had a variety of benefits.

These ships were balanced, in larger battles, by more nimble smaller ships (which also experienced changes in dimensions and new sail configurations), which resulted in different approaches to battle tactics. One scholar suggested Winstanley was working off his bitterness at the privateers. I don't know whether it's true or not, but it certainly helped reinforce England's status as a leader on the high seas. It led to a tremendous domination of the seas that was critical in fighting off challenges—including our own—for many years. Other countries countered those changes in time, naturally, either by copying them or finding their own improvements. And then, before we knew it, there were steam ships, and then diesel-powered engines, and now nuclear power plants at sea. We have come a very long way from sail.

And a long way from bowlers and top hats, too. Maybe your mother has mentioned it, but her grandfathers (both of them) wore hats until they died. My father liked a grey felt fedora with a black band, and her other grandfather always wore a straw Panama. Lovely hat, that one. Both of them. But to tell you the truth, Lauren, I never much liked hats myself. I don't know that I've ever admitted that to anyone before, though your grandma figured it out a long time ago. The day after my father's funeral, I put my own black wool fedora into its box in my closet and only ever took it out again for funerals. I sometimes think of this as a betrayal of my father and my grandfather, but I just feel lighter without a cover on my head. Maybe keeping that hat in a box helps keep certain thoughts locked away, too.

But after all these years, I've never stopped thinking about Henry Winstanley. He was a great man who did great things, when he could have simply gone home and rested on his laurels. It inspires me—but it also shames me. When it was all over with the Co., I could have done anything. I was only 46. I could easily have gone back to school and become the teacher I'd longed to be, and helped young people to study and learn from the past. Or I could have been an archivist and preserved history. Or a researcher, or a public historian. I could even have found a way to help set public policy with an eye to past lessons we might learn from. Had I taken the time to study Henry Winstanley's life in this depth much sooner, perhaps I would have.

Do you know, Winstanley was actually 52 when he *started* building his first lighthouse, and 62 when his last was completed—and he braved the wild winds and seas of Eddystone Rocks to do it? And me? My grand legacy was to help oversee the failure of a company that was started by my great, great grandfather and was regarded as the best in the country in its heyday, followed by spending 22 years managing accounts payable for a medium-sized clothing retailer. *That* company did a far better job of navigating change over the years than the old Co. did—and all without any help from me.

I'm proud of much of what I did. Of my family, and the home and life I built with them. But I could have done more. Not as much as Winstanley, perhaps, but more than I did. A great deal more. You know, your grandmother actually suggested yesterday that I write a book about our dear Henry. At first, I thought she was daft. The thought of taking on such a large project at my age? Mad as a hatter. But, now? I may be old, but I think I will look to Henry's fine example. If he could do all he did without the benefits of electricity or cement or databases for research, well, the least I can do is bestir my old bones to write a book.

Meanwhile, learn from my mistakes, my dear granddaughter. Be strong, be bold, be great. Build a towering beacon and make your light shine over the roiling seas around you. And in the meantime, write soon and tell me more about your plan to travel to Plymouth to learn more about our mutual friend. I can't wait to hear all the details!

Best of luck with your exams.

Love,

Granddad

P.S. I'm attaching a picture of Winstanley's second lighthouse in all of its absurdly ornate glory.

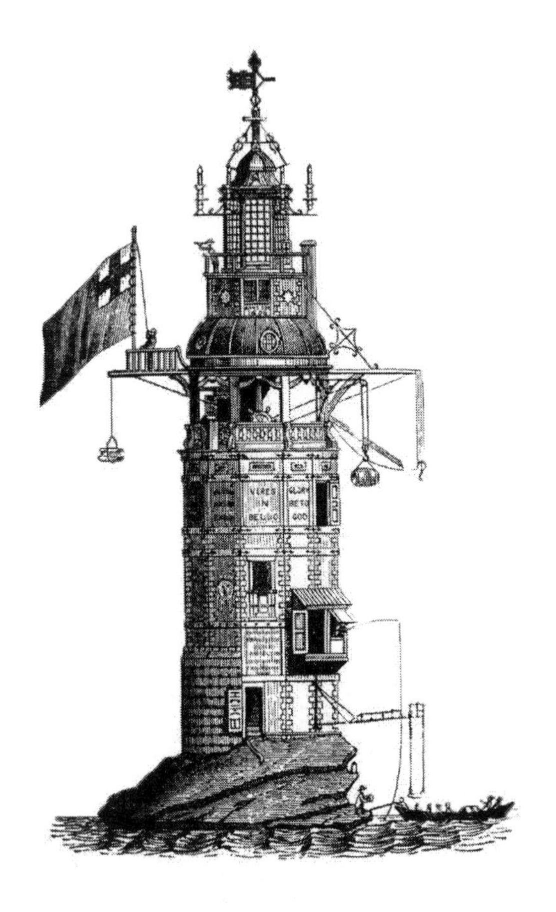

*****

Meriah Crawford Bio

Meriah Lysistrata Crawford is an associate professor at Virginia Commonwealth University, as well as a writer, editor, and private investigator. Among her publications is the co-written novel *The Persistence of Dreams* (https://ericflintsringoffire.com/book/the-persistence-of-dreams/), which involves a seventeenth century painter and a time-traveling West Virginia town from the year 2000. For more information about her work, or if you'd like to confess to a crime, please visit www.meriahcrawford.com or connect with her on Twitter: @MeriahCrawford or Facebook: www.facebook.com/meriah.crawford.

# # # # #

Corsairs and Tenzans by Philip S. Bolger

Early Morning, January 5, 1944
200 Miles off the Coast of Italian Somaliland

"Why are we even out here?" Leutnant Heinrich Metzger griped as he flew his Fw200 C-4 Maritime Patrol aircraft.

"Because it's our job," Leutnant Schmidt deadpanned in response, while Schmidt was keeping his eyes on the aircraft's radar.

"Well, obviously," continued Metzger. "I mean why are we flying out here in what's probably a typhoon? Why does command think the Americans and Japanese are going to come this way? If I were the head of their alliance, I wouldn't."

Of course you wouldn't, thought Schmidt. *You'd order all troops to stay safe and warm and dry and then still find a way to complain about it.* Schmidt did not remember a time his fellow pilot was not constantly complaining—about the heat, about being reflagged from a bomber squadron to a patrol squadron, about being based in Africa, about missing out on the action, about having to fly combat missions, or any number of other paradoxical nonsense. If it wasn't lies, it was exaggeration—Metzger's "Typhoon" was a mild storm at best, one the Fw200 would easily be able to handle.

"They did beat the Dutch," said Schmidt.

"Oh wow, big military power there, the fascist Netherlands," Metzger said, rolling his eyes. "This Oahu Pact, they declared war, what, eight months ago? We've been at war since '39. We've taken the Polish, the French, the British, and will soon have the Soviets. Why would they even want to fight us, the world's premier military power?"

"Did you forget about the sub contact last night? Several Italian ships took damage."

"The Italians always whine," said Metzger. "I doubt their ships are anywhere near as damaged as they say. I had to work with them in North Africa, you know."

Maybe that's who you picked up all this complaining from, Schmidt thought.

"And that's the thing about submarines," Metzger said. "It could've been a rogue Briton, or one of their commonwealth lackeys. It isn't like they come up to surface and announce who they are and why they're shooting at you."

Schmidt didn't have time to respond, as his cathode ray screen began showing a surface contact. Schmidt looked again, and made sure he had the right readout.

"Metzger, pay attention," he said. "Radar's got something. Looks like…dead on from us. Distance is 30 miles or so."

The two pilots looked at each other. Metzger's eyes were wide.

"Oahu Pact?" Metzger asked.

Schmidt nodded.

"Well let's not dawdle," said Metzger. "For all we know, we're right over their AA and they just haven't seen us yet. Break off, we'll alert command."

* * *

Admiral's Wardroom, IJN *Musashi*

"I trust you've enjoyed your stay, commander?" Admiral Yamamoto Isoroku asked.

"Yes sir," replied Commander Bailey.

"A bit different from US vessels, I assume?"

"Definitely different from the subs I'm used to," said the commander, grinning. "Less cramped, and the food's better."

Admiral Yamamoto smiled slightly at that.

The admiral was wearing his blue, high-collar uniform, with gold on the collar and braids on the sleeves. He had abstained from wearing his medals, choosing function over form. His leather gloves, the admiral's only concession to wet weather gear, sat next to his plate—he'd taken them off to eat. Though he normally ate in private in his quarters, he craved a bit of companionship, so he'd come to the wardroom.

"Did you ever think you'd serve on a Japanese ship?" Admiral Yamamoto asked.

"No sir," said Bailey, shaking his head. "Truth be told, we expected we'd fight you."

Admiral Yamamoto chuckled slightly at that. "When your president and our emperor signed the Oahu Pact, I was quite surprised. I too, had envisioned our nations on a crash course in the Pacific. I am glad we chose warmer relations instead."

The wardroom was deserted, save for the American liaison, who had been onboard the ship less than a week. The two had shared a brief breakfast. Commander Seth A. Bailey was a hulking Texan with the kind of confident can-do attitude Yamamoto found common among American career officers. The admiral imagined the big man must've been quite uncomfortable onboard the tight quarters of a submarine. Bailey wore tan fatigues with USN markings, most of which Yamamoto recognized.

Bailey nodded. "Likewise, sir. Especially with Europe under the Swastika, we need to stick together."

Yamamoto did not want to tell the US officer how much the destruction of the British Monarchy had perturbed the Imperial Navy. The Nazis had made it clear, despite their nominal affinity for monarchs in places like Spain and Italy, that they would dismantle any rival power structure given time. The American did not need to know about the insecurities of Japan, Yamamoto decided.

"Sir," Bailey spoke up. "I don't mean to be rude, but could I clarify, make sure I know what assets we've got? Last time I did anything with surface ships was nearly a decade ago."

"Of course," said Admiral Yamamoto, hiding his slight concern that the big Texan had not retained the information. "We have one battleship division, consisting of this ship, *Musashi*, and its sister, *Yamamoto.* We have the remnant of your battleship division, USS *Alabama*, since USS *Maryland* was crippled by the Dutch."

"Well at least the carriers are fresh," Bailey said with a wince. "I am familiar with our task force, but I am not familiar with yours."

"We, like you, have cruisers with our carriers," Yamamoto said.

He does not need to know we lack the oil to bring the Kongo*-class with us all the way out here*, Yamamoto thought. That had been the subject of much contentious debate within the IJN's staff.

"*Soryu* is about the equivalent of our *Yorktown*?"

Yamamoto smiled thinly.

"More or less."

"For obvious reasons, I get the destroyers," Bailey said, and Yamamoto favored the submarine officer with a smile.

"Rear Admiral Truog was not as happy that I insisted on a heavy escort for the carrier task forces," Yamamoto replied.

Bailey rolled his eyes, then realized what he'd done.

"Sorry, sir, surface commanders always want more destroyers," Bailey said. "They don't understand how happy we submariners are when they strip the screen around the capital ships. Do you have six destroyers to a screen like us?"

"Not usually," Yamamoto answered. "Ours run flotillas of four."

He really does not understand surface combat that well, Yamamoto thought, surprised. Bailey had only arrived on the ship with the recent change of command, so it was probably unreasonable to expect him to have a perfect grasp of the situation.

The man is also quite young for a commander. The Americans seemed to promote their officers far more rapidly than the IJN.

"What do we think the Germans have, sir?" Bailey asked. "Intelligence seemed confused when they briefed me."

That is something common for both of us, Admiral Yamamoto thought as he considered the question. The man wished he had a better answer, but intelligence was unclear on what, precisely, was coming, besides a combined force of German and Italian ships.

"We can expect them to also have a sizable battleship presence," Yamamoto replied. "Thankfully neither of our opponents invested heavily in carriers, but we are close enough to their African colonial holdings that they may have shore-based aircraft that come after us."

Bailey nodded again.

The admiral was one of the only Oahu Pact leaders to have seen heavy combat—he cut his teeth at the battle of Tsushima Straits, fighting the Russians. It cost him two fingers on his left hand. He had a role quelling the rebellions in the 1930s, as well—it was Yamamoto who ran down the naval cadets who had attempted to assassinate the Prime Minister, and Yamamoto who testified at the 1936 Army Treason Trials. Some of the Americans had seen action in the Great War, as had some of the Japanese officers, but none of them had been part of a fleet action before. Yamamoto, in many ways, was the only logical commander of the joint force.

Before Yamamoto and Bailey could continue their conversation, a junior officer burst through the wardroom hatch. Clad in wet weather gear and soaked from the ongoing rain, the officer nearly blurted out a report.

"Sir," he said. "Ensign Takeda reporting with a message from the Officer of the Watch. The American destroyer pickets report contact. Enemy patrol aircraft, followed by heavy gunfire. It's their main force, as we feared."

"We do not fear, Ensign," said Yamamoto, neatly folding his napkin next to his plate. "We expect. Then we react. Has the destroyer screen fixed an enemy?"

"Not yet, sir," the watch officer said. "They've reported several targets and reported taking fire, but the storm is causing trouble getting a good fix. They're attempting to develop a better picture before breaking contact."

Yamamoto nodded. One of his favorite things about working with the Americans was their commanders' tendency to take the initiative. Yamamoto glanced out the wardroom's porthole and grimaced.

"Still raining? I assume the carrier aircraft are grounded?" said Yamamoto.

"Yes sir," said the officer. "Carrier Division 1 reports the rain is still too heavy to scramble aircraft. The Americans also report no flight operations."

This posed a problem. The aircraft were the big strength of the Oahu Pact fleet. The '41 Pearl Harbor War Games had proven their utility, but they would be useless under such a cloud of rain.

"You said the destroyers had radar fixes. Do they know what of?" asked Yamamoto.

"Initial report is unclear," said the action officer. At that moment, a sailor ran up and hurriedly passed a paper into the officer's hands. The officer read it, and his eyes went wide.

"Sir, Admiral Oshima of the Carrier Division reports his destroyers are in contact with the enemy as well," the officer said. "They've identified several large radar contacts and are taking heavy plunging fire."

Yamamoto grimaced. If the Germans had used the storm to move up heavy guns, it would be difficult to counter.

"A formidable enemy," said Yamamoto. "We cannot let this aggression go unanswered. Instruct the battleships to prepare for combat. Get us into a position to support either the Japanese screen to the North or the American to the South. Whichever is taking heavier fire, the battleships will move to support."

"Yes sir!" the messenger said, and as he hustled to the bridge, the alarm bells began clanging. In the great turrets of *Musashi*, the gun crew began the arduous process of loading the heavy Type 94 naval guns. On the deck, crewmen donned helmets and manned AA guns as petty officers shouted excitedly while the rain poured down on the deck. In sickbay, the doctors prepared to receive casualties, the smell of antiseptic and rubbing alcohol clogging the air, while damage control teams closed watertight doors in preparation for combat. The engines set to flank, and the mighty battleship was on its way towards the fight. The first contacts had been reported by the forward destroyer screen, almost 25 miles west. The Imperial Japanese Navy's twin battleships, *Yamato* and *Musashi*, steamed towards their adjusted position, supported by USS *Alabama*. The battleship line formed as they headed towards combat.

On the *Musashi*'s flag bridge, Yamamoto listened as his various task groups reported in. As the ships passed within 15 miles of the destroyer screens, Yamamoto heard reports from the carrier groups—still no aircraft in the sky. The American battleship, *Alabama*, was relaying contact reports from American destroyers. Unfortunately, the reports were only general, as the heavy weather was preventing the radar returns from delivering targetable data. Soon after, *Yamato* and *Musashi*'s systems picked up the same contacts.

They are far closer than we thought, Yamamoto thought. *Five miles from the destroyers is far too close.*

Looking out across the roiling sea, the clouds showing perhaps just a sign of breaking, he viewed *Yamato* and *Alabama* moving on line. On the horizon, he saw little through the haze of rain.

Well, at least there won't be a long, tedious run in, he thought. All around, officers buzzed and barked orders as the ship sailed towards its destination.

"Sir," reported a signals officer. "*New Orleans* reports the loss of three friendly destroyers to surface gunfire, originating somewhere in the Northwest. USS *Clark* remains in contact. Rear Admiral Truog is calling again, asking for more support."

"Tell him the battleships are on their way," said Yamamoto. "He must hold for roughly an hour."

In actuality, Admiral Yamamoto's estimate was slightly optimistic. Playing a game of deadly tag in the gloom, Admiral Truog managed to drag the Axis battleships back towards the Oahu Pact force in exchange for most of his destroyers. *Yamato*, *Musashi*, and *Alabama*'s arrival came as an unpleasant surprise to the Axis light forces harrying their Pact counterparts, with a *Hipper*-class heavy cruiser dying spectacularly under the American battleship's guns. Yamamoto's counterpart, Vice Admiral Erich Bey, temporarily turned his force away to give his Italian contingent time to catch up. Contrary to the Condor crew's scuttlebutt, the Italians' *Littorio* had been the only vessel damaged by the British submarine's torpedo spread. Although slowed to just under twenty-two knots, the vessel maintained the ability to use her main battery.

Thus, it was shortly after 1100 that *Bismarck*, *Tirpitz*, *Littorio*, *Roma*, and *Vittorio Veneto* hove south to engage *Musashi*, *Yamato*, and *Alabama*. With the skies clearing, both sides scrambled to launch from their carriers.

* * *

USS *Yorktown*

Ready Room

The cramped room was full of aircrew and pilots as Lieutenant Commander Nathan "Skip" Leibowitz shuffled in. Without pausing, he headed to his specific seat next to the rest of his flight—Lieutenant Hall, Lieutenant Mallek, and Ensign Broward.

At the front of the room, Commander Hart, the squadron commander of VF-42, stood in front of a chalkboard.

"Good morning, men," he said. "You may have heard the scuttlebutt—we've found the Jerries."

A quick murmur rose but stopped almost as quickly—the appetite to hear more overrode the wish to talk about it.

"Our destroyers are in contact. We've already lost a few, and the main force is engaging as we speak. Not sure how many of theirs we got, but Intel says the Krauts used the storm to move close. The enemy feels confident. That's their mistake."

Hart drew a few icons on the blackboard, in quick succession.

"We've drawn the short straw," he continued. "We'll be escorting in a flight of our pals from Japan—an outfit our liaisons have designated "Naginata Squadron."

"Nagi-whatsit?" Asked Ensign Broward, a big burly pilot that Leibowitz knew to be a perpetual groaner. Broward was one of those guys who only worked well when he was miserable.

"It's a type of Japanese spear," Leibowitz offered in his Minnesotan lilt. "Now why don't we all keep ourselves quiet while the commander finishes the brief, okay?"

Leibowitz privately wondered why the squadron would have such an unusual name. From his encounters with the Japanese, they tended to use unnamed, numbered squadrons. His curiosity was not enough to interrupt the commander's briefing.

Hart nodded in appreciation, and continued speaking.

"Naginata Squadron is the Fleet Main Air Effort," Hart continued. "Their mission is to sink the battleship *Bismarck*, the enemy's flagship."

Hart motioned to a functionary, who rushed up with a blown-up photograph of the battleship. Leibowitz's breath caught in his throat—*Bismarck* was truly a monstrous ship. He saw some of the men in the room look wary.

"Lot of anti-air on that," came a rumbling from Leibowitz's right. There was a certain value in quantity of lead you could sling skyward, and *Bismarck*'s builders had understood that.

"We don't want to get close," said Hart. "Just get the torpedo bombers into position. We'll be the third wave of attacks against this beast."

"Third wave, sir?" Asked Broward. Hart nodded.

"*Lexington*'s got first dibs—fast-flying dive bombers. Think of them as a jab. We're the uppercut."

The usually grim Broward grinned at that.

"Now," Hart said. "The Jerries aren't going to just give us that shot. They'll be sending planes up after our pals from the Orient. That's where we come in."

A series of flash cards were passed around among the pilots. Before he even received his, Leibowitz knew what they were going to be—Zeewolfes, plus some Italian planes that Leibowitz privately doubted would even work. The flash cards confirmed that.

"These aircraft are being flown by men with a lot more combat experience than we've got," cautioned Hart. "But they're still cherries when it comes to carrier operations. Those Zeewolfes, the ones on the cards you're seeing, those are brand new Kraut planes, based on their successful model that beat the Russians. Besides them, be on the lookout for anything coming from the shore. We know the Italians have airbases in their African holdings. Intel isn't sure if they coordinated with the German fleet, but I'd rather be safe than sorry."

Leibowitz flipped through the cards. He didn't see anything surprising. He tucked them into his leather jacket.

"Are there any questions?" asked Commander Hart.

A hand shot up beside him, and Leibowitz fought the urge to fix its owner with a hard glare. Lieutenant Hall was an upstart kid out of Philadelphia. Guy was a track star and the stereotypical fighter jock. Leibowitz had his own thoughts on the young pilot's attitude, but kept those to himself unless his wingman screwed up.

"Yes sir, I've got one. What do we get for shooting down the most Krauts?"

You might want to be a little more concerned with doing your job and keeping my tail clear, Leibowitz thought, this time letting his glare sweep over his wingman. Hall shrank back down in his chair.

Commander Hart grinned, noting both the rebuke, and that it had been received.

"A pat on the back, maybe a handshake," Hart said. The various pilots murmured to themselves. Hart asked if there were any other questions, but there weren't.

"Pilots man your planes," the intercom crackled. "I say again, pilots man your planes."

"Well, there's our casting call," Hart said.

* * *

USS *New Orleans*

Goddammit, Rear Admiral Jacob Truog swore, watching as USS *Winslow* split in half from an Italian 15-inch shell. *Any time that Japanese admiral wants to close with the heavy ships, I'd appreciate it.*

New Orleans' guns cracked away at a target. Truog forced himself to ignore reports on the heavy cruiser's effectiveness. The vessel had lost her radar to a salvo from the big German brute that had been annihilated by *Alabama*, so odds were she was missing much more than she was hitting.

"Sir!" an officer interjected. "*Yorktown* reports she is launching aircraft."

About damn time, Truog thought.

There was the sound of ripping canvas, followed by the high singing of steel fragments going past the flag bridge's open hatches. Screams and calls for corpsman told Truog that the splinters had found some casualties.

"Well make sure they know where we are," Truog said sarcastically. "I guess we can leave out the part about us maybe not being here much longer if those flyboys don't hurry up."

* * *

Leibowitz nervously touched the Star of David he held around his neck. In his ears, he could hear squadron radio chatter, and the back and forth with *Yorktown*'s tower. Leibowitz was anxious. He was hot in his flight leathers—the equatorial heat made wearing such a pain, but he knew he'd need the warmth when he was up above the clouds. He'd been sweating since before he'd sat down in the cockpit, and the slimy feel of his helmet and the strap of his goggles made him all the more anxious to get into the air.

His plane sat on the deck, along with Hall's. The gull-winged Corsair was painted in typical naval camouflage—blue top, white bottom, with the American roundels prominently displayed so he wouldn't get misidentified and shot down by a friendly in a fight. The 2,000-horsepower radial engine thrummed along happily, waiting to propel Leibowitz through the sky. Leibowitz checked his instrument panels for the fiftieth time, then shook his head.

Nervous as a bride on her wedding night, Leibowitz thought, briefly glancing at his wife's picture taped to the top of the instrument panel. Leibowitz hadn't been in combat, but they'd scuffled often enough with the Australians who had fought the Germans in North Africa. After each mock combat, the groups of pilots had sat down to discuss what the Americans had done right and wrong.

"You have to be more aware," one of the Aussies, a double ace, had said. "It's not just awareness of the enemy, but of yourself. You must know what's working, what's not, and how much fuel you've got—be a damn shame to win a dogfight and go down in the drink because you weren't paying attention to your fuel levels."

A dead pilot from a crash is just as dead as one torn apart by 20mm cannon, Leibowitz thought. Leibowitz also, when he was feeling particularly anxious, thought about how awful it would be to be stranded in the deep ocean, treading water and hoping none of the local marine life was feeling too hungry.

Something the controller said broke Leibowitz out of his reverie. He never heard what the island had directed, but saw that the sailor at the end of the flight deck was motioning with his paddles. Pulling into position, Leibowitz watched as the man signaled for Hall to take off.

Well here goes, he thought as Hall's Corsair taxied forward. The dark blue fighter sailed off *Yorktown*'s bow, dipping just a bit as it cleared the edge of the flight deck before clawing into a climbing turn.

The flight control officer motioned again. Leibowitz taxied forward, and hit the throttle. His stomach lurched as his Corsair cleared the carrier. As the storm broke, the cloud ceiling receded.

"Blue Two, Blue One," Leibowitz said into his radio. "Let's get up to angels three and head to the RV."

"Roger," Hall acknowledged. The two planes began climbing. The Corsair was Leibowitz's third aircraft, after a trainer and a stint in the Buffalo. Of the planes Leibowitz had flown, the Corsair was easily his favorite. The gull-winged fighter was a beast and didn't do well going slow…but if you could crank it up to speed, you could dive or turn with the best of them. He flew up through the breaking clouds, Hall slipping back into position. Turning, he took a heading for the rendezvous as the rest of the flight caught up.

Let's go find our friends, he thought.

* * *

Aerial Rendezvous Point Able

Lieutenant Yoshida Ichiro was happy to be in the air. In the cockpit of his B6N Tenzan Torpedo Bomber, he felt like he was the instrument of the heavens, here to dole out justice. Well, technically, it would be Ensign Fujiwara Shinji, his weapons operator, or possibly Petty Officer Matsui, the tail-gunner, doling out justice, but it was Yoshida's responsibility to fly the plane to the right position.

His two crewmen were young. They'd both been cycled in after the skirmish off of Haiphong with the French that had precipitated the current conflict. Yoshida didn't yet know the other two crewmen very well, but they'd come recommended. The officer had written his wife, Reiko, saying that being responsible for such young men had reminded him of his own daughter, Megumi. Reiko's response had icily noted that it was good he was getting practice as a father, given that he'd had so few opportunities to do so in the past year.

It wasn't that Yoshida was old—he had not yet hit his thirtieth birthday—but after seven years in the Imperial Japanese Navy, including peacekeeping tours in the Philippines and Manchukuo, he had become aware of some of the truths of the military that junior men do not realize. Yoshida had seen no combat as a Tenzan pilot yet, but to him, it was merely a new platform for the same kind of job, a new window into war. He did not share the young men's lust for glory and battle.

Still, he was required to do his duty to the Emperor, and to his nation.

The B6N Tenzan was the IJN's newest torpedo bomber, fielded right before the declaration of war against Axis Europe. Yoshida's plane was painted teal on the fuselage and white on the undersides. The only exceptions to the subdued colors of the plane were the distinctive Rising Sun emblem of Japan. The plane was also painted with the squadron markings for the 44th Attack Squadron, or Sento Hikokai 44, known onboard *Hiryu* as Naginata Squadron.

Orbiting at the RV point, he saw the American Corsair fighters that were to be their escorts. Yoshida did not understand command's decision to have the Americans escort his flight—the Zeroes onboard *Hiryu* should've been enough, but Yoshida had heard good things about the Corsair.

The gull wings make them easy to pick out, he thought. *In any case, it is always better to have escorts than not. Plus, if I must coordinate with them, I know my English is good enough.*

"Think the gaijin are up to the task?" asked Fujiwara. "I've heard they're nothing but cowboys that don't even train for their tasks."

"Nonsense," said Yoshida. "Have some respect. I've trained with the Americans. They're every bit as capable as us."

"Yeah," opined Petty Officer Matsui. "Yoshida-san was at the '41 Pearl Harbor wargames. He'd know."

Fujiwara stayed quiet, harboring whatever prejudices he held in silence. That was fine by Yoshida. He needed the young gunner to hit his targets. What he thought about foreign affairs was none of Yoshida's business.

"What did you fly in '41, sir?" asked Fujiwara. "Still bombers, right?"

"I flew the Aichi E13," said Yoshida as he checked his instruments. "Off the back of *Yamato*."

"You flew with the admiral?" asked Matsui, surprise in his voice.

"No," said Yoshida. "The admiral was still using *Nagato* as his flagship at the time. I was the spotter for *Yamato*."

"Well," said Fujiwara. "Much better to be on a torpedo bomber, sir. We'll be the ones to sink the big ships!"

The voice of Yoshida's flight leader broke over the radio, informing him to get in formation. Yoshida assumed a wing side position alongside another Tenzan, and two American Corsairs led them in.

As they crossed the sea, just above the fading storm clouds, Yoshida thought about purpose.

* * *

The Skies above the Indian Ocean

"Red One, Blue One," said Leibowitz on squadron communications. "Got about three hours of fuel left. We've just passed Waypoint Charlie."

"Red One acknowledges," replied Hart. "No enemy contacts yet. Everyone, keep your eyes peeled."

Hall was flying 500 feet to Leibowitz's port side. Broward and Mallek were off to Leibowitz's starboard. Behind him, Leibowitz could see the four Japanese Tenzans they were escorting, though not well—the torpedo bombers were keeping their distance and preparing for their own strike. If intel was right, they'd be over their targets soon enough.

Suddenly, tracers arced down from above, passing right in front of Leibowitz.

"Tally ho! Enemy fighters!" he barked, pulling up abruptly to scan for his assailant. He didn't have to look long—a Zeewolf screamed down in front of him. It was only due to sheer fortune, or the opposing pilot's mistake, that Leibowitz lived. The German's wingman followed right behind him, having inexplicably not fired.

"Fighters, one o'clock high!" Broward called into the flight radio channel. Leibowitz turned to look at what his subordinate had seen and felt the blood drain from his face. Four Zeewolf were diving, opening fire as they came. Instinctively, Leibowitz kicked his rudder, but still felt two thumps as shells hit his fuselage.

Broward never had a chance. The Corsair was perforated by 20mm rounds, one going right through the top of the cockpit. At this distance, at this speed, Leibowitz couldn't say for sure whether or not he saw the blood spatter.

Shit, shit, shit, he thought. The first flight of Zeewolfes had made the mistake of breaking off their dive to try and turn in after the Tenzans.

"Blue Four is down," Hall reported over the radio. "I'm in pursuit."

"Get your ass back into position Blue Two!" Leibowitz barked, reefing his stick over to dive towards the enemy fighters. The Corsair rattled with the Gs, and he felt his vision darken as he brought the big fighter around just on the edge of a stall.

The German flight leader realized his error just as he was about to fire at the Japanese torpedo planes. Unfortunately, it was far too late for him to do anything, as Leibowitz squeezed his trigger. The six .50-caliber streams ripped the Zeewolfe's starboard wing off, the structure nearly flying back to hit Leibowitz as he hurtled by.

"Splash one!" Hall called out as his flight leader pulled up. Looking back, Leibowitz saw his wingman had ignored his orders and gone after his own Zeewolfe. Even as the German fighter fell away in flames, Leibowitz saw two more flights of Germans joining the fight.

The next sixty seconds were total chaos, as the second wave of Zeewolfes split their attentions between the escorting Corsairs and vulnerable Tenzans. Realizing they had the single flight of Corsairs temporarily outnumbered, the Germans struck and moved away. The tactic worked briefly, as the Tenzans were vulnerable targets. Two of the Japanese craft tumbled from the sky, their wings shorn by German cannon. The remainder, including Yoshida's, conducted evasive maneuvers as they attempted to make room for the American pilots to intercept.

It was at that point that the rest of VF-42 arrived, Commander Hart having made the decision to abandon *Yorktown*'s dive bombers in order to help his Blue Flight. Striking two of the Germans in the bounce, the tables were quickly turned as three Zeewolfes spun down into the Indian Ocean.

Leibowitz felt sweat pouring down his spine as he reached the top of his Immelmann turn. Spotting a Zeewolf closing in on a Tenzan, he traded altitude for speed to bring himself down on the German's port side. Just as with Leibowitz's last victim, the Zeewolf was focused on the Tenzan in front of him, its tail gunner firing ineffectively back at the closing German.

Boy is this bastard in for a surprise, Leibowitz thought angrily. He pulled the trigger on his joystick, and six fifty caliber machineguns barked at once, spitting streams of tracers. The three-second burst arced behind his target, and Leibowitz skidded desperately to add more lead. Belatedly realizing his danger, the German panicked and broke to port, greatly easing Leibowitz's gunnery problem. Nearly stalled, the German's vulnerable underbelly rolled towards Leibowitz at barely one hundred yards. The subsequent burst slammed up through the unarmored belly.

I must've caught something good, Leibowitz thought in a mixture of jubilation and horror as the Zeewolf lit up like a torch. He arced back around to give the enemy plane another burst, then stopped as he watched the enemy pilot pulled the canopy back.

I'm not a damn Nazi, he thought, thinking to reports of the Germans' actions over Great Britain. As he passed the doomed pilot, he saw that his opponent was wreathed in flames as he jumped.

"More bogeys coming in!"

"Let's cover our friends, gents!" Hart's voice crackled over the squadron radio. "Get them some space!"

How many carriers do the Krauts have out here?! Leibowitz briefly wondered. He saw a Zeewolf nail a Tenzan with a deflection shot, then die himself as two separate Corsairs shot the German to pieces. The VF-42 pilots had to break to avoid one another, and the dead German's wingman turned to follow one of them. Seeing that his own wingman had gone missing again, Leibowitz chased the Zeewolf. He was too late as the German's cannon fire set his prey ablaze.

Goddammit, Leibowitz raged. The Nazi waited an extra moment too long, perhaps hoping to shoot at the Corsair's pilot. Leibowitz dipped in right behind the German, and put enough .50 caliber rounds downrange to end the enemy pilot's victory streak. Unlike his latest victim, he did not remain, immediately breaking away from the burning Zeewolf to clear his own tail. Suddenly, the skies around him were clear.

"Blue Flight, status report," Leibowitz barked.

"Blue Three damaged, I splashed one."

"Blue Two, joined up with Gold Three."

"Red One, Blue One, my flight's scattered all over the place," Leibowitz said. "We're rejoining up on our charges."

There was silence.

"Anyone hear from Red Flight?" Leibowitz asked.

"This is Red Four," came a shaky, familiar voice. "Red One collided with Red Two, Red Three was shot down."

Oh shit, Leibowitz thought. He had just become a squadron commander.

"Bandits, three o'clock!"

Sure enough, there was another wave. Leibowitz banked right, and the Corsair turned hard, rumbling as it did, the G forces sinking Leibowitz into his seat. He flew head on into the enemy formation. To his right, he saw Hall moving in.

Those must be different Germans, he thought. The airframes didn't look like Zeewolfes, being more slender, but they still looked threatening to the Tenzan flight. He lined up on the leader as the two groups slashed into one another, firing a burst then breaking left. He heard Hall give a victory whoop as he pulled up, then turned around to see that Blue Two had come in and finished what he started. The enemy aircraft, despite being more slender, seemed much more clumsy and fragile than the Zeewolfes.

"Blue leader, this is Naginata leader," an accented voice said over his radio. "We have eyes on the enemy main force. We are engaging."

"Roger," acknowledged Leibowitz, his arms shaking from fatigue. "We'll keep the top covered. Let's make some space for 'em, boys!"

* * *

The Bridge of the IJN *Musashi*

Admiral Yamamoto was concerned, although his face remained impassive as the *Musashi* shrugged off another Italian battleship shell. Rear Admiral Truog was doing what he could with his remaining vessels, but the Axis light forces were starting to have enough of an advantage that a second torpedo attack was certainly in the offing. The first had heavily damaged USS *Alabama*, even as that vessel had seen off the *Roma* with a salvo of plunging fire. The *Yamato*, while still floating, had been forced to flood her main magazines.

If I had a choice, I would send her out of the line, Yamamoto thought grimly. *But she is absorbing fire, and her secondaries are part of the reason the Axis are being very careful before they commit another torpedo attack.* Even more importantly than the two destroyers she had destroyed, *Yamato*' guns had crippled *Littorio* and gravely injured *Vittorio Veneto*. The Italian vessels had clearly not been designed to fight at long distance; their decks lacked the ability to stand up to plunging fire. As Yamamoto listened, the initial air strikes were swarming the damaged ships.

"Admiral," the action officer said. "Fleet air main effort reports contact with *Bismarck* battle group."

It is about time, Yamamoto thought. As if on cue, the Germans' next salvo thudded into the flagship. *Their* shells were fully functional and effective, if not as deadly as their designers had likely hoped at this range.

"Excellent," said Yamamoto. "Direct all aircraft to engage."

* * *

Lieutenant Yoshida piloted his B6N closer to the target. Behind him, his bombardier excitedly called out the targets they were overflying.

"That's a Z-class destroyer! And a *Hipper*-class cruiser! We've found the enemy main force!"

Matsui radioed the initial sighting as Yoshida accelerated. He kept it steady, trying to ignore the bullet holes in his starboard wing. The engine was sounding a little funny, too, perhaps a machine gun round had nicked it, but his instruments were showing nothing out of the ordinary, so Yoshida kept his mind on the task at hand.

"Excellent," said Yoshida. "Let's keep an eye out for *Bismarck*. Soon as we see her, we're dropping."

He looked again at the reference picture on his dashboard, before looking back up. Through the broken clouds, punctuated by plumes of fire and smoke, Yoshida saw it. His heart raced. The mighty battleship had been damaged by an earlier attack by American dive bombers—its rear turrets appeared to be inoperable, with one smoking, badly. The radar mast was shorn off, as were a number of communications antennae. Yoshida knew he was here to deliver the killing blow. Just to be sure, he checked the profile against his target card, before looking back to make sure he was still flying on target.

"That's *Bismarck*," he said, as Matsui notified the squadron.

The six remaining B6Ns dropped low and level, over the water. As they did, they invited fire from *Bismarck*'s escorts. The beast's screen opened up with everything they had, tracers snaking out towards Yoshida and his comrades. One of the rounds slammed hard into Yoshida's windscreen, startling him with the impact. The rush of slipstream through the cracks made an eerie whistling sound as Yoshida leveled off.

Now comes the hard part, Yoshida thought. Off to starboard, one of his wingmen suddenly splashed into the water as flak blew out the B6N's engine. Far above, he saw the American Corsairs stop a sudden rush from enemy fighters.

Not as many of them as there were when we started, Yoshida thought. He stayed level, no longer worried about the threat from above, then checked his airspeed. Muttering, he dropped a few knots to get back within range and then fought to keep his aircraft at optimal height.

He had not come this far to have his weapon hit too fast or at the wrong angle and thus fail to arm or go off-course.

Look at the size of that thing, Yoshida thought, looking at the smoking, burning German battleship. He kept the Tenzan steady, the run seeming like an eternity even as his mental countdown told him it was less than ten seconds. The entire world seemed to move in slow motions, each piece of it spiraling at once—the German and Italian ships shooting anti-air, the other Tenzans off to his left and right, the breeze coming through the cracked cockpit windshield with more than a hint of an oil and smoke smell. It was terrifying—Yoshida knew he was vulnerable at this height and speed. It was also, in an odd way, quite serene with the falling water from splashes and spray.

From behind, Fujiwara gleefully announced release. The torpedo dropped from the B6N, and the aircraft lurched upwards as the weighty munition headed towards the surface. The torpedo hit water as Yoshida accelerated and then rapidly pulled up, evading the latest round of flak and machinegun bullets from the nearby ships. The other Tenzans dropped their torpedoes in the water and peeled out of the free-fire zone.

The five Type 91 torpedoes sped through the water towards the *Bismarck*' port side. Aboard *Bismarck*, her captain realized that he would not be able to avoid the five weapons from Yoshida's drop and the seven coming in from starboard. In a last minute effort, the man rang for all flank and turned towards the seven weapons, hoping to outrun the five from port.

The maneuver may have worked had *Bismarck* not been damaged. Two torpedoes missed entirely through the luck of the draw. One hit, through sheer chaotic fortune, a German Z-class destroyer, dooming the escort craft. All seven of the torpedoes from starboard were successfully dodged.

Unfortunately, *Bismarck*' evasive maneuvers weren't quite enough to get the warship out of trouble. The first torpedo hit, right on the ship's stern, the explosion blossoming directly beneath the painted swastika. The blast flooded the battleship's steerage compartment, and a nearby damage control crew was torn to shreds by fragments.

The next torpedo hit the ship's port side, exploding against the battleship's belt. The damage wasn't enough to penetrate into the vessel's vitals, but killed several of her crew and weakened her plating.

Yoshida's torpedo also struck the port side of *Bismarck*, but the pilot wasn't sure how much damage had been done. Aboard *Bismarck*, the damage control teams began their work. As Yoshida gained altitude, he saw, dispiritingly, *Bismarck*' two bow turrets open fire again. He'd failed.

Yoshida saw the rest of his flight align. His flight leader ordered the formation to return to base.

Yoshida shook with the energy of fear and disappointment. He did not come this far to fail. He would not just surrender now.

He broke formation, ignoring his squad mates' complaints on the radio, taking his Tenzan on a dive.

"Lieutenant!" shouted Fujiwara. "What are we doing?"

"Finishing this," growled Yoshida.

Visions raced through his head—his Tenzan crashing into the bridge of the *Bismarck*, the explosion killing the German admirals and staff members. A hero's funeral at home. The Nazis in full retreat. The smiles of his ancestors.

But as he turned to align his aircraft for the final approach, more visions passed through Yoshida's head—Reiko and Megumi crying over a flag-draped coffin, a jingoistic speech offering them no comfort. His parents unable to live peacefully without his care. His town decrying him as just another selfish samurai man, a relic from before modern times. His plane crashing into the side of *Bismarck* and doing no more damage than a fly crashing into a mountainside.

Yoshida righted himself, ignoring the increasingly frightened demands of Fujiwara.

As he brought the plane up, narrowly escaping the enemy anti-aircraft fire, he saw something—his torpedo had done more damage than he thought. *Bismarck* was moving, but slowly, and locked in a circle!

As he flew off, he radioed into his squadron leader the updated battle damage assessment, and hoped it would get to the right people in time.

* * *

USS *New Orleans*

The enemy gunfire had let up. It hadn't stopped, but Rear Admiral Truog had some room to breathe. Overhead, Pact and Axis fighters dueled in sprawling furballs as dive bombers broke the cloud cover to attack enemy ships. The air was filled with the smell of smoke, cordite, and oil, tainted just a little bit with what Truog recognized as the unmistakable stench of death.

New Orleans' AA defenses rattled off as an Italian dive bomber poked its way through the air coverage. Truog thought about trying to man one of the AA guns himself, but made the wiser choice to take cover against a nearby bulkhead. The 20mm shells shredded the enemy aircraft, and a sailor whooped as the enemy plane caught fire, impacting the water in front of the ship.

Damage control had got the A turret working again, and *New Orleans* was firing as much as it could, but Truog knew the screen was all but destroyed. He had started with two destroyer divisions—eight in total. *Clark* was all he had left, and *Clark* was sinking.

* * *

IJN *Musashi*
The Flag Bridge

The *Musashi* wasn't quite dead, but the big battleship was roughed up. Admiral Yamamoto was bleeding from his head. Blood obscured his vision, and smoke clogged his lungs as the smell of gunpowder, oil, and death strangled his nostrils. The ship's captain was considering abandoning ship.

We must hold on, Yamamoto thought. With *Yamato* now immobilized and *Alabama* sinking, *Musashi* was the only heavy unit left. With Admiral Nimitz roughly four hundred miles away on the rapidly closing *Ranger*, sacrificing the command and control of *Musashi* would doom the ships that accompanied her.

Still, I may not have much command and control left as is, he thought. His chief of staff was dead, torn in half by fragments of *Musashi's* heavy armor. Many of his staff had joined the man in death or were being dragged to the nearest makeshift sick bay. Commander Bailey, the American liaison, was helping drag wounded off the bridge.

Too many guns, he thought. *We were foolish to think Musashi and Yamato were the equal of any two of their vessels.* Even without penetrating *Musashi's* hide, the German and Italian vessels had done grievous damage

"Sir!" a signals officer said. "The gunnery officer reports *Bismarck* is circling, crippled!"

"*Bismarck*? How?" asked *Musashi's* captain.

"Torpedo bombers, sir," the signals officer said. "They managed to hit her stern!"

"Likely damage to the steerage compartment," remarked Yamamoto. He strode to the speaking tube down to the navigational bridge "Captain, let us finish this!"

Musashi's captain acknowledged, and *Musashi* came about to turn her broadside to the German battleship. Even as the secondaries began to engage the Axis destroyers that reacted to the maneuver by initiating a torpedo run, the gunnery officer laid his director onto the circling German. *Musashi's* three heavy turrets matched as the gunnery officer took two long minutes to make sure he had the *Bismarck*'s pattern down. All three turrets tracked on its path, then in beautiful unison, all nine guns fired.

The shock caused the battleship to leap in the water, nearly knocking Yamamoto off his feet. Closing his eyes against the concussion, after several breaths he opened them and raised his binoculars.

* * *

In his cockpit, Yoshida prayed, while above him, Leibowitz scanned the skies for any lingering Germans.

* * *

Aboard *Bismarck*, Vice Admiral Bey watched the smoke waft back from the Japanese battleship and knew what the sound of ripping canvas meant. Even as the men around him crouched, the German admiral remained defiantly upright. He had watched the massive Japanese battleship guns destroy his Italian counterparts and maul *Tirpitz*. Now, with a crippled flagship under his feet, Bey was well aware that his fate could be sealed.

* * *

It was not a perfect salvo. The majority of it was long, the last shell in the pattern hitting *Bismarck*'s heavily armored deck amidships.

* * *

Yoshida could not see what was happening to the enemy ship, but from behind him, his two crewmen cheered.

"*Musashi* has the range!" he heard Matsui shout.

"Not quite," Fujiwara replied. "But I am sending the correction!"

* * *

Onboard *Musashi*, the heavy guns were busy being reloaded. With some damage to the hoists and reduced power, it was an arduous process. After two of the longest minutes of her crew's life, the triple turrets roared again. Unknown to *Musashi's* gunnery officer, the hit had slowed *Bismarck's* circling speed, and the nine shells landed in a close pattern just forward of the German battleship's bow.

The process repeated once more, then again, each successive salvo resulting in another couple of hits. Even as *Musashi* evaded the German destroyers' final torpedoes, her guns fired for a fourth time.

For years afterwards, historians would debate exactly what killed *Bismarck*. Was it the torpedoes? Was it unexploded ordnance from the dive bombers? Or was it the naval gunnery from *Musashi?* They'd all take credit, but the truth was, *Bismarck* would've survived, were it not for all three. Four of *Musashi's* rounds impacted, although only the first hit was necessary. The shell punched deep into the vessel's forward magazines before exploding, its hot fragments doing the rest. In a series of volcanic blasts, the vessel's forward section disappeared in a ball of flame.

* * *

B*Ismarck's* demise coincided with the arrival of the second wave of strike aircraft from the Oahu Pact's carriers. With their German counterpart's fighters either decimated or in the process of refueling, the second wave wrought havoc upon the former Axis screening vessels. The overall Axis commander, Admiral Erich Lutjens, ordered a general retreat from the carrier *Graf Zeppelin.*

As the *Ranger* task force, including the Japanese carriers *Akagi* and *Kaga*, reached maximum range, the weather continued to favor the Oahu Pact's pursuit. For the pilots who had been forced to abandon their aircraft in the early afternoon, PBY Catalinas and H6K Flying Boats rounded up the survivors. By nightfall, the attack aircraft had managed to finish the retreating Italian battleships, with only the threat of land-based airpower and the need to try and save the damaged *Yamato* and *Musashi* preventing Admiral Nimitz from conducting a general pursuit. Even without it, the Axis fleet had lost all five battleships it began the day with.

* * *

IJN *Musashi*
The Flag Bridge
Three weeks later

"Well, I wish we were meeting under better circumstances, Admiral Yamamoto, but it is good to finally make your acquaintance," Admiral Chester Nimitz said, extending his hand.

Admiral Yamamoto gingerly accepted the American's gesture. While his wounds were far from major, it still hurt to move rapidly.

"Welcome to Singapore," Yamamoto said, gesturing for the man to sit down.

How odd the world is, Yamamoto thought. *Here I sit with an American admiral in a former British base preparing to discuss what comes next.*

"Thank you, Admiral," Nimitz replied. He nodded at Commander Bailey. "I trust our liaison has worked out well?"

Yamamoto smiled.

"I believe you have seen the citation I wrote for him?" Admiral Yamamoto replied. He enjoyed the look of surprise that flitted across Bailey's face.

"Yes, I have," Nimitz said. "I think Commander Bailey will be joining one of the Corsair pilots on my flagship for a presentation in the coming weeks."

Bailey was completely agog at that statement. Lieutenant Commander Leibowitz was already famous through the Oahu Pact for his actions during the Battle of the Horn and immediately following. The war's first ace after downing a couple of Condors, it was an open secret that Leibowitz would be getting a Navy Cross, if not the Medal of Honor.

"Very good," Yamamoto replied. "However, you did not come here to discuss presentations."

"No, I did not," Nimitz said, his face going grim. "With the heavy losses, I understand your government has asked for a temporary pause to offensive operations?"

"Yes," Yamamoto said, his tone neutral. The loss of *Yamato* had shaken the Navy Staff. Taken under tow, several of the battleship's transverse bulkheads had suddenly buckled under the strain of an Indian Ocean gale. Thankfully, only a skeleton crew had gone down with her, but it was still a most unpleasant coda to the Battle of the Horn.

"There are those in Washington who wonder if your reluctance is a sign of continued mistrust towards our nation," Nimitz said diplomatically. "Given the reports of the Italian Navy's mutiny, followed by the Germans seizing their ships as well as those of Britain and France, it would appear that now was a perfect time to strike *somewhere.*"

"I understand," Admiral Yamamoto replied. "But, as you are well aware, our nations have spent much of the last two decades preparing to fight one another. That we lost one of our two largest vessels and had the other one crippled has led some of the more unsavory members of our government to claim a conspiracy."

Nimitz nodded at that.

"You and your men fought well," he stated simply. "Well enough that ol' Adolph has apparently put a couple of his senior admirals up against the wall."

Yamamoto raised an eyebrow at that.

"While that worked for the Royal Navy once, I think he will find that less than helpful in the long term," Yamamoto replied. "It could be argued that I should have retreated rather than stay and fight once I realized the Italians were not nearly as damaged as we believed."

"I would have done the same in your shoes if I had two vessels like this one," Nimitz stated. "I do, however, have nine battleships and five carriers. Please impart onto your government that I would truly love to have several more I could count on."

Yamamoto nodded, standing. Nimitz followed suit.

"I will fervently do so," he stated. "With the hopes that this is not the last time we will work together, Chester."

*****

Philip S. Bolger Bio

Philip S. Bolger is an army veteran who left active duty service to work as a cog in the Military-Industrial Complex while pursuing his passion for writing. "Corsairs and Tenzans" is his first published short story. His debut novel, the Urban Fantasy adventure "The Devil's Gunman," was released in January of 2019. In his free time, he enjoys history, wargames, and pen and paper RPGs. He lives in the heart of Northern Virginia with his partner, Victoria, and their two dogs: Robert the Bruce and Francois Guizot. Philip can be reached at philipsbolgerauthor@gmail.com or via Facebook at his page: https://www.facebook.com/philbolgerwrites/.

#####

For a Few Camels More
by Justin Watson

There—there they were; the faintest flicker of white against a deep black gap in the nighttime ocean. The shadowy form swayed up and down in Masayoshi's reticle. It *was* a ship, her stern running lights just now visible. Now with a point of reference, Masayoshi methodically swept the periscope left and right, making out two more black blots of similar size and at least one smaller ship trailing them. The ships were flanked on one side by the darkened mass of the island of Sumatra, on the other by the Malay Peninsula.

"*Kuso*," Masayoshi murmured as he leaned back from the periscope. Only the ping-whine of the hydrophone set and the beeping of the radar from the control room below answered his low curse. The two men standing in the conning tower with him held their tongues while the Captain thought.

We're in a stern chase with them now. I'd hoped to intercept them before they entered the narrow part of the strait.

"Down scope," Masayoshi ordered, and the quartermaster, a young enlisted man who'd served under him during the last year of the war, sent the periscope column down.

Captain Tanaka Masayoshi was a small, whipcord thin man. He'd always been slight of stature but the starvation conditions of '44 and

'45 had given him a permanently cadaverous appearance. With cold black eyes and a perpetual scowl, Masayoshi's aspect was that of an angry revenant hunting the sea lanes for victims.

Reaching into a breast pocket on his dungarees, Masayoshi retrieved a pack of cigarettes, tapped one out and lit it with a long, satisfying inhale. The soothing burn of nicotine entering his lungs didn't soften the hard lines of Masayoshi's face, but the tension in his shoulders eased fractionally.

If only they were Nat Sherman's.

Though Japan did not officially name her submarines, his crew had unofficially dubbed their vessel the *Funayurei* after the vengeful sea-ghosts of Japanese legend. Most of the men on this boat had served under Masayoshi during the war and the youngest amongst them were already in their mid-twenties. That was one of the reasons the fledgling reborn Japanese navy had come knocking at Masayoshi's door for this job. He was one of only four Japanese submarine captains to survive the war, and his old crew was likewise intact.

Admiral Komatsu had given him one of the three surviving I-201 submarines for this mission. Like her sister ships, this boat had never seen combat, finishing the war tied up to the pier at the Kure Naval Yard. She was shorter than many of her peers from the war years, sleek and deadly, capable of dizzying speeds beneath the waves and armed with the fastest torpedoes with the highest blast yield of any such weapon yet conceived.

Like the legendary ninja of Masayoshi's home city of Koga, the *Funayurei* was meant to fall upon an enemy swiftly and silently, execute merciless violence, and slip away before her foes could retaliate. Even Masayoshi's deadened soul sung in response to the anticipation, the untapped martial potential in her very steel.

No, you clever bitch, Masayoshi took another hard drag and left the cigarette clasped between his lips as he descended the ladder from the conning tower into the control room. *What's dead should stay dead.*

With a much diminished beam compared to most subs, the interior of the I-201 submarine was inhumanly cramped, even by submariners' standards. The torpedo data computer, or TDC, as well as the table holding the navigational plot, were both within three feet of the ladder. The TDC was a fancy new model twice the size of what they'd had in the war, with a plethora of knobs, switches, and dials. Its finicky electronic components were the reason *Funayurei* was the first Japanese submarine equipped with air conditioning.

Soft, Masayoshi took another deep drag off the sub-par cigarette. *Still, who likes sweating their testicles off?*

"Captain," a tentative, young voice spoke up from the chair in front of the TDC. "Is it wise to smoke while we're submerged?"

Masayoshi turned to the officer manning the TDC, Lieutenant Komatsu. Tall and handsome, somehow neat-looking despite two weeks at sea with no showers, he was Masayoshi's weapons officer, the admiral's nephew, and the only stupid sonofabitch who wasn't here for the pay. He was also the only one who knew how to work the new TDC, which was why he was sitting there instead of an enlisted operator. That usefulness might have saved his life already on this voyage because his enthusiasm grated on both the crew and his captain.

"Don't worry, Lieutenant, the boat needs the nicotine. She's addicted too," Masayoshi said, letting smoke roll out of his nostrils as he turned away.

"I only saw four ships, but visibility is shit," Masayoshi said. "What time is moonrise tonight?"

"Sir, moonrise is at 0013 hours,"

A sailor with iron-shaded hair and a craggy face spoke up from where he stood between the helmsman and the planesman.

"Sounds like our convoy, Captain," said Chief Petty Officer Hiroshi in a gravelly voice, not taking his eyes off the ballast indicators.

Masayoshi nodded. "Probably."

"Captain," Komatsu said, an edge of eagerness creeping into his voice. "We can be close enough to commence our attack at dawn."

"No, I don't think so," Masayoshi said. "The escorts are dispersed throughout the convoy, we could kill one of the escorts and perhaps a freighter as well but the other two would have us then. We're fast underwater, but not faster than a destroyer; we'll need open ocean and deeper waters to escape."

"Sir," Komatsu said. "If this convoy gets to Indochina unscathed, we will not get paid."

Cutting to the heart of the matter for once, Masayoshi thought. *Perhaps the boy is a little more self-aware than we give him credit for.*

"I know that, Lieutenant, and they won't," Masayoshi said, stepping over to the maneuvering board, motioning for his Weapons Officer and Chief Petty Officer to follow. "Fall back out of visual range. Once we're beyond visual, surface and match course and speed with the target."

"Surface?" Komatsu said, belatedly adding, "Captain?"

"We may have to track them through the whole strait, Lieutenant," Masayoshi said. "That's a three day transit. Our batteries could carry us for two of those days submerged at about half our target's speed. No, we'll run barely surfaced through the night up until zero-four-hundred hours. Then we'll submerge and close the gap a bit."

"Yes, sir," Komatsu said, nodding slowly. "When do you anticipate commencing our attack on the convoy?"

Masayoshi's scowl deepened.

"When I'm damn good and ready," he growled around the glowing cigarette planted in the corner of his mouth. "Set the watches, two hours apiece, two lookouts and the officer of the watch on the bridge at all times. You take last watch. Nothing's likely to happen in the next few hours so I'm going to get some sleep. Wake me if I'm wrong or if we get to 0400, and I'm not up."

* * *

Standing on the portside of the main gun turret of the French destroyer *Marceau,* formerly the Kriegsmarine destroyer *Z31,* Captain Louis Lefebvre grimaced at the sight of one of his merchant shipping charges falling behind the others.

A bull of a man, with a full but carefully manicured red beard and a sharp widow's peak, Lefebvre often walked the deck of the *Marceau* a few times to clear his head before going to bed. A long-service sailor, he adjusted his gait for the way the waves rolled and pitched the destroyer without conscious effort.

Through his binoculars, Lefebvre could see the top deck of the merchantman lined with armored vehicles secured to the ship with chains. This particular ship, the *Oroville,* was festooned with boxy hulls of enough Panzer III tanks to equip a light armored regiment. Shaking his head and muttering imprecations upon the heads of all merchant sailors, Lefebvre turned on his heel and stalked aft across the deck and ascended the ladder to the Combat Information Center with the grace of a much younger man.

"Commodore on deck," a seaman announced as Lefebvre stepped through the hatch into the CIC. Although his rank was actually captain, Lefebvre was commander of the entire convoy and not this particular ship; ergo he received a verbal promotion to Commodore.

The CIC was crowded with analog charts as well as radio and radar sets. All of the electronics were state of the art. Credit where it was due, the Germans had refitted the old destroyer with some of the newest stuff coming out of Siemens & Halske as part of the sale to their French clients. Personally, Lefebvre believed that was because they wanted to see if the shit would work with French asses on the line before they trusted German lives with it. In the middle of the night the conversation in the CIC was muted, but enlisted technicians and operators still worked their machines and updated status boards with inexorable, if bored, efficiency.

"As you were," Lefebvre said reflexively, encouraging the CIC's crew to continue their normal operations.

Lieutenant Commander Henri Allard, captain of the *Marceau*, looked up from a glowing green radar screen and nodded at his commander. Allard was of medium height and build with black hair and an easygoing manner.

"Good evening, sir," he said with a wry smile. "Shouldn't you be asleep?"

"I could say the same to you, Henri," Lefebvre said. "Do we have *Oroville* in radio contact?"

"Yes, sir, should we raise them?" Allard asked.

"Yes, do."

It took five minutes for Oroville to answer.

"Marceau, this is Oroville, what is it, over?" A sleepy, irritated voice answered.

Both Allard and the young radio operator's faces wrinkled in disgust at the unprofessionalism. Lefebvre held out a hand for the radio's microphone.

"*Oroville*, this is Commodore Lefebvre," he said. "Are you having engine troubles? Over."

"Uh, no, sir, but this pace is burning fuel awfully fast," the voice said, still audibly annoyed but more deferential.

"You're not here to conserve fuel, *Oroville,* you're here to accomplish the mission," Lefebvre said. "Need I send a detachment of marines to help you remember that? Speed up and get back in formation. Out."

Lefebvre handed the microphone back to the young seaman before the *Oroville* had a chance to respond and jerked his head to the right, indicating that Allard should join him out on the deck.

"We have to tighten them up, Henri," Lefebvre said as they stepped out into the damp night air of the Malacca Strait. *Oroville* was closing the gap and allowing his other warships, the torpedo boats, really pocket destroyers *Lorrain* and *Alsacien,* to likewise assume a better defensive posture. The *Marceau* herself was a full destroyer, a veteran of many battles.

"Easier said than done, sir," Allard said. "It's been a long voyage already, and both our men and the merchies know that there hasn't been any enemy naval activity more than five kilometers from the Indochinese coast in three years."

"There's a first time for everything," Lefebvre murmured.

"Sir, respectfully, where would the Viet Minh even find a warship with the range to trouble us this far out?" Allard said.

"Where did they find enough artillery, mortars and small arms to outfit a whole army?" Lefebvre retorted. "By some reports the *Rubis* and *Minerve* have been running covert supply missions for the Viet Minh on the Americans' payroll. If they were to repurpose them to engage us, and we aren't prepared, they could clean sweep this convoy."

The *Rubis* and *Minerve* were French submarines that had escaped capture by the Nazis and defected with the rest of the Free French diehards to the United States after the fall of Britain.

"De Gaulle's men are fanatics, but I can't believe even they would aid the Viet Minh against their own countrymen," Allard said, his normally placid expression betraying alarm.

"Why not?" Lefebvre asked, bitterly. "As far as they are concerned, we are Nazi collaborators and traitors."

Allard was quiet for a long moment, staring at his commander.

"Do you regret not joining them, Louis?" Allard asked, gently.

Lefebvre exhaled slowly. Allard rarely used his first name, but Lefebvre did not correct his familiarity. Allard had served as Lefebvre's XO aboard the *Guepard*, a Free French destroyer. As long as an ally was actively fighting the Nazis, Lefebvre, Allard and the rest of their officers and men had been committed to continuing the war.

But then the Germans had invaded England and London had capitulated. All Churchill's pretty words about fighting to the bitter end were reduced to ash. There was no Allied realm left to continue the fight. The Americans accepted the Free French defectors and granted them asylum, but they proved unwilling to enter the war against the Nazis, even as they willingly wielded their new French clients against the Japanese.

Lefebvre surrendered his command to the Germans without further resistance. The Vichy government rewarded his compliance a few years later with the resumption of his service and even a promotion in the new French Navy; in the service of the Greater Reich, of course.

"No, Henri, I don't regret it," he said, sadly but firmly. "The war has been over for ten years. De Gaulle and his remaining men are fucking fools. Damn the Americans for indulging them in their delusions."

The two men stood together staring out into the rippling black sea for long silent seconds, both of their minds churning with past tragedies and uncertain futures.

* * *

The sake he'd brought with him aboard the *Funayurei* let Masayoshi sleep, but it didn't keep the nightmares away. In his sleep, he heard once again the endless bleating of the hydrophone amidst a dozen enemy propellers, felt the blast of depth charges rattling his boat like a tin can. He saw a woman's corpse amongst a ruined house, half retaining its former delicate beauty, half charred and shredded into so much meat. In a small shack by the sea he held a young boy's body in his arms in ghastly repose, eyes open and staring, features pinched from malnourishment and pale from fever. He remembered the cold metal of the Nambu pistol's muzzle under his chin. He was sitting in that same shack back on the coast of the main island. Release was so close, all he had to do was apply a little more pressure and it would be over, but some bastard wouldn't stop knocking at his door.

Can't a man even kill himself in peace?

His eyes fluttered open. Outside his cabin door he heard a muffled voice.

"Captain, it's 0400," Komatsu said. "You told me to wake you."

Masayoshi groaned and wiped a hand over his face to clear the moisture. Unlike the conn, his cabin was not afforded the luxury of air conditioning, and even sleeping in nothing but a pair of skivvy shorts he awoke slick with sweat. He swung his legs over the side of the bed and forced himself erect.

"I heard you," he growled at the door. "Be out in a minute."

Five minutes later when Masayoshi opened the door to his cabin, Komatsu was still standing there. Masayoshi checked his stride and glared at the younger man.

"I can take your change of watch brief in the conn, Lieutenant," he said.

"Yes, sir, of course," Komatsu said, too quickly. "I would request a word in private, Captain."

Fuck me, what now?

Masayoshi sighed and stepped back, motioning for Komatsu to step inside the cramped sleeping quarters. The lieutenant stood in front of his narrow writing desk at rigid attention.

"Alright, Komatsu," Masayoshi said as he shut the door, sealing them both into a space less than six feet across. Masayoshi didn't sit, but stood with his arms crossed. "What is it?"

"First of all, sir," said Komatsu. "I want to apologize for questioning you in front of the crew."

Masayoshi grunted noncommittally.

"Something else?" Masayoshi said when his XO seemed to be having trouble continuing his side of the conversation.

Komatsu's eyes flicked nervously to the door and then locked back onto Masayoshi's face. The captain could see the younger man steeling his resolve.

"Sir, I mean no disrespect, but why are we taking such a timid course?" Komatsu said.

"I explained my reasoning," Masayoshi said, rubbing a hand across his jaw. *Not that you were owed an explanation.*

"I understand, Captain, but—" Komatsu looked at a loss for words for a moment, then the next sentence came in a rush. "Captain, you are Tanaka Masayoshi."

"Last I checked, yes, I was," Masayoshi said, and his temples throbbed at what he knew was coming next.

"You sank three American destroyers and the aircraft carrier *Hornet* with a boat nowhere near as fast or quiet as an I-201," Komatsu said. "If you can infiltrate a carrier battle group and destroy a flattop surrounded by the best surface warships the Americans had to offer *and survive*, what threat are a destroyer and two torpedo boats built back in the 30's?"

Masayoshi pressed the heel of his palm into his right eye, willing the sudden headache to go away.

"We attacked the *Hornet's* carrier group alone because we had no other choice," Masayoshi said, trying not to snarl. "The Americans were at the very doorstep of the mainland. We threw everything we had at them and still they barreled through. It was desperation, not tactical brilliance, that drove me into that course of action, and I wouldn't risk it again if I had any other choice."

"Our mission, though, sir—"

"Our *contract*," Masayoshi corrected. "You're still thinking like we're the Imperial Navy. We are not. We're mercenaries, Lieutenant; contracted pirates, and we don't get paid if we don't survive."

"Sir, if these contracts go well, you know it could mean the rebirth of our Navy," Komatsu said, and the zealot's gleam in his eye made Masayoshi feel physically ill. "With enough funding, we could all be back in Imperial uniform."

"I don't care," Masayoshi said. "War is war, it doesn't matter what tailor you go to. I do it because I'm good at it and these men would be wasted under a lesser officer." *Like you.* "Everything else is a distraction." *Like you.*

"But, sir, the glory of the Empire—"

Masayoshi took a step forward, glaring black-edged hatred up into the younger man's face. The lieutenant hit his head on a bulkhead support trying to back up.

"FUCK the glory of the Empire," Masayoshi hissed. "Fuck the uniform and fuck the Emperor."

Komatsu looked as if he were about to throw up, and his lower lip quivered. Masayoshi continued his assault.

"We need this job in the first place because that limp-wristed twit sitting on the throne allowed his generals to start a war we had no chance of winning and then refused to surrender until the Americans had turned our cities to ash. We're not here to serve him, we're here to do a job, and we're going to do it, but we're going to *survive* to collect our pay.

"If you die out here for the glory of your Emperor, your oh-so-honorable uncle the Admiral will make sure that pretty young wife of yours wants for nothing. If these men die, their families will not be so fortunate. Some of the more attractive widows might luck out and end up the kept woman of but one American officer, perhaps even one who washes regularly, but most will have to choose either watching their children die slowly or sucking twelve cocks a day to get the rations they need. The glory of the Empire means nothing to me compared to that. Not. A. Fucking. Thing."

Komatsu's eyes were wide and round. Masayoshi thought the young officer might cry. He didn't give a shit.

"I suggest you jettison your 'three-cheers-for-the-emperor' bullshit," Masayoshi concluded. "Your duty is to these men. Everything else is a fucking lie. No response is expected, Lieutenant, and you are dismissed."

* * *

Rolling walls of thick gray smoke billowed across the waters of the Malacca Strait, reducing visibility to less than a hundred meters. The crew of *Marceau* coughed and spat at their stations; the reduced air quality, piled on top of the heat and humidity, served to maximize the misery throughout the convoy.

"Where the hell did all this smoke come from?" Lefebvre asked as he stepped back into the CIC.

"Forest fire on Sumatra, sir," Allard said. He was standing near the hydrophone operator. "We talked to the Brits at Fort de Kock via radio. According to them, massive fires are pretty common this time of year. We have bigger problems, though."

"What is it, Captain?" Lefebvre said, eyebrows drawing sharply together.

"Tell him, Chauncey," Allard said to the sandy-haired enlisted man who sat at the hydrophone, earphones clamped over his head.

"Sir, I picked up something submerged on active sonar," the young sailor said. "But it was very faint. The acoustics in this part of the channel are terrible."

"Too faint for a positive identification, I assume?" Lefebvre said.

"Yes, sir," Chauncey said. "It was a submarine, sir, I'd bet my ass on it, but I have no idea whose submarine it is."

"You have bet your ass on it, son," Lefebvre's red bearded face split in a wide grin to take any sting off the remark. "Good work, Chauncey. Keep listening and tell us if you hear anything else."

"I already checked with the Brits about the contact, as well," Allard said when they stepped away from the hydrophone station. "They say they don't have anything in the Strait. It could be the Americans keeping tabs on us, or maybe you were right, and they do have *Rubis* or *Minerve*."

"Possibly," Lefebvre said, chewing on his lip unconsciously. "What if the Americans sold a few submarines cheap and provided volunteers the way they have for the air war?"

"A few jets is one thing, sir," Allard said. "Even their old World War II subs aren't cheap. The Viet Minh couldn't pay for them even at cost."

"Still…" Lefebvre murmured to himself for a moment. "*Alsacien* is out, her captain is too timid for this kind of work, but Bisset; he's audacious enough for the job. Tell the *Lorrain* I want them to fall behind and assume a search pattern across the strait. Hug the coast and wait at least one hour before using active sonar. We've established there are no friendly submarines operating in the area; if he detects a submarine in that time, report it to us and follow it. If it displays hostile intent, he is to engage on my authority."

* * *

Even during the day, *Funayurei* slowed and came up to periscope depth occasionally for twenty-second stints. The chance of the French spotting the slender periscope head was slim, especially if they kept the exposure to less than half a minute. Masayoshi and most of his men had sailed the Malacca Strait before, so they weren't as taken aback by the smoke as their French enemies, but it was still a nuisance, especially since they were only an hour or so out from the Singapore Strait where they hoped to make their attack.

"Down scope. Can't see shit anyway," Masayoshi said. "Fucking forest fires."

He was in the conning tower again with his quartermaster and a phone talker.

"Sir, one contact behind us now," Sakai, the radar operator called up to the conning tower. "Range estimate five kilometers."

"Are you sure?" Masayoshi leaned down to talk into the control room from the tower.

"Yes, sir," Sakai said. "And only four of the enemy vessels are ahead."

Masayoshi thought for only a second.

"Officer of the Deck, come about to one-eight-zero," he snapped.

"One-eight-zero, aye," Komatsu acknowledged. "Helm, left full rudder. New course one-eight-zero."

"Left full rudder aye. My rudder is left full. Coming to new course one-eight-zero," the Helmsman echoed a third time.

They hadn't even completed the turn when Ito spoke up.

"Sir, new contact, it's the other torpedo boat," Ito said. "He's pinging us with active sonar now."

"Understood," Masayoshi said.

"We can't outrun them, sir," Komatus said from his position at the TDC below. "The *Ebling* class can make close to forty knots."

"Understood." Masayoshi nodded again; everything but the tactical problem before him forgotten. They were in between this ship and the rest of the convoy. If the convoy's other escorts turned, they could close a noose around *Funayurei* while they were still in the Malacca Strait. They were unlikely to survive a coordinated depth charge attack from three vessels in this shallow, narrow waterway.

There was another option, in a few kilometers they could peel south between Rangsang and Karimunbesar Islands, but that detour gave the rest of the convoy good odds of making it to Saigon before even the speedy I-201 class sub could catch up with them. Then his men wouldn't get paid.

Masayoshi slid down the ladder into the control again to confer with his crew.

"Komatsu, what kind of forward armament do they have on that boat?" He said.

"Just their 105mm gun, sir," Komatsu said. "No forward depth charge throwers and their torpedo tubes are lateral."

"Understood," said Masayoshi. "In that case, all ahead full. Komatsu, stay on the TDC and prepare to calculate a firing solution."

"Yes, sir," Komatsu said. This time, Masayoshi could not bring himself to begrudge the young man his enthusiasm. Masayoshi's own blood sang with impending battle.

"We're going to close to one thousand meters and fire all four tubes. I want a good spread, he'll probably start zig-zagging any moment," Masayoshi said, loud enough for the whole control room to hear. "Once we've fired, we're going to dive thirty-degrees down bubble until we're damn near scraping the bottom and pass underneath them. We don't have a lot of water to play with and if our fish don't end him, he's going to be pissed and in a position to do something about it."

With that, Masayoshi crawled back up the ladder into the conning tower.

For several agonizing minutes Masayoshi stood with Irikawa, his quartermaster, and Yoshi, his phone talker, in the claustrophobia-inducing confines of the conning tower, while *Funayurei* closed the distance. Masayoshi couldn't stop himself from drumming on the periscope column, itching to give the order to reduce speed and bring the scope up.

But if they slowed too soon, they would be an easy target for the torpedo boat, and if he tried to put the periscope up at full speed, he was likely to rip the damn thing off. There was nothing to do but wait. Three more minutes, two…one…thirty seconds, twenty…ten…

"Officer of the Deck, signal engines to reduce to one-third," Masayoshi shouted down into the control room. "Up scope!"

After the officer of the deck repeated the order to the engine room, and they felt the boat slowing, the quartermaster sent the scope back up. Masayoshi gripped the periscope's handles like a drowning man grasping a preserver and put his eye to the piece, zeroing in on the enemy in a matter of seconds.

"New bearing three-four-niner," Masayoshi said as he depressed the switch on the periscope to get a radar reading.

"Bearing three-four-niner," the QM called down.

"Three-four-niner, aye," Komatsu said, his hands flying across the state-of-the-art TDC like a concert pianist performing a well-practiced concerto.

In the circle of the periscope's field of view the enemy ship began to zig zag as he'd predicted, and a plume of gray smoke blossomed out of its bow gun turret. The shriek-crack of the round passing overhead caught up almost a full second later, followed by the splash and detonation well behind them.

"Officer of the Deck, come starboard two zero degrees and maintain course for twenty seconds, then come port two zero degrees," Masayoshi shouted down the ladder. "Let's see if we can't get a better angle."

Masayoshi leaned into the sway of his boat as they fought to envelop the approaching French torpedo boat. His heart beat rapidly, but not painfully, and he found his lips curling in a smile. They were in the last bit, the breaths between life and death.

Masayoshi tweaked the scope left and right as the boat maneuvered, keeping the enemy in his reticle even as the *Funayurei* banked beneath him. Another gray cloud erupted from the French vessel, this time the freight train sound of the artillery round flying through the air was only a breath behind, the splash-detonation close enough to be felt as well as heard.

"New bearing mark, two-five-niner," Masayoshi said, his voice unstrained by the enemy's fire.

"Bearing two-five-niner," Hiroshi called out, with Komatsu echoing immediately.

Well, that's a little better. Hiroshi studied the white-capped bow wave preceding the torpedo boat intently for a few seconds to estimate speed; they didn't have the time for the sonar operator to count propeller RPMs.

"Target speed, three-six knots, range one-five-zero-zero meters," he said.

"Three-six knots, aye, one-five-zero-zero meters, aye!" Komatsu acknowledged.

Now for the tricky part.

With a practiced eye, Masayoshi estimated the average course of the torpedo boat's to-and-fro progression across the water and compared it to the orientation of his own vessel in his mind's eye for the last bit of data Komatsu would need for a firing solution.

"Target angle," he said, "port two-one-zero."

"Port two-one-zero, aye," Komatsu said, almost shouting in excitement. "Calculating firing solution."

Masayoshi took several deep breaths. On an unaware target, he would've taken several predictive measures from the TDC and matched them against the target's actual position to verify the firing solution, but a third splash-detonation behind them that Masayoshi felt in his fillings indicated they didn't have time for that security margin.

"Got it!" Komatsu said, his professional façade cracking. "Solution calculated for four torpedoes fired at two second intervals."

"Make tubes one through four ready for firing," Masayoshi commanded, his heart racing with excitement, his knuckles white on the periscope handles as he waited for the torpedomen to come back with, "Up!"

"Final solution, match bearings…Shoot One!" He said, and instantly the trill of a Type 95 torpedo speeding through water filled the hydrophone.

"Tube fired electrically!" Komatsu provided.

Masayoshi waited another heartbeat, "Shoot Two...Shoot Three...Shoot Four. Down scope. Dive officer, thirty degrees down bubble! Make depth ninety-meters."

"All torpedoes running true, Captain," Ito supplied from down in the control room as negative gravities sent all their stomachs into their throats.

A fourth artillery round from the enemy shook the boat hard enough to knock the navigator to the deck even as their fish churned towards the enemy. The *Funayurei's* hull groaned under the strain of the dive and the increasing water pressure. For twenty seconds, they heard nothing over the hydrophone, for thirty seconds, and forty-five, nothing.

That means only one fish left...

THOOM. The sound of a torpedo hitting a hull over the hydrophone pick-up was an old, well-loved song to Masayoshi and his men. The reverberation of the detonation through the water was powerful enough to jostle Masayoshi against the column of the periscope and make his ear ache, and over the blast they heard steel bending, breaking, shearing, and being sent to the bottom of the ocean. The crew was too professional to cheer, but there was a muted, collective grunt of approval and few dark chuckles at the death of the diminutive French vessel.

"Sir, we have fulfilled the terms of our contract," Komatsu said, formally. "Should we set course for Haiphong?"

Despite Komatsu's best efforts to keep his tone neutral, Masayoshi picked up on the hopeful, almost pleading note in the boy's voice. He looked around at the rest of his crew, saw the eager tension in their posture. He realized that he was smiling himself, that he felt better today than he had in six years.

Damn you, girl, Masayoshi silently cursed his vessel, but could muster no real heat for her.

"We have six more torpedoes, Lieutenant," Masayoshi said. "We can't very well go home with unexpended ordinance."

"Yes, sir," Komatsu said, grinning broadly. Masayoshi shook his head, but when he looked around at his men, felt their pride, their belief in themselves, and he could not bring himself to regret this fool's errand. If the price of feeling the steel of a warship binding their souls together once again was their death—so be it.

"They won't be prepared for our speed," Masayoshi said. "My bet is they'll put their big destroyer at the rear of the convoy in hopes we follow directly. With their torpedo boat in lead, we'll swing wide—wider than any other sub could and hope to catch up to them, then approach their lead ships, unload on them and run for the open ocean."

Komatsu's face split in a grin.

"Banzai, Captain."

"Oh, shut the fuck up," Masayoshi said, but even in his own ears, the reproof lacked bile.

They had their first kill, and the hunt was still young.

* * *

Lefebvre found himself with little to do except listen to radio traffic. *Lorrain* was gone with most of her crew. God be praised, their proximity to Sumatra had enabled rapid rescue of the remaining survivors, about forty in all, but the ship herself was already a wreck at the bottom of the strait and tomb to most of her crew; *his* men.

They had no idea where the attacking submarine was.

Allard didn't need his boss sticking his nose in *Marceau's* shipboard operations, and the *Alsacien* was leading the rest of the freighters toward Saigon. So Lefebvre stood, trying to appear the stoic commodore on the bridge as *Marceau* traced a wide back and forth search pattern a few miles behind the rest of the freighters.

A loud SNAP drew his gaze away from the ocean to one of the manual plotting boards. There a young sailor with jet black hair and an over-prominent nose gave a shamefaced, "Pardon." In his right hand the boy held the remnants of a grease pencil snapped in two from him pushing too hard on it.

Apparently my attempts to appear calm and unconcerned are of limited utility to the men.

Lefebvre looked at the hands on the clock set to local time above the bridge hatch. It was 1704 hours, less than two hours since the *Lorrain* had died. The tension of action delayed was unbearable, and Lefebvre knew that all his men were feeling the strain of it. For all they knew, the American, or whoever was manning that submarine, had already retired from the pursuit, or they could be under another torpedo attack any second. Once in action, his crew would know what to do, it was the interminable waiting in the dark that wore on the stoutest of warriors.

Fortunately, they were now leaving the Singapore Strait and within the hour they would be within the combat radius of the Fock-Wulfe 200 patrol aircraft out of Tourane Airfield in Da Nang. If the enemy captain chose to pursue into those waters, he'd find his chances of survival rapidly diminishing. The next minutes were the most dangerous.

"*Marceau,* this is *Alsacien,*" a tinny voice came over the radio speaker set to the convoy command net. "We have contact to our starboard at one-five hundred meters, submerged and constant-bearing, decreasing-range...oh, shit, fish in the water!"

Lefebvre's fatigue evaporated like a drop of butter on a red-hot skillet at the report of torpedo attack.

"Captain, bring us about," he said. "If *Alsacien* can't stop him from getting in amongst the merchies, we'll be too late to do anything but avenge them."

Orders given, Lefebvre went back to practicing his stoic glare, but his mind was churning furiously.

How the hell did they get ahead of us?

* * *

"Match bearings, Shoot One and Two," Masayoshi said and watched in satisfaction as the Type 95 torpedoes churned white trails through the water, their kerosene-oxygen engines propelling the largest warhead of any submarine-launched torpedo at unrivaled velocity.

The French torpedo boat must have detected them a second before they fired because it started a sharp bank to port, but it was too late. Masayoshi's timing was too good, and Komatsu's operation of the new TDC too precise.

The first torpedo caught the target right between the propeller shafts, sending the aft quarter of the vessel bucking into the air in an orange-gray cloud, dipping the bow into the ocean for a moment. The spray of water from the submergence and resurfacing of the ship's forward quarter hadn't even settled when the second torpedo took her amidships. Even from a kilometer away, Masayoshi could hear the enemy ship's steel spine rend and snap amidst the noise of the blast.

"We got him," Masayoshi affirmed without taking his eye away from the periscope.

"Sir, the destroyer has broken off its search pattern," Sakai reported from the Radar station. "It's headed towards us; estimate at least thirty-knots and accelerating."

"Sir, that's the *Z31*," Komatsu supplied. "According to our friends, the French did equip her with forward-firing mortars capable of delivering depth charges."

"Understood," Masayoshi acknowledged as he swept the periscope over to the lead cargo ship. "Officer of the Deck, come port ten degrees. Match course with the lead freighter."

"Aye, Captain," the officer of the deck acknowledged. "Left standard rudder, come port ten degrees."

Masayoshi swayed easily with the ship as it made a sharp left turn.

"Sonar," Masayoshi said. "Find me the smoothest bit of rock on this part of the ocean floor."

"Aye, Captain," Ito acknowledged the order

"Here's what we're going to do," Masayoshi said between his knees. "We don't have time for a fancy firing solution, so we're going to get to point blank range on the lead freighter and give her two torpedoes, then we're going to ground and shut down. After a few depth charges we'll release oil and detritus from Ballast One."

"What if the French aren't fooled?" Komatsu asked from down below.

"Even if they're not, sir," Chief Hiroshi spoke up. "That destroyer captain will have to get his other cows back inside the fence fast. For all he knows, we may have friends coming too."

"So we take two combatants and a freighter," Komatsu said. "And live to get paid."

Masayoshi leaned back from the periscope for a second, looked appraisingly down at Komatsu and allowed the slightest upward twitch of his lips.

"We'll make a pirate of you yet, Lieutenant."

* * *

Lefebvre's jaw worked as he saw the *Alsacien* gutted by two torpedo impacts.

Sacre merde, they were too fast, and too fucking big. The Americans aren't supposed to have anything like that.

"Commodore we have a fix on the enemy," Allard said. "But he's danger close to the *Oroville*."

"The *Oroville* is already dead," Lefebvre said. "Fire at will."

* * *

"Shoot Three and Four!"

At knife-fighting range, it only took seconds for the *Funayurei's* torpedoes to reach the ponderous freighter and rip her guts out, filling her hold with water and dragging her inexorably into the depths.

A heartbeat after the *Funayurei* sent two torpedoes speeding into the French merchant ship's hull; two nearby explosions rocked the submarine almost as if in sympathetic reaction. Masayoshi was thrown against the wall of the conning tower, but his phone-talker steadied him with an outstretched hand.

Whoever is working those mortars is pretty good, and bold. I didn't expect them to start firing so close to one of their freighters.

"Down scope," Masayoshi shouted, releasing the handles of the periscope column.

"Dive officer, put us on the bottom," Masayoshi shouted. "Let's cuddle up to that patch of sand Ito found us."

The ocean floor in this part of the straight was just beyond *Funayurei's* test depth and the steel of the hull groaned under the rapidly increasing water pressure. Komatsu gave a swift surreptitious glance to the bulkhead. Just as they were coming level, another two explosions rocked their submarine.

"Captain, should I jettison the oil and detritus?" Komatsu asked.

A third pair of depth charges detonated above them and Masayoshi's ears began to hurt from the concussion, which carried even through the steel of *Funayurei's* hull.

"Wait, son," Masayoshi said, grinning at the young man's discomfiture. "They'll suspect the ruse if it's too early. We've got to take a little more before we send up the oil and debris. Don't worry, the Chief was telling you the truth, time is on our side."

Two more detonations shook the submarine, just minutes ago a mighty predator, now meek prey, hiding at the bottom of a very large pond. Masayoshi grinned, hoping his men didn't see that it was just another way to grit his teeth.

* * *

"Weapons, what's our status on depth charges?" Lefebvre said over his shoulder.

"Sir, we are down to one-third our load-out," the officer in charge of the *Marceau's* weapon systems reported.

Well, that's not good.

"Commodore, look, starboard, one-hundred-ten degrees," Allard said, binoculars pressed to his face. "We've got an oil slick and debris."

Lefebvre's head swiveled and he saw the same black mass Allard did, along with what looked like some papers, buckets, a few uniforms...

"Captain Allard, do you see any corpses?" Lefebvre said. "I can't see any."

"No, Commodore," Allard said. "But that doesn't mean—"

"I know, Henri," Lefebvre said. "But this asshole is a wizard. I want to be sure."

Allard nodded, though he didn't look happy at having to loiter and wait for further evidence of a kill that might not come.

"Captain, message from *Nice,*" A radio operator spoke up. "The *Oroville's* survivors are all aboard the remaining ships, they are ready to proceed."

"Acknowledged," Allard said quickly. He turned back to his superior and lowered his voice.

"Sir, the Army needs what's left of our cargo," he said.

Lefebvre glared at the inky black slick atop the ocean's surface for three long seconds. Finally, he gave one short, sharp nod.

"Agreed, Captain," he said. "Make course for Saigon. Let's get the fuck out of here."

* * *

Well, I didn't miss this *shit,* Masayoshi thought as he lit another cigarette.

Two more detonations caused the flame to flicker a bit and singe his hand. He frowned and snapped the zippo shut.

The next expected pair of blasts didn't come. The *Funayurei* and her crew waited for five minutes, ten, twenty…

"Sonar, what do you pick up?" Masayoshi said in a low voice.

"Three sets of screws, Captain," Ito answered, also keeping his voice down. "Headed north."

There was a collective sigh and several tired smiles at that news.

"Rig for silent running," Masayoshi said. "We'll stay rigged silent until nightfall. Then we can recharge the batteries and start making our way back to Haiphong. Any questions?"

No one had any except Komatsu who took a step next to his captain and asked, in a very low voice, "Sir, was that what the war was like?"

"Not at all, Lieutenant," Masayoshi said, smirking. "The war was actually tough."

* * *

Sometime Later in Saigon…

Lefebvre, resplendent in a summer-weight Navy blue dress uniform, stepped out of the impromptu court room the Indochina command had made of the former governor's house. His expression bespoke a deep lack of confidence in the company he'd just been keeping.

"I swear I should just retire," Lefebvre murmured.

"They're not going to force you to?" Henri Allard, also in summer-weight blue dress, fell into step with his commander.

"No, when I explained the capabilities of the sub we were up against and pointed out what an embarrassment such an intelligence failure was to their command, they began to see reason," Lefebvre said. "In fact we're going to take one of the destroyer squadrons that was blockading Haiphong and secure our own lines of supply."

"Has it occurred to them that the Vietnamese may have wanted exactly that so their own seaborne resupply can continue unmolested?"

"I explained that possibility to them," he said. "But General de Lattre is insistent that he needs the shipments to keep coming regardless; he says he's massing for something big."

Allard didn't respond to that. The two men walked toward the Cercle Sportif Saigonnais in companionable silence for several seconds.

"I notice you didn't claim the sub kill for *Marceau*," Allard said.

"No, I didn't, Henri," Lefebvre said. "I have a feeling we've not seen the last of that particular bastard."

* * *

And in Haiphong…

The piers of Haiphong were awash with a cornucopia of ships, including several massive I-400 submarines whose crews were offloading ammunition, small arms, mortars, even jeeps, howitzers and at least one jet fighter in multiple pieces. But the most interesting sights to Masayoshi were the three other sleek I-201 hulls tied on piers next to the *Funayurei.*

Komatsu stood next to his captain, examining the new fast attack submarines silently.

"They'll be joining you on your next patrol," an accented voice spoke up in Japanese behind them.

Masayoshi turned to find a short, bespectacled white man with dark brown hair and an offensively blunt face approaching them. He wore khaki pants and a white button-down shirt, already stained with sweat in the heat and humidity of the Indochinese coast.

"Good evening, Captain," the short man said. His Japanese, while imperfect, had risen above the level of unintentional insult. "My name is Feldman. I'm an advisor to the Coalition Government of Vietnam. Chairman Ho and General Giap have asked me to relay their thanks for your efforts and an invitation to dinner at their headquarters."

Masayoshi exchanged a brief glance with Komatsu.

Who the hell are Ho and Giap?

"Well, since they're paying the bills," Masayoshi said. "It would be our pleasure."

"Excellent," Feldman said. "I'm also to relay from my own superiors our pleasure at your fine work off the coast of Singapore. Your kill bonuses for the freighter and both torpedo boats have been confirmed and will be wired to your chosen accounts today. Additionally, given the risks you took fulfilling your contract, we've authorized full VIP ration status and housing allowance for all of your men's families, to be honored for the duration of the occupation."

Masayoshi's eyes widened, he was taken aback at the influx of largesse from his former enemy.

'That is exceedingly generous," Masayoshi said, knowing he sounded standoffish and suspicious.

"Your performance was exceedingly superior," Feldman said smoothly. "This is a direct reward for performance above and beyond what we expected. I personally want to be clear that you are incurring no debt to us accepting these improvements in the bargain."

Masayoshi's impression of the Gaijinn improved as heard the precision and propriety in Feldman's words.

"Hai," Masayoshi said, and inclined his head sharply.

"The last thing, Captain," Feldman said as he returned the shallow bow, "is that Admiral Komatsu asked me to bring you a carton of these."

Reaching into a pack slug over one shoulder, Feldman retrieved a familiar brown and white carton…

It can't be—but it is!

"Thank you, Mr. Feldman," Masayoshi said fervently as he accepted the full carton of high-quality cigarettes.

I guess the Americans aren't all *bad.*

"It is my honor, Tanaka-san," Feldman said, bowing slightly. "Thanks in part to you; we will keep the Reich out of Indochina and perhaps drive him from this part of the world entirely. Good day to you."

After Feldman had gone, Masayoshi stood next to Komatsu the Younger, holding a carton of cigarettes that Komatsu the Elder had gifted him. After some internal deliberation, Masayoshi secured a single pack out of the carton, tapped out two cigarettes and handed one to Komatsu.

"Here, Lieutenant," Masayoshi said as he proffered the cigarette. "If you're going to be a submariner, you have to develop some vices. People who are too pure don't survive in boats."

"Thank you, Captain," Komatsu said, accepting the cigarette.

Masayoshi lit the brown and white Nat Sherman cigarette and inhaled with deep relish. A few drags of the quality tobacco took days of stress off his shoulders. He handed his lighter over to Komatsu, who lit his own cigarette inexpertly and coughed a bit when he tried to inhale his first drag.

"Captain, may I offer a candid comment?" Komatsu said after a long silence.

"Must you?" Masayoshi said. "I was enjoying the quiet."

Komatsu didn't say anything further, but Masayoshi could sense the unsaid words in Komatsu's head like a mosquito buzzing in his ear.

"Oh, alright, Komatsu," he said. "What is it?"

"Sir, I just wanted to say that it's been an honor to serve under you. I understand why you feel the way you do, but I hope to someday serve alongside you in a real navy."

"Boy, you're going to make me take back my cigarette," Masayoshi said.

"Captain, surely you realize survival isn't enough," Komatsu said. "Men need purpose. Service to the Empire *is* that purpose. We are more than ronin."

Masayoshi said nothing for many seconds, gazing out on hundreds of ships unloading millions of tons of military materiel. This massive logistical effort was all bankrolled by the Americans and represented what they could do for a clandestine, low-profile operation.

We never stood a chance.

"Maybe it *is* our purpose," Masayoshi finally said. "But if we're going back into the business of war, I pray to every ancestor and

Kami who will listen that we have chosen the winning side this time."

*****

Justin Watson Bio

Justin Watson grew up an Army brat, living in Germany, Alabama, Texas, Korea, Colorado, and Alaska while being fed a steady diet of X-Men, Star Trek, Robert Heinlein, DragonLance, and Babylon 5. While attending West Point, he met his future wife, Michele, on an airplane, and soon began writing in earnest with her encouragement. In 2005, he graduated from West Point and served as a field artillery officer, completing combat tours in Iraq and Afghanistan, and earning the Bronze Star, Purple Heart, and the Combat Action Badge. Medically retired from the Army in 2015, Justin settled in Houston with Michele, their four children, and an excessively friendly Old English Sheepdog.

#####

Per Mare Per Terram
by Jan Niemczyk

1st May 2005

HMS *Bulwark*, Trondheimsfjord, Norway

Operation FISH HOOK was the first major NATO counter-offensive not mounted in direct response to a Warsaw Pact operation. In one form or another, the planners at HQ Allied Forces North had been working on something like FISH HOOK almost since the day Norway joined NATO, so they had a lot of past experience to draw on when working on the final plan. FISH HOOK would also see the Striking Fleet, Atlantic, emerge from its fjord bastions to support the operation and hopefully provoke the Soviets into mounting a major attack against it rather, than the assets of FISH HOOK itself.

The timing of FISH HOOK was always going to be an issue—firstly the initial Soviet thrust had to be brought to a halt along the main defence line in Troms. Once that was achieved, it was hoped that Soviet combat troops could thoroughly be locked into battle and FISH HOOK would be launched once they were fully committed to breaching the line. By 1st May, it was felt that this had been achieved, and with the arrival of the balance of II Marine Expeditionary Force, 7 Canadian Brigade Group and the leading elements of 10th (US) Mountain Division, it was felt by Commander in Chief, Allied Forces, Northern Europe (CINCNORTH) that the initial phases of FISH HOOK could begin.

To this end, the UK/NL Amphibious Force began to board British and Dutch ships which had been sheltering in the Norwegian fjords, and, apart from 4 Marine Expeditionary Brigade, which was already ashore, the remaining portion of II MEF would remain aboard its ships.

The paratroopers of 5th (UK) Airborne Brigade were also due to be relieved by 7 CBG, although some Paras would remain with the Canadians and continue to broadcast radio traffic that would suggest that the brigade was still in place. Two battalions of Norwegian infantry were also attached to the FISH HOOK force.

- Extract from *'The Battle for the North—the Nordic countries and World War Three'* by Generalløytnant Christian Stubø, Norwegian Army (retired) and Generalmajor Thor "Eeo" Eriksen, Royal Norwegian Air Force (retired).

* * *

Major Robert Williams, RM, CO of X-Ray Company, felt happy to be back aboard HMS *Bulwark* after the days of inactivity 45 Commando and the rest of 3 Commando Brigade had to endure. After the brief period of the war's first few days, the 'Booties' had been placed in Commander North Norway's (COMNON) reserve; they had continued to train and were occasionally mobilised to prepare to reinforce the Main Line of Resistance in Norway. However, the forces already in position had always managed to deal with Soviet attacks every time without their help. The fact that 3 Commando Brigade and its attached Dutch elements were being loaded onto British and Dutch amphibious ships suggested that something big was brewing. Williams' excitement was somewhat tempered by the fact that he had been summoned to a briefing aboard the flagship of the Commodore, Amphibious Warfare (COMAW), Commodore Michael Ramsey. The last time that had happened, he had ended up leading a dangerous company sized raid to evacuate a Norwegian coastal fort under siege by Soviet forces; his ribs were still sore after being blown off his feet by a mortar round.

"Evening, Bob," Lt. Colonel Winchester, Williams' Commanding Officer said in greeting. "I'm afraid we've been given a rather 'interesting' job by brigade."

"Why do I not like the word 'interesting,' sir?" Williams replied, rhetorically.

Following Winchester to the Amphibious Operations Room, the major was interested to see that along with the usual suspects—Brigadier Larkin, the brigade commander, Commodore Ramsey, COMAW, several RN and RM staff officers, and their liaison officer from the Norwegian Costal Rangers, *Kapteinløytnant* Petersen, there were also three officers from the Royal Fleet Auxiliary present; Williams recognised one of them as Captain Sam Duncan, master of RFA *Sir Tristram.* The other two he had not seen before, but guessed that they were the masters of the other two *Round Table*-class LSLs assigned to the UK/NL Amphibious Force.

Well, something is clearly afoot, he mused, feeling suitably intrigued that the masters of these three aging ships and not their counterparts in command of the modern *Bay*-class were attending this meeting. Williams took his seat and waited for the briefing to begin.

"Good evening, ladies and gentlemen," Commodore Ramsey said, taking his place at a podium at the far end of the AOR. "No doubt you are wondering why you are all here; well, you people have been assigned a special task as part of Operation FISH HOOK."

With that, Ramsey brought up a map of northern Norway on the screen behind him, and Major Williams got his first look at what he was going to be asked to do.

"Bloody hell," he muttered under his breath. "Looks like a good chance to earn a V.C. Posthumously."

* * *

4th May

RFA Sir Tristram, Lopphavet, Norway

Captain Sam Duncan peered out from the bridge of the LSL into the gloom, trying to make out the village of Hasvik on the nearby island of Sørøya with no luck. Like all Norwegian settlements in Finnmark, it had been evacuated and subject to the 'scorched-earth' policy intended to deny the Soviet invaders any shelter. The Norwegians had also removed all the navigation markers at the mouth of the thirty-eight kilometre long Altafjord and liberally seeded it with mines.

Hope these ship pilots recall where they left all the 'presents,' Dunlop thought, thinking of the other four ships in this small convoy. *Or that none of them have a heart attack, seeing as only the Norwegians know where the minefields are.*

Ahead of his ship, Duncan could just make out the frigate HMS *Alacrity* carefully picking her way towards the straight between the island of Stjernøya and the mainland. Although he could not see them all astern, his experience allowed him to visualize the other ships in line astern—RFA *Sir Bedivere*, RFA *Sir Galahad,* and HMS *Avenger.*

Every one of us is an old ship, Duncan thought. *Which, of course, makes us all expendable.*

Even if FISH HOOK was a complete success, there was a good chance that the LSLs, at least, would be Constructive Total Losses (CTL).

Thank goodness we can at least defend ourselves somewhat. For this mission each of the three Landing Ship, Logistics had been modified with steel plate and Kevlar armor. Moreover, in addition to the two 40mm Bofors the ships had been armed with at the beginning of the war, additional armament including 20mm cannon, 12.7mm Brownings, 7.62mm GPMGs, and even M134 miniguns had been emplaced. Perhaps the most interesting modification had been a change to the LSLs paint scheme and pennant numbers, which were now Soviet in style. Furthering the ruse, each ship was now flying the Soviet naval pennant, rather than the Blue Ensign of the Royal Fleet Auxiliary.

The additional weapons were manned by RN personnel attached to the ships. Rounding out the crews were all of the RFA sailors who had volunteered to remain with the ships. Duncan thought wryly of the intensive refresher training every RFA member, himself included, had received in both the use of the additional weapons as well as the personal arms they all now carried.

Feel like a bloody buccaneer, he thought. *The Marines are the ones supposed to be doing the fighting.*

The reason for the modifications to the ships were below decks—the Marines of 45 Commando with attached engineers, signals personnel, and various support troops from its parent brigade, plus two troops from the Blues and Royals, and another two troops of Challenger 2s from 5 Royal Tank Regiment.

As part of FISH HOOK the marines and sailors would seize Alta and its important airport in a *coup de main.* Once the airport was secure, more troops from 3 Commando Brigade could be flown in by helicopter to expand the beachhead. Simultaneously at other points along the coast, troops from the USMC's II MEF would be coming ashore, whilst 5th Airborne Brigade would be making the first British combat drop since 1956 to secure an airhead for follow-on forces. The latter included two battle groups from the Norwegian Brigade North.

The operation's next phase would be the most delicate. Under the command of II MEF, the American, British, Dutch and Norwegian forces would expand and hold their bridgehead, which would cut-off the Soviet forces currently engaged in combat along the main NATO defensive line to the south from re-supply.

It will be a thing of beauty if it works, and total carnage if it does not, Duncan thought.

"Time to the next course change?" Duncan asked the Norwegian pilot.

"Two minutes, Captain."

"Good."

Duncan was satisfied that so far all was going well, and evidently their disguise was working. He knew there were several observation posts ashore and that the fjord was covered by a number of artillery batteries, all capable of blowing his ship and its sisters out of the water.

* * *

Below decks, Major Williams finished putting his rifle back together, having taken an opportunity during the voyage to clean it. The men of his company, seeing his example, had all begun doing the same. Williams put the last parts of the rifle back into place and loaded a magazine. Hearing some stirring towards the entry hatch, he looked up and spotted a messenger from the headquarters troops making his way towards him. The man stopped to speak to other sub-unit commanders as he made his way to Williams, and Williams impatiently drummed his fingers on his rifle.

"How long?" Williams asked the messenger, anticipating his message.

"Thirty minutes, sir," the sergeant replied.

"Right, I'll start to get my lads ready to move."

* * *

USS Iwo Jima
Off Sørøya, Norway

The Landing Forces Operations Centre of the LHD was crowded—filled, as it was, with the staff of II MEF, plus liaison staff from the UK/NL Amphibious Force and 5th Airborne Brigade. There were also personnel from the Striking Fleet, Atlantic and the ASW Striking Force present.

Lieutenant-General Douglas S. Burns watched the amphibious 'plot' as the situation developed. He could see that marines from 2nd Marine Regiment had seized the airport at Hammerfest by vertical envelopment using MV-22B Ospreys and were now fighting their way through the town against troops from 77th Motor Rifle Division. Other troops from 2nd Marine Division had landed successfully, either by Osprey or LCAC, and more men and equipment were now being ferried ashore.

The British and Dutch Marines also seemed to be doing well, having taken Hasvik and a few other small settlements around the entrance to Altafjord to secure for follow-on forces. However, these landings would only be worthwhile if the *coup de main* to seize Alta worked out. Burns could see that effort was now approaching the most dangerous phase as the group of British ships closed in on Alta.

The only fly in this very nice ointment might be the Brits' drop, Burns thought. Radio contact with the paratroopers had been fragmentary, but from what could be gleaned from them was that the wheels had come off this particular part of Operation FISH HOOK. It seemed as if there were far more Soviet troops in Lakselv than had been expected, and casualties amongst the NATO side had been heavy.

"We've sent them into another Arnhem," Burns muttered as he looked at the part of the display showing Lakselv.

"I hope not, sir," the liaison officer from 5th Airborne commented. "One Arnhem is quite enough for the regiment."

"I think you need to modify your plan, Colonel," Burns told him. "Clearly your second lift can't be an air-landing insertion of engineers. You need infantry reinforcements in there now. What do you have available?"

"2 Royal Green Jackets and the Gurkhas both have reinforced companies of airborne-qualified troops which we can send in right now. Our brigade commander has already been in contact with CinC-UK Land Command and 1 Para is boarding aircraft as we speak."

The news that one of his British subordinates had gone outside the chain of command of AFNORTH, never mind II MEF, caught Burns by surprise. However he gave the brigadier full points for initiative and reacting so quickly.

"Wow that was quick work, Colonel; pass on a Bravo Zulu to the brigadier when you get a chance."

"Well, we always included them in our contingency planning; in fact, I believe they have spent the last few hours hoping there was a crisis that would call for their deployment. I'll make sure your 'well done' gets passed along, sir."

Burns chuckled.

"They missed the Falklands, didn't they?"

"Indeed they did, sir; got stuck in Northern Ireland, despite their best efforts to join the Task Force."

"So they won't have wanted to miss this op then," Burns observed. "Glad we were able to oblige."

* * *

Alta, Norway

Alta was garrisoned by troops from 131st Motor Rifle Division, who were currently the immediate reserve for the assault on the Lyngen Line. Much of the division was spread out between Alta and the Main Line of Resistance, leaving only one motor rifle battalion and elements of its tank battalion in Alta itself. Surrounding the town were additional forces consisting of mainly engineers, signals troops, artillery, and a variety of other rear-area troops. There were also a couple of Border Troops-manned *Grisha II*-class corvettes anchored off the town.

It was the corvette *Rubin* that first spotted the convoy of British ships approaching. As a re-supply convoy was expected sometime in the next day or so, the watch currently on duty was not overly concerned, however, they did attempt to contact the ships by blinker light. The reply they received was a little confusing, even if it did seem to be in Russian, so the officer in charge decided to summon the captain. However, this all took time, and by the time he reached the bridge and realized that the signals were not in the code of the day, it was too late; the British frigates were within point-blank range.

114mm shells from HMS *Alacrity* tore into the corvette, blasting it apart and killing most of the crew. HMS *Avenger* engaged the second corvette, *Izmail*, and the smaller ship blew up spectacularly after half a dozen hits. The sound of gunfire could not be disguised and alerted every Soviet soldier in Alta. However, by now, the three *Round Table* ships were only a minute from their designated landing beaches.

To offer as much covering fire as possible, both frigates engaged targets in town. Knowing that they did not have to worry about collateral damage, as every Norwegian civilian had been evacuated, the frigates' gunnery officers were able to be profligate with their ordnance. Both vessels' priority target was a battery of A-222 Bereg 130mm coastal defence guns. Mobile weapons, the Beregs were more than capable of sending all five ships to the bottom within minutes.

Airborne reconnaissance had located the battery, and *Alacrity* and *Avenger* blanketed the area with shells. The weight of the frigates' fire more than made up for the naval bombardment's inherent inaccuracy, as five of the guns were destroyed by the hurricane of high explosives. Unfortunately for the convoy, however, the now deceased battery commander had decided, for reasons he took to the hereafter, to move one of the guns to a new location.

This remaining Bereg engaged *Alacrity*, straddling the frigate twice within a few seconds. In less than a minute the gun scored a hit, and a 130mm shell exploded in the warship's funnel, blasting it apart. *Alacrity* rapidly reversed course, smoke and flames pouring from the area around her destroyed funnel. A second shell burst in her hangar as she attempted to withdraw. Fortunately she was not carrying a helicopter and all of the aviation fuel had been landed, but the impact still killed over a dozen crewmembers.

Before the Bereg could finish *Alacrity* off, two Harrier GR.9s dropped a load of RBL.755 cluster bombs on its location, and the anti-tank bomblets destroyed the gun, its crew, and its nearby ammunition. While the crew of *Alacrity* fought to put out the fires started by the pair of 130mm shells, the two Harriers climbed back to altitude and circled the town, allowing other aircraft to make attacks, with attention being especially paid to any armored vehicles. This far in the Soviet rear area, the only surface-to-air missile threat came from man-portable weapons and, by remaining above the effective ceiling of these weapons as much as possible, the NATO aircraft were able to get on with their jobs relatively unmolested.

While the Harriers were putting paid to the coastal defense gun, *Sir Tristram* grounded on a gravel beach only a few meters away from the edge of Havenevien airport. Located in an industrial estate on the edge of town, the beach was perfectly situated for the LSL to open her bow doors and drop her ramp. The added mixed armament of cannons and machine-guns engaged a variety of targets, to include a BRDM-2 that had unwisely gotten a bit too close to the LSL. Before the crew could get off a contact report, the reconnaissance vehicle was riddled by a mixture of 40mm and 20mm shells which set it alight.

The Scimitars and Challenger 2s that the ship had carried raced off to secure the airport, followed closely by a company of marines on foot. The final vehicles off the LSL were Trojan and Terrier engineer vehicles, part of the Royal Engineers team that would hopefully restore the airport.

Across the bay, *Sir Bedivere* and *Sir Galahad* were able to land their armored vehicles and marines onto a quay and the car park of a hotel so the men did not even get their feet wet. The troops and vehicles from *Sir Bedivere* moved rapidly down the E6 road towards Alta itself, forming a blocking position, while those from *Sir Galahad* moved into Elvebakken to cover the flank of the troops securing the airport.

* * *

Major Williams ducked as several 82mm mortar bombs burst rather too close for comfort. He decided that establishing his company HQ this close to *Sir Tristram* was not one of his better ideas as the ship was now attracting all manner of Soviet fire from mortar bombs and heavy machineguns down to rifle fire. The sound of her guns returning fire was also somewhat distracting.

"Sooner she gets out of here the better," he said to his assembled 'O' Group. "Well, no matter, we can't stand around here all day, gentlemen, we've an airport to secure. Let's push on."

* * *

If I leave now, there's a good chance I'm going to end up looking like the Herald of Free Enterprise, Captain Duncan thought. *The damn crew has to get the hatch up manually before we get a hole we can't fix.* His vessel had already been struck by hundreds of small arms rounds, most of which had punched through the hull with relative ease. If not for the *ad hoc* armor, there probably would have been dozens dead and wounded among his crew.

Kaboom!

The LSL shook, and Duncan was briefly blinded by a flash. When his vision cleared, he could see that something, probably a mortar bomb, had burst on the upper deck, starting a fire.

Well, that tears it; we can't stay here, regardless of what might *happen*, Duncan thought. *For those mortars will* certainly *destroy us.*

"I need that ramp closed now!" he barked. "Officer of the Watch, stand-by to withdraw from the beach."

"But the ramp, sir?"

"I'll take my chances; besides we'll be going astern. Tell the men below they have five minutes to get the ramp up."

* * *

USS Wisconsin

Off Sørøya, Norway

Blam!

The half-century old battleship shook as another 16-inch salvo crashed out, throwing nine car-sized shells at a target onshore. The gunfire support *Wisconsin* was providing to the 2nd Marine Regiment in Hammerfest was proving to be crucial in their fight against troops from the 77th Motor Rifle Division for control of the town. Every time the Soviet infantry had managed to form a cohesive defensive line against the advancing marines, their positions had been blasted to pieces by a few salvos from the battleship. To the Soviets' horror, they had found the 16-inch shells were powerful enough to throw even armored vehicles through the air. What they did to men had led to several squads and platoons to simply break and run, despite their commissars' best efforts.

Wisconsin was now methodically demolishing all the Soviet artillery batteries within her range. As with the British frigates, the battleship had started with A-222 Beregs. Despite her best efforts, a handful of surviving guns were currently preventing any amphibious ships from landing heavy equipment directly to the quay. Indeed, the 130mm guns were even making the transit of fast vessels like the LCAC somewhat perilous, as well as preventing destroyers and frigates from closing with the coast to provide more responsive naval gun fire with their 5-inch guns.

With not much to see from the bridge, Captain Craig Flack, USN, the battleship's captain, had decided that it was best to fight his ship from the CIC. It might be dark and claustrophobic, but at least he could watch the flat-screen TV that was currently displaying the footage being beamed back from one of the battleship's RQ-2 Pioneer UAVs. There was a brief flash on the screen as the latest salvo reached its destination, obliterating the target.

"Good shooting, Weaps." Flack remarked to the Weapons Officer, Commander Leverett. "Shame we don't have color on this thing, like the chair farce's Predators."

"Thank you, sir, I'll pass that along," Leverett replied. "The new Fire Scout will have color and much better cameras than the Pioneer."

"That's nice, Weaps, for whoever gets to have one on their ship, but it does squat for me now. Watching a black and white TV is like being back in the seventies."

* * *

As the explosions from *Wisconsin's* salvo began to subside, Staff Sergeant Dennis Novak, 1st platoon, A/1-2 Marines, rose from the temporary shell scrape that marked the furthest point of his platoon's advance into Hammerfest. Or into the collection of rubble and charred wood splinters that marked where the town had once been. What structures had survived the Norwegian demolitions during the evacuation of Hammerfest had been destroyed by a combination of naval gunfire support, close air support, and the Soviet efforts to defend their positions.

We even got the damn chapel, and that thing survived the Germans, Novak thought sadly.

"Move, move, move!" Novak yelled to his marines. "Do you want to live forever?"

The shells from the battleship had created some useful ready-made fox-holes for the marines to drop into once they had crossed the open ground between their positions and those of the Soviets. Novak dropped down into one of the holes, discovering that he was sharing it with a disembodied left leg. He fired a couple of short bursts from his rifle before dropping back into cover, finding that the platoon's commander, a young 2nd Lieutenant and his RTO had joined him.

"Those battleship shells sure help a lot, Staff Sergeant," the platoon commander, 2nd Lieutenant Thomas Dewey, commented.

"Amen to that, LT," Novak replied. "Without the 'Big W,' I doubt we'd have made any progress at all, especially since the Russkies have got armor, and we don't. No way would we have been able to ship in heavy equipment either."

"Any news on that?" Dewey asked. "I haven't been paying attention due to our friends up ahead."

"I heard on the battalion net that an artillery firebase is getting set up at the airport, and we should have some tanks and LAVs on the ground pretty soon."

As if on cue all three marines heard the distant squeaking of tracks and the whine of gas turbine engines. The first of a platoon of four M1A1 Abrams tanks from Company C, 2nd Tank Battalion, hove into view.

"Now that sure is a sight for sore eyes." Novak commented approvingly.

* * *

Alta, Norway

Captain Duncan could see that for some reason RFA *Sir Bedivere*, which was now ablaze, had failed to back off from the quay that she had landed her vehicles and troops on. In a scene reminiscent of Bluff Cove, flames were licking up her superstructure. Duncan's own ship, *Sir Tristram,* was damaged but operational, as was the other LSL, *Sir Galahad*, so he decided he might just still be able to do some good.

"Take us alongside the *Bedivere's* stern," he ordered the helmsman. "We'll see if we can take off some of her crew."

"Aye, aye, sir," the helmsman replied. Swallowing hard, the man put the *Tristram's* helm over. Duncan had five long minutes to think about his decision as they headed towards the blazing LSL. Then there was the sound of metal scraping against metal as *Sir Tristram's* bow rubbed up against the stern of *Sir Bedivere*. Damage control parties from the former directed fire-hoses onto the fires burning just forward of the latter's superstructure.

"Hold her there!" Duncan told the helmsman as he watched members of *Sir Bedivere's* crew leap from the burning LSL onto *Sir Tristram*. Rather fortunately for both vessels, the surviving Soviet defenders of Alta were now too occupied with the attacking Royal Marines and tanks to pay much attention to the two LSLs still close to the shore. The third LSL, RFA *Sir Galahad*, was making her way back up the fjord with the damaged HMS *Alacrity*. Duncan turned from watching the departing vessel to see that one of *Sir Bedivere's* surviving officers, a Second Officer—a rank equivalent to a naval lieutenant—managed to make his way to the bridge of *Sir Tristram* to report.

"How bad is it, son?" Duncan asked.

"We've lost her, sir; she's beyond saving," the man replied. "Only reason she hasn't sunk is because she's beached; engineering spaces and the tank deck are partially flooded, and the fires are likely to burn everything that is not under water."

Duncan winced at the news.

"Most of the reserve ammunition is in the flooded holds," the man continued. "Captain Batten is getting the last of our crew off at the moment; he'd appreciate you keeping your bow where it is for as long as you can."

"I've no intention of going anywhere," Duncan said. "Do you need any help getting crew off?"

"It would be appreciated, sir."

"Speak to Chief Officer Masters; he's down on the tank deck. Tell him I've ordered that he is to give you any help you need."

"Thank you, sir."

The smoke-blackened officer ducked out of the bridge and hurried back down to the tank deck. Duncan turned his attention back to events forward. He could see that while his damage control parties were not bringing the fires under control, they were at least preventing them from spreading aft.

"Not sure how long I can hold her here before we start to damage the bow doors, sir," the helmsman reported.

"Do your best; we'll shore up the doors if we need."

* * *

I feel like I'm looking at Ypres, Major Williams thought to himself. *Wait, no, Passchendale.* Between the initial Soviet attacks, Norwegian demolition, and now what FISH HOOK had done, Alta looked like a moonscape. At least the lack of civilians meant that there was no need to worry about collateral damage, something demonstrated very well by a Challenger 2 fitted with a dozer blade. Having had a Soviet stronghold pointed at it, the tank shrugged off machinegun fire and a lone RPG before firing a HESH round into the already badly damaged building.

Poor bloody bastards, Williams thought as the structure imploded. His horror increased as the MBT used its dozer blade to bury any surviving occupants alive, then followed that up by driving over the wreckage on the way to its next objective.

The treadheads seem to be a bit more ruthless than I expected, Williams thought.

The Royal Marines did not often work with heavy armor, so they were taking the opportunity to use the advantage the tanks gave them to the fullest. The combination of surprise, speed, aggression, and firepower meant that 45 Commando had very quickly secured a lodgement, allowing more marines from 42 Commando and an artillery battery from 29 Commando Regiment, RA, to be flown in to Alta Airport by helicopter to reinforce them.

There was the sound of ship's horn from the harbour. Williams turned to see that more reinforcements had entered the fjord. With the Soviet coastal batteries eliminated, a second convoy of landing craft, this time belonging to the army, set off from the amphibious holding area. Consulting his notes, Williams realized this was probably the remainder of the 5 RTR coming ashore. Smaller RM-manned LCU and LCVP also set off down the fjord as 3 Commando Brigade began to build up its strength in the Alta beachhead.

We're about to be a very large bone choking off the Soviets' throats. With that pleasant thought, Williams turned back to leading his company.

* * *

A Few Hours Later

The Lynx AH.7 helicopter carrying Brigadier Robert Larkin, the commander of 3 Commando Brigade, touched down by the brigade forward HQ. The landings were going well enough that Larkin felt that he could transfer from HMS *Bulwark* to ashore.

"How are things going, Dick?" he asked his Chief of Staff, who had established the forward H.Q.

"Doing very well, sir," Major Richard Capewell replied. "40 Commando and the Dutch 1st Marine Combat Group are now ashore. 42 and 45 Commando have captured most of their initial objectives. The balance of 29 Regiment and its guns should be ashore soon.

"The really good news is that the first Norwegian troops have arrived at the airport. I watched them raising their flag; got me rather emotional, I can tell you."

Brigadier Larkin smiled. "Looks like we are in good shape, Dick."

* * *

Major Williams took a moment to look back at the harbour. He could see smoke coming from the beached RFA *Sir Bedivere;* her surviving crew had been evacuated to *Sir Tristram* which had now departed the fjord. It was a stark reminder that success had been bought at a price, which was still being paid.

Williams' company was advancing up the E6 towards the village of Nerskogen, following three Challenger 2s from 5 RTR. The marines had come to appreciate the tank's support and fire-power. It had been a nice change to put armor before flesh and have three 120mm cannons at their disposal. One tank in particular had proven especially helpful; it had clipped a garden shed, which had against all the odds survived intact, causing it to topple over. To the marine's delight they had found a number of almost brand new shovels, spades, and picks which they would be able to use to dig in.

The tanks advanced slowly through Nerskogen while the marines cleared the village, not that it took very long, given there were no intact buildings. However, evidently some Soviet troops had managed to find a place to shelter as an RPG round suddenly shot out and slammed into the side of the turret of one of the Challengers. Rather like shooting a rhino with a pellet gun, all the rocket did was make the tank mad. The turret traversed round and, after a moment, the coax began to spit fire. Under cover of tank's fire, the marines 'pepper potted' their way towards the source of the RPG round. Once in range, grenadiers placed several 40mm grenades into the position.

Williams' attention was drawn from the counterattack by the 'pop, pop' of small arms fire as his marines engaged other fleeing Soviet troops whose positions had become untenable.

That anti-tank ambush didn't go quite the way they had planned, obviously, he mused with a grim smirk.

A waving hand drew his attention, and he turned to where his radioman, Marine Paul Young, had sought a position to obtain better reception. Whatever the man was now hearing, his facial expression said he did not like it.

"Boss, battle group has just passed a message to go firm," Young said.

"What? We've got them on the run," Williams replied incredulously. "Another few hours and we could link up with the Septics.

"Give me that," he said, taking the Bowman's handset. "This is X-Ray One Sunray; repeat your previous message, over."

"*X-Ray One Sunray, you are to go firm at your present location until further orders, over.*"

"I've got the enemy on the run, what the hell is going on, over?"

"*Do as you're told, X-Ray One Sunray.*" The voice of Lt. Colonel Winchester said, irritation clearly evident, even over the radio. "*This is not a Chinese Parliament, out.*"

Williams handed back the radio handset, absolutely mystified. On the face of it, the order went against all military logic—once an enemy was on the run, he should not be given a chance to rest or regroup. All Williams could think of was that something had happened elsewhere that had affected the brigade as a whole.

"Well at least we'll get to use those spades and shovels now," he commented to his radioman.

* * *

Skaidi, Finnmark, Norway

The MV-22B Osprey landed almost precisely on the intersection between the E6 and Highway 94 (Rv94). Staff Sergeant Novak sprinted down the rear ramp and took cover in the trees while the Osprey off-loaded the remaining marines, who joined him in the trees, sheltering while other MV-22Bs landed to drop off the rest of the battalion.

Novak took a good look around him. The small village, like all the settlements he had come across in Finnmark, had been very effectively razed. Across the intersection he could see what might have once been a shop and small gas station.

The briefing given to Novak's platoon had been that they were to secure the intersection between the E6 and Rv94. The use of the word 'intersection' had given them the impression that it would be something much grander.

"Intersection; now there's a joke," the senior NCO muttered under his breath.

"Well, it looked more important on the map," Lieutenant Thomas Dewey, Novak's platoon commander, remarked. The man pointed in one direction. "The E6 is the most important north-south road in Norway and the west coast of Sweden."

"Looks like a two-lane back home to me," Novak said. "But if it's this big all the way up, it means the Soviets can't move much on it."

"Well, we got to get a move on." Dewey said. "The Brits have been told to hold up so the flyboys can concentrate on supporting us."

Novak and Dewey's conversation was suddenly interrupted by the squeaking of tracks and the rumble of diesel engines that announced the approach of a Soviet column. The first vehicle, a BTR-90, was followed by a pair of MTLBs. Behind them was a long line of trucks, indicating that this was a supply convoy.

"Contact!" Novak shouted, his cry simultaneous with several others down the line.

There was no time for any finesse or to call in any outside support, as one of 1st Platoon's anti-tank gunners immediately engaged the BTR-90 with a Predator SRAW. The rocket hit the APC at the base of its turret, cooking off the 30mm cannon's secondary ammunition in a large fireball. As Russian infantry began abandoning the APC, Novak threw a pair of smoke grenades to blind the MTLBs' drivers. With both the sudden obscuration and the demise of the BTR-90 in front of him, the first MTLB's driver instinctively slammed on the brakes. Half asleep, his counterpart in the next MTLB did not see the manoeuvre, thus causing a chain reaction that saw the both MTLBs and a truck piling up.

"*Go, go, go!*" Dewey shouted, operating under the principle that attack was the best defence. The marines pushed forward, destroying the stalled MTLBs with grenades rather than use valuable anti-tank missiles or their AT-4s. With the slight rise interrupting the convoy, the two MTLBs and BTR-90 of the rear escort were able to disgorge their infantry. Unfortunately for the Soviets, when the BTR-90 tried to manoeuvre around the stalled trucks, it found that the road was too narrow, while the truck drivers attempting to escape the now attacking marines did not make the motor riflemen's job any easier. The BTR-90 finally managed to bump across a grass verge onto a minor village road that ran parallel to the E6 and opened fire on the marines.

"Get that dammed BTR!" Novak yelled as 30mm shells shot over his head.

"We've got incoming choppers!" another marine yelled.

"Ours or theirs?" Novak wondered.

* * *

The answer to Staff Sergeant Novak's question had been "both." Almost simultaneously, a pair of Soviet Mi-24VM Hinds and two marine AH-1Z Vipers arrived over the battlefield; rather than providing close air support to either side, they instead engaged each other.

The marine Vipers had the advantage—not only were they faster and more agile than the Hinds, but they were also armed for air-to-air combat, and their crews regularly practised for helicopter versus helicopter engagements. One Hind was brought down by a couple of bursts of 20mm cannon fire, while the second was felled by an AIM-9M Sidewinder.

With the immediate threat to them eliminated, the two marine Vipers pulled back and circled awaiting directions from the FAC on the ground. These were not long in coming, and the troublesome BTR-90 was blasted to bits by a Hellfire missile, and the two remaining MTLBs riddled with cannon fire. Since the marines on the ground could handle what was left, the FAC ordered the Vipers to fly up the E6 and attack any other Soviet troop columns that posed a threat.

* * *

Staff Sergeant Novak got to his feet and slowly made his way down the line of trucks, some of which were now on fire. A few of the drivers had not made it out of their vehicles, and he could smell the sickly-sweet odour of burning human flesh. For a moment it looked as if all the Soviet troops were either dead or fled, however, a figure holding a rifle with a banana shaped magazine suddenly popped out from between two trucks. Novak brought up his rifle and put a three-round burst into the soldier, felling him.

"Now what was the point of that, you stupid bastard?" Novak muttered as he loaded a fresh magazine into his rifle.

With no further threats, the marines spread out, taking up defensive positions to protect the intersection. Two hours later, they had the satisfaction of seeing their handiwork bear fruit as a column of M1A1s and AAV-7A1s approached down Highway 94; part of the column joined the marines already in place, while the majority headed south down the E6 to link up with the British and Dutch marines.

* * *

5th May

Sitrep from COMNON to CINCNORTH.

From: COMNON

To: CINCNORTH

For information: CO II MEF, COMSONOR

Subj: Op FISH HOOK

FISH forces now all but fully landed, Forward HQ 3 Cdo Bde now established ashore. Secure perimeter in place, landing of supplies continues. Armored battle group formed from troops of Brigade North now landing.

4 MEB now established ashore and has pushed south to link up with 3 Cdo Brigade, forming continuous beachhead.

Position of HOOK forces rather more precarious. Most airborne-capable elements of 5 AB Bde are now on the ground; however, the perimeter of the airhead is not large enough to allow air-landing elements to be inserted. Supplies are being landed by parachute and LAPES.

Brigade commander believes he can expand airhead enough to allow rest of brigade to be inserted if he is given sufficient air support. If not forthcoming, his brigade will need to wait for arrival of FISH forces.

Air reconnaissance suggests that major Soviet counterattack will be launched against HOOK forces in the next 24-48 hours. Troops currently on the ground will have difficulty in holding any major attack, especially if it includes armor. Therefore, it is requested that majority of available air support be assigned to

HOOK forces. Will assign majority of suitable aircraft under my command to HOOK.

* * *

6th May

Indre Billefjord, Finnmark, Norway

The US Marines were using their air mobility to leap forward again; this time 1/2 Marines were being dropped on the small village of Indre Billefjord. A fishing village once home to around 256 people, Indre Billefjord had been lain waste by the retreating Norwegians, like so many other villages and towns in Finnmark. Only the church remained standing among the devastation.

The Marines had been warned not to enter any buildings that had been left intact, or to pick up any object they spotted on the ground, no matter how interesting or enticing it looked. The Norwegians had been very thorough when it came to booby-traps.

* * *

Staff Sergeant Novak made sure that the magazine was seated properly in his rifle as the Osprey he was traveling in made its final approach to the landing zone. On emerging from the aircraft, he was surprised to find that the LZ had already been secured by members of Force Recon and Norwegians from the Finnmark Landforsvar; the later had been operating covertly behind enemy lines but had emerged into the open when the first marines had arrived.

"Spread out, guys!" Novak shouted to his marines. "We don't know if there are any Russkies in town, but we should assume that there might be!"

The marine infantrymen spread out, clearing any possible hiding places before pushing further out to form a defensive perimeter. Once the perimeter was secure, Ospreys and Super Stallions began to lift in more troops and heavy equipment.

The only Soviet troops they encountered were a group of Traffic Directors and a couple of lorry drivers whose vehicles had broken down. Unsurprisingly, they rapidly surrendered to the heavily armed marines and were soon evacuated by Ospreys bringing in reinforcements.

"Okay, Marines, good work," Novak told his men once they had dug in.

Satisfied that all was well he reported to his platoon commander, who was speaking to the company commander.

"We're all squared away, LT, no more hostiles within our part of the perimeter."

"Good work, Staff Sergeant," Lieutenant Dewey replied.

"Those Traffic Directors give you any trouble, Staff Sergeant?" the company commander asked.

Novak smiled and shook his head.

"They all but crapped their pants when they saw us coming, Captain. I think that directing traffic is supposed to be a cushy billet in their army."

* * *

Within an hour of the first marines arriving, a battery of M777 howitzers from 1/10 Marines was in position, and marine engineers were busy constructing a forward operating base for aircraft. Initially, it would only be for helicopters and Ospreys, however it was intended that it would soon be able to take Marine and RAF Harriers.

While the Marines at Indre Billefjord could not yet quite support the British and Canadian troops, they could engage Soviet forces on the other side of the fjord, and the howitzer battery was soon engaging armored vehicles advancing towards the Anglo-Canadian positions. Once the FOB was operational they would also be able to provide almost constant air support.

The HOOK forces had not quite been relieved, but an important step among many had been taken towards that ultimate goal. At best, friendly forces should reach them within the next 48 hours; at worst the Marines had established a safe line of retreat.

* * *

7th May
Signals between FISH HOOK and CINCNORTH

From: Com FISH HOOK
To: CINCNORTH
Copied: COMNON, SHAPE

FISH forces now all ashore and have consolidated their beachhead; marines from 2(US) MEB and 3 (UK) Cdo Bde now form a single lodgement. If possible, would like troops from COMNON or CINCNORTH reserve to be released for garrison duty within the lodgement; also request transfer of 4 (US)

MEB from COMNON to own command to reinforce advance north as soon as 10th (US) Mtn Div is operational. If 4 (US) MEB cannot be released, would instead request that balance of Brigade North be assigned to my command.

HOOK forces continue to hold out against weak Soviet attacks and are no longer in danger of being overrun. Advance forces from 2 (US) MEB have established a FOB close to HOOK perimeter and are now able to provide support with artillery and aviation. Once additional battalion is air lifted into FOB, I am confident that an expanded lodgement can be made with HOOK forces in advance of link-up with ground column.

For reasons not fully understood to me, Commander 3 (UK) Cdo Brigade has requested that a token unit from his force be included in troops that link up with 5 (UK) Abn Bde; I have given permission for X-Ray Company, 45 Cdo to be detached for this reason. Neither Cdr 3 Cdo nor senior liaison officer from 5 Abn have responded in detail when requested to explain importance of this, but felt that if British forces wished to be involved in relieving their countrymen I could see no problem with that.

X-Ray Company will be attached to US Marine battalion due to fly into the FOB and be included in force making link-up within the next 24 hours.

* * *

From: CINCNORTH
To: Com FISH HOOK
Copied: COMNON, SHAPE

COMNON cannot currently release 4 (US) MEB as it is holding an important part of the Lyngen Line. It is also currently the only major non-Norwegian formation in the front-line; therefore it is important politically that it remains where it is. COMNON intends to use the brigade as part of the spearhead of an eventual counter-attack.

However, COMNON is willing to release the balance of Brigade North to your command. A significant armored force may be of more use to you than another brigade of marines, especially if the Soviets mount a major counter-attack from the Kola.

I endorse decision to detach X-Ray Company, 45 Cdo to take part in link-up with HOOK forces. RM and Parachute Regiment have important historic relationship, it will be important to former that they take part in relief of later.

For your information, Swedish/Finnish force in Finnish Lapland is making good progress against Soviet troops. This makes it likely that our troops along Lyngen Line will be able to mount offensive sooner rather than later, as Soviet troops opposite them are now effectively cut-off. Will need your forces to act as anvil to the hammer of COMNON's troops; does make counterattack from Kola much more likely. With effective elimination of Soviet Northern Fleet, Striking Fleet, Atlantic will be available to provide air support for the foreseeable future. However, be aware that a major operation about to be launched in Germany may temporarily restrict the availability of transport aircraft. Please advise if this will effect ability of HOOK force to conduct combat operations.

* * *

From: Com FISH HOOK
To: CINCNORTH
Copied: COMNON, SHAPE

Have enough organic rotary and fixed-wing assets to continue to supply HOOK force if number of C-130 aircraft is reduced or eliminated altogether. Expect full link-up with ground column to take place within the next 48 hours in any case.

Have enough troops from FISH force to act as anvil when COMNON launches counterattack. Very pleased to hear of good progress in Finnish Lap-

land; anything that keeps the Soviets occupied is good in my book. Similarly hope that operation in Germany is successful.

* * *

9th May

Outside Igledas, Finnmark, Norway

Major Williams always felt slightly claustrophobic when riding in an armored vehicle; as Marine Commando he always had visions of being trapped in an APC after it had been hit by an ATGW or RPG. He did make an exception when it came to the Bv-206S and BvS-10 Vikings used by 3 Commando Brigade, but only because he knew a lot about the capabilities of those vehicles. However, he could not help but think this American vehicle was a death-trap.

"You doin' okay, Major?" the vehicle commander asked.

"Fine. Thanks, Sergeant," Williams replied. "How long till we get to the RV?"

"About ten minutes," the commander replied.

"Okay." Williams said, thinking that was ten minutes too long.

* * *

Sergeant Lee, a member of the Canadian Merville Company attached to 5th Airborne Brigade, had been snoozing when the sound of approaching armored vehicles woke him up. As with most combat soldiers he was able to go from fast asleep to full wakefulness almost immediately.

"*Weapons tight, repeat weapons tight. Friendly armor approaching.*" The radio headset in his left ear said.

"Gents! Weapons tight!" he yelled to his section. "Friendly armor approaching!"

Knowing that he was about to witness a historic moment, Sergeant Lee sat up on the lip of his rifle pit. The first two vehicles to appear out of the gloom were a pair of LAV-25A1s, followed closely by a quartet of M-1A1 tanks. AAVP-7A1 Amtracks followed next, the cheerful marines waving to the Canadian and British paratroopers as they passed by. Most of the vehicles passed through without stopping, heading to the other side of the perimeter to take up their positions. However, Lee was intrigued to spot a group of Amtracks halt by 2 Para's battalion H.Q.

* * *

Major Richards, the Acting CO of 2 Para, was also slightly puzzled as to why the group of Amtracks had halted beside his Command Post. He guessed that perhaps the American column commander wanted to talk to him for some reason. His puzzlement soon turned to dismay, and he groaned audibly as he saw the camouflage pattern of the marines who debussed from the vehicles.

"Better contact brigade," he sighed to the battalion adjutant. "We've just been relieved by the 'Booties.'"

"*Our* Booties, sir?" The adjutant queried as he emerged from the tent.

"I'm afraid so." Richard confirmed. "We're never going to live this down."

* * *

Major Williams stretched his back to get all the kinks out of it once he had stepped off the rear ramp of the AAVP-7A1. He looked around and spotted the two Para officers watching the arrival of his company.

Should be good payback for Stanley, he thought to himself as he strode towards the two men.

"Major Williams, Officer Commanding X-Ray Company, Four-Five Commando," he stated as the two men glanced up. "I'm looking for the CO of 2 Para."

"You've found him," the senior of the two Paras replied. "Major Richards, acting CO, 2nd Battalion, The Parachute Regiment. Welcome to Lakselv, Major Williams."

"Thank you, Major Richards," Williams said. "My orders were to report to you before heading to brigade H.Q."

I'll bet they were; somebody wants to make sure as many people as possible know we were relieved by the 'Booties,' even if it was only a single company, Richards thought.

"Well I suppose I should say something like 'I stand relieved' before passing you on to brigade, Major Williams," he said with more friendliness than he felt.

"Thank you, Major Richards; always a pleasure to work with the Paras."

***

Nyby, Finnmark, Norway.

While he had often worked with British marines, Staff Sergeant Novak had never worked with British airborne troops; however, they seemed like professionals, at least for 'army pukes.' His platoon of A Company, 1/2 Marines was dug in just to the rear of the forward positions of 3 Para, having moved in hopefully unobserved by the Soviets. When the expected Soviet attack came, the Marines had been given strict instructions not to engage until ordered.

Doesn't make a lot of sense to me, Novak thought. *Standoff is our friend. I guess someone has a plan.*

* * *

Where are the enemy helicopters and jets? Colonel Anatol Sokolov wondered. Sokolov kept his face impassive as his regiment advanced, but kept glancing nervously into the skies.

"*Comrade Colonel, we have reached Phase Line Moskva,*" his lead battalion reported. "*Continuing to advance.*"

As he monitored the division command net, Sokolov felt strangely reassured about the lack of airpower.

They are all concentrating on the 115th Guards Motor Rifle Division over on E6 Highway, Sokolov thought. *To be fair, they likely seem like a larger threat. No matter, we will achieve penetrat…*

The first sign of the enemy were anti-tank missiles that reached out to destroy some of his leading recce vehicles, tanks, and MTLBs. Sokolov cursed at the contact reports, immediately ordering the regimental artillery and supporting divisional rocket battalions to conduct a 'hurricane' artillery bombardment.

"All battalions push through!" he yelled into his radio. "We do not have time for a methodical attack."

The artillery seemed to have done its work, as his forward troops soon reported seeing the enemy beginning to drift back. The general smiled.

Looks like we will beat the 115th into Lakselv after all.

* * *

"All right, Mates?" The British Para sergeant said as he dropped down into the foxhole that Novak and another Marine were occupying. "Never thought I'd be glad to see Marines." He added with a grin that showed several missing teeth, confirming what Novak thought about the Brits and dental hygiene.

"Always happy to save airborne from themselves, Buddy." Novak replied. "Now it's time for us to kick some Commie ass."

As the Soviets passed over the now abandoned British positions, Novak's radio crackled with the order to open fire. Javelin and TOW missiles flashed out from the Anglo-American positions, while mortar and artillery fire lashed the Soviet rear. The surprise volley caused the lead Soviet battalion to stagger to a stop; their burning vehicles blocking the roadway and the un-swept surrounding terrain seeming an unsafe proposition. As the lead Soviet units were sorting themselves out, 1st / C / 2nd Tank and two platoons of LAV-25s from 2nd LAR Battalion joined in the execution. The artillery and mortar fire briefly lifted to allow attack helicopters and fixed-wing aircraft to join in the attack.

Colonel Sokolov lived just long enough to realize he had been drawn into an ambush. He was trying to think of a way to get out of it when a salvo of MLRS rockets fired by O Battery, 5/10 Marines obliterated his command vehicle and the accompanying headquarters.

* * *

A short distance away, the lead regiment of the 115th Guards Motor Rifle Division also ran into an ambush. As at Nyby, the British defenders appeared to retreat after a short initial engagement, and the Soviet troops then ran into the massed firepower of USMC units. With the lead units stopped, they had their follow-on forces engaged by attack helicopters, fixed-wing aviation, and long-range artillery. The massacre was almost complete.

In less than an hour, the NATO defenders had effectively destroyed the equivalent of two Soviet divisions, sending the survivors retreating east towards the border. The Soviets did have other troops available in the Kola, but these were lower readiness formations, and it would take time for them to be made available for another attack.

* * *

USS Iwo Jima
Off Sørøya, Norway.

"We've done it, sir! We've done it, sir!" Major Andrew Rawson, USMC, said excitedly as he burst into the stateroom of the commander of II MEF.

"What have we done?" a groggy Lieutenant General Burns replied, swinging his legs out of his bunk.

"We've met all of our objectives, sir—our forces now form a single lodgement. We've also defeated the last Soviet forces that pose an immediate threat."

A now fully awake Burns got to his feet, grabbing his uniform jacket. He exited the stateroom, heading towards the amphibious operations room with Rawson following in his wake.

"Any news from CINCNORTH, or COMNON?" he asked.

"While we were completing our operations, 4 MEB, Norwegian troops from their 6th Division, and the army's 10th Mountain Division mounted an attack Skibotn. They took the village and are now sitting astride the road out of Finnish Lapland."

"So there goes the Soviet's last land-based supply lines," Burns commented.

* * *

"Well, ladies and gentlemen, I go away for a couple of hours sleep and you complete FISH HOOK," Burns said to the Operations Room staff. "A very well deserved Bravo Zulu to you all; I'm sure we'll all be getting one from CINCNORTH and the Supreme Allied Commander Europe soon too.

"Now to serious matters—where is the Soviet air force? We've been damned lucky that our air cover has been able to protect us from what they've sent against us."

"The Soviet Northern Fleet is out, sir," the senior naval officer on the staff, Captain David Garcia, USN, replied. "Intelligence suggests that the Soviets have been saving their air assets to go after Striking Fleet, Atlantic."

Burns 'harrumphed' in disapproval.

"Damn fools; with half of what they probably plan to use against the carriers, they could have caused us very real problems. Still, looks like the airedales will be in for a tough fight."

The general turned to Major Rawson.

"How long has it been, Major?"

"Sir?" a puzzled Rawson asked.

"Since the war started, Major."

"Ah...thirteen days I think, sir...yes, thirteen days," Rawson confirmed.

Burns smiled.

"Then it has taken NATO thirteen days to win its first major victory of the Third World War. It won't be our last."

*****

Author's Note:

This story is an adapted extract from my continuing web novel, *The Last War.* Readers who have read the original story will notice some differences; these have been necessary to make the story work as a stand-alone work.

I want to thanks all those who helped with making both this story and *The Last War* a better story than it would otherwise be.

*****

Jan Niemczyk Bio

Jan Niemczyk was born and brought up in Scotland, where he currently lives. He has long had an interest in military history, aviation, naval warfare and horses. He also has an interest in the Cold War. Mr Niemczyk is the author of the web novel *The Last War*, an alternative history where the USSR has survived into the early 21st Century (https://groups.yahoo.com/neo/groups/jans_fiction/files). He is currently employed in the public sector.

#####

Fate of the Falklands

by James Young

Chapter 1: South African Medals and Intemperate Notts

HMS Invincible

1400 Zulu (1100 Local)

3 May 1982

Lieutenant Commander David "Rusty" Ethell did not even have to look up to know who had stormed into No. 801 Squadron's wardroom. Lieutenant Commander Nigel 'Sharkey' Ward was a distinctive fellow with his beard and full head of brown hair, and even more so when his temper was up. The stormy tempest that was pitching the *Invincible* violently up and down apparently matched the squadron commander's mood.

Well, guessing his discussion with Captain Black was not exactly a happy one, David thought. *Of course, when you refer to the Flag's air captain as a 'bell end' who does not know his 'head from his arsehole' when it comes to the Sea Harrier, ensuing discussions are almost certain to be unpleasant.*

"The *Conqueror* has had a bit of trouble," Ward said without preamble, catching David by surprise.

"Wait, what?" he asked the squadron commander as he stretched. Whereas Ward was of average height and build, David had maintained the tall, athletic frame he'd had when playing as a backup midfielder for Dartmouth.

"She was trailing that Argie cruiser, the *Belgrano*, south of the Falklands," Sharkey continued, his face concerned. "Flag sent permission for her to sink the bitch; apparently she tried and had one of her fish go premature right out of the tube."

David winced even as Ward continued.

"Apparently, torpedoes aren't supposed to do that," Sharkey observed drily, "so now the submariners are rightfully skittish about their kit. I don't blame them, as it appears *Conqueror* was badly shaken up, lost her sonar, and is now headed back for repairs."

"Bloody hell, are we the only people who are going to do our job?!" David exclaimed, then calmed himself.

"Come now, it's not nice to besmirch the crabs," Sharkey chided, his tone belying any indication of seriousness. "I mean, it's not like the other side's covering itself in glory."

"Yes, well, we'll see how things go once the weather clears with that runway getting extended," David muttered. "Been nice if that damn bomb raid had managed to go through rather than leaving No. 800 Squadron to try and pull off the impossible."

Sharkey shook his head at the mention of the RAF's attempt to crater Port Stanley's runway. Launched from distant Ascension Island, the use of a positively ancient Vulcan bomber had apparently gone horribly awry, with the main bomber and its two accompanying Victor tanker aircraft still missing.

"Well at least the Harrier chaps managed not to get lost, swallowed by a storm, or snatched by a bunch of UFOs," Sharkey observed, speaking of the eight RAF Harriers that had flown directly from the merchant vessel *Atlantic Conveyor* to the *Hermes*.

"We're a bit far from Bermuda," David replied. "Plus, after that Black Buck cock-up, the crabs had to be seen to be doing something." Standing, he crossed the compartment towards where a fresh pot of tea had just been placed on a serving table.

"Between Doug breaking his collarbone," Sharkey said, "and Lieutenant Curtis getting appendicitis, I'm starting to think this whole thing is turning out a little bit cursed."

Lieutenant Commander Doug Hamilton had been No. 801's executive officer when the British Task Force had departed Plymouth. He had been descending a ladder from the *Invincible's* island when he had lost his footing and tumbled down to the lower deck. In what the vessel's surgeon had dubbed a freak accident, the officer had happened to strike the unyielding steel at just the right angle to snap his collarbone. That this had been followed by Lieutenant Curtis' appendix trying to rupture was taken as a bit of an ill omen by several of the Sea Harrier pilots. That the squadron commander was succumbing to these feelings did not bode well for morale.

Of course, I was flying a desk this time last week, so maybe I'm too rusty to know better, David thought. Like Sharkey, he'd started his career as a Phantom pilot off the old *Ark Royal*, the Royal Navy's last "full deck" carrier. The two of them had become professional acquaintances during the Sea Harrier's initial acceptance trials, which was part of the reason Sharkey had recommended David replace Hamilton after the latter's accident.

"Not cursed," David countered. "Just suffering the after effects of a decade spent neglecting military funding and material."

As if on cue, the *Invincible's* deck began to vibrate as the carrier accelerated into the heavy seas. Sharkey cursed as the wardroom's wait staff moved quickly to rescue dishes before they vibrated off to the deck below.

Builder's fault—that should have been fixed before she was accepted, David thought, disgusted. *Makes it bloody hell sleeping.*

"Robin thinks that shaking is going to be the death of the younger chaps," Sharkey observed, referring to Lieutenant Commander Robin Kent.

"Robin's on to something," David replied. "What the bloody hell are we up to, speeding up in this sea?"

"That's the other thing I was going to mention—we're hunting the *de Mayo*," Sharkey said calmly. David looked at him, not bothering to hide his surprise.

"While I am certain an elderly carrier and her air group of a handful of obsolete American fighter bombers is hardly a threat to be ignored, at last report she's the opposite direction of the Falklands," David said drily.

"Yes, and there are a lot of folks back in London who think Flag is being far too cautious," Sharkey continued. "Especially in light of the *Conqueror's* difficulties and the *Splendid's* inability to actually find anything flying an Argentinian flag. Seems the Defence Minister has made some derisive comments about awarding Rear Admiral Woodward the South African Medal since he's staying so far east."

"Maybe John Nott would like to come out here to the South Atlantic since he appears so keen for a fight," David snapped. "Perhaps he can get those other idiots in Whitehall to explain who thought it was a good idea to sell the Argies Type 42 destroyers while he's at it."

"Well, you don't have to worry about the destroyers," Sharkey said. "Flags has decided that No. 801 squadron and the RAF chaps are the folks to have a go at the Argies while we play goalkeepers back here with *Invincible*."

"Are they mad?! You're the most experienced Sea Harrier pilot in the fleet, and, unless I'm mistaken, the crabs have no idea how to attack a ship at sea!" David exploded. The *Invincible* lurching through a particularly heavy swell interrupted his heated rant, his knee catching the table's underside. Cursing, he took a few seconds to regain his composure.

"Hell, given the rotorheads seem to be the only people who can hit things as of late, I'd sooner have them take a go with their Sea Skuas than a bunch of crabs and those idiots in 800 Squadron on a suicide run."

"I have been assured by Captain Black that my objections, which closely mirror yours, have been noted," Sharkey stated. "He also has pointed out that we, unlike No. 800 Squadron, bagged a couple of Mirages and a Canberra on Sunday."

David shook his head at that.

"Well, if Rear Admiral Woodward thinks that eight Sea Harriers are going to be enough to stop the Argentinians once the weather clears as expected tomorrow, he's probably going to be sadly mistaken."

"I think the intelligence wags are certain the Argentinian Air Force won't have time to react to us heading west before we get the *de Mayo*," Sharkey stated. "Especially if they're trying to relocate some fighters to Stanley before we get a chance to hole the runway."

"The crabs had better hurry up and see to that," David stated, bracing himself as the *Invincible* rolled with a particularly heavy swell. "I don't fancy fighting a carrier battle *and* dealing with land-based air if it comes to that."

There was a clatter from the mess, followed by some cursing.

"Well, good thing we've already had lunch," Sharkey said. "I suppose there's one advantage to the Task Force still being on London time."

Just another political decision that I sincerely hope does not bite us in the ass, David thought. The Admiralty had directed the Falklands Task Force to keep all their clocks on London time in order to simplify staff coordination and planning. Looking at the clock on the bulkhead, David fought back a wave of melancholy.

I hope the kids aren't giving Mum too much trouble, he thought, thinking of his mother who had suddenly inherited two teenagers in her London flat. *Have to try and keep them from becoming orphans.*

"I want to thank you for integrating into the squadron so smoothly," Sharkey said, then continued as if he were reading David's thoughts, "I know it's tough for you after Barbara."

"It's been eight months," David replied stiffly. "The kids know what I do for a living, even if Mum thinks I'm insane."

Sharkey nodded. "Still, by all rights you should be leading a section, not flying as my Number Two."

David gave Sharkey a wry grin.

"Last thing we need is me leading some just as green fellow off that deck to his doom," David said. "I'm just now at the point where I feel like I won't accidentally shoot my own arse off with one of those Sidewinders."

"Don't take this the wrong way, but I'm more worried about you shooting off *my* arse," Sharkey said. "But point taken."

"Too bad the Admiralty shot down using a couple of the test Sea Eagles after all," David observed. "Be nice to have something as good as the Exocet to throw at that Argentine carrier."

Sharkey shook his head.

"The carrier will be easy," he replied. "It's the two destroyers with her that concern me."

* * *

ARA 25 de Mayo
1800 Local (2100 Zulu)

The groaning of the *25 de Mayo*'s hull as she pounded through the waves was not the only thing keeping Ensign Juan Vila on edge. Certainly it was a major factor, as he half expected to hear the screech of metal and sound of alarms that would indicate the pounding seas had breached the elderly vessel's hull. Far more pressing, however, were the words that had just come out of Lieutenant Commander Alberto Philippi's mouth.

Tomorrow. We will strike them tomorrow. As the 3rd Naval Escuadrilla's deputy commander continued to speak about the British task force somewhere to the *25 de Mayo*'s southeast, Juan's mouth began to go dry.

We're all going to die, Juan thought, his heart pounding in his ears. *I should have joined the Army like Hector did. Freezing on some damn island has to be preferable to this.*

"Ensign Vila, am I boring you?!" Lt. Commander Philippi asked sharply, jerking Juan back to the present.

"No, sir," Juan said, his voice quaking. There were several snickers and muttered comments, and Juan felt blood rushing up to his face. Philippi's face switched from sternness to being almost genial in an instant, his brown eyes gentle as they regarded Juan.

"Do not worry," Philippi stated earnestly. "Yes, there are many British ships, but our attack is but one of many scheduled for the morning. Even the Air Force will get in on the act, which is quite unlike them so far."

There was nervous laughter around the table at Philippi's obvious joke. The gathered Skyhawk pilots were well aware that, so far, it was only the Air Force that had actually fired shots in anger.

"All joking aside, do not worry—we will have plenty of cover before we attack their carriers."

Juan hoped his skepticism did not show. While the young ensign was far from the most experienced pilot in the room, even he could do math.

We brought three Skyhawks aboard today, he thought. *That is the entire squadron of eleven aircraft. The reconnaissance pilots think that there are over twenty ships in that task force.*

"You seem unconvinced, Juan," Philippi continued, favoring him with a smile. "If you are that concerned, Ensign Juarez can go in your place."

Juan felt his face flush for entirely different reasons than before. He could see Juarez, one of the Escuadrilla's "spare" pilots, shift forward in his seat.

"I am no coward," he replied, then added a belated, "sir."

"I was not implying that you were," Philippi replied. "However, I do not want any man in this room to believe that we are forcing him, at gun point, to fly on a suicide mission."

"Nor do I," Lieutenant Commander Castro Fox, the squadron's nominal commander, quickly chimed in.

Odd how they pulled Philippi off a desk for this, Juan thought. *It's like they thought there was something wrong with Lieutenant Commander Fox but did not want to embarrass him.*

"Speak honestly, Juan," Philippi continued. "What is bothering you?"

"I just do not understand how we will penetrate their air defenses," Juan said.

"By coming at them from a different direction than they expect," Philippi replied. "This storm should clear by dawn, and the weather officer predicts the wind will be out of the south. We'll be able to launch with full fuel and bombs provided the catapult holds out."

That's a mighty big 'if,' Juan thought uncharitably. Even as a junior officer, he was well aware that the *25 de Mayo*'s cantankerous catapult was just as likely to break sometime during launch operations as get the entire squadron off her deck.

"How is the Air Force planning on finding the British fleet tomorrow?" Juan heard one of the other pilots ask from behind him.

"When the Neptunes regain contact after the storm is through, the location will be shared with the Air Force."

Philippi stated the words with such conviction that Juan almost believed him. Of course, it was highly unlikely the Air Force would have time to arm their aircraft, launch them, and the groups reach the area before the British realized the *25 de Mayo* had turned to head west.

"It is clear over the mainland," Philippi said, as if reading his thoughts. "Since the Air Force does not have to worry about the British attacking, they have already armed and prepared the planes. Civilian navigators and auxiliaries will guide them out here."

That's dangerous, Juan thought, seeing the looks of surprise as he looked around. *It's a recipe for the civilian planes to stumble into the British carriers or, even worse, their Harriers.*

"Those are brave men," Lieutenant Commander Fox observed, getting assent from several of the surrounding pilots.

The door to the 2nd Escuadrilla's ready room opened to reveal Petty Officer Gimenez, assistant to the *25 de Mayo*'s chaplain.

"Gentlemen, confession will be closing in two hours," he stated. "Chaplain Diaz gives his compliments and also says he will be giving any religious services you wish beginning one hour before dawn."

Nice of him not to state 'last rites,' Juan thought grimly.

"Thank you, Petty Officer Gimenez," Lieutenant Commander Philippi said. The man nodded, then closed the hatch behind him. After a pause, Philippi continued.

"The Neptunes will launch an hour before dawn. The 2nd Escuadrilla will launch with their Etendards an hour after that."

Juan looked at the map as Philippi continued to outline the Argentine attack plan.

If the British somehow close the runway at the Malvinas, the Air Force is going to have a serious problem, he thought. *Even with the runway, that's a lot of aircraft going to one spot.*

"Once the Air Force has recovered to Puerto Argentino, they can refuel then fly home," Philippi said. "As for us, we will return to the *de Mayo*."

Of course, if the Neptunes do not find the British in the morning, this will all be for naught.

"You must expend your bombs on the British carriers," Lieutenant Commander Fox stated, standing. "Even if the 2nd Escuadrilla manages to hit them with a missile, even if they are ablaze, we must all hit the carriers."

The squadron commander paused, clearly considering his next words carefully.

"The Americans had a famous squadron commander named John Waldron," Fox said slowly. "On the eve of the Battle of Midway, he gathered his pilots together, much like we are tonight."

Fox slowly scanned each of the men in front of him, meeting each of their eyes.

"When asked by his men what he expected of them, Waldron responded with a simple statement: 'Go in and get a hit.'"

Juan saw Philippi wince slightly, but had no time to consider why the man seemed in pain.

"That is all I will ask of you all," Fox said simply. "Get some rest. We will start preflight an hour before dawn."

* * *

Chapter 2: Trackers in the Dark, Trackers in the Deep

Gold Two

0900 Zulu (0600 Local)

4 May

"Gold Leader, Gold Leader, I have possible trade for you," *Hermes*' Anti-Air Warfare Controller's (AAWC's) voice crackled in David's headset. "Launch immediately. I say again, launch immediately."

Well, that chap sounds a bit worried, David thought. *Of course, it's a bit early for trade so I'd be slightly concerned as well.* Turning, he looked over at

Sharkey's Sea Harrier. The small, charcoal grey fighter was just barely visible across the *Invincible's* still-dark deck. For not the first time, David found himself cursing the inconvenient fact that his nation had chosen to go to war in a wholly different hemisphere.

I should be enjoying the beach with the kids right now, not freezing my ass off closer to Antarctica than London, he thought. *Oh well, at least the storm broke.* David wasn't sure when the gale had finally ended, but it had been sometime before they'd been awoken for operations. The *Invincible's* bow pitched up and down underneath clear, starry skies.

"Roger!" Sharkey replied. "Gold Flight launching."

David turned his head back into his own cockpit as the crew chief sprang up the ladder beside him. The two men quickly ensured everything they'd checked off a half hour before when David had climbed into the aircraft was still correct, then started the Sea Harrier's turbine. As the power plant whined to life, he then proceeded to check the twin Sidewinders, the pair of 30mm Aden cannons and, finally, the Blue Fox radar that was likely his only hope of finding a target in the pre-dawn darkness.

"Sharkey, any idea of what the trade is?" he asked over No. 801 Squadron's net.

"You know as much as I do, Rusty," Sharkey replied. David could hear the squadron commander's annoyance.

"Sharkey, it's a slow-moving contact, right around 250 knots, keeps porpoising in and out of radar at around forty miles, bearing one four five off the bow," *Invincible's* AAWC chimed in.

Once again, I question Rear Admiral Woodward's decision on flagships, David thought. To date, *Invincible's* crew had reflected on the fact they'd been recently exercised while the *Hermes*' had been going through a refit when Argentina had invaded.

"Roger, Control," Sharkey replied. David watched as the squadron commander rotated his aircraft's nose around to align with the light carrier's "ski jump" bow. Using his rudder pedals and stick, David jockeyed his fighter into position off of Sharkey's starboard wing. With swift signals from the flight deck launch officer, the lead Sea Harrier hurtled down *Invincible's* deck and off the edge into the gloom.

Bit different than launching from Ark Royal, David thought. *Probably won't ever get used to not seeing the glow of afterburners.*

Following the launch crew's flashlights, David aligned his fighter with the carrier's bow. As the bow neared the bottom of its natural pitch, he was waved forward. Advancing the throttle, he felt the Sea Harrier spring forward into its roll, and he shot down the deck and up the ski jump. Rotating the Sea Harrier's vectored thrust nozzles as he cleared the ramp, David pulled gently back on the stick to begin climbing away from the *Invincible.* Scanning the sea, he could see the wake of the HMS *Broadsword* off the carrier's bow as the frigate kept pace with her charge. Roughly five miles ahead, the HMS *Antrim* maintained an anti-submarine watch.

"Gold Leader, trade is at bearing one eight zero true, range four oh miles, speed two three oh," *Hermes* AAWC finally answered.

"Say again bearing and range!" Sharkey spat tersely. "Bloody one eight zero true and that range would put the trade on the other side of the damn Falklands!"

Even forty miles is a bit far for trade to be hanging around, David thought. *Not that we have the best information on the 25 de Mayo's air group, but that's a good five hundred miles from her last estimated position.*

"Gold Leader, correction, trade is oh two oh from your current position, speed now two five oh," came a different voice from *Her-*

mes' control room after a long pause. "Range is now six five miles and moving away from us. Target is radiating."

Bloody hell, it is an Argentine, David thought. *That's not good at all.* Looking at his map, he realized that their prey was likely well within radar range of the *Invincible's* support group. As the British task force had come north, it had detached the tanker RFA *Olmeda* and ammunition ship RFA *Resource* in the company of the frigate HMS *Yarmouth.*

At least, I hope it's a Tracker, as anything else means the Yarmouth is well and truly fucked, David thought. *Even a Tracker might see her off.* The *Yarmouth* anti-aircraft armament was a short-ranged Seacat SAM and some 20mm cannons. That meant the frigate was barely able to protect herself, never mind either of her charges, from air attack. The Argentine S-2 was capable of carrying a large bombload, even if attacking in the clinging darkness was insanity.

"Gonna have to kick it in the ass, Gold Two," Sharkey said, clearly doing the same calculus in his head.

"Roger Gold Leader," David said, advancing his throttle to remain on the other Sea Harrier's wing. As he maintained position, he began to manipulate his radar controls, hoping the Blue Fox could help them find their prey in the darkness. After a few moments, he got a contact...then two more that told him he'd found *Yarmouth* and the two auxiliaries.

"Contact!" Sharkey barked. "Bearing two seven oh, ten miles!"

"I don't have anything yet," David said, cursing his radar.

"Pulling up," Sharkey said. "He's down on the waves and I don't want to fool with him in the darkness."

"Gold Leader, target is transmitting radio signals," *Hermes* AAWC reported.

"Guess we don't have a choice," Sharkey muttered. "Stay up high, Gold Two."

David watched as Sharkey dipped his wings, and the Sea Harrier dove into the darkness. Pulling up at one thousand feet, he leveled off began to make a broad orbit toward the *Yarmouth* while keeping his eyes down towards the ocean's surface.

"Gold Leader, Fox Two!" Sharkey said after a long two minutes. With a bright flash, a streak of light briefly outlined Gold Leader's wing before springing off in a snakelike path. The Sidewinder's rocket lit up the ocean below, and David realized just how low the Argentine aircraft was flying as it fled Gold Leader. His brain had not processed the information before the AIM-9L exploded as it merged with the S-2's port engine. The detonation was immediately followed by a larger one as the patrol aircraft's wing tank ignited and horrifically outlined the Grumman for a brief moment before it tumbled into the ocean.

"Splash one Tracker," Sharkey said flatly.

"Gold Leader, *Coventry* reports additional trade, range five oh miles, angels twenty-five, speed two seven oh," *Hermes'* controller reported almost simultaneously.

"Bloody Hell," David muttered, bringing his Sea Harrier around. The Tracker's debris continued to burn on the ocean even as Sharkey climbed to resume lead position as they reversed towards HMS *Coventry*. The big Type 42 destroyer was the middle ship in a twenty-mile long picket line with her two sisters, *Sheffield* and *Glamorgan*.

"Why isn't she shooting the damn thing then?" Sharkey muttered.

"Gold Leader, be advised contact is squawking a civilian transponder," *Hermes* reported. "Flags wants positive identification before engagement."

This better not be another one of their damn 707s, David thought angrily. Looking at his map, he cursed. *Of course, if it's another aircraft, it's technically just outside of the Exclusion Zone we put around the Falklands. Could be another Brazilian airliner, so Flags is right to be cautious.*

* * *

Unknown to either the *Coventry* or the approaching Sea Harriers, the aircraft was indeed a Brazilian 747. The airliner's flight crew had been monitoring "guard," the international rescue frequency. As such, they had heard the panicked, repeated radio reports of the *25 de Mayo*'s doomed S-2, to include its reports of British aircraft. Not wanting to stumble into a shooting war, the jumbo jet began transmitting its flight plan on multiple frequencies, to include its location.

Thirty thousand feet and sixty miles behind it, a lone Argentinian Neptune patrol craft heard the 747's transmissions, triangulated from the S-2's hurried position, and the radar signals its own electronic warfare officer was picking up from *Coventry*. After a quick consultation in the darkened cabin, the patrol craft began its own transmissions, first on the Argentine Navy's monitored frequencies, then the Air Force's.

* * *

ARA 25 de Mayo
0700 Local (1000 Zulu)

Uncertain of his footing in the predawn gloom, Juan paused before stepping from the *25 de Mayo*'s island superstructure onto the carrier's deck. It was a foolish decision, as the press of his squadron mates reacting to the alert klaxon and order to man their planes popped him out of the opening like a cork. Staggering like a drunk, Juan managed to regain his footing despite being weighted down with his flight gear.

"Get your batteries in and let's go!" Lieutenant Commander Philippi snapped at him. "The *Hercules* has detected an enemy aircraft to our west!"

As if on cue, there was the sound of a missile launch from the 25 *de Mayo*'s starboard side as the *Hercules* opened fire. Mouth agape even after Philippi's admonishment, Juan watched as the Sea Dart's flame briefly illuminated the Type 42 destroyer's hull before the missile's motor boosted it off the deck. A brilliant comet, the weapon shot up for a second then arced rapidly out towards the northwest.

Am I watching a foreshadowing of my own death? Juan thought as the missile shot out of sight.

"Goddammit Vila, *snap out of it!*" Lieutenant Jerges, another of the Skyhawk pilots shouted, cuffing Juan on the shoulder. Juan turned and followed the man towards the gathered Skyhawks, briefly looking up as the *Hercules* fired a second Sea Dart. Lieutenant Commander Fox came rushing from the island behind him, a flight map clutched against the strong wind blowing perpendicularly across the flight deck.

"Gather together men!" Fox shouted. "Quickly!" Juan watched as the man nearly stumbled as the 25 *de Mayo* began to turn into the wind. The carrier's deck crew was towing an S-2 Tracker into position.

I wonder how those men are feeling now? Juan thought. Word of the Tracker's demise had already spread throughout the ship, with one version of the rumor claiming the aircraft's pilot had screamed like a banshee as he died. Others stated he had bravely transmitted right until the end. Juan had known Lieutenant Manuel Forches from childhood. He doubted the stocky, brooding father of two young girls had dishonored himself.

I hope he managed to see the chaplain, Juan thought, remembering Manuel's solo with their parish church choir in Buenos Aires. *His poor family has now lost both of their sons, one to the security forces and the other to the British.*

There was one more ripple of sound that broke Juan's thoughts, as this time the *Santísima Trinidad* tried her luck from four miles astern of *Hercules*. As the young ensign turned to look at the second destroyer, Juan was startled to see three more vessels in line abreast, signal lamps blinking as they began passing up the *25 de Mayo*'s port side. After a moment of high pulse rate, he recognized the shapes as the three corvettes *Drummond*, *Gerrico*, and *Granville*.

"Ensign Vila, grab a corner of the map!" Fox barked as he stepped towards his Skyhawk. Juan complied, helping two other pilots hold the laminate down on the fully loaded fighter as the wind shifted straight down the *25 de Mayo*'s centerline.

"We have confirmed the position of the British fleet!" Fox shouted, his voice barely carrying against the wind and the noise of the S-2 Tracker being moved into position to launch on an anti-submarine patrol. "Unfortunately, as you just saw, an enemy reconnaissance aircraft from Ascension has found us as well. The Air Force has begun launching and will be in position to strike in an hour. We will follow..."

Fox was cut off by the sound of the Tracker's engines revving up as the larger patrol aircraft prepared to take off. The carrier's flight deck officer dropped to one knee and pointed down the deck. After a moment, the Tracker jerked forward as the catapult fired...then seemed to move sluggishly as a gout of steam shot up around its wheels. Before the gathered Skyhawk pilots' horrified eyes, the Tracker shot off the bow without nearly enough airspeed. Dipping almost gracefully beneath the bow, the S-2 smacked into the water ahead of the *25 de Mayo*. Even as the carrier's helmsman tried to pull the vessel's helm to starboard and the collision alarm sounded, the 25,000-ton vessel ran down her own aircraft. The brief shudder as the hull ripped the Tracker and its crew to shreds stunned the entire Skyhawk continent into a brief silence.

Madre de Dios, Juan thought.

"Gentlemen!" Lieutenant Commander Philippi shouted. "We have a strike to plan! Give Lieutenant Commander Fox your attention!"

Juan watched as brightly colored flight deck crew ran out towards the catapult. He turned back as Lieutenant Commander Fox started talking.

"We will launch and rendezvous with the Etendards at Point Bolivar at 0830," Fox stated. "They will lead the attack with their Exocets, and we will follow to attack the British carriers."

But what about the Air Force? Juan thought, briefly glancing at his watch.

"The Air Force will destroy the British fighters so that we have a clear run in," Fox continued. "Remember, go in and get a hit."

"Lieutenant Commander Fox!" a man yelled, running across the flight deck towards the gathered Skyhawk pilots. Fox signaled to the other man, waving him over.

"The XO says they will repair the catapult in ten minutes! You are to make sure your men are ready to launch at that time!"

Fox spared the other man a hard look, and Juan realized the flag lieutenant had been utterly casual in speaking to the squadron commander.

"We will be ready, *Lieutenant*," Fox snapped. "Give Commander Hernandez my regards."

Before the young officer could respond, Fox turned back to his squadron.

"Gentlemen, mount your planes."

* * *

Chapter 3: A Day of Heavy Trade

HMS Invincible

1130 Zulu (0830 Local)

4 May

"So in light of the Tracker and whatever the hell aircraft has spoofed the picket line, we managed to talk our good friends over on *Hermes* into sparing two of their number as reinforcements," Sharkey said. "Hopefully that lot will get in and smash the carrier now that RAF found her for us."

"Good to see the crabs are good for something," Lieutenant Steve Thomas observed, shaking his head.

801 Squadron, minus the two alert Sea Harriers currently airborne, was gathered on the deck inside of a parked Sea King helicopter. With its doors closed to block the wind, the large helicopter was serving as an impromptu briefing room on the *Invincible's* flight deck. The seven remaining serviceable Sea Harriers were arrayed on the small carrier's deck, with the armament and refueling crews crawling over Sharkey and David's recently landed aircraft.

I can't believe that damn Brazilian bastard would not stop broadcasting for seventy miles, David thought angrily. *It's like he was worried we were going to assassinate him if he stopped talking.*

"Easy Steve," Flight Lieutenant Paul Barton, RAF, said in return to Thomas' jibe. "Last I checked, there's eleven blokes about to follow you Navy lot out to bomb that carrier."

"That and the Nimrod which found her is going to have to go into internment in Brazil," Sharkey allowed. "Got near missed by one of their Type 42s."

There was a moment of silence at that thought.

"Guess their missiles are working then," Barton said grimly. There had been some discussions with the intelligence blokes on rather or not the Argentineans had been performing proper maintenance on the Sea Darts.

"In any case, that's *Hermes'* problem," Sharkey said, then pointed at several diagrams he'd drawn on the map. "The only missiles we're concerned about are the ones that might be carried by a damn Etendard. Those circles are Exocet range from the pickets, and we're not to pursue any trade further than that."

Before anyone could respond, the helicopter door opened.

"Lieutenant Commander Ward, the captain wanted me to inform you that your request for *Hermes*' to reduce the strike by two Sea Harriers was denied," the tall pilot said. "He passes along his apologies."

Now did Captain Black send His Highness to deliver the news so that Sharkey wouldn't shoot the messenger, or because he was the nearest available officer? David wondered, watching Sharkey's lips compress into a thin line.

"Thank you, *Leftenant*," Sharkey said formally. The man nodded in return, then started to close the door. Before he could finish doing so, the *Invincible's* alert klaxon began to sound, followed by the intercom clicking on.

"All pilots man their aircraft! I say again, all pilots man your planes!"

"Well that tears it!" Sharkey snapped. "Excuse me, Your Highness," he said, pushing past Prince Andrew and heading at a quick walk towards his fighter. The rest of 801 squadron followed suit, David suddenly aware that he'd been up for several hours on night alert prior to their interception of the Tracker.

"Black Flight's engaged with four Mirages!" the *Invincible's* air officer shouted.

Oh shit.

* * *

The Argentine Air Force had been as good as its word to the ARA. From multiple airports across the nation's southern half, the Fuerza Aerea Argentina (FAA) had swiftly scrambled from its alert buildings, to its revetments, then as rapidly as possible into the sky...where it had blundered eastwards into the brightening dawn.

Among the first aircraft to stagger into the sky in the pell mell rush towards the British fleet was a civilian Learjet. From a volunteer squadron dubbed Escuadron Fenix, the aircraft was manned by a pair of civilian pilots who had been flying with a cargo airliner in Buenos Aires barely two weeks before. Belatedly realizing they had no formal mission, the Learjet had found itself being directed to turn on its transponder and wait until it was joined by a flight of four Mirage III fighters before proceeding to the British Fleet's reported position.

It was this *ad hoc* flight that was first detected by the HMS *Coventry* at a distance of seventy miles. Due to the Mirages' proximity and the strength of the still active transponder, the destroyer's air traffic controller was uncertain that he was not seeing another civilian aircraft. It was for this reason that he directed Black Flight out to intercept at twenty-five thousand feet.

It was only the two Sea Harrier pilots' professionalism, their immediate reaction to being locked onto, and the FAA pilots' unfamiliarity with their weapons that allowed the British pilots to survive the next thirty seconds. All four Mirages engaged with their single R530 radar-guided missiles, but only one pilot had managed to properly complete the entire procedure necessary for a head-on launch. His missile was spoofed by the cloud of chaff dispensed as the Sea Harriers immediately broke for the deck while calling urgently for *Coventry* to open fire.

* * *

"Dammit, dammit, dammit! Get off the deck!" Sharkey yelled to No. 801's pilots. With almost simultaneous starts, the seven remaining Sea Harriers began to spool their engines.

I really hope that the Argentines are all nice enough to come in the next hour or so, David thought worriedly. *It might get kind of sticky here if we start to run out of Sea Harriers and they keep sending aircraft.* His preflight complete, he turned to look at *Hermes*. The last of No. 800 Squadron and the RAF had finished forming up, and the large gaggle of Harriers began to turn to head north.

"Gold Leader, Gold Leader, hold your flight," David's headset crackled.

"This is Gold Leader, say again?" Sharkey asked incredulously.

"You are to hold on the deck," *Invincible's* air officer said sharply. "Captain's orders!"

As David watched, two Sea Harriers broke off from the departing strike and began heading west.

"Sharkey, No. 800 is sending two fighters west," he said quickly. "We're the reserve."

"Goddammit!" Sharkey muttered. "Shut down then, no need burning fuel."

* * *

The reason for dispatching the two No. 800 fighters was Black Flight's enmeshment with the four Mirages and the appearance of at least twelve more contacts on *Coventry* and *Glamorgan's* radar. Having fired two missiles at the fleeing Learjet without result, the *Coventry* turned her attention to the dozen fast-closing fighters. As Black Leader continued to call for help as he and his wingman went defensive, the destroyer began to work up to full speed and turn towards the six contacts on her port bow.

The aircraft in question were six FAA Skyhawks, each delta-winged attack aircraft carrying a pair of 500-lb. bombs. Unlike their ARA brethren, the FAA had never practiced a coordinated attack against an armed ship underway. Believing themselves safe at one hundred feet, their squadron commander's violent destruction twenty miles from the smudge of smoke on the horizon quickly disabused of that notion. The brown and black puffball had barely begun to dissipate before it was joined by the second section leader's destruction; *Coventry*'s anti-air team was one of the best in the fleet.

Screaming and cursing in Spanish, the four remaining Skyhawks dipped even lower, advancing their throttles to full speed. At fifty feet, the South Atlantic seemed to reach for them, but the black shapes of two more Sea Darts passed harmlessly overhead to explode harmlessly behind. The *Coventry*'s radar refused to maintain lock in the intervening two minutes before the Skyhawks closed the distance, even as the destroyer's 4.5-inch gun began to engage. Surprisingly, one of the shells detonated close enough to damage one of the approaching fighters, its wing streaming fuel as the pilot gritted his teeth and continued to close.

The four fighters released in sequence, the trailing pair belatedly realizing that they were almost certain to catch fragments if their comrades hit. Or, at least, they would have caught fragments if the single bomb to slam into *Coventry* had not hit the large vessel amidships, pierced the side, then come to rest in the vessel's operations center in a bow of sparks, smoke, and spall rather than a shattering explosion. Despite killing several of the individuals present, stunning the captain, and starting a persistent fire, the bomb's only success was rendering the Sea Dart useless against the next onslaught.

The six Daggers coming in from the *Coventry*'s starboard bow were only belatedly engaged by the vessel's small arms, as *Glamorgan* switched her missiles to assist Black Flight. Opening the spacing between their pairs, the Daggers struck in quick succession. In a cruel twist of fate, an armorer's error in the hurried pre-dawn loading had led to all six aircraft being equipped with 1,000-lb. retarded bombs rather than the low drag ordnance that had been actually ordered. Thus, the two 6th Air Brigade bombs that hit the *Coventry,* and the four that missed close aboard, all functioned as designed.

The first struck the destroyer's bridge, ruining that structure and causing the sympathetic detonation of the smaller weapon in the operations room. In a stroke, the vessel's leadership was removed as the captain, executive officer, and gunnery officer all died at their posts. The second weapon detonated in the destroyer's hangar, causing a secondary explosion as the vessel's Wessex and several anti-submarine torpedoes went up in a gout of bright flame. The four near misses all dished in portions of the *Coventry*'s hull, with the total damage immediately transforming the vessel from a man of war to a ship *in extremis.*

* * *

"*Coventry*'s hit!" someone on the *Invincible's* deck called out. Looking to the west, David could see the start of black smoke on the horizon, even as another four smoke trails shot off into the sky.

"Black Leader, splash one Mirage!"

"Blue Leader, tally-ho four Daggers!"

"Green Leader, tally-ho two Canberra!"

"Apex Leader, tally-ho four Skyhawks!"

Glad to see the Hermes' lot join the party, David thought.

The next fifteen minutes was chaos, as the Sea Harriers merged with the incoming Argentinean air strikes. The fighters' intervention seemed to save the *Glamorgan* from destruction, but not damage as the vessel was hit by two bombs that did not detonate. *Coventry*, burning like a beacon and unable to protect herself, was finally hit by three more bombs. In exchange, the two remaining British destroyers and the Sea Harriers confirmed at least fifteen kills, with another pair of Argentinean attackers damaged by cannon fire and several more forced to jettison their bombs.

The pickets are going to start running out of missiles if they keep firing at that rate, David thought, watching *Invincible's* own Sea Dart launcher begin to track some unidentified target. The *Brilliant* began to accelerate and draw away from the carrier, surging ahead to place herself between *Invincible* and the next wave of Argentinean attackers.

We came too far west, David thought bitterly. *Of course, the* 25 de Mayo *is now well within range.*

"Gold Leader, go ahead and get airborne," came the order from *Invincible's* island. "Hold astern and don't foul the Sea Darts' arc of fire."

David started his engine, wearily snapping his oxygen mask over his face as he listened to the continuing fight. Black Flight, out of Sidewinders and low on fuel, dutifully turned astern from *Invincible*.

"All stations, all stations, *Brilliant!* Handbrake, I say again, Handbrake!"

The radio warning sent a chill through David. Handbrake was the warning call that a vessel had detected the signals of a Super Etendard's Seranto radar. That could only mean one thing—Exocet!

* * *

Leopard Three
0900 Local (1200 Zulu)

Juan tried to control his breathing as he focused on staying with Commander Fox's Skyhawk. The reason for reinforcing the *25 de Mayo* with the entire ARA's inventory of A-4s had been the expectation that at least one or two would have some sort of maintenance failure. In an occurrence that almost seemed to be God answering the chaplain's fervent prayers for safe operations after the Tracker incident, all eleven aircraft had made it airborne. Furthermore, they had inexplicably remained unseen by the large gaggle of British aircraft heading the opposite direction towards the *25 de Mayo.* Thus all eleven Skyhawks, carrying a pair of retarded 500-lb. bombs apiece, were now skimming towards the British carriers at just under fifty feet over the ocean.

A sneeze could kill me, Juan thought. Motion ahead and to starboard caught his eye, as four shapes popped upwards from the ocean almost as one.

The 2nd Escuadrilla, he thought. The large, dark Super Etendards had been late to the rendezvous, but caught up with the Skyhawks on their way to the British task group. After popping up for roughly ten seconds, first the flight leader, then the other three aircraft, each released a single Exocet. All four missiles ignited, their engines accelerating them to just under the speed of sound. The flight of aircraft executed a sharp, immediate turn to starboard.

Heading for home, Juan thought. Fox waggled his wings, the signal for his two wingmen to shift to line abreast formation. Juan noted several plumes of smoke ahead of them, with two thicker than the others on the southwest horizon. The Exocets moved out of sight, moving at over two hundred miles faster than the A-4s. Looking at his map, then his watch, Juan gritted his teeth.

Four minutes, he thought.

* * *

Gold Two

1203 Zulu (0900 Local)

"*Invincible! Invincible! Missiles inbound!*"

The urgency in Sharkey's voice was scarier than anything else David had experienced in his life. The fact that he had just departed the *Invincible's* ski ramp and had no available airspeed to maneuver made Gold One's warning all the worse. Ahead of him, flame and smoke burst from the *Broadsword's* bow as the frigate launched first one, then immediately a second Sea Wolf missile.

"Break to port, Gold Two!" Sharkey barked. "Now, now, now!"

Working on it, Sharkey! David thought, his throttle maxed. As his airspeed moved just past three hundred knots, he dipped the Sea Harrier's nose down and away. In his peripheral vision, he saw a streak of motion surrounded by smoke and a flaming halo as *Invincible's* own Sea Dart fired. Chaff rockets burst around the maneuvering carrier, and a Sea King began to lift off the carrier's deck.

"Splash one missile!" someone reported over the task force network. Then David was concentrating on flying his Sea Harrier just above the waves, hurtling past *Invincible* below her deck and on the carrier's port side. There was a flash of motion across his rearview mirror from left to right. David whipped his head around just in time to see the streaking Exocet, decoyed away from the *Invincible*, continue on to strike the HMS *Brilliant* on her starboard side. Even as his mind was registering that detonation, a second missile touched off the frigate's Sea Wolf magazine.

Blimey, David thought, the task group net a bedlam of differing voices. He turned his head to the left as he swung wide astern. Turning to look out to the north, David's pulse started to race as he sighted several delta-winged shapes rushing in from the north east.

"Gold One, Gold Two, tallyho, trade bearing oh three oh true, range seven miles!" he reported quickly while preparing both his Sidewinders. He brought the Sea Harrier's nose on line with the rapidly swelling aircraft.

"Last calling station, this is *Invincible*," came the voice of their carriers AAWC. "Say again trade!"

I don't have time to repeat myself, you bloody idiots, David thought. The closure rate between himself and the opposing squadron was over supersonic. As he fought to bring the nose on line with the flight leader, the port Sidewinder growled that it had a target. Even as he thought the angle to be impossible, David squeezed the trigger. The AIM-9 leapt from his port wing, flew the quick snake pattern that gave the missile its namesake, then hit the enemy leader square on at two miles. Tracers flew past David's canopy as another A-4 fired a wild snap burst at him, then the enemy aircraft were clear of him.

"Gold Leader, Fox Two!" he heard Sharkey bark.

Dammit, I forgot to give out a warning call, he thought, hauling the Sea Harrier around in a tight turn. The fighter shuddered as his nose came around.

"This is Gold Two, splash…"

"Friendly fighters, get clear!" some shouted over the radio.

* * *

The frantic call was from the *Broadsword*, the frigate's air action officer trying to clear the range for the vessel's three remaining Sea Wolf missiles. Never intended as an area defense weapon, the anti-aircraft missile system was having trouble determining what contacts were Gold Flight and which were the trade that had seemingly appeared out of nowhere.

Already befuddled by the Exocet attack and a near collision with the *Invincible* as that vessel had turned to narrow her aspect, the *Broadsword's* combat action center still managed to serve their role as the *Invincible's* goal keeper. With the Sea Wolf requiring manual reload, the frigate only had three shots remaining. As the Skyhawks passed three miles' range, the first missile came off the rails.

* * *

Leopard Three

Juan jerked his stick over to avoid the debris that had been Leopard Two hurtling back towards him. If he had not already fouled himself, the second fiery death of a comrade in under two minutes would have caused him to wet himself once more. With a primal scream, he squeezed the trigger for his two cannon as his aircraft approached the British frigate that had just killed his friends. Several bright flashes told him that his rounds had hit, then he was flying just over the hostile vessel. There was a loud *bang!* as a cannon shell hit his wing, and for one terrifying moment Juan thought the Skyhawk was going to roll into the ocean.

No! he thought, fighting the stick back. Cursing, he saw that it was too late for him to turn and hit the smaller British carrier. Before him, however, was the British flagship, its bow swinging slowly, ever so slowly, towards him. To his port, he could see another British frigate, possibly the sister to the one that had just killed Jaguar One and Leopard Two, fully engulfed in flames. Beyond the *Hermes* there was another frigate moving at full speed, the vessel's turret seemingly in a seizure.

Focus, Juan thought to himself. The A-4 was a simple weapons system, its forward gunsight also serving as the bomb sight. He aligned himself with the *Hermes*' starboard bow, time seeming to slow as he tried to remember his training. Tracers shot by his canopy as he closed, 20mm cannon and machine guns shooting towards him from around the deck. Biting his tongue, Juan waited until his sight had dragged across the flight deck and toggled both his bombs.

The two weapons separated cleanly from underneath the Skyhawk's wings, retarding fins jerking open. Even as Juan's A-4 jerked upwards from the suddenly released weight, the Mark 82s slowed immediately from the increased drag. Both weapons' fuzes armed, their noses snapping downwards as they hurtled into *Hermes*. The first weapon, just barely on target, plunged through the flight deck edge and exploded as it passed into the hangar deck. The second punched through the center of the flight deck just abeam of the island, passed through the hangar's deck bottom at an angle, then burst in a passageway two decks down.

Juan saw the detonations in his rearview mirror.

"Yes! Yes!" he screamed, even as the final British vessel fired at him with small arms.

I did it, Commander Fox, he thought. *I went in and got a…*

At some level, his brain registered the Sea Harrier's shadow sliding in behind his aircraft. Before that could be a fully formed thought, the small fighter's cannon burst put one shell into his engine and two more into his cockpit. Whether he would have died from shock or blood loss as the explosions tore his left leg and arm from his body became academic, as the sudden loss of power sent the Skyhawk pitching into the South Atlantic.

* * *

Gold Two

David pulled up and over his third kill, screaming in impotent range as he looked back at the blazing *Hermes*, *Brilliant,* and now *Broadsword.*

Well at least the bastards missed Invincible, he thought. Captain Black had thrown the carrier's helm hard over at the last moment, causing the four Skyhawks to miss close aboard. *Hermes*, larger and less nimble, had first taken two bombs from the lone Skyhawk, then what looked to be four more from the next pair. David resisted the urge to chase the quickly escaping A-4s, as there was a good chance Sharkey and he were the last two Sea Harriers with any appreciable fuel this side of the group that had gone after the *25 de Mayo*.

"Gold Leader, Gold Two," David said, looking about for his flight leader. His arms began to shake from the exertion of having turned back into the fray and pursued the Skyhawks against orders.

"Gold Two, Gold Leader," Sharkey replied, his voice shaken. David could see why, as another secondary explosion shook the *Hermes.*

I hope they put the ordnance away from this morning, he thought. *If that fire reaches the bomb magazines,* Hermes *is finished.* As if to demonstrate his point about secondaries, the wreckage that had been HMS *Brilliant* suffered another massive detonation as her anti-submarine torpedo magazine went. There was clearly additional damage beneath the waterline, as the frigate began to slowly roll on her beam ends.

My God, we cannot stay here and pick up survivors, David thought. *We're too close to the Argentine coast.*

"I have one Sidewinder and roughly three quarters of my cannon left," David said.

"Gold Flight, need you to head west towards *Glamorgan*..." someone began to say over the radio.

"Negative, Gold Flight," Captain Black's clipped voice came over the radio. "Maintain position, cover rearming and rescue operations."

"This is *Glamorgan*! We have..."

"You will stand by, *Glamorgan*," Black barked. "Look east of your damn vessel, you bloody idiot."

There was a long pause.

"*Glamorgan* is engaging hostile aircraft. God save the Queen."

We've lost the war, David thought. He suddenly had to swallow hard to keep from vomiting, the realization like a hard punch to the abdomen. *Regardless of what happens next, it's over.*

Hot tears began to run down David's face at the realization. As he listened to the *Invincible* organizing rescue operations, the slight tears became full blown sobs of frustration.

* * *

Epilogue

HMS Invincible
2200 Zulu (1900 Local)
4 May

David rubbed his eyes, then opened the manila folder that Sharkey had just handed to him. The two men were in Sharkey's cabin, the squadron commander having summoned David to follow him from the cacophony of No. 801's wardroom. *Invincible* had recovered the fifteen Harriers that had survived the strike on the *25 de Mayo.*

I imagine it's quite striking to return to find your own carrier looking like the one you just pummeled, David thought grimly as he began to read the flimsy. He got about halfway through then stopped, paused, and reread it.

"Well the Iron Lady has clearly had quite enough," he said, his face ashen. "I hope the Admiralty realizes ordering *Splendid* to finish off the entire task force basically condemned a couple thousand Argentinians to die in the ocean."

"I think after seeing the footage of *Hermes,* our good Prime Minister may not give a damn," Sharkey said.

She will when there's camera footage of young Argentine sailors frozen to death in life rafts, David thought. Apparently *Splendid*, already on the way to the reported location, had arrived to find the burning *25 de Mayo* and settling *Santísima Trinidad* with four Argentine vessels in attendance.

Guess the ensuing two hours demonstrated the decisiveness of nuclear submarines, David thought. *Also showed that the* Conqueror's *torp problems had just been a fluke.*

"Keep reading."

David resumed reading, got through two more paragraphs, then slammed the page down.

"Oh, how nice of the Americans to *finally* decide to intervene with a firm hand," he snapped. "I am so glad they have now decided to freeze all Argentine assets in the United States due to the 'act of overt aggression.' It was just as bloody overt when it occurred several weeks ago!"

"You'll note that both sides are being 'highly encouraged to extricate themselves from the conflict area while diplomacy is once again tried,' correct?" Sharkey observed grimly.

"Yes," David snapped. "And that the USS *Saratoga* and USS *Constellation* battle groups are en route to help 'monitor the situation' and 'prohibit additional loss of life.'"

Sharkey shrugged, then gestured his shoulder astern.

"Our last big deck carrier is currently burning herself out thirty miles behind us," he said bitterly. "Successive governments have made bad choices, and here we are."

I thought they might be able to save Hermes, David thought with a sigh. *Too bad about the secondary explosions shattering the fire main.*

"What is our plan?" David asked.

"With Rear Admiral Woodward in the infirmary, and the weather likely to go to shit in less than a month?" Sharkey snorted. "I think the plan is to hope that the good Secretary Haig doesn't attempt to take liberties with Prime Minister Thatcher or Her Majesty's interests."

David took a deep breath, then stood.

"Well, if it's all the same to you, Sharkey, I'm going to turn in," he said. "The idiots in suits will do their part or not, but the fate of the Falklands is out of our hands."

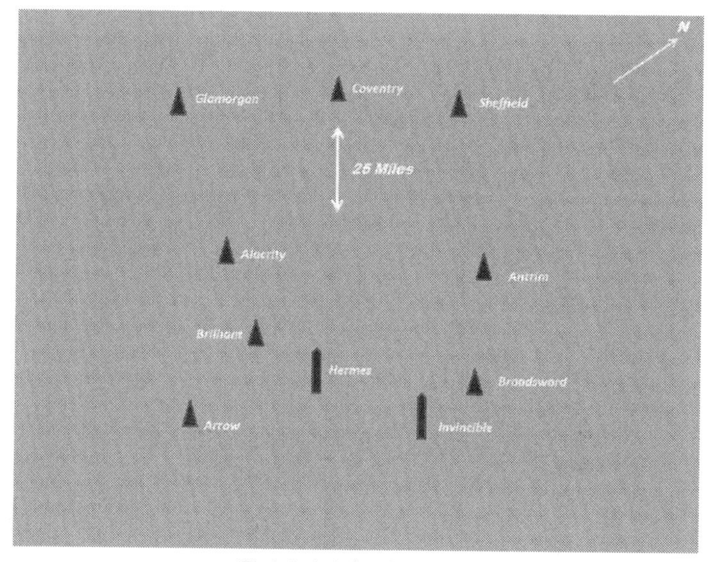

British TF Sketch

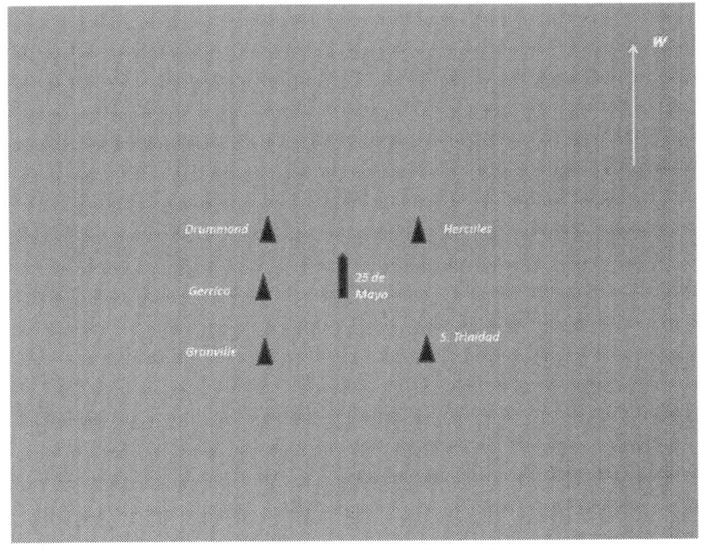

Argentinean TF Sketch

#####

About the Editors

A Dragon Award finalist, Chris Kennedy is a Science Fiction/Fantasy/Young Adult author, speaker, and small-press publisher who has written over 20 books and published more than 50 others. Chris' stories include the "Occupied Seattle" military fiction duology, "The Theogony" and "Codex Regius" science fiction trilogies, stories in the "Four Horsemen" and "In Revolution Born" universes and the "War for Dominance" fantasy trilogy. Get his free book, "Shattered Crucible," at his website, https://chriskennedypublishing.com.

Called "fantastic" and "a great speaker," he has coached hundreds of beginning authors and budding novelists on how to self-publish their stories at a variety of conferences, conventions and writing guild presentations. He is the author of the award-winning #1 bestseller, "Self-Publishing for Profit: How to Get Your Book Out of Your Head and Into the Stores," as well as the leadership training book, "Leadership from the Darkside."

Chris lives in Virginia Beach, Virginia, with his wife, and is the holder of a doctorate in educational leadership and master's degrees in both business and public administration. Follow Chris on Facebook at https://facebook.com/chriskennedypublishing.biz.

James Young is a Missouri native who escaped small town life via an appointment to the United States Military Academy. Deciding that beating wasn't enough, he moved to the Midwest to obtain a doctorate in U.S. History from Kansas State University. Fiction Dr. Young's first love, and he is currently the author of the *Usurper's War* (alternate history), *Vergassy Chronicles* (space opera), and *Scythefall* (apocalyptic fiction) series, all of which are available via Amazon. As a non-fiction author, Dr. Young has won the 2016 United States Naval Institute's Cyberwarfare Essay contest and the U.S. Armor Center's Draper Award. You can find him at his blog (https://vergassy.com/), FB Page (https://www.facebook.com/ColfaxDen/), or on Twitter (@Youngblai).

* * * * *

The following is an

Excerpt from Book One of The Psyche of War:

Minds of Men

Kacey Ezell

Available from Theogony Books

eBook, Paperback, and Audio

Excerpt from "Minds of Men:"

"Look sharp, everyone," Carl said after a while. Evelyn couldn't have said whether they'd been droning for minutes or hours in the cold, dense white of the cloud cover. "We should be overhead the French coast in about thirty seconds."

The men all reacted to this announcement with varying degrees of excitement and terror. Sean got up from his seat and came back to her, holding an awkward looking arrangement of fabric and straps.

Put this on, he thought to her. *It's your flak jacket. And your parachute is just there,* he said, pointing. *If the captain gives the order to bail out, you go, clip this piece into your 'chute, and jump out the biggest hole you can find. Do you understand? You do, don't you. This psychic thing certainly makes explaining things easier,* he finished with a grin.

Evelyn gave him what she hoped was a brave smile and took the flak jacket from him. It was deceptively heavy, and she struggled a bit with getting it on. Sean gave her a smile and a thumbs up, and then headed back to his station.

The other men were checking in and charging their weapons. A short time later, Evelyn saw through Rico's eyes as the tail gunner watched their fighter escort waggle their wings at the formation and depart. They didn't have the long-range fuel capability to continue all the way to the target.

Someday, that long-range fighter escort we were promised will materialize, Carl thought. His mind felt determinedly positive, like he was trying to be strong for the crew and not let them see his fear. That, of course, was an impossibility, but the crew took it well. After all, they were afraid, too. Especially as the formation had begun its descent to the attack altitude of 20,000 feet. Evelyn became gradually aware of the way the men's collective tension ratcheted up with every hundred feet of descent. They were entering enemy fighter territory.

Yeah, and someday Veronica Lake will...ah. Never mind. Sorry, Evie. That was Les. Evelyn could feel the waist gunner's not-quite-repentant grin. She had to suppress a grin of her own, but Les' irreverence was the perfect tension breaker.

Boys will be boys, she sent, projecting a sense of tolerance. *But real men keep their private lives private.* She added this last with a bit of smug superiority and felt the rest of the crew's appreciative flare of humor at her jab. Even Les laughed, shaking his head. A warmth that had nothing to do with her electric suit enfolded Evelyn, and she started to feel like, maybe, she just might become part of the crew yet.

Fighters! Twelve o'clock high!

The call came from Alice. If she craned her neck to look around Sean's body, Evelyn could just see the terrifying rain of tracer fire coming from the dark, diving silhouette of an enemy fighter. She let the call echo down her own channels and felt her men respond, turning their own weapons to cover *Teacher's Pet*'s flanks. Adrenaline surges spiked through all of them, causing Evelyn's heart to race in turn. She took a deep breath and reached out to tie her crew in closer to the Forts around them.

She looked through Sean's eyes as he fired from the top turret, tracking his line of bullets just in front of the attacking aircraft. His mind was oddly calm and terribly focused...as, indeed, they all were. Even young Lieutenant Bob was zeroed in on his task of keeping a tight position and making it that much harder to penetrate the deadly crossing fire of the Flying Fortress.

Fighters! Three o'clock low!

That was Logan in the ball turret. Evelyn felt him as he spun his turret around and began to fire the twin Browning AN/M2 .50 caliber machine guns at the sinister dark shapes rising up to meet them with fire.

Got 'em, Bobby Fritsche replied, from his position in the right waist. He, too, opened up with his own .50 caliber machine gun, tracking the barrel forward of the nose of the fighter formation, in order to "lead" their flight and not shoot behind them.

Evelyn blinked, then hastily relayed the call to the other girls in the formation net. She felt their acknowledgement, though it was almost an absentminded thing as each of the girls were focusing mostly on the communication between the men in their individual crews.

Got you, you Kraut sonofabitch! Logan exulted. Evelyn looked through his eyes and couldn't help but feel a twist of pity for the pilot of the German fighter as he spiraled toward the ground, one wing completely gone. She carefully kept that emotion from Logan, however, as he was concentrating on trying to take out the other three fighters who'd been in the initial attacking wedge. One fell victim to Bobby's relentless fire as he threw out a curtain of lead that couldn't be avoided.

Two back to you, tail, Bobby said, his mind carrying an even calm, devoid of Logan's adrenaline-fueled exultation.

Yup, Rico Martinez answered as he visually acquired the two remaining targets and opened fire. He was aided by fire from the aircraft flying off their right wing, the *Nagging Natasha.* She fired from her left waist and tail, and the two remaining fighters faltered and tumbled through the resulting crossfire. Evelyn watched through Rico's eyes as the ugly black smoke trailed the wreckage down.

Fighters! Twelve high!

Fighters! Two high!

The calls were simultaneous, coming from Sean in his top turret and Les on the left side. Evelyn took a deep breath and did her best to split her attention between the two of them, keeping the net strong and open. Sean and Les opened fire, their respective weapons adding a cacophony of pops to the ever-present thrum of the engines.

Flak! That was Carl, up front. Evelyn felt him take hold of the controls, helping the lieutenant to maintain his position in the formation as the Nazi anti-aircraft guns began to send up 20mm shells that blossomed into dark clouds that pocked the sky. One exploded right in front of *Pretty Cass'* nose. Evelyn felt the bottom drop out of her stomach as the aircraft heaved first up and then down. She held on grimly and passed on the wordless knowledge the pilots had no choice but to fly through the debris and shrapnel that resulted.

In the meantime, the gunners continued their rapid fire response to the enemy fighters' attempt to break up the formation. Evelyn took that knowledge—that the Luftwaffe was trying to isolate one of the Forts, make her vulnerable—and passed it along the looser formation net.

Shit! They got Liberty Belle*!* Logan called out then, from his view in the ball turret. Evelyn looked through his angry eyes, feeling his sudden spike of despair as they watched the crippled Fort fall back, two of her four engines smoking. Instantly, the enemy fighters swarmed like so many insects, and Evelyn watched as the aircraft yawed over and began to spin down and out of control.

A few agonizing heartbeats later, first one, then three more parachutes fluttered open far below. Evelyn felt Logan's bitter knowledge that there had been six other men on board that aircraft. *Liberty Belle* was one of the few birds flying without a psychic on board, and Evelyn suppressed a small, wicked feeling of relief that she hadn't just lost one of her friends.

Fighters! Twelve o'clock level!

*****

*****

The following is an

Excerpt from Book One of the Salvage Title Trilogy:

Salvage Title

Kevin Steverson

Available Now from Theogony Books

eBook, Paperback, and Audio Book

Excerpt from "Salvage Title:"

The first thing Clip did was get power to the door and the access panel. Two of his power cells did the trick once he had them wired to the container. He then pulled out his slate and connected it. It lit up, and his fingers flew across it. It took him a few minutes to establish a link, then he programmed it to search for the combination to the access panel.

"Is it from a human ship?" Harmon asked, curious.

"I don't think so, but it doesn't matter; ones and zeros are still ones and zeros when it comes to computers. It's universal. I mean, there are some things you have to know to get other races' computers to run right, but it's not that hard," Clip said.

Harmon shook his head. *Riiigghht,* he thought. He knew better. Clip's intelligence test results were completely off the charts. Clip opted to go to work at Rinto's right after secondary school because there was nothing for him to learn at the colleges and universities on either Tretra or Joth. He could have received academic scholarships for advanced degrees on a number of nearby systems. He could have even gone all the way to Earth and attended the University of Georgia if he wanted. The problem was getting there. The schools would have provided free tuition if he could just have paid to get there.

Secondary school had been rough on Clip. He was a small guy that made excellent grades without trying. It would have been worse if Harmon hadn't let everyone know that Clip was his brother. They lived in the same foster center, so it was mostly true. The first day of school, Harmon had laid down the law—if you messed with Clip, you messed up.

At the age of fourteen, he beat three seniors senseless for attempting to put Clip in a trash container. One of them was a Yalteen, a member of a race of large humanoids from two systems over. It wasn't a fair fight—they should have brought more people with them. Harmon hated bullies.

After the suspension ended, the school's Warball coach came to see him. He started that season as a freshman and worked on using it to earn a scholarship to the academy. By the time he graduated, he was six feet two inches with two hundred and twenty pounds of muscle. He got the scholarship and a shot at going into space. It was the longest time he'd ever spent away from his foster brother, but he couldn't turn it down.

Clip stayed on Joth and went to work for Rinto. He figured it was a job that would get him access to all kinds of technical stuff, servos, motors, and maybe even some alien computers. The first week he was there, he tweaked the equipment and increased the plant's recycled steel production by 12 percent. Rinto was eternally grateful, as it put him solidly into the profit column instead of toeing the line between profit and loss. When Harmon came back to the planet after the academy, Rinto hired him on the spot on Clip's recommendation. After he saw Harmon operate the grappler and got to know him, he was glad he did.

A steady beeping brought Harmon back to the present. Clip's program had succeeded in unlocking the container. "Right on!" Clip exclaimed. He was always using expressions hundreds or more years out of style. "Let's see what we have; I hope this one isn't empty, too." Last month they'd come across a smaller vault, but it had been empty.

Harmon stepped up and wedged his hands into the small opening the door had made when it disengaged the locks. There wasn't enough power in the small cells Clip used to open it any further. He put his weight into it, and the door opened enough for them to get inside. Before they went in, Harmon placed a piece of pipe in the doorway so it couldn't close and lock on them, baking them alive before anyone realized they were missing.

Daylight shone in through the doorway, and they both froze in place; the weapons vault was full.

*****

*****

The following is an

Excerpt from Book One of the Earth Song Cycle:

Overture

Mark Wandrey

Now Available from Theogony Books

eBook and Paperback

Excerpt from "Overture:"

Dawn was still an hour away as Mindy Channely opened the roof access and stared in surprise at the crowd already assembled there. "Authorized Personnel Only" was printed in bold red letters on the door through which she and her husband, Jake, slipped onto the wide roof.

A few people standing nearby took notice of their arrival. Most had no reaction, a few nodded, and a couple waved tentatively. Mindy looked over the skyline of Portland and instinctively oriented herself before glancing to the east. The sky had an unnatural glow that had been growing steadily for hours, and as they watched, scintillating streamers of blue, white, and green radiated over the mountains like a strange, concentrated aurora borealis.

"You almost missed it," one man said. She let the door close, but saw someone had left a brick to keep it from closing completely. Mindy turned and saw the man who had spoken wore a security guard uniform. The easy access to the building made more sense.

"Ain't no one missin' this!" a drunk man slurred.

"We figured most people fled to the hills over the past week," Jake replied.

"I guess we were wrong," Mindy said.

"Might as well enjoy the show," the guard said and offered them a huge, hand-rolled cigarette that didn't smell like tobacco. She waved it off, and the two men shrugged before taking a puff.

"Here it comes!" someone yelled. Mindy looked to the east. There was a bright light coming over the Cascade Mountains, so intense it was like looking at a welder's torch. Asteroid LM-245 hit the atmosphere at over 300 miles per second. It seemed to move faster and faster, from east to west, and the people lifted their hands to shield their eyes from the blinding light. It looked like a blazing comet or a science fiction laser blast.

"Maybe it will just pass over," someone said in a voice full of hope.

Mindy shook her head. She'd studied the asteroid's track many times.

In a matter of a few seconds, it shot by and fell toward the western horizon, disappearing below the mountains between Portland and the ocean. Out of view of the city, it slammed into the ocean.

The impact was unimaginable. The air around the hypersonic projectile turned to superheated plasma, creating a shockwave that generated 10 times the energy of the largest nuclear weapon ever detonated as it hit the ocean's surface.

The kinetic energy was more than 1,000 megatons; however, the object didn't slow as it flashed through a half mile of ocean and into the sea bed, then into the mantel, and beyond.

On the surface, the blast effect appeared as a thermal flash brighter than the sun. Everyone on the rooftop watched with wide-eyed terror as the Tualatin Mountains between Portland and the Pacific Ocean were outlined in blinding light. As the light began to dissipate, the outline of the mountains blurred as a dense bank of smoke climbed from the western range.

The flash had incinerated everything on the other side.

The physical blast, travelling much faster than any normal atmospheric shockwave, hit the mountains and tore them from the bedrock, adding them to the rolling wave of destruction traveling east at several thousand miles per hour. The people on the rooftops of Portland only had two seconds before the entire city was wiped away.

Ten seconds later, the asteroid reached the core of the planet, and another dozen seconds after that, the Earth's fate was sealed.

* * * * *

Get "Overture" now at:
https://www.amazon.com/dp/B077YMLRHM/

Find out about Mark Wandrey and the Earth Song Cycle at:
https://chriskennedypublishing.com/

* * * * *

Made in the USA
Middletown, DE
27 December 2019